THE END WOULD COME
AT MIDNIGHT LOCAL TIME.
AND IT WAS ONLY SECONDS AWAY . . .

"Seven . . . Six . . . Five . . ."
Suddenly his heart was pounding, there was a tightness in his chest, and a thrill of fear surged through him. Yet somehow he kept counting down with the rest of them, the grin fixed on his face even as his heart and soul braced for doom and nothingness.

"Four . . . Three . . ."
The voices grew louder, more manic, as the moment came. It seemed to George that he caught a look, a wild panic, in more than one person's expression. And suddenly he knew he was not the only one caught wondering, not the only one who would deny worrying tomorrow—*if* there was a tomorrow.

"Two . . . One . . ."
Like a leap over a precipice, the moment came on, unstoppable . . .

ROGER MacBRIDE ALLEN
and
ERIC KOTANI

AVON BOOKS ◆ NEW YORK

SUPERNOVA is an original publication of Avon Books. This work has never before appeared in book form. This work is a novel. Any similarity to actual persons or events is purely coincidental.

AVON BOOKS
A division of
The Hearst Corporation
1350 Avenue of the Americas
New York, New York 10019

Copyright © 1991 by Roger MacBride Allen & Eric Kotani
Published by arrangement with the authors
Library of Congress Catalog Card Number: 91-92044
ISBN: 0-380-76060-6

First Avon Books Printing: October 1991

AVON TRADEMARK REG. U.S. PAT. OFF. AND IN OTHER COUNTRIES, MARCA REGISTRADA, HECHO EN U.S.A.

Printed in the U.S.A.

RA   10 9 8 7 6 5 4 3 2 1

For
Freeman Dyson
Kim Stanley Robinson
Stanley Schmidt
J. Craig Wheeler

Prelude

Sirius System

Years before and trillions of kilometers from Earth, it begins.

Back in time and deep into space, the fate of the lesser of two stars is about to be sealed. It will be tortured by its companion and then destroy itself, erupting in the most violent form of explosion possible in the modern universe.

The doomed star is a white dwarf, orbiting a more massive white star. The larger star is a hundred times the size of the dwarf, the two forming a classic binary system. Their complex, orderly dance, two suns revolving about each other in perfect symmetry, has been stable for millions of years. But now order is overthrown.

Deep inside the greater star, the delicate balance of radiation pressure pushing outward against gravity pushing inward breaks down when the internal temperature rises slightly.

The temperature rise is a little thing, a minor flux—and the first step in the long and torturously complex path toward system-wide disaster. For inevitably—indeed, by definition—the star's increased heating means increasing its radiation output. And all things expand when they heat. The bloated, hotter, more energetic plasma can no longer be contained by the star's gravity field.

Thus an ancient battle between two old antagonists—gravity and radiation—renews itself. It is the battle between these two forces, each attempting to kill the star, that makes the star live. The heat and other electromagnetic radiation tend to make the star expand, while the pull of gravity tends to make it contract. Gravity forces enough heat and pressure by its compression to spark and maintain thermonuclear fusion and massive heat.

Without gravity, the heat and other radiation would kill the star by forcing it to expand out into a diffuse hydro/helium cloud too thin to allow fusion. Without heat and other radiation, gravity would kill the star by crushing it down into a dark, cold, wizened ball.

It is the dynamic *between* the two forces, the struggle of one against the other, that causes the star to shine.

But now, inside the larger star, that delicate balance is thrown into chaos. The shift in temperature, in radiation pressure, is minute—almost unmeasurable—but it is enough.

Massive storms boil out of the star's interior as gravity and radiation strive against each other to reach a new equilibrium. Flares, plasma arcs, and spicules rage across the photosphere. Massive jets of hydro/helium plume up from the greater star as it throws enormous quantities of matter clear of its gravitational field. Much of the plasma escapes to interstellar space, but some of it is drawn down by the gravity well of the smaller star, an elderly white dwarf. Even in this first plume event, gigatons of matter are transferred from the greater to the lesser star.

But this first plume is strongly affected by the magnetic lines of force connecting the two stars, forming a bridge between them, pulling a disproportionate amount of the larger star's escaped mass down onto the lesser star.

Yet the storms still rage across the face of the greater star. More jets and plumes blast out from its surface, matter still escapes—and more and more of that matter accretes onto the surface of the white dwarf. The situation grows more untenable by the moment, the likelihood of a hellfire explosion becoming greater and greater.

This tragedy is played without an audience. No living thing is present in this star system to name these stars, or study them—or witness the gathering disaster. Here, these are but two nameless balls of fusion fire.

But light travels, moves endlessly across the interstellar blackness. To a place that has named these suns, and called them Sirius A, the greater star, and Sirius B, the lesser. Light moves slowly across the great distances of space: for nine years after the fact, Sirius will shine unchanged in terrestrial skies.

It will be nine long years after the initial, destabilizing event in Sirius A before the first hint of the coming catastrophe reaches the telescopes, and the naked eyes—and the minds—of Earth.

Chapter 1

September 1997
Tucson, Arizona

George watched the cool, quiet streets of night slide past as he made his way home, driving slowly, like a man who was not in a hurry.

It had been a long night, and one spent doing another man's research; tonight he had just been working the night shift, doing data reduction for Stowton, his thesis advisor. Graduate students in astronomy did not tend to draw exciting duty.

Tonight I really ought to head straight to bed, George told himself as he pulled up in front of his apartment complex.

But that resolution was no more convincing than it had been the night before, or the night before that. He looked up at the window of his one-bedroom apartment on the second floor: nothing but an empty bed and an empty night waited for him there. Night and the slow, sleepless crawl to dawn.

Night. Night and early morning—those were the times with meaning to an astronomer, the times to be awake. George's mind was still racing; was restless, nervous about the coming morning, not yet made up on the decision that would shape the rest of his career.

George stepped out of his tired old car and locked the door. He shoved the keys into his pocket and stood there, indecisive.

No. He wouldn't, couldn't go home yet. He needed to unwind, cool down, or he wouldn't sleep at all tonight . . . Not good when tomorrow was the big day. He turned around and walked in the opposite direction, away from his apartment, toward the Wranglers' Bar. A shot or two of Maker's Mark Kentucky bourbon might calm him down enough to see him through another night.

But it had to be Maker's Mark, George told himself again. The good stuff, not whatever cheap bar bourbon was on hand.

Maker's Mark. The Wranglers' was just about the only place in his neighborhood of Tucson that stocked it. He would go there again tonight, no matter how rough a spot it was. It felt good at least to have made a decision, to have a destination and a purpose. At least there were some decisions he was still capable of making. Except, of course, going to the Wranglers' for a shot after a night on the mountain was becoming a ritual, a habit. Maybe he should worry about that. But not tonight. Not tonight.

It was a short walk to the Wranglers', with not too bad a crowd inside tonight, by the looks of things—but instead of relief, George felt a certain pang of disappointment. Truth to tell, he got a secret thrill from hanging out in a place with such a rough-and-tumble reputation.

George paused at the entrance, then pushed his way through the swinging doors and up to the bar. He took a stool off to one end of the counter to avoid unwelcome conversation with other customers, trying to look like he belonged, trying to blend in.

George was twenty-six years old and of medium height. A mop of light brown hair framed a face with a broad forehead, a rather undistinguished nose, and a square jaw. George Prescott presented a most unremarkable appearance—except perhaps for his green eyes, their gaze piercing and firm.

The bartender came up and nodded toward him. "What'll it be?"

The bartender still has to ask, George told himself. That was something. It had not yet become such a ritual that the man set down George's order without being asked. "Maker's," he said. "Straight up, with ice water on the side."

The bartender nodded and served him. George took a sip of the bourbon and let the familiar taste slide through his mouth. He didn't actually have to swallow—the smooth whiskey just seemed to merge into his being without any conscious effort on his part. A warm glow began to spread through his body, and George's naturally optimistic world view started making a very tentative return. He caught the barkeep's eye and signaled for another round.

As the bartender was pouring George's drink, two strangers came into the place. George glanced idly at the door, and the bartender looked as well, with a bit more professional interest. "Oh, hell," the barkeep said, "not them again." He turned to George and shrugged, then nodded at the newcomers. "Get a lot of them in here," he said apologetically, obviously assuming George would know who "they" were.

"They cause you trouble?" George asked, almost at random.

"The ones who come in here do. But I've tended bar for some of their services. There, you can meet some real nice folks. When I call the Church to complain about jerks like these, they say they've never heard of them. All I know is, I wouldn't want to be in a dark alley with any of the ones who show up here."

That didn't sound promising, whatever it meant. "Ah, hell," the barkeep went on. "Here they come. They never take a booth."

The two tough-looking strangers turned and walked up to the bar. Much to George's dismay, they took seats on either side of him. They were dressed in leather jackets and blue jeans, with long, shaggy hair and beards that needed trimming. George had the two of them sized up as standard-issue biker hoods until one of them spoke.

"Praise be to you, brother barkeep," the shorter of the two said. That surprised George a bit. Then he noticed that both of them wore several crosses around their necks. One even had an intricate pendant that combined a motorcycle wheel, a stylized set of handlebars, and a cross.

Suddenly it all fell into place. *Wonderful,* George told himself. *Christriders.*

The shorter of the two riders smiled at the bartender and gestured toward himself and his friend. "The usual."

The bartender looked hard at each of them. Clearly they were not among his favorite customers. "Money first," he said, stone-faced.

The two newcomers smiled right back at him, perfectly cool. Beatific and warm as their grins seemed, there was more threat than friendship in their faces. "Of course," the shorter one said, pulling out a wallet and slapping a twenty on the counter. "That should cover us for a while."

The bartender grunted noncommittally, picked up the twenty, worked the register, and slapped their change down on the counter, closer to his side, where he could get at it to pick off the tab for their next rounds. He poured each of the two a double shot of Wild Turkey.

Bikers for Christ. What was the official name? The Church of the Road—that was it. George vaguely remembered reading about them a few months back. In the old days, evangelicals had not been likely to look, dress—or smell—like these two. But they were reputed to do good work, on occasion. Disaster relief, repairing shelters . . . that sort of thing. Their charity work earned them a grudging respect, and some people liked to think they were a calming influence on other biker groups.

Even so, no one really knew if the Riders were truly evangelicals, or merely talking the talk and walking the walk. If it was a scam, it was working: their membership was way up, and their treasury was bulging with donations—though it was whispered that some donations were not entirely voluntary. Times were changing; times were strange.

The taller of the two Christriders, seated to George's right, turned toward him and grinned, showing a pair of gold-capped teeth.

"Praised be the name of the Lord, my friend," Gold-Teeth said. "I bear good tidings. The Second Coming of the Savior will be soon. Let us rejoice!"

George grunted noncommittally, silently cursing his bad luck in choosing the wrong stool. But, on second thought, these two probably would have cornered him wherever he sat. He didn't know if they were true religious fanatics or just bullyboys, but George had a theory that both types had an uncanny skill for seeking out people who most wanted to be left alone.

These days, he got lots of chances to test such theories. The nuts were out in force these days, inspired by the close of the second millennium.

And there were still three years to go. George shook his head. By the time it actually got here, the year A.D. 2000 was going to have a lot to answer for. Not long ago, George would have been a bit more tolerant of the occasional crazy, but he had little patience for such nonsense in his present mood.

"Will you not praise God with us, brother?" Gold-Teeth asked again, and his breath made it clear this was

not the first bar he and his friend had been in tonight.
"Will you not aid us in toasting the Second Coming of
the Savior?"

Now he got it. In this context, helping to praise God
meant standing for the next round of drinks. Whatever
remaining shred of respect George had for the Christrider movement vanished in that moment. Cadging
drinks in the name of the Lord did not go down well
with him.

Sanctimonious freeloaders, he thought. His annoy-
ance and the bourbon combined in him to make him a
bit less cautious than he should have been. He turned
to the man and asked, a bit more belligerently than was
altogether wise, "The Savior is coming? How do you
know that?" Too late he realized how much of an invitation to bend his ear he had just offered.

"Events on Earth match the prophecies of Revelations," the Rider said, a certain slurriness to his voice
as he let the tired phrases roll off his tongue. "The acts
of man and the events of nature portend that the Shout,
the Trump, and Judgment Day itself are close at hand.
There shall be a new star in the heavens, and the Second Coming shall be at hand."

Somehow it sounded like lip service, not deeply held
belief. But still, they had to be parroting what *somebody* believed. George hadn't seen anything special in
the news that matched what he knew of Revelations,
but he knew that wouldn't bother a Rider, or anyone
else in one of the millennial cults. They could bend any
event to match the weird, hallucinatory images of Revelations. He decided to argue on a slightly different
tack.

"Isn't it a bit presumptuous to assume that anything
people do could affect the timing of God's decision to
do something—or that God's actions are bound by human interpretation of prophecy?"

"Oh, there's no question of interpr'tation. Th' signs
are all around. Ya just gotta know 'em," Gold-Teeth
said. The Rider seemed to notice his slip into the ver-

nacular, and his face grew grim as he tried to concentrate. "Besides, it isn't just human events on Earth. All th' scholars agree. There will be fantastic signs in the heavens just before the Second Coming of Jesus Christ. New stars an' bright comets shall split th' sky."

The Rider slapped George on the back and leaned in toward him. "Why don't you come to the church down th' road and learn these things for yourself? Repent before th' final Judgment, and avoid eternal damnation!"

George, feeling his drink just a bit, got genuinely angry. He had no use for any sort of demands for repentance from strangers. There was enough on his plate without some leather-jacketed Bible-thumper getting in his face. Besides, he was an astronomer, and the idea that stars and planets could be at the beck and call of pseudoreligious gibberish got him good and angry.

"Thanks just the same. I've got nothing to repent, and a two-thousand-year-old paranoid delusion isn't going to frighten me," he said. "Stars and comets just don't foretell the end of the world."

Gold-Teeth set down his drink with a cold anger. A pretty, young blond waitress was at the bar, waiting for refills to take back to her table, and had overheard the argument. Her presence seemed to force his anger up higher. George saw Gold-Teeth's eyes flick from George to Gold-Teeth's silent companion, to the waitress, and then back to his fellow Rider. George cursed under his breath, and realized too late he had gone too far. Christ or no Christ, bikers don't like to be challenged in front of women. Especially not with a fellow Rider as a witness.

The bartender frowned. He had been keeping a close eye on the Riders, and seemed to judge the argument was about to get out of hand. After handing the fresh drinks to the waitress, he stepped over to the three at the bar.

"How dare you speak against the Holy Scripture?" Gold-Teeth was demanding of George. "Who do you think you are, to question the sacred words in the Book of Revelations?''

George swallowed hard and tried to make his voice steady, reasonable. "I'm an astronomer," he said. "I ought to know a little about what goes on in the sky."

Gold-Teeth growled warningly, and his friend grabbed George by the shoulder and shoved his face into George's.

"Are you saying Revelations is a lie, white-bread?" the second Rider demanded, his breath hot and alcoholic, his eyes red and rheumy, less than a handbreadth from George's own. George, speechless with surprise, could do nothing but stare back into those too-close eyes.

The tableau held for an endless moment before the bartender intervened. "Okay, fun's over, you two. Pick your fights somewhere else tonight. Drink up and take it outside." His look delivered the unvoiced "or else."

Judging from the way he carried himself and his bulging biceps, the bartender also served as the bouncer. Judging from the Riders' reaction, he was good at the job. To George's surprise, the Riders backed off. Maybe they had tangled with this barkeep before. *Or maybe they're hoping to be meek enough to inherit the Earth,* George thought sardonically. Without speaking further, the two men lifted their glasses, knocked back the last of their Turkey, scooped up their change, and left.

Maybe the bartender had come to his rescue, but George got the distinct impression that he was no longer welcome here either. But Maker's Mark was sipping whiskey, not rotgut to be swigged in a hurry. And it might not be such a bad idea to give the Riders time to clear off. Coolly ignoring the bartender's glare, he sat there, nursing his drink, savoring its smoky flavor. At last he emptied his glass. He settled his bill and headed for the swinging doors, enjoying the warm glow of the whiskey, glad the Riders had departed without incident.

He should have known better.

The two of them jumped him as he stepped out the door. In that instant, George's reflexes and martial arts training took over. He stepped out of the way of the first attacker, turned ninety degrees, and grabbed at Gold-Teeth, slamming him headfirst into the wall of the building. The Rider dropped like a stone, out cold. The second Rider, the short one, delivered a straight punch to George's face before George had the chance to face him fully. George ducked his head to the right, just barely avoiding the punch, then slammed down on the biker's head with his forearm. There was the unpleasant sound of a breaking bone, and George saw his assailant fall to the ground, striking his head on the hard pavement.

The bartender-bouncer came running out with a baseball bat, ready to break it up, but the fight was over.

''Okay, you bozo yaboos, get the hell away from my bar!'' he bellowed. But the two Riders were in no shape to go anywhere. Gold-Teeth was completely out cold, and his buddy was stunned.

George lifted his hand and felt a harsh spasm of pain. He suddenly realized that the breaking sound had come from his own forearm. Too late, he recalled his karate instructor's admonition not to strike anything hard with his forearm. That idiot's head must have been full of rocks.

The bouncer was prodding the second Rider with his bat, and George decided it might be smart to get out of there before he got the man's attention back. He had had enough trouble for one night.

Cradling his broken arm, he turned and walked back the way he had come.

Of course, there was plenty of trouble left to happen: struggling to hail a taxi with his good arm; a painful ride over rough streets in a cab with a bad suspension;

the emergency ward of the local hospital, where the attending physician asked entirely too many questions that George was in no mood to answer; the pain, and then the numbness, of a broken arm set in a cast and loaded up with painkillers.

Not a good night, all things considered.

It was in the small hours of the morning that George finally got back to his lonely apartment, his right arm in a cast and sling. At least the X rays had revealed a clean break. Even so, George would be wearing the cast for the next four weeks.

He stood in the hallway, in front of his own door, struggling to fish his keys from his pocket one-handed, his broken arm throbbing with numb pain that seemed to leak out from behind the painkillers and flare up every time he managed to bang the cast against his chest. The awkward maneuver reminded him just how difficult life was going to be with a broken arm, but at last he extracted the keys. It took a minute to work the tricky lock one-handed, but finally the door swung open, revealing a dark and empty space. George breathed a sigh of relief and stumbled inside, glad to be home, to be at the end of all effort.

But then he reached over and flicked on the lights. George had thought he was used to having only half the furniture he should have, but tonight all the missing things seemed to loom out at him—all the possessions that his ex-girlfriend Trish had gathered up and taken away when she had moved out six months before: the missing stereo; the half-barren bookshelf; his dining room chairs sitting in forlorn formation around her vanished dining room table. Somehow, he had never quite found the time, the money, the energy, to go out and replace it all. The idea of scrounging the local Goodwill for furniture was just too depressing.

He crossed to the kitchen nook and sat down on the one lonely stool that remained. Empty and gone—everything was empty and gone.

He thought of the long night just past, and the effort it had taken to get back here.

Sitting there, alone in the too-bright aseptic yellow light, George wondered what, exactly, the hurry had been.

Chapter 2

Tucson, Arizona

George got moving more than a little late the next morning, and had to rush to get to his office in the Department of Astronomy at the University of Arizona. He was starting his fourth year as a graduate student there, but four years of practice didn't seem to be making things any easier: every step of the journey toward a doctorate was a struggle for him.

At last he stood before the shabby building that housed his office. Not knowing why, he realized that he did not want to go in. *You can't stand out in the street forever,* he told himself at last. His broken arm still rewarding every abrupt move with a new twinge of pain, he made his way into the scruffy environs of low-budget academia. Should he even have come in at all? Surely a broken arm was excuse enough for taking a morning off. He *would* have called in sick today—

except for the meeting with Stowton, his thesis advisor. He had already avoided this conference longer than was strictly wise. Canceling again today would just be asking for trouble.

He had hoped to keep the story of his broken arm somewhat quiet—at least for a day or two—had hoped to hide behind the mountain of research materials piled up on his desk . . . but Philby was in the office. Today *would* be the one day a week they were both scheduled with office hours. George cursed his luck. Philby, a rather persistent fellow graduate student with whom he shared an office, descended while George was still struggling to pour himself a cup of coffee from the pot in the hallway.

"Jesus, George, what the hell happened to you?" Philby demanded.

George shook his head mournfully. That was it: There was no escape from Philby's inquisitiveness. The man was completely immune to any tactful hint, and would hang all over George until he had the full story. The news of his misadventures would be all over the place by lunchtime. George spent the next hour or so recounting every detail of the story, not only to Philby, but to the constant parade of graduate and undergraduate students who wandered in and out. He thought more than once of turning tail and heading home, taking a sick day. He certainly didn't get any work done until Philby wandered off to bother someone else. But retreat wasn't really an option—not when his appointment with Stowton was looming. He was supposed to settle on the theme of his doctoral dissertation today.

Trouble was, he still didn't know what his thesis was going to be about. No, that wasn't quite right. It was going to be about galactic core modeling, a subject that George found about as exciting as watching paint dry.

What he *wanted* to do was modeling of Type Ia supernovae, the dramatic process wherein white dwarf stars accreted so much mass from companion stars that their internal stability was destroyed and they blew themselves up.

Unfortunately, he also knew his advisor's views on supernovae: that they were a dead end. Stowton had told him that supernovae were played out six months ago, when George had put forward his initial ideas for a thesis. And therein lay the problem: Stowton seemed to have a point.

George Prescott stared unhappily at the stack of scientific journals on the desk in front of him and moodily drummed the fingers of his unbroken left arm. It had all seemed like such a great idea six months ago. Type II supernovae had been studied, yes, but he thought Type Ias were practically virgin territory.

For six months, George had spent whatever time he could spare from his teaching and assisting duties struggling to put together a credible thesis proposal on Type Ias.

Even at the start, he had been prepared for the idea that it might take a lot of research to turn up the material he needed. Still, he had plunged into his work with gusto. Unfortunately, months in the library had done nothing but show that Stowton was right: supernovae had been done to death. In fact, Stowton was even righter than he had thought. George had performed a thorough literature search and found out the unsettling truth: it wasn't just the Type IIs that had been worked over.

Even the Type Ias had been chewed over pretty carefully. He had been counting on at least the Ias being an uncharted area. But Ias had been worked over enough to produce acknowledged experts in the field: Smith and Garnet. They had produced a paper on the subject a decade before, and it was still considered definitive. Its highly detailed model of the Type Ia's interior was accepted—or at least left unchallenged—as the standard. More depressing still, their work had been promptly accepted on publication ten years ago—and then promptly forgotten. As best George could tell, neither

Smith nor Garnet had ever published anything else on the subject of Type Ias again.

Somehow, by the time he had worked his way through the literature, none of that surprised George. He had read Smith and Garnet's paper a few years back, long before he started his thesis research. He remembered being distinctly uninspired by it. Even for a scientific paper, it was more than a bit dry. He *had* hoped to dig it out and plug their formulae into his own work, use their results as a launching pad for his own research.

But there was very little that could be lifted off that pad. Their paper was *too* complete, leaving no scope for further inquiry. To change metaphors, it was as if Smith and Garnet had squeezed the last blood out of the Type Ia supernova rock. Even ten years later, nothing more had been said—perhaps nothing *could* be said.

The conventional wisdom of the astronomical community was that any work left unchallenged for that long was probably correct. Otherwise, in all that time, someone would have spotted the flaw. The further conventional wisdom was that the topic was probably damned uninteresting, utterly barren, leading nowhere. If no one had done a follow-up, that strongly implied that there were no follow-ups *possible*.

That was the trouble with neat endings in science: An answer was supposed to lead *somewhere,* lead to new problems, new questions, new areas to explore. But Smith and Garnet's paper seemed to have closed doors rather than opened them. They had defined Type Ias so completely, so rigidly, that there didn't seem to be any loopholes left. Their mathematical formulations were very solid, and left little room either for alternatives or refinements. There was nothing more to be said. Stowton wanted George to join the throng studying galactic cores. And unless George came up with a miracle now, this morning, it looked very much as if it *would* be galactic cores. Damn it. Why had Smith and Garnet been so damned thorough? Their model left nothing to chance, left no options open.

But, inevitably, Philby finally came back and started asking damn fool questions about George's arm again, and that reminded George how much his arm hurt. He lost his train of thought, and then his temper, as he stacked his papers back into some sort of order and left, no clear destination in mind, his arm hurting like hell, no further forward with the idea of a revised supernova model than before.

He stepped out into the sunlight and began to walk the campus. A stupid idea, anyway. Hell, he had spent the last six months struggling to find a loophole in Smith and Garnet. What had possessed him to think he could crack it in one more morning? He sighed deeply. Years of study into the lives and times of galactic cores seemed to be looming up before him.

At last George made his way to the campus's cavernous main cafeteria. The place was every bit as noisy as usual, filled to bursting with chattering undergraduates. The nearly stale smell of mass-production cooking floated in the air. But sometimes crowds could afford a person at least some sort of privacy.

George worked his way through the food line, made his selections, and sat down square in the center of the huge, anonymous room. It wasn't a particularly homey or pleasant place, but at least here no one was likely to bother him.

Sitting there, alone, he found himself thinking not just about Stowton, or supernovae, or galactic cores, but about something that cut a little deeper; that seemed to matter more than what the subject matter of his thesis might be:

Trish.

But why the devil should she pop to the surface right now? She had walked out months ago.

George certainly had enough else to worry about at the moment, but getting home to the half-empty apartment last night with his arm snapped in two had brought her very much to mind. He had long ago concluded that her leaving had been for the best. After all, how much in common had they had? What part could she have played in his life, in the long run? Or he in hers?

—Look at the way she had left him. Trish had dropped out of her own graduate program and moved back in with her old boyfriend, a lawyer she had dated when he was at the university. The key point in her decision seemed to be that her new-old boyfriend had just accepted a junior position in a thriving local firm that specialized in corporate law. Maybe it was oversimplifying, but what it boiled down to was that Trish had opted for the lawyer and his money over the scientist and his intellectual pursuits. Trish had as much as admitted she didn't really love her lawyer friend. She had come close to saying flat out that his money was the prime attraction.

He would never be rich, George knew, but there was more to life than money. He looked around himself at the cafeteria, and considered the campus beyond those four walls, and the world of academia of which it was a part. Maybe some people on campus were difficult, and maybe the surroundings weren't all they could be, but intellectually—and emotionally—it was far more satisfying than chasing a dollar. In point of fact, Trish, depressingly enough, hadn't really been that much of a loss.

Trish had sold herself; he hadn't. That thought cheered him up, at least a bit.

So when Stowton pitches galactic nuclei, I'll say no, George told himself. *I'll stick with supernovae.*

He looked up from his meal, startled. When had he reached those conclusions? What place in his subconscious had volunteered the idea of turning Stowton down? He hadn't been consciously aware he was even *thinking* of saying no. His vision of his astronomical career had changed a lot if he had decided not to cave in. Up until this moment, he had been ready to go along, to get along by playing the game. True, the canonical galactic nucleus modeling bored him, but it was the safe road to career advancement.

But the hell with that. Let Trish sell herself for money—he wouldn't. Hell, you could get your arm broken just trying to have a quiet drink by yourself. What was the point in playing it safe?

Supernovae: he would stick with his first love, supernovae. Apparently, getting his arm broken had changed George's outlook. If life was that full of unpleasant surprises, who was to say that the nucleus modelers couldn't fall flat on their faces? How would it feel, if he were part of that project, if and when it did fall apart? What would it feel like to throw away years of hard work for something he didn't even care about?

And yes, he had another motive. George wanted to be famous, or at least have a chance to be famous in the world of astronomy, and being a team player on a galactic nucleus project was not likely to make that happen.

On the other hand, George knew fully well a good-sized, close-up supernova was long overdue. A luckily timed supernova could make it all happen for him. Several astronomers had hit the limelight right after the supernova of 1987 in the Large Magellanic Cloud.

But he wanted even more than that. He wanted his name to ring down the ages as the man who learned to *predict* supernovae. It might take years—or even decades—but George believed he could construct the computer models that would let him do it. The rest would be simple: spot an unstable star in its presupernova stage, predict its explosion, and wait for the explosion to happen. The fame would be unending.

Of course, for that little dream to come through, he not only would need to achieve a breakthrough in modeling, but would have to arrange for a supernova to light up during his career. Both were unlikely events, to put it mildly. Which was why he had been willing to go along with the galactic nucleus project. It, at least, was reliable.

But no. Better to fail trying for something he really wanted.

George was a gambler; for the past couple of years he had supplemented his meager graduate student stipends by playing poker, and by slipping over to Las Vegas to work the blackjack tables. He understood risks, and stakes—and gut feelings. Today his gut was saying there was no point in playing it safe. Maybe it hadn't been true last week, but right this moment, he was willing to bet on the long odds that there would be a predictable Type Ia supernova in his lifetime, perhaps even early in his career.

Suddenly he felt better, felt more determined and confident than he had in a long time. Making this decision felt *right*.

But how? Garnet and Smith were bulletproof.

Wait a second. That was true—but only *if* George used their model, their math, their underlying assumptions. George had planned to do just that.

But astrophysics had grown up a lot in ten years. While there had not been any world-shaking breakthroughs, there *had* been refinements, lots of them. Perhaps no one of them would be enough to topple the Smith-Garnet edifice, but perhaps the cumulative effect would be enough. Taken as a whole, their arguments appeared unassailable. But maybe—maybe—they could be chipped away piece by piece.

George leaned back in his chair and stared off into space.

Suppose he cooked up a new model from scratch? That way he could make sure that all the basic assumptions that went into the theoretical model were his own, make sure that they were as realistic, as accurate, as possible. *That* was the tack to take. It would take some serious computer time even to construct a new framework for his model, but that was all right. He had an idea, and that was the main thing. He started making a mental list of possible lines of attack, possible minor weaknesses in Smith and Garnet.

George sat there, his unfinished sandwich before him, staring into space. Time, which had been crawling past before, seemed to gather momentum and move forward briskly. He was lost in thought, thinking on new approaches.

Some time later—a minute, an hour—someone jostled George's chair and he came back to himself with a start. He glanced at his watch. Damn! It was almost time for his meeting with Stowton. He wolfed down his bacon-lettuce-and-tomato sandwich, cleaned up his tray, and hurried back to the astronomy building.

The faculty wing's hallways were kept up a bit better than down in graduate student turf, but there was still more than a hint of academic scruffiness about the place. But then, all status symbols were relative. George stopped in front of a door with a rather overstated brass plate that proclaimed the occupant to be Professor Wilton Stowton, and knocked on the door.

Wilton Stowton, Ph.D., sat behind his ancient desk, looking over his office. Here he was, back at it, after a summer spent pursuing more rewarding duties. The faculty offices allocated to the astronomy department were an improvement over graduate students' quarters, but not by very much. Why, Stowton wondered, not for the first time, was it such a privilege to sit here in this tenured, shopworn chair, hand-holding the graduate students who flowed past him year after year?

He heard the knock at his door and automatically checked his desk calendar to see who was on the other side. It was appointment day, and a steady stream of students had been coming through. The name *George Prescott* was inked in, and he let out a small sigh. George was one of the difficult ones—and the rumor mill was reporting that he had demonstrated that again the night before. "Come in," Stowton said.

George Prescott entered and closed the door behind him.

"Sit down, George," Stowton said, trying to muster more enthusiasm than he felt. "I hear that you had quite a time last night."

George shrugged, flinching as he jarred his still tender arm. "Yes, sir, I did. It could have been a lot worse, I suppose," he said, his voice almost surly, betraying just how unhappy he was to be here. There wasn't anything Stowton could say to that, but Prescott didn't seem about to say anything else. The silence hung heavy and awkward in the room, making Stowton distinctly uncomfortable. Well, trundling around campus with a freshly broken arm couldn't be fun. Or was it the subject of this appointment that made Prescott unhappy? Either way, it was bad form on Prescott's part to be so openly sullen.

Stowton regarded his recalcitrant student with misgiving. If only Prescott would learn to pay heed to advice from his professional betters, he could go a long way in his career.

At last the professor spoke. "Well, then, down to business. Have you decided on the theme for your dissertation? I still think a detailed modeling of the accretion disk surrounding a supermassive black hole is a good topic. There's a strong interest in active galactic nuclei right now, and accretion-disk modeling would be useful."

George shifted in his seat and cleared his throat. When he spoke again, it was in a more civil and controlled tone. There was that about Prescott, Stowton thought. He knew his stuff, and could at least talk science graciously.

"I don't know, sir. I know a lot of theorists are working on the accretion disk problem, but the boundary conditions still aren't clearly established. There's just too little data. I don't like making assumptions about things I know so little about."

Stowton returned his student's gaze equably. "Don't just throw the idea away. Galactic centers are very big right now. If you applied the magnetohydrodynamic computer code developed by Swann, you could carve out a nice little niche for your research career doing galactic—"

"I don't want to do galactic nucleus work," George interrupted. "I'm interested in Type Ia supernovae. I've been grinding through school too long to be satisfied with working on something I don't care about." He paused, then went on in a calmer voice, "And to be honest, Dr. Stowton, I don't want to spend my life, my career, in a niche."

"All right, maybe that wasn't the best choice of words. But, George, be reasonable. Supernovae have been sucked dry. They've been done to death. Galactic core studies are hot right now. Yes, the data points are lean—but that just means you'll have the chance to gather the data yourself if you get involved." Stowton hesitated for a moment. "I know it sounds absurd, but you can't just choose your dissertation topic on the grounds of what interests you. You've got to keep your eye on the job game. Play the game right, and there'll be a job and even a big NSF or NASA grant waiting for you when you get your Ph.D. But if you pick an unfashionable topic for your thesis, you'll have a hard time even getting a postdoc job, doing research for hire. And how satisfying will that be?"

But George had made up his mind. "Dr. Stowton," he said firmly, "I appreciate what you're saying, but supernovae are the reason I'm here in the first place. When I was a teenager I read about the eighty-seven supernova, and that was what hooked me on astronomy. Besides, it's the Type IIs that have gotten all the attention and all the papers. Type Ia supernovae are completely different, and not much work has been done on them. Well, except for Smith and Garnet, of course," George admitted, in a tone that showed he knew fully well how much wind Smith and Garnet took out of his sails.

Stowton contemplated his charge skeptically. "I still think you ought to give another thought to accretion disk modeling," he said. "If you still want to work on Type Ia supernovae after thinking it over for a few more days, bring back a thesis proposal. Okay?"

George brightened visibly. "Okay. I will, Dr. Stowton. I'll think about it."

The two made their good-byes, Stowton muttered some vague words of sympathy over George's broken arm, and then he watched the younger man leave.

Good for him, he thought. Oh, he'd been quite sincere and well-meaning when he urged George toward accretion-disk modeling, but that didn't mean he couldn't admire Prescott's determination. Stowton stared at the door that had closed behind his graduate student. He saw the likely track of the young man's future if he stuck to his supernova guns, and it was not a promising path. But at least it would have the virtue of letting the man be true to himself. Certainly *that* was worth something.

Worth quite a good deal indeed.

As George stepped out of the office, he practically ran into a short, cheerful-looking woman who beamed a sunny smile up at him. Jessica Talmadge: cute, perky, brown-haired, she was the sort of person it was almost impossible to dislike. She was getting her Ph.D. at Harvard, but she was completing her thesis work at Kitt Peak, the site for the various telescopes of the National Optical Astronomy Observatory and U. Arizona's Stewart Observatory. Stowton was on her thesis committee, and overseeing her work in Tucson.

"Hi, George," she said. Her eyes shifted downward and widened as she noticed his broken arm.

"Oh, dear, I didn't know you had hurt yourself."

George braced himself for the inevitable next question about how it had happened, but it never came. Instead she reached out a gentle hand and patted the cast so softly, even his sensitized arm could not feel the movement. "Listen," she said, "if you need help with anything while you're in that thing, just give me a holler. Okay?"

"Thanks, Jessica. I sure will," George replied genially, knowing she really meant it.

"Okay, gotta go," she said. "I'm next up with Stowton. Wish me luck."

"You?" he said. "You've never needed luck in your life."

She smiled again and waved good-bye before knocking on Stowton's door and disappearing inside.

George watched her go, thinking that their brief conversation revealed a good deal about Jessica. She didn't know about his broken arm, although she must have seen practically everyone in the department on her way to Stowton's office. In other words, she had not listened to the prime piece of departmental gossip. And she hadn't asked how it had happened, merely offering help instead. Jessica would not intrude on his privacy, but she wanted him to know that she was there if he needed her.

George shook his head and turned to walk down the hallway. Jessica Talmadge wasn't a great beauty, but she had a first-rate mind. She was regarded by her male classmates as too brainy, even intimidating—Philby, for one, would have nothing to do with her. But there were few higher recommendations than that to George's mind. Philby's taste in women was atrocious.

Why didn't he have enough sense to get involved with a woman like Jessica? George wondered. Why instead had he gotten himself tangled up with a cold-hearted calculator like Trish?

Why? It didn't matter. After all, if he could explain how the human heart worked, he wouldn't need a supernova to get famous.

Boston, Massachusetts

The blast had shattered the frame of the house, and then set it ablaze. Now, a day later, what had been a home was a charred, collapsed ruin. But the man standing in the driveway had his back to the house; his attention was elsewhere.

The tall, heavyset man with thick, nut-brown hair looked up into the still-lightening sky, dark blue with the promise of dawn. It would be a clear, bright morning, the sort of morning that was supposed to be full of hope, full of promise. But promise and hope could no longer exist in this place. A tear slid down his cheek, but his face was expressionless.

Here and now, there was only the taste of death. It was not the sky, but the ribbon of smoke sliding upward into nothingness that the man was watching. Watch it go away, see the wispy cloud of blackness that is left when the cleansing fire has done its work; watch the blackness dissipate to nothingness—or at least seem to do so. Appearances were deceiving. That much he had learned. At last the man looked down at the small blaze, gleaming bright in the half-darkness of dawn, that was producing the smoke.

Dr. Desmond Potter stood in the driveway of his ruined home and watched his files burn. That was almost the last of them. Each a patient, each a complete catalog of a mind's darkness and sorrow and loss. But sadness and pain were not the worst of it. There was also evil.

All but one of the files were gone now—all but the worst.

He looked down at what he held in his hands, at the one remaining file. He opened it, touched a page or two, and then drew his hand back. Surely this file was the most evil, the most hate-ridden of them all, the one with the deepest and blackest sins. The case notes on his last patient: *Gibbons, Conrad P. Occupation: letter carrier. Unmarried. Age 47 at time of first consultation. Initial diagnosis: paranoid schizophrenic.*

Dr. Desmond Potter closed the file and shut his eyes for a moment. At last he opened them again and stared at the manila folder. It was unscuffed, unscarred, new-looking. That right there was the proof that he was at fault, for he had been treating Conrad Gibbons's case for five years, ever since the man had become con-

vinced his shift supervisor was the Antichrist, a role
Gibbons later assigned to Desmond Potter. The file
should have been worn, rumpled, much-used, much-
consulted.

Now it was far too late to read anything in it; Potter
knew all he needed to know. The police had told him last
night . . . told him that Gibbons was the man who murdered Desmond Potter's family, blown up his house with
a bomb in a package. Told him that Gibbons had then
walked into the police station, confessed to the crime in
a cool, collected manner, and then calmly drawn a pistol
and shot himself through the head. Potter's wife, Dorothy,
was dead, his five-year-old daughter, Jane, was dead; but
they had not been the target. He, Desmond Potter, was
meant to have that privilege. Their deaths were a mistake—Gibbons's last mistake.

A spasm of reaction seemed to shudder over him.
With a flinch of revulsion, Potter threw the manila
folder onto the flames and watched as it shriveled into
twisted black ribbons and knots of ash.

The last of his files—but not the last of the things he
needed to burn. Desmond went back to his office and
pulled his diploma off the wall, snatched down his license to practice psychiatry. He stuck the diploma under his arm and held the license in both hands. There
it was: the grand, proud document that boldly declared
he was qualified to judge another's mind, declare it
healthy or diseased, dangerous or harmless. He stared
at the thing, his sight suddenly blurry, his eyes swimming with tears.

Not tears of sorrow, though—not anymore. That time
was gone, although it might be back. These were tears of
anger, a seething, blistering anger. He smashed the frame
against the edge of his desk, showering the room with
broken glass. Ignoring the broken shards still clinging to
the frame, he pulled the wooden strips apart, ripped off
the backing, and snatched the stiff parchment out, dis-
carding everything else. The diploma was bonded to a
thick piece of wood; it would burn just fine as it was.

Back outside. He walked to the smoldering embers of his fire and tossed the diploma and license onto it. The flames licked higher, catching on the paper and the wood. He imagined his anger as the thin trail of smoke, a thread of darkness and impurity launching itself up into heaven and to judgment. But that was gone now, the hatred and the fear and the anger roasted away in the clean yellow flame of judgment.

And how soon would come the day for Potter's own judgment? Not just before the authorities, the medical board, but before the Judge of All? One of his notepads had escaped the hottest part of the fire and he kicked it back in with a careful toe. The flames engulfed it, and he watched the pages of notes shrivel up and die in the flame, curl into black, mute tongues of accusation that crumbled to nothing just as they seemed about to speak to him.

Desmond Potter knew what was in that folder. Enthusiastic scribblings, describing Gibbons in detail. Similar delusional patterns could be found in any of the literature, but Potter had never seen such a case, or treated one himself. He had seen it all as a wonderful challenge: a challenge to bring this man back to reality, to demonstrate to him that his fears were groundless, the danger illusory.

But then Gibbons had chosen to act, to defend the world against the angel of darkness.

Potter had been out at the store when the package had arrived. Only his wife and daughter had been home when the firebomb's timer engaged. Now there was nothing but the charred and shattered remnants of the house to show where they had died. Potter turned and looked toward the wreckage, his heart pounding. Nothing left . . . nothing whatever.

Only his office, in a detached side building, had survived the tremendous blast and subsequent fire. There was a message in that, he knew. Desmond Potter was being told that he could go on if he so chose. With the charred embers of his house, his home, his life, plainly visible through the picture window, he could sit there and counsel his patients, tell them he knew what was best for them. Someone was telling him he could go on.

But was that someone—no, no sense being coy about it—was *God* testing him to see if he would accept or refuse the chance? Which path was correct?

It was, of course, far too late for such questions.

But what did God want of him? Even as he asked the question, Potter marveled at its strangeness. It had been years since he had thought in such terms, since he had brought God into the equation. Was this his own madness beginning? Or his blindness ending?

Never mind. Did God want him to stay, to soldier on, to start his practice again and stand against this shattering disaster? Was this a test of his strength of character?

Or was it a punishment for his arrogance, a warning to turn aside?

Stay or go—which was it to be?

That was the test, the challenge before him. Desmond Potter looked deep into the scudding ashes of the fire as the blackened curls of paper were caught by the wind.

No. He could not, would not, go any further down the path that had killed his wife and daughter. He did not know if God willed him to leave or stay, but in a sense, it did not even matter. He *could* not stay.

A gust of wind snuffed out the last ember of the fire, and Desmond Potter turned and walked away. Where he would go, what he would do, he did not know.

Even as he walked down the street to nowhere, a part of his mind that seemed to be watching from afar knew that he was descending into a delusional state of his own, falling into madness.

And even as he recognized that, he realized one last thing:

He no longer cared.

Chapter 3

January 1998
Ithaca, New York

Kenji Yamada was getting tired of being Ken.

He stood by his office window and stared at the snowdrifts outside, realizing that he was getting a little tired of *that*, as well. American weather—or at least upstate New York weather—was like the country itself: it went to extremes.

But weather was an incidental. It was the way Americans fouled up his name that got to him, that told him perhaps it was time to start thinking about going home to Japan.

Ken: they called him *Ken*, even on five minutes' acquaintance. Ninety-nine times out of a hundred, it didn't bother him. But then that hundredth person would come by, and Yamada could feel his blood pressure go through the roof.

32

Usually it was someone like today: the father of one of his graduate students had blundered through the campus on a visit, mortifying his daughter at every turn.

Kenji Yamada shook his head and sighed. Janet Spencer was a fine student, but her father—Spencer the elder—was an oversize, loudmouthed buffoon who had clearly never had an idea in his life, and was plainly suspicious of people who had. And *he* had called Yamada not only by his first name, but by a diminutive form of it. Not even Kenji, but *Ken*.

Back home, it might be years, or even never, before the closest and most intimate friends would get to a first-name basis. Here, it was the accepted privilege of a total stranger. Spencer had even seemed to think Kenji should regard it as an honor to be addressed informally.

None of that was fair, or rational, of course. Things were different in the States—the tradition, the culture. Of course Americans would use the American form of his name. And, Kenji Yamada reminded himself, Ken was the form he himself had chosen, back in the days when his enthusiasm for things American had been greater. No matter what the rules were back home, here the use of a first name was a matter of no great import.

The United States was a more informal country than Japan, and most times, Kenji Yamada *liked* that. After all, he had left Japan because he had thought it too rigid, too formalized and regimented for him. Yamada allowed himself a tiny smile as he remembered that sentiment. Not anymore. Now he found himself longing for a little order, a little discipline.

And now he had the chance. It might take months to arrange, but he had a ticket home, a job waiting. He turned back to his desk and looked at the letter again. It was from ISAS, Japan's Institute of Space and Astronautical Science, one of the most prestigious institutes in the country—and they were tendering him a standing offer of a full professorship.

Nor was that his first offer of work in Japan. Some months ago, Noboru Hayashi had asked him to join his company as a consulting scientist. Hayashi was one of Japan's greatest industrialists, the founder of a leading electronics firm. Now he wanted to move his company into the area of applied hydrodynamics. Hayashi Industries was pursuing a contract to develop advanced flow sensors for natural gas pipelines in Siberia.

Yamada was an astrophysicist, specializing in thermodynamics and gas flow theory. On the face of it, there was nothing in pipeline operations for an astrophysicist, but appearances could be deceiving. The same theoretical models that predicted the movement of ionized gas across space could easily be adapted to the behavior of pressurized gas moving at high speed through a cylinder.

Now the invitation from ISAS. Exciting challenges, prestige, and he would be working in Tokyo: home.

Yes, Yamada thought, making up his mind. It would take time to arrange an orderly departure from his duties at Cornell, but he would do it. He couldn't place the whole blame for the decision on Janet Spencer's father, but certainly that little incident had made it easier.

But there was another letter today, one that made him feel good about the time he *had* spent in the States. There were some young minds out there that he had helped along. This one was from George Prescott, one of Yamada's graduate students. Yamada smiled fondly, remembering the obstinate young man as one of the few really bright spots of his terms as a visiting associate professor at the University of Arizona. George's problem also involved gas flow, though in the highly specific environment of an unstable star. George had written to say more about his ongoing assault on the citadel of Garnet and Smith. Good, solid, determined work, it looked like. Yamada especially admired George's grasp of flow-dynamic mathematics. Too bad he'd be back home before George could have the work done.

Home. He smiled to himself. Of course, three years from now, he'd probably be longing for things American, sick and tired of everything Japanese, and packing his bags again.

February 1998
Tucson, Arizona

Six months, George told himself as he waited for the computer to complete its latest run. Six months since his meeting with Stowton, six months of long, hard work, sixteen hours a day, seven days a week, but it was paying off. If all went well, he'd have his thesis paper done, his doctorate all but clinched, by summer.

And it was going to be one hell of a thesis at that. He was way ahead of all the previous work done in the field. Garnet and Smith? Amateurs. Incompetents. George shifted uncomfortably and shrugged to himself. Well, all right. It was unfairly harsh to dismiss his predecessors so completely. After all, they *had* worked ten years ago, and a lot had been learned in the meantime. Not just about supernovae and stellar structure, but about the art and science of modeling real systems inside a computer. And to be completely fair, George had about a thousand times more computer capacity available than they had had.

But the real news was that George Prescott now understood Type Ia supernovae better than Garnet and Smith ever had. That did not alter the fact that Garnet and Smith had done their best, working with poorer information and less powerful tools. They did not deserve his contempt. In his calmer moments, George managed to keep that in mind.

But then, George hadn't had any truly calm moments in a long time. Day and night, sleeping and awake, he was caught up in the thrill of the chase, that heady feeling of things coming together, the gut feeling that he was onto something big. It all blurred together: His mind was working every spare moment. Not just mornings in the library, and evenings at his office, but in stolen minutes here and there in his classes as the students bent over their quizzes, in the line at the cafeteria, during his walks back and forth across campus.

Every hour, every minute, it seemed, his brain was working over the problem, searching out the mysteries. Waking in the middle of the night, back at his apartment that no longer seemed so lonely, flinging off the blankets, firing up his computer, linking into the campus mainframe when a sudden inspiration hit. Searching the library stacks, the computer data bases, panning for nuggets of data-gold in the endless numbers and charts. Everything else in life seemed to take on a shadowy half-reality. George was losing weight, his skin taking a bit of a pallor most unnatural for someone living in the Southwest. But nothing else seemed to matter. He was chasing something big, and the end of the chase was in sight.

The computer run ended and George brought the latest results summary up on-screen. There were the numbers and the graphic display, but he barely dared to believe the results he was getting. They were too good, too exciting. There *had* to be a mistake.

No. No, he told himself firmly. Numbers were numbers, and facts were facts. They had to be believed, accepted. And the long and the short of it was that his model calculations showed that a white dwarf star of even intermediate mass could go supernova.

It had long been known that a white dwarf in a binary star system could accrete matter from its companion, and that accretion could produce a global thermonuclear runaway. Result: the white dwarf could blow up in a supernova explosion. That much wasn't news. It was the question of the star's *mass* that broke things wide open.

Even before Garnet and Smith, theoretical work had shown that a white dwarf star at least twenty percent more massive than the sun could go supernova. The kicker was that George's results indicated that a much *smaller* white dwarf could go supernova. Under certain circumstances, the mass of the supernova progenitor could be as low as that of the Sun itself.

That was news, big news, if it was true.

The trouble was, George could not prove it was true. George could not assemble the white dwarf in the lab and see if his numbers were accurate. No one could.

Although the physics of the internal structure of a white dwarf star had been under study since Chandrasekhar's original work back in the 1930s, all of it was theory. No terrestrial physics laboratory could duplicate the extreme conditions that existed in collapsed stars, where the density was a thousand kilograms per cubic centimeter. A dice-sized chunk of a white dwarf would weigh about a ton. It seemed unlikely in the extreme that there could ever be any way to reproduce such conditions on the surface of Earth.

All that humanity had learned about the interior of white dwarfs, or about any star, it had discovered through the use of theory, mathematical models, and computer simulations based on limited observational data.

What George had done was still mere theory, mere modeling. But by using more up-to-date physics, better programming, faster computers, and more recent observational results, George had been able to bring his model a lot closer to realistic conditions. Previous models had been overly simplistic, glossing over vital details of convective motion and electron capture by atoms. His model borrowed a lot of techniques from the climate modelers who were making such strides in understanding the movements of Earth's oceans of air and water. They simulated flow behavior at a much finer scale; their techniques brought him much closer to approaching the complexity of a real-life star's interior.

His model told him that white dwarf stars were a lot more likely to blow than anyone had ever dreamed. George smiled at the screen, and he was astonished to find himself overcome by a fit of yawning. He suddenly realized how tired he was, and how much he had been running on adrenaline these last few days. Time to go home and get some sleep.

George stored his results and powered down his computer monitor. He stood up, stretched to ease the crick in his back, shifted his shoulder to get some movement into the arm that he had broken. It still got a little stiff now and then. He shut off the light in the office.

He left the building and walked out into the chill air of the night. The crisp air woke him up a bit. It felt good to get some exercise, even if it was just a leisurely walk home. He had spent too much time of late hunched over computer terminals.

There were several quick ways back to his apartment, but George chose to walk one of the longer routes, one that took him a block or two out of his way. There was a vacant lot, with the streetlight in front of it burned out. The buildings to either side of the lot blocked out most of the city's background light. Here, in this spot, he could do something that many astronomers really did not do much anymore: he could look at the stars, the points of light that had set humanity to wondering about itself so long ago. There they were, the bright stars of early spring, constellations spangled low across the southwestern sky: Orion, the Hunter, with his dog, Canis Major, the Big Dog, nearby. And there, in Canis Major—Sirius, the Dog star, brightest of all the stars, save the sun itself.

George took in a deep breath, and felt the cold air tingling through his lungs. *Nothing between us,* he thought. *Right now there is nothing between me and the stars except thin air and a few wisps of interstellar gas.* The mystery, the distance, the grandeur and beauty of those points of light, had inspired thousands of years of study, of thought, of wonderment and worship. And he was a part of that heritage, buoyed up by it, adding to it.

A wave of pride and excitement washed over him.

He was privileged to be among the generation that knew the most, had learned the most, about those stars. Further privileged to be a member of the elite, the fraternity that studied them, and drew that knowledge out.

Now, tonight, he himself had added to the sum of that knowledge, swung open the door to let out truths no one else had ever found. That was enough, more than enough for him, even if there was never anything else to his career. He lowered his gaze, turned, and walked toward home.

Boston, Massachusetts

Tonight, the screaming did not start until well after three in the morning. That in itself was unusual. Saturday nights were usually the worst, the wildest. Until just a moment ago, tonight had been strangely quiet. But it didn't matter. Desmond Potter was awake before the screaming started, staring into the dark gloom of his cubicle's ceiling.

No, call the thing by its name. It was not a cubicle; it was a cell. This place was a prison as much as it was a shelter. That you knew just in the name of the facility. The Commonwealth Avenue Security Shelter.

How long had he been here? Weeks? Months? His last clear and certain awareness of time was from before he came here. Desmond had wandered the streets of Boston for nearly a week before the sweepers picked him up.

That was how he had come here this time. But he had been at the shelter before, many times. But those times didn't count, for then he had come to the shelter for wholly different reasons, by wholly different means. First he had come protesting the shelter's very existence, and then he had come attempting to minister to its hapless inmates.

In the final analysis, of course, the name *security shelter* did not go deep enough. In cold truth, this place was neither shelter nor prison: it was an insane asylum, for none but the insane ever stayed there long. The merely indigent were placed elsewhere, the criminals and drug dealers hauled off to jail or thrown back out on the street. Only the demented remained here.

A madhouse, in every sense of the word. Calling it a homeless shelter merely put a new name to an old form of establishment. It, and the similar centers across the nation, had been established, not as treatment centers, but in shamefaced civic self-defense. Before the security shelters were opened, the lunatics had been taking over the cities, until society simply could not tolerate it anymore. The rights of the insane to act insane were an imposition the sane could no longer accept. Suddenly the First Amendment was no longer interpreted as protecting a maniac screaming abuse at passersby, or defecating in public. Antiloitering and antivagrancy laws were passed and enforced for the first time in generations.

And when the street-sweepers picked you up, the place you landed was here, or someplace like it. From here, the thugs and druggies were dragged off to the real jails. The hard-luck cases were packed off and moved on, sometimes even helped with a buck or two, or even, at incredibly rare intervals, with job placement.

Even some of the crazies could get themselves put back together—regain their sanity, more or less. A few hot meals and a decent place to sleep brought on more than one miracle cure. The shelter warden was only too glad to get the newly sane cleaned up and moved out.

And that left no one behind but the hard-core crazies, the cases that no one wanted. All the security shelters were like that: a transitory population that belonged somewhere else, and a permanent core population that didn't belong anywhere at all.

Now Dr. Desmond Potter was an inmate where once he had been a doctor, though that, of course, was an irony only he was aware of. The shelters didn't try too hard to track down the people the sweepers brought in, and the sweepers didn't try at all. They scooped you up and dropped you off, and that was that. There wasn't much point in attempting to trace the crazies. After all, the inmates of these places had spent their whole lives falling through the cracks. Half of them couldn't remember their own names—or if they could, as Desmond could, they weren't telling.

He lay in the dark and listened as the screaming reached a new crescendo before someone—guard or inmate—cut it off with a punch to the gut. Desmond felt a sudden pang of sympathy for the mad screamer. There was one man at least who knew what it meant to be here: it meant he was insane.

Except, in some interior part of himself, Desmond did not *feel* insane. That rational splinter of his mind was still there, always seeking the clearheaded explanation, looking for the reason, the answer, that would make it clear why his wife and child had died, why he was in this place. But those were really side issues.

What he really wanted to know was why the world was the way it was, and how much longer it would stay that way.

Sooner or later, Judgment would come, and it would come for him. For he, Desmond Potter, and no one else, had set Conrad Gibbons free. What a sin of pride that had been! What arrogance to imagine he could restore a lost soul to health. What criminal, sinful, venal sloth to let him free upon the landscape rather than go to the trouble of institutionalizing him. The lawyers, the other doctors, had wanted it—but no. *He* had promised them all there would be no trouble. Gibbons's raving, his bizarre outbursts and threats, were a harmless means of escape, nothing more, a way for an introverted personality to let off some steam, assert itself.

Besides, it was such a struggle to arrange for an involuntary commitment. No point in it, when Gibbons was on the verge of a cure. The treatment was going well. Gibbons's religious delusions were sure to crack soon, and he would step back into the real world. In the meantime, Potter told himself, Gibbons made for a fascinating study. His delusions were making a not uncommon transference, but one that Potter had never seen before. The patient was beginning to see, not his boss, but his doctor as the Antichrist. His shift supervisor he now perceived as a mere underling of the Prince of Darkness.

Some compartment of Potter's mind seemed to be watching the rest of him, noting the new transference that was taking place, as the doctor now took up the patient's symptoms, if not his delusions. God was involved here: God was punishing, or testing, or both.

God—there was an idea that Desmond Potter had not much concerned himself with for many, many years, ever since he had walked out of the seminary and into the larger world, in the mid 1960s.

Back then, full of the bloom of youth, in the middle of the tumult of America generally and Boston specifically, God had seemed utterly irrelevant. God could not—or worse, would not—feed the poor, succor the anguished, heal the sick. Desmond had abandoned his father's dream of a son in the priesthood and launched into the real-life, here-and-now battles against the social ills that plagued the nation and the world.

Or perhaps the there-and-then battles, Desmond Potter thought. The towers of the city were barely visible from here, but they seemed close and accessible compared to the causes to which he had given himself in those years.

Yet his rejection of God, his passionate battles for social justice, his deep-set need to rebel against his father—those had been the very things, the driving forces, that had shaped the path of Desmond's life. Those inbuilt drives had guided him toward a life spent helping others. And those attempts to help, in their turn, led him to a belief that diseased minds were the root cause of humanity's problems—that one self-deceiving

neurotic could spread pain and sorrow throughout all
the lives he touched. From there, to psychiatry. From
there, and the modest aid he was able to afford a few
patients, to the foolish arrogance that he could cure all
minds, all illnesses. And from that arrogance it was but
the briefest journey to a plummeting Fall, a crashing
drop to this place beside the smoldering ruins of his
work and his life, the ashes of his family.

And to this place.

The screaming started up again.

Tucson, Arizona

George Prescott lay on his back, snoring loudly, as
if his body were struggling to rest itself as hard and
relentlessly when asleep as George worked it when he
was awake. But then the snores stopped, and he shifted
position suddenly, drawing his knees up and raising his
left arm in defense against some unseen foe. He was
dreaming, his face twitching, twisting back and forth,
his eyes sliding back and forth under closed eyelids, as
if he were in search of something.

Suddenly his eyes snapped open, his mind instantly
wide-awake.

Sirius: that was it. No, he couldn't drag a white dwarf
into the lab, but he could do the next best thing—he
could look out the window at a white dwarf that was
practically right next door. Sirius, the brightest star in
the sky. Except the dwarf itself was invisible to the
naked eye, of course.

What time was it? The clock by his bed showed
6:00 A.M. He might as well get up. George swung
himself out of bed and drew his robe on. He stepped
to the bathroom, and splashed water on his face while
he thought it through, trying to remember the first-
year astronomy detail he had memorized for some
long-forgotten quiz. He started to shave, going through
the motions on automatic as he thought.

Sirius B: the nearest white dwarf, and a companion to Sirius A, a spectral type A0 main-sequence star. The mass of Sirius B, perhaps the best-determined of all white dwarfs because of its early discovery and proximity to the sun, was almost exactly one solar mass.

A very interesting numerical value indeed. Especially since his new model put the lower limit for a supernova at just a shade *above* a solar mass.

It was almost embarrassing that he hadn't thought of Sirius before. Sirius was so damned *obvious*. It was so close and bright and clear that whole generations of astronomers, concentrating on the effort needed to detect the distant, faint, and dim, had regarded it an overbright bore.

But there was a flaw in George's sudden inspiration. He was studying unstable white dwarfs in their role as Type Ia supernova progenitors. That let the Sirius system out: Both stars were rock-solid steady. Not the least bit of fluctuation or variability. *Damn!* So much for early morning inspiration. He finished shaving with far less enthusiasm than he had begun, and slunk into the kitchen to make coffee.

He had regained his spirits a bit by the time the coffee was ready. After retrieving the fat Sunday paper from the apartment hallway, he sat down on his beat-up couch, set his mug down on the coffee table, and started scanning the headlines on the front page. In the old days, Sundays had been spent around the kitchen table, but he still hadn't gotten around to replacing the furniture Trish had taken with her. By now, it seemed quite natural to have breakfast on the living room couch rather than at a table.

The paper wasn't very interesting today. The usual political dustups, more unrest in sub-Saharan Africa, another pitched battle between the two drug-gang alliances in Los Angeles. Eighty dead this time, bad enough that the Christriders were checking into the situation, offering their services as mediators. Very few gangs had the nerve to turn down any offer from the

Riders. He shook his head over the praise the Christ-riders were getting and all the good publicity they were garnering. *As if the Riders were only in to stop the bloodshed,* George thought. *Can't anyone see the Riders want a piece of the action themselves?* But no one the paper quoted was even voicing that as a possible concern.

Then it struck him. The paper was full of praise for the Christriders' good works, and pointing to the organization as a hopeful sign for the future. Everyone knew the Riders were okay—everyone but George.

He felt a twinge in his healed arm, as if he needed a reminder the Riders were thugs. Bitter experience had taught him that it didn't pay to accept the accepted wisdom.

So why are you? The question almost did not seem to come from inside his own mind, almost seemed to have popped in from outside. That was illusion, but the sensation, just as much as the question itself, brought him up short. He let the newspaper fall into his lap. What accepted wisdom? he wondered.

And then it hit him: Sirius. Everyone in astronomy *knew* that everything worth learning about Sirius had been discovered years before. There was nothing more to see. That was why nobody looked anymore.

Just like Type Ias, George told himself.

And suddenly all thoughts of relaxing over the newspaper were gone. Today was meant to be spent in the library, searching.

By late afternoon, George had gleefully discovered a whole new part of his world where everything he knew was wrong. He was even starting to get used to the sensation. Amazing things could happen when you started poking around in the stacks and the data bases.

Sirius B was about as stable as the San Andreas fault: George had convinced himself of that. Oh, the information wasn't right out there where it was easy to find— but it was there. The conventional, accepted wisdom of

Sirius was surely easy to locate. A dozen references blandly stated that Sirius B showed no measurable variance in brightness. But there were other, harder-to-find sources that flatly contradicted that.

There were, for example, two items in the journal *Nature,* one published in 1985, the other in 1986. The first article was by a pair of German astronomers, who cited several references from the Babylonian and Roman period, including none other than Cicero himself, all of whom spoke very clearly and specifically of Sirius as a *red* star, not the bright white star seen in modern skies. The clear implication was that one of the two stars had been bright red back then.

The idea fit in with a few other points of classical culture. Apparently the ancient Romans used to sacrifice a red dog to celebrate Sirius the Dog Star, it being the brightest in the constellation of Canis Major. George shook his head when he noted that connection. How many astronomers even stopped to think that Canis Major meant Big Dog?

But that was off the point. The central fact was that *stable stars did not change color.* If Sirius had been red two thousand years ago, then one of its two component stars had gone seriously off the rails. But which star? And by what mechanism?

It took George a while to stumble across the second article, but when he did, he knew he had struck pay dirt. It was written by a trio of American astrophysicists who offered an explanation for the color change. The paper suggested that Sirius B, the white dwarf, had experienced a surface thermonuclear runaway, which caused it to become, albeit temporarily, a red giant star. Sirius B had stayed in the giant stage for several centuries and then transmuted back into a dwarf.

George was elated. Obviously the Sirius system was recently unstable; to an astronomer a millennium was but a blink of the eye.

But there was more. George found several references that seemed to suggest the larger star, Sirius A, was slowly evolving off the Main Sequence of the Hertzsprung-Russell diagram, likewise mutating into a red giant. It was a process that would ultimately take millions of years, but it did suggest that Sirius A was not entirely stable either. When a star showed signs of moving off the Main Sequence of the H-R diagram, that star was at least potentially in very serious trouble.

The idea of the H-R diagram was simple: In crudest terms, you charted the absolute brightness of a star at the standard distance of ten parsecs against its temperature. Set up a graph such that overall brightness was measured on the vertical axis, with dimmest at the bottom and brightest at the top. Measure temperature, or spectral class, horizontally, with hottest at the left and coldest at the right.

When the brightness and temperature of a large number of stars are plotted onto such a chart, it quickly becomes apparent that most stars fall into a small band of values known as the Main Sequence, running from the upper left to the lower right. Virtually all stars, except for giants, supergiants, and white dwarfs, charted right smack into the Main Sequence band. Brightness and color were closely related to each other, so much so that the H-R diagram had great predictive value. If a researcher could determine a star's spectral type and its luminosity class precisely, he or she could immediately know its absolute brightness, and thus calculate its distance from its observed apparent brightness.

But there were telling exceptions: stable white dwarfs—old, wizened stars that remained unchanged for millions of years—and stars of all types that had gone unstable one way or another.

The giants and supergiants had relatively cool surfaces, but were so large that their overall brightness was tremendous. Most giants and supergiants, cool in temperature and bright in light, found themselves in the upper right-hand corner of the H-R diagram. White dwarfs like Sirius B were very hot, but so small they

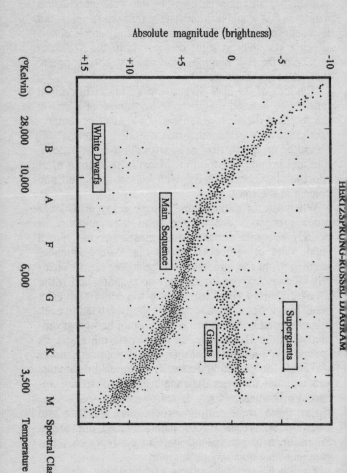

HERTZSPRUNG-RUSSEL DIAGRAM

did not give out much light overall. They wound up in the lower left of the chart.

But the Main Sequence was where most mature stars spent most of their lives. Departing from it almost always spelled catastrophe.

Suppose the Sirius system was on its way to renewed instability. *That* would be something. It was mere speculation, of course, but it was an intriguing idea. So how would it work? How could it happen?

George started doodling out notes and diagrams on a fresh piece of paper. First off, the mass transfer rate from Sirius A to the white dwarf, which was infinitesimal at the moment, would have to increase immensely. That was obvious. Maybe that was what had happened to Sirius B in Roman times. Sirius A ejected just a little extra matter, and just enough of it got sucked up by Sirius B to increase the temperature at the surface and force a mini thermonuclear runaway, which did not quite become a nova because of the limited quantity of nuclear fuel available for it.

Once the excess energy and material were dissipated into space, Sirius B would settle down again until the next time Sirius A bled off part of its atmosphere to its companion. Maybe, the next time, there would be enough matter accreted by the white dwarf to start an honest-to-God surface thermonuclear runaway. For that to happen to such a close, bright star, so near Earth—*that* would be something. If it occurred, it would be a tremendously dramatic event, the sort of thing that would catch the public's attention, send all the astronomers in the world scrambling to repoint their instruments.

George shook his head and blinked. This whole line of reasoning was based on flights of fancy. It was fine to think of the Sirius system as a place to test his revised model of white dwarf instability, a place to get some baseline data. But toying with the idea of Sirius itself going unstable, brightening and changing color dramatically . . . Sirius! One of the most observed, best-known, most placid star systems in the sky. It was almost an article of faith that Sirius was a stable, boring star. To suggest it might alter its behavior—well, it was like suggesting the pope was conducting orgies in the Vatican. George needed to have some pretty good evidence before anyone would admit the possibility, let alone believe him. Hell, he'd have to have incredibly good evidence just to convince *himself*.

And maybe, just maybe, George admitted, he was getting ahead of himself. He had been going out into this research spoiling for a fight, eager to prove the big guys wrong. Well, he had been successful at that, all right, at least to his own satisfaction. Maybe a bit *too* successful. Was he finding things that weren't there, working up evidence that didn't exist?

He needed someone to check his calculations and spot where he had added instead of subtracting. More modest ideas than this one had been shot down by someone catching an elementary flaw in the math or the theory, the author blinded to the error by his own excitement—or ego. George definitely needed to discuss his ideas with someone to make sure he was not completely off on some wild-goose chase.

But who? Certainly not his office mate, Philby. Not unless he felt like getting laughed off campus. And he certainly couldn't ask Stowton.

He tried to think of anyone who might listen without laughing or sneering. There was a sudden twinge of ghost pain in his right arm where it had been broken, and he suddenly remembered the one person who hadn't made a dumb joke or asked any annoying questions when it had happened:

Jessica Talmadge. How many times since that day, half a year before, had he meant to look her up, talk to her, get to know her better—or just thank her for her kindness? Somehow the moment had never come. He had been too wrapped up in his research. Or perhaps, be it confessed, he had never worked up the nerve.

And somehow he had utterly failed to develop any other sort of close friendship in the department this year. Even the few friends he had made in previous years seemed to have dropped by the wayside. For a moment, George felt a deep pang of loneliness. He thought of Trish for the first time in months.

But never mind. He *had* to talk this thing through, bounce the ideas off someone else, and Jessica was almost the only game in town. That much decided, he stood up, gathered his belongings, stuffed his papers in the shabby briefcase that was the trademark of a graduate student, and left the library. It was a short stroll across campus to the astronomy building, and George spent every second of it struggling not to lose his nerve.

He felt ridiculous. After all, he was simply going to ask a colleague her opinion. He wasn't asking her out on a date or anything. Well, maybe he should; he certainly didn't want to thrash this out in front of Jessica's rather humorless office mate. Okay, then, he *would* ask her out for a drink, if the office mate was around. Strictly for the sake of ensuring a private discussion, of course. That was perfectly reasonable, and it even had the merit of being true. Not that the errand's legitimacy had any bearing on the way his pace quickened as he entered the building and headed toward her office. By that time, Sirius B was far from the first thing on his mind.

The end result of this rather convoluted line of reasoning was that he was altogether crushed to find Jessica in sole possession of her office, working on something at her computer, keyboard in her lap. Privacy was theirs here and now, which blew his excuse for buying her a drink right out of the water. But all of a sudden that didn't matter. He stood in the open doorway, a bit out of breath, for some reason suddenly feeling very much at ease.

For a long moment, George stood there, leaning in the doorjamb, just looking at her. Her usual warm smile was absent now, replaced by a look of almost fierce concentration as she stared at her computer terminal. Her short brown sun-lightened hair framed her face nicely. Her complexion still retained a fair degree of its tan, the inevitable result of a vigorous summer spent outdoors in the desert Southwest. She was wearing a blue short-sleeve blouse, and her arms revealed themselves to be strong, muscles well-defined under the skin. Her fingers moved gracefully as she worked at the keyboard. Blue eyes, a pert nose, and it didn't matter that her face was a bit too round, that her mouth was perhaps a shade too small, a bit too thin-lipped. She was nice to look at. George even forgot his errand for a moment, too wrapped up in the simple pleasure of watching her work.

Finally the moment ended. Jessica worked through whatever it was on the computer and looked up, a bit surprised to find that she had a visitor.

"George!" she said with a smile. "How long have you been standing there?"

"Not long. I didn't want to break your train of thought. Have you got a minute?"

"Sure. Just let me save what I've got here." She typed something on her keyboard and put it to one side, then turned to face George as he snagged the chair from behind the other desk and pulled it around beside Jessica's.

"So," she asked. "What's up?"

George took a deep breath. "I think I'm onto something. In fact, a whole series of things."

Jessica cocked her head and looked at him strangely. "Maybe you'd better start at the beginning."

"Well, I'm not even exactly sure where the beginning is. I wanted to do my dissertation on Type Ia supernovae, but a couple of heavy hitters had worked them over pretty well. I could see there wasn't anything left to do."

"But it didn't stay that way," Jessica suggested. "I've kicked open a few closed doors like that myself. Amaz-

ing how much they didn't learn once they were sure
they knew it all.''

George smiled. ''I never thought of it that way, but
that's exactly what this has been like. The long and the
short of it is that I'm convinced that the classic model
of Type Ia supernovae is flawed. They fixed the minimum mass for a white dwarf to go supernova at about
1.2 solar masses. I get a value closer to 1.05, possible
lower. And there were other errors, every bit as serious.''

Jessica raised her eyebrows and let out a low whistle.
''Boy, someone must have really dropped the ball doing
the math.''

''Not really. That's the fascinating thing. Based on
what was known then, their work was perfectly fine.
It's just that there's been a lot of work since, in astrophysics and elsewhere. Each advance was modest by
itself, really, but the cumulative effect of all the little
corrections has been tremendous.''

Jessica pointed to George's briefcase. ''Show me,''
she said.

Feeling more than a bit nervous, George pulled out
his notes and slid his chair closer to her desk, so he
could spread them in front of her. And with that, their
conversation slid out of standard English and into the
tight, cryptic jargon of astronomy and astrophysics.
George went over the research and recalculation he had
done during the last six months; and then quickly
brought her up to speed on the evidence he had found
suggesting that Sirius B was far more variable than most
astronomers thought—and that Sirius A was showing
signs of departing the main sequence.

There was an odd, spare magic to the technical conversation they shared. The words were dry and terse,
as full of acronyms and numbers as anything else—but
there was a *connection* between the two of them, by
which each understood the other instantly. Neither had
to ask the same question twice; each grasped every explanation almost before it was given.

Neither of them noticed the passage of time. There was nothing but the interplay of ideas, papers shuffled back and forth, sketches and quick calculations and doodled diagrams scribbled here and there, a few quick checks of this reference or that.

But at last they emerged from their shared concentration, and Jessica knew everything George knew. George felt a momentary twinge of disappointment that it was over. But he also knew it was not the ending of their communion together, but the beginning. Not some schoolboy romance, perhaps not romance at all. That didn't matter. He had found what he had been looking for, longer than he knew: someone he could talk to.

Jessica shoved the last of the papers back and stretched. "Okay," she said. *"I'm* convinced. You've got the theoretical work on medium-mass white dwarfs and Type Ia supernovae nailed down pretty tight. *That* you could present, and people might listen. It might be a big enough discovery to score you some points."

"But what about the rest of it? The discussion of Sirius A and B's instabilities?"

"Fascinating," Jessica said, her eyes meeting George's. "But close to impossible for you to present or publish. It's speculation—too many ifs. You probably wouldn't get past the referee for the *Astrophysical Journal.* Even *Nature* wouldn't touch it. They might if you had your doctorate and a prestigious position somewhere—but you're an unknown graduate student."

George nodded sadly. One of astronomy's dark little secrets: it was not socially acceptable to start a controversy unless you had at least an associate professorship. "I figured you'd say that. But dammit, if Sirius A does change in its spectrum, if it is really starting to take off from the main sequence—then someone ought to be watching for that. No one ever observes Sirius anymore—"

"Amazing how much they'll miss since they're sure they won't find anything," Jessica said with a smile.

George smiled back, something he hadn't done

enough of in a long while. "Yeah, the same old story. But if it *does* happen someday, someone should be watching for it, so we have as long an initial data baseline as possible. Besides, it'd just be *fun* to follow it. As it is, I couldn't justify any observing time for this myself, especially since I can't predict when changes will occur. They may not happen for years, even centuries."

"And unless you go public, nobody else will be looking for changes in Sirius. After all, everyone knows it's a rock-steady standard-issue boring star." Jessica leaned back in her chair and stared at the cracked and peeling ceiling, chewing her pencil. "What about the amateurs?" she asked at last.

The world's professional astronomers were vastly outnumbered by the amateurs. Some of them were organized in clubs, while others worked alone. Many of them possessed first-rate hardware and real skill. In some ways they were purer astronomers than the professionals: The politics of academia and science didn't get in the way of their work—at least not as much. Without the distractions of career building and ambition, the amateurs were driven by little more than enthusiasm for the night sky.

The professional astronomers traditionally maintained close but slightly awkward relations with the amateurs. A bit embarrassed by their puppy-dog enthusiasm, a bit annoyed when one of them stumbled across a discovery the pros had missed, they still relied on them for the sort of routine, ongoing observations that effectively blanketed the heavens, covering far more of the sky than the pros ever could by themselves. The conventional wisdom among the professional astronomers was that the amateurs served as something of an early-warning system, providing a network of lower-powered instruments that at times could alert the *real* astronomers where to point the big guns. The network was effective: most new comets were discovered by amateurs.

"I bet you *could* get the amateur astronomers interested in this thing," Jessica went on. "You just said yourself, professional astronomers couldn't afford to burn up observing time watching for something that might not happen in their lifetimes. But the amateurs don't have to worry about budgets or hogging telescope time from each other. And Sirius is the brightest star in the sky—it would be dead easy for them to observe. If one of them got to spot Sirius A leaving the main sequence or caught the beginning of a thermonuclear runaway on Sirius B—well, that's the sort of prize they live to chase."

George nodded thoughtfully. "That makes sense," he agreed. "But how do I let them know about observing? I can't publish it without getting laughed out of the profession."

"You wouldn't get laughed out. Some people won't take you seriously, but you're only offering this idea as a possibility. You're floating a trial balloon, not stating a certainty."

Gorge rubbed his chin. "True. But it still might be smart to use some kind of low-key way to offer the idea. How about if I gave a paper, a five-minute presentation at the next AAS meeting?"

Jessica nodded thoughtfully. "Maybe AAS. Or else you might consider the Astronomical Society of the Pacific. Neither of them is too strict about the content of poster papers or five-minute papers. AAS is probably the best bet. Besides, with a five-minute talk or a poster, you wouldn't have to say too much in the preconvention abstract." Jessica grinned mischievously. "*That* should make you feel safer." The abstracts offered summaries of the papers to be given, but gave the five-minute talks and the poster papers little more than a few sentences.

George considered the suggestion. Maybe a five-minute talk would be just the right slot for a dicey paper like this one: a short presentation that was public, but not too public. A poster paper might be *too* low-key. A poster presenter simply stuck the paper up on the board and then hung around, prepared to discuss his ideas with anyone who'd listen.

Jessica's advice made sense, but it was more than a bit disheartening. He had come into her office with news that could turn astronomy on its ear; and suddenly he was reduced to scheming out ways to avoid embarrassing himself.

"Think a five-minute paper's the best I can do?" George asked.

Jessica nodded, suddenly serious again. "I think so, George. If they'll even let you do that much."

Chapter 4

February 1998
Boston, Massachusetts

Father Francis Xavier O'Rourke, S.J., despised few things so much as Boston winters.

Considering his present circumstances, that was not good. Not only was he back in Boston, however briefly, and not only was that city caught in the throes of the nastiest winter in years, but to cap it off, by all accounts, today was one of the worst days of the whole miserable season.

It would be.

The one day Father Francis had to travel across town, the one day he could have used some cooperation from the weather—that *would* have to be the day it all turned doubly miserable, bad enough to shut down the trolley lines and make driving an invitation to suicide. Still, he could get there by walking. Just barely.

That didn't matter, though. Today he had a debt to pay. Desmond Potter was missing, and Desmond Potter was his friend, going back all the way to the seminary. The Church had lost a good priest when Desmond had left to pursue his interest in psychiatry.

And he had been a good psychiatrist, until the final disaster. Desmond Potter had done many good works for Boston, and for Francis's parishioners, back in the days when Francis had a Boston parish to run. But then the Church had shipped him out to the blessedly mild and reasonable climate of Southern California. Coming back from there to here on Church business only served to remind him why he had been glad of the California posting.

Francis had lost track of Desmond during the years in California, and had been shocked to learn the news when he made a casual attempt to look up his old friend. Something over a year ago, an ex-patient had blown up his wife and child, destroying Desmond's house. The assailant had killed himself, and Desmond Potter was missing, presumed dead. End of story.

Another vicious blast of wind caught Francis square in the face and he hunched over again. Today's storm was the sort where the wind howled and the snow came down in a stinging, needle-sharp torrent that felt like a sandblaster gnawing away at any part of your body you were foolish enough to leave exposed. No one went outside who could possibly avoid it—but today Father Francis was forced to traipse halfway across the city.

He gritted his teeth and hunched over more, tried not to see the dismal cityscape that surrounded him. The gray snows of yesterday were a dismal underpinning for today's onslaught, and all the snows of the last two grim months lay in moribund heaps beneath that. In layers thick and thin, light gray and dark, the snow heaps were a dreary sedimentary history of the whole horrid season.

Every year it was the same. As the winter progressed, the snow would take over the city. There would be no place to put it all, and so it would sprawl every-where, heaping up anyplace it wanted, wherever it could be shoved even partly out of the way. Plowed to the sides of the roads, shoveled to the edge of sidewalks, avalanching off roofs, it stayed where it landed, in mounds and heaps and overhangs that slumped over and collapsed and had to be moved out of the way again and again.

And still new snow would come, and there would be no place to put the freshly shoveled stuff but atop the snows of yesterday. And the plows would come again, thrusting up another layer in the towering walls of snow.

And so the mounds, the hummocks, the hills of plowed and shoveled snow, grew and merged into min-iature mountain chains, running virtually the length of every street. Many of them were taller than a tall man. Father O'Rourke was of medium height at best, and he could not see over most of them, but only straight up and down the narrow path cut between the snow heaps.

By now, midway through February, the streets and sidewalks had become long, meandering trenches, bul-warks dug in a long, grim—and failing—attempt to hold against the enemy, winter.

But the most depressing sights were the cars, frozen in place like so many ghost ships locked in an arctic sea of ice. Father Francis paused by one of them, and shook his head sorrowfully. He might be a man of God, but he was also a bit of a car enthusiast. As best he could tell, that was a late-model Saturn under there—a very stylish little car, a pretty thing. At least it had been pretty before the plows had buried it well past the door handles.

The wheels, the hood, the rear deck—all of them were engulfed by the snow. Only the passenger com-partment was even partially exposed. A new gust of wind caught at the father and he moved on, heading west on Commonwealth, shaking his head sadly over the fate of the car. By the time it melted out in spring, the paint would be gouged and scraped, perhaps some of the windows cracked by the weight of the snow, the tires more than likely gone flat.

The priest passed a similar automotive victim a few hundred yards on. On every block, it seemed, were cars that no one had dug out in time, the day the first heavy snows had come. That was a fatal error. Fail to excavate your car before the plows came, and it would be too late. For when the plows did come, they would heap more snow atop the cars. If—no, *when*—another snow came, and another plow came past, that would only make it worse. After a while the snow would congeal and compress into a gray-black ice as hard as iron, and those unlucky cars were frozen in, for months at a time.

Father Francis walked grimly on, remembering the long years he had served here. This time he was only in town for a few days, but he remembered, down in his bones, how a Boston winter lasted, how long it felt. Boston winters were the closest he ever cared to get to understanding the concept of eternity.

For a Boston winter never ended—not really. Not deep in one's memory. The sky gray, the snow gray, the people gray, the gritty slush that slopped everywhere most decidedly gray. And then the snow would come again, in the gloomy afterlight of evening; even *it* would seem gray. January, February, and sometimes it seemed February again, on into March. There was nothing but a frozen and changeless gray world. Until you finally decided it truly would never end.

But then it did. The snows would fade away, the clouds would part, flee across the sky, and the world would be reborn. All would be made new.

All but memory. For even in the balmiest days of midspring, when the New England freshness and green seemed to invade the city's heart and let it be born anew—even then you would remember those gray and endless days, and recall the depths of your own depression.

And perhaps that was the point, Father Francis told

himself as he walked toward the Commonwealth Avenue Security Shelter. Even after something as bad as a Boston winter, there was spring, there was life. There was hope. Even if hope had to be edged with the remembrance of pain and experience. Even in the depths of winter, hope was necessary, and possible.

That, after all, was the message he had come to deliver.

It had taken him a long time to track down Dr. Desmond Potter. It had taken a lot of time merely to confirm the man was nowhere to be found, at least not under his own name. There had been no sign of him since he had vanished from the ruins of his own property over a year before. There had been a bit of a hue and cry in the papers for a few days when Desmond disappeared, but by now it was just one more forgotten case in the files, so far as the overworked police were concerned.

The police said that Desmond was dead, or had skipped out, left the city, perhaps the state and the country, to start over somewhere new. But none of Desmond's bank accounts had been touched, none of his credit cards used, no checks cashed. It was as if Desmond had walked out, deliberately leaving everything behind. He had even left his wallet behind, with his credit cards and a considerable amount of cash still in it. The police seemed to have reached the unspoken assumption that Desmond had killed himself, doing it in some way that had left no trace. Perhaps he had jumped off a boat with weights on his feet, one sergeant suggested.

Father Francis had resisted that notion. There was no way to know for sure, of course, but he could not quite believe that Desmond was capable of such an act, no matter how desperate his situation. The man had talked far too many people out of suicide; Francis could not believe he would try it himself.

And there was the money, the wallet, the way it had all been left behind. It had been found stuffed in a

drawer, not put in any special place. There had been
no note left behind. And the crumbled remains of the
bonfire in the driveway—that told Francis a different
story from what it told the police. Desmond had not
destroyed any of his personal papers, had not burned
family pictures, or destroyed anything that spoke of
Desmond Potter, the man, the husband, the father.
What he had destroyed instead were case notes, scholarly papers, certificates and diplomas: in short, he had
killed Dr. Desmond Potter, the psychiatrist.

Following this line of reasoning, therefore, Father
Francis concluded that Desmond Potter was alive. In
which case the money he had left behind spoke vol-
umes. He abandoned it because it was tainted, earned
in the profession that had betrayed him so completely.
He had left without a dime in his pocket.

And that, in itself, was a clue, *the* clue that had led
Father Francis to Desmond Potter. For without money,
Desmond could not have gotten far. Well, yes, he could
have hitchhiked his way out, or simply decided to walk.
But if his intention was to lose himself, then there were
few better places to do that than a city he knew well.

Desmond, therefore, was in the Boston area, and
somewhere in the Boston area where a person without
money could exist. And in this day and age, there were
precious few places where *that* was possible.

Father Francis had battled his way through endless
phone calls, hectored any numbers of officials, and
called in more than one personal favor before he got
access to the computerized photo files stored in the
bowels of the Boston city computer system. The per-
missions had taken days. Once he had a description of
Desmond fed into the computer, the search had taken
minutes. A John Doe answering Desmond's description
had been taken to the Commonwealth Avenue Security
Shelter a few days after the attack on Desmond's house,
and was still there.

It had to be him.

At last he reached the brow of the hill, and the bleak,

barricaded entrance of the security shelter. It was a dismal old place. Francis had some vague recollection that it had been a car dealership thirty years before, and then Boston University had used it for a while before ceding it to the city. Now all the windows were bricked over, and a high steel mesh fence topped with accordion wire surrounded the building.

Father Francis paused at the entrance, then stabbed a finger into a button marked *access*. After a moment, an armored camera atop the gate swiveled down to get a look at him. There was a low buzzing sound, and the gate swung open. He stepped inside the perimeter and made his careful way up the ice-sheathed stairs. The heavy steel doors swung open just as he reached the top stair. A blast of overheated air slapped him in the face as he stepped into the harsh, too bright, yellowish light of the security vestibule. The outside doors slammed shut behind him and his glasses fogged over for a moment as he stood in the small compartment. He spotted another inspection camera and pulled the hood of his parka back. He took his gloves off, unwrapped his scarf, and pulled his fogged-up glasses off to give the camera a good look at him. Father Francis had a thin, patrician face, a sparse thatch of graying hair, deep blue eyes, and a long, beaklike nose. "Father Francis O'Rourke," he volunteered before any disembodied voice could challenge him. "Here to see John Doe inmate number 11729."

There was a moment's pause, and then the inner door swung open. The harsh odor of disinfectant redoubled as he went inside. He found himself in a large, barren room, forty feet on a side, the air stale and overheated. A surly man in the gray coverall of an inmate was pushing a broom around. He glared at the priest, clearly suspecting him of treading in mud and slush from the outside. Father Francis looked around and saw a guard booth along one wall. "Father O'Rourke," the priest repeated, simultaneously feeling a bit unnerved and foolish. "For inmate 11729."

A bored, suspicious guard sat in the booth behind bulletproof glass. "Interview room two," his voice boomed out from a speaker. "The transit guard will bring 11729 down from the dayroom."

There was a line of numbered doors in the far wall. Father Francis crossed the aseptic linoleum, opened the one marked 2, and stepped inside a small room with scruffy soundproofed walls. There was a table with two chairs in the center of the room, and another door in the opposite wall. Somehow this room seemed a bit chilly, as if it had nothing to do with the barren, overheated wilderness of the front room. Father Francis sat uncertainly in the chair on his side of the table.

Without preamble or warning, the door on the opposite side of the wall swung open, and a dark, swarthy, unshaven man came in, walking with a firm, aggressive stride. Father Francis gasped. It was Desmond, all right. Up until this moment, he had not been sure.

But if this was Desmond, it was not the Desmond he had known. The priest had prepared himself for a change in Desmond's appearance, but not this much of one. The intake ID photo he had seen downtown did not convey it all. The beard, the gauntness, even the haunted look in the eyes—all that had been there. But no photo could convey the anger that seemed to crackle around this man, or the way his hands automatically knotted up into fists when he did not need them. Yet if anger was at the core of this man, there were other things layered on top of it. Resignation, dejection, were written in the droop of his shoulders. Before he saw Francis, his face seemed bored and preoccupied, as if he had expected this to be another iteration of some unpleasantly familiar ritual. He slumped down into the seat of his side of the table.

Then he looked up to see Francis, and his face went altogether blank, betraying no emotion whatsoever. *That would be a vital survival skill in this place,* Francis told himself. *Mask any emotion that could be re-*

garded as a weakness. Like being surprised. "Hello, Desmond," he said, forcing his voice to an even calm, keeping his own face steady.

"Hello, Frank," Desmond Potter said at last. "I thought you were going to be another of the goddamn socials coming to lean on me."

Something had changed in Desmond's voice, become harsher, more guttural. Even the words he chose were different—harder, colder, tougher. "Socials?" Francis asked, though he could guess the meaning.

"Social workers, do-goods, shrinks like I used to be," Desmond said carelessly. "They come in, try and get us to clean up our act." He drummed his fingers on the table, nodded toward Francis. "So what are you here for?"

Francis swallowed hard and looked at his friend. "I'm here for you, Desmond. I've come to get you out of here."

Desmond's eyes flashed with sudden alarm. "No!" he said. "I can't come out. This is where I belong. Where I deserve to be."

"Because of what happened to your family." Francis didn't make it a question.

"Yes!" Desmond said. "I could have prevented—"

"Nothing." Francis spoke the word in a flat, harsh voice, but then tried to calm himself. These were delicate matters. "In the course of my searching for you, the police allowed me to see the file on the man who—who killed your family and then himself. What I saw there chilled my soul. I have read his diary, seen the list of people he intended to kill—and the list of people he *had* killed. Your wife and daughter were not his first victims. Did you know that?"

Desmond looked up sharply. "No. But that can't be right. I *treated* the man. He told me everything. He told me all his revenge fantasies, and they were pretty horrific. He would have told me if he had killed."

That was it. There was the thing Desmond needed to hear. The priest leaned forward across the table, his eyes bright, his expression eager, urgent. *"That* is your failing—your only failing—in all of this: your arrogant belief that you knew, and understood. *No* man tells another everything. *No* man can know a fellow being with perfect understanding, and that is doubly true for a madman. Only God can know the deepest inner workings of the human soul, and the blackness of Gibbons's soul was the deepest and most tortured I can imagine.

"How could you claim to understand Gibbons, when that power is given only to God? The one thing that is certain here is that the man could not even begin to comprehend himself, to tell delusion from reality. It's entirely possible that Gibbons was no longer aware that he had killed before, or was so lost in his own delusions he could not distinguish his fantasies from his real actions. Perhaps he thought he was imagining it all when he delivered that package to your home."

"But I should have seen all that. I should have spotted it, and stopped him."

There was something in Desmond's voice that told Father Francis the man was asking for absolution, and the priest was glad to offer it. "No, you could not have. No one could have stopped him. He was too skillful at what he did. He fooled the whole world, paid his rent, held down a job. His sessions with you were paid for by the postal workers' health plan. He built up a whole life, or at least the shell of one, to camouflage the monster inside. Maybe in your sessions you breached the first layers of his defenses—but how many layers were there?

"Gibbons was a catastrophe waiting to happen. He spent his whole life concealing the true depths of his madness, his monstrosity, from public view. He was a past master at hiding it. You could have not seen who or what he was. No one who lived in the real world could possibly understand his warped, diseased view of things.

"Sooner or later, he was going to fixate on someone again. Once he chose you, there was nothing you could do to stop him, because it was impossible for you to know what he was. And bear in mind that it was *you* he was trying to kill, not your family. *You* did not place your family in danger. Blame his incompetence for their deaths, not your failure to stop him.''

''But I *am* to blame, for living,'' Desmond cried. *''I* should have died. *I* was meant to die—''

''No one *should* have died. *No one* was meant to die. A deranged man fixated on you and murdered your family when he tried to kill you. Period. He is to blame for his actions, for their deaths. Not you, not your profession, not your attempts to help him.''

''But—''

''Desmond. This is me, Frank. The two of us could never lie to each other. Look me in the eye, right now, and tell me you truly believe you are responsible for these deaths. Can you do that?''

Desmond Potter looked up at his old friend, and their eyes met for a moment that seemed to last an hour. At last Desmond sighed and looked away. But something long dead seemed to have come back to life in his eyes. ''No. No, I can't. Not anymore. When I first came here, yes. But you have a lot of time to think in a place like this, and I've spent the last month or two telling myself everything you've just said.''

''Then why in the world are you punishing yourself?'' Francis demanded. ''Why do you think that you belong in a place like this?''

''Because I do!'' Desmond said, suddenly standing up. ''Because we *all* do. That's the terrible secret I've discovered. I have spent over a year in here, Francis. A year with the sort of madmen I never truly imagined still existed. The kind that were too far gone for me, for any doctor to reach. And what I've come to realize is that Gibbons isn't the exception—he's the rule. I have seen the true face of humanity in here, and it is dark, and getting darker.''

Father Francis looked up into his friend's face, fear

in his heart. What had this man seen, what dark visions had he conjured up for himself in this place?

"I'm taking you out of here," the priest said at last. "What you have seen is not humanity, but merely one dark corner of it, and *you don't belong in that darkness*. You're not a madman. Even if you consider what this place is supposed to be, instead of what it is, you don't belong. It's supposed to be a shelter for the poor, and you are no pauper. You have money. A lot of it."

"What money?" Desmond demanded. "What money that isn't tainted by the way I earned it? Lying to people, telling them I could help."

"But you *did* help them, hundreds of them directly as your patients, and many more by helping the community. You just got through saying that you were wrong, that you knew Gibbons was not your fault. Can you honestly say that you helped no one? Or even that you failed to help the vast majority of your patients? And even if you grant, irrationally, that the money you earned by your own toil is tainted—what moral victory is gained by letting the bank keep it? Besides, even ignoring the money you had in the bank, there's the question of the insurance settlement."

Desmond looked startled. "Insurance? I never even thought about that—"

"Your house was blown up," Francis said, a trace of irony in his voice. "I'd say that was grounds for a claim. I've checked into it, and it's quite a tidy sum. I doubt even you could perceive *that* money is tainted. It's yours, and you are entitled to it. Either you accept it or the insurance company keeps it, and I don't see what *that* accomplishes. The long and short of it is, you are a wealthy man."

"I have no use for money. Not anymore."

"Nonsense. If you told me you had no use for fancy cars and elaborate dinners and shopping sprees, that I could accept. But money can buy many things far more worthwhile. It can buy you the chance to do some good."

Desmond sat down and nodded vaguely, drumming his fingers on the table. "All right, all right. So what do you suggest I do?"

"I think you should come back to California with me. As far away from this nightmare as possible. There's a Jesuit retreat in Santa Barbara. I can arrange for you to stay there for a while. Stay there and rest . . . and heal."

"Then what?" Desmond asked.

Francis relaxed a bit. He knew the signs, knew he had talked Desmond into it. "That," he said, "is entirely up to you."

April 1998
Tucson, Arizona

George Prescott had a star in a box. In fact, two of them. At least that was how he thought of his model. He patted the side of his home computer, knowing fully well the image was irrational on more levels than one. For starters, he was using the computer as a terminal, and the model itself wasn't even *in* this box. It was in the department's miniframe, buried somewhere in the bowels of the astronomy building, linked to his home computer by phone lines. Even down at the department, his imagined star in a box wasn't anything but a mathematical abstraction lodged in a miniframe computer.

George yawned enormously and grabbed, unseeing, for another slice of pizza, his eyes still glued to the screen. He sat at a makeshift desk jammed into one corner of his apartment's living room, the once-neat room half-buried in reference books and computer printouts, massive flowcharts taped to the wall. Night had fallen long ago, and the room was dark. There was no illumination but a desk light and the glow from the computer screen, and George's face looked strange, lit from below and glowing with strange shades reflected from the screen. He rubbed a grubby hand over his stubbly, unwashed face and murmured a string of formulae as he read them off the screen, talking himself through an intricate revision in his math.

His model of the Sirius system was getting better; no, more than better. It was getting *real*. The complex formulae, the elaborate data sets, the simulated convection patterns and heat transfer rates—all of it was beginning to act like a real pair of stars. Today, this very day, was a day of major triumph. He punched a few keys and watched the visuals again. There it was. His simulated Sirius B went through a pseudo red giant phase and then returned to its normal state as a white dwarf, just as the real star had two thousand years ago. He watched as the pinprick of yellow-white swelled out to become a huge, dim red star far larger than Sirius A, and then retracted into itself again, shrinking back down to a dot of burning-bright white. George felt a wild sense of excitement. It was a rough match, a crude match, but it was a triumph nonetheless. His star in a box was getting real.

But his eyes were starting to swim again. Time for a break. He broke out of the visual simulation, saved his latest version of the coding sequence, stood up, and stretched.

He smiled as he looked down at the work he had done so far. The Sirius simulation was all right, but it was merely one specific data point. There was one part of his data he was dead-certain of, and it ought to be enough to get him some real attention—and it ought to be valid for all white dwarfs in binary or multiple star systems: the minimum mass value for a white dwarf to go supernova was dropping like a rock. Well, maybe that was overstating the case, but not by much. The accepted minimum mass for a supernova progenitor in all the textbooks was 1.20 times the mass of the Earth's sun. But George's first pass through the data, all those many months ago, had shaved it down to a hair over one solar mass. Every pass since then had whittled away a little bit more of that number. Now the minimum was down to just over 95/100ths of a solar mass.

And Sirius B weighed in at almost precisely 1.00 solar mass. For the thousandth time, George thrust that thought from his mind. That was craziness. But the things he had found out today were making that craziness seem just a bit closer to sane.

He started pacing the darkened apartment, restless. He was up too late again, mostly because he had made yet another wild-eyed discovery. And once again, he had made it, not by searching the sky, but by combing the library.

There is a story in astronomy, a true one, but with the force of legend nonetheless. In 1978 a Dr. James W. Christy had noticed that a series of images of the planet Pluto were ruined, the image of the planet elongated, blurred, stretched. In short, Pluto had a bump in one side. That was a not-uncommon flaw in long-duration telescopic exposures. The slightest jarring of the telescope could knock things out of kilter, resulting in a doubled or blurred exposure.

He, and many other astronomers, had seen other elongations in other photographs of the planet, and assumed that they, too, were flawed, defective. But then Christy noticed that none of the *stars* in the photographs were elongated, and that the bump in Pluto's side was moving. He dug out older shots of Pluto, and found the same bulge in some 1965 images. A series of images taken over a six-day period in 1970 made it plain that the bulge was moving clockwise around the planet.

The flaw in the image, the rejected data from the defective images, was nothing more or less than Pluto's moon. Christy named it Charon, and got his name in the history books.

George had gotten to know that story extremely well in the last few weeks. He had found his own lumpy photos, so to speak, by trawling through various spectra of the Sirius system taken over the years.

George sat down at the computer again and called up a series of spectra to the screen. Some of the spectra were older than he was, some taken the week before.

What he had found in the library was a whole series of slightly odd spectra of Sirius A just like the ones on the screen. Spectra that, if taken as correct, showed the star subtly out of kilter. Nothing dramatic, but just strange enough to get another exposure. A day or two after the unusual spectra, everything would be fine again.

Since everyone knew Sirius A just was stable, in no danger of leaving the main sequence within the next million years or so, everyone simply ignored the small, telling oddities. But George was not convinced of that stability. He was willing to believe the oddities were real.

And with the blinders of preconception off, he had established that there were several periodicities to the spectral shifts. They would come and go over a period of a few days for a few years, and then vanish. There was a series of strange spectra on and off in the 1900s. Then a long period of normalcy. Then another series of oddities in the 1940s and 1950s. And, just recently, another flurry of them had cropped up. Even today, no one seemed to be aware that anything was wrong. Not when spectra taken a few days later showed that everything was just fine on Sirius A.

Unless, of course, you assumed the unnoticed data was significant. In which case Sirius A was no more stable than Sirius B. George no longer doubted that the larger star was headed off the main sequence. Indeed, it was no doubt responsible for Sirius B's instability.

George imagined himself sitting down to write the paper, the actual words on the page. That part of the process was far off, but thinking about it helped to sharpen his thoughts, keep them organized.

To sum up, then: Sirius A has not been observed regularly or with great attention in this century. As a result, evidence that its brightness fluctuated has been scant, and that which has been collected has been discounted as errors in measurement. Since nobody was expecting to see light variations in Sirius, nobody did. Any putative variations were dismissed as observational errors.

When taken at face value and plugged into model calculations, these measurements resulted in indications that Sirius A was undergoing nonlinear oscillations, several overlapping cycles of variability with periods of a few years to a few decades.

The kicker was that, if George had the cycle lengths figured correctly, the beat periods of the various cycles were going to coincide within a year or so to produce a maximum oscillation. He could not predict when that might happen with any precision, in part because of the paucity of the observational data.

An odd thought came to George. He was used to thinking in terms of the data points as they came to him, which was, of course, only sensible. But if his data were correct, and he was predicting the evidence of Sirius brightening to arrive at Earth in the next year or so—then that meant the actual event, the brightening, had already happened, though the light carrying that information was still on the way.

Strange thoughts, exciting thoughts. Good old Sirius. No one else paid it much attention, but to George, there was a lifetime of excitement 8.9 light-years away. He leaned back in his chair and smiled around a mouthful of cold pizza, thinking back on how he had tracked it all down. That first time, the first day he had pulled it all together. That had been a red-letter day, and not just because the numbers had worked. That had been the day, the first day, he had really talked to Jessica, gotten the chance to do more than meet her.

He glanced at the cluttered wall behind the computer. There was a photo of Trish there, too, but merely because he had never gotten around to taking it down. On an impulse, he did so now, lifted the frame off the nail in the wall.

It was Jessica's photo that he wanted to look at. A smile on her face as the camera caught her looking over her shoulder. She was wearing a light blue cotton pullover that set off her eyes. The hours and days they had spent together, first merely as colleagues, and then, later, as closer friends, were among George's fondest memories. He missed her terribly.

And with that thought, the smile faded from his face. Photos were all the Jessica George was going to see for a while. She had finished up her work at U. Arizona, and headed back east to Harvard to finish her thesis.

Jessica already had a tenure-track assistant professorship at Caltech lined up. She would start there next fall, after a year and a half of postdoc work at Harvard in order to complete her current project. It was an amazingly rapid advance, considering the current job market. But if anyone deserved a fast track in an astrophysical career, it was Jessica, so far as George was concerned.

He was bitterly aware that his own career was having a slow start. But the thought of being slow reminded him: There were two other things to look at on that wall. A clock and a calendar. The semiannual meeting of the American Astronomical Society was getting closer by the minute, and he wasn't going to be ready.

He tossed the half-eaten slice of pizza back into the box and returned to his work.

Interlude

Sirius System

Go back in time a small distance of years, move a handful of light-years across space.

Far from Earth, in a star system distant in time and space, great events are at hand. At the time they happen, they can have no immediate effect on Earth. Indeed, from Earth, it is impossible to detect them. But, as in a pond of still waters struck by a stone, the results of the event will move outward from the center in waves that will strike at Earth long after the event itself is over.

Sirius A is still ejecting gigatons of matter. Though the two stars, Sirius A and B, are separated by twenty astronomical units, three billion kilometers, a disproportionately large share of the matter being thrown out from Sirius A is being accreted onto the white dwarf, the flow preferentially guided by the magnetic field lines connecting the two stars. An immense quantity of hydrogen/helium gas cloud is accumulating at the surface of Sirius B.

But the flow rate, and the rate of accretion, rapid though they be, are not sufficient to start a thermonuclear runaway at the surface of Sirius B.

A surface runaway is a lesser, survivable crisis for a star. It produces a nova, rather than a supernova, outburst. While the words—nova and supernova—are similar, the events are not. In a nova, only the accumulated outer layers, the surface layers of the star, blow off into space. The star's core survives, and can even attain a new stability, unburdened by the unbalanced pressure of too much surface matter bearing down. A nova can be a purgative, a way to regain health and stability and avoid the danger of a greater destruction.

But a supernova explosion is tremendously more powerful than any mere squall on the star's surface. In a supernova, the star's core itself explodes. Afterward there is, for all intents and purposes, no star left.

Though it has been so in past crises, this time there will be no relatively gentle nova-like event to alleviate the pressure on the core. No mere surface disruption can save the star now.

Instead, the accretion matter continues to arrive at Sirius B, bearing down on the matter at its core, increasing the density and temperature there. Inside the core, the heat and pressure increase until the carbon and oxygen become hot enough, compressed enough, that they are ready to start fusing into heavier atoms. For a time, Sirius B survives on the razor's edge, appearing to bear up well under the troubling infall of matter from Sirius A.

And yet beneath the false calm, the star's fate trembles in the balance. If the mass transfer from the larger star would but stop, the white dwarf could settle down, safely absorb the new matter, and survive.

But the mass transfer does not stop. Sirius A pulses

with new energy. New flares and extravagant explosions jet gigatons more mass out into space. More matter falls on Sirius B. More pressure bears down on the core.

Finally the flashover happens. Deep inside the star, two atoms join into one: a carbon-oxygen fusion event that releases more energy. In nanoseconds the energy is roiling the surrounding region of the star, setting off new fusion events, until a chain reaction begins. Now the speed of events increases abruptly. Time must be measured in nanoseconds, rather than days or weeks. The star itself will not survive long enough for a second hand to sweep once across a clockface.

In far less than a second, the region of fusing atoms spreads out from a dot the size of a match head until it encompasses a volume hundreds of kilometers across. The fusion explosion gathers force with horrifying speed, each new fusion of carbon and oxygen releasing more energy, more heavy particles.

A runaway nuclear fusion ignites the central regions of the white dwarf. Now the star is doomed.

Sirius B topples off the razor's edge, and into the abyss.

Within a few seconds of the first ignition, the fires of fusion engulf over eighty percent of the star's total mass. Mass converts to energy, and atoms are destroyed and reborn in the hottest of all fires.

The catastrophic explosion propagates out toward the surface of the star at some ten percent of the speed of light.

Though it has the mass of the sun, the dense dwarf star is only about the size of Earth, and seconds after the core disruption, the shock front of the colossal explosion reaches the surface of the white dwarf.

At that instant, a blazing ball of flame, fated to become brighter than all the rest of the Galaxy combined, flashes into being. The entire surface of the star lifts off into space. It swells outward from the core, moving at incredible velocity. The plasma shell that moments before had been the star's surface blooms out like a deadly blazing flower.

The superheated shell expands through the orbits of Sirius B's few worlds, slamming into the three wizened, ancient planets that were all Sirius B had. Three small planets, none so large as Earth's moon, evaporate like so many drops of water caught in a blowtorch flame. Rock vaporizes, planetary crusts are shattered by the supernova's shock wave. Worlds boil away, shatter into trillions of fragments, but the wall of fire will not even suffer such broken shards to survive. It smashes them down further into molten nothingness, into vapor and gas, and they are seen no more. The last traces of the lost worlds are caught up in the interior wave fronts and flung outward, dead ashes cast into limitless space.

The star is dead.

The supernova is born, and growing.

The newborn supernova gathers its power and moves outward with a speed and power unimaginable. It takes only twenty seconds from the moment of the initial explosion for the expanding shell to grow from the size of Earth to the size of Earth's sun. In only eighty minutes it grows to the circumference of Earth's orbit.

The shell expands out into space at one tenth the speed of light. Its exterior is extremely bright, but its interior surface is all but opaque to most of the electromagnetic spectrum.

Inside the shell, the remnant of Sirius B's core is a roiling maelstrom, a witch's caldron of fusion reactions spewing out hard radiation and energetic particles of all kinds.

Because the remaining crust of the white dwarf, containing some fifteen percent of its total mass, is at first optically thick, the extremely energetic photons from the supernova explosion are contained within the shell, bottled up. They cannot yet escape.

Thus, the core conditions are not yet observable in any form of electromagnetic radiation. The rapidly expanding gaseous shell is in effect a giant bottle that holds all the core radiation—X rays, gamma rays, and other forms of high-energy photons—inside itself. It bounces the gamma rays and other radiation back and forth across the interior. Energized photons are de-energized by the Compton effect, and then reenergized by the inverse Compton effect. None of this interior radiation can escape. Yet.

However, the rapidly inflating shell itself has started off its career as the skin of a hot white dwarf star, with a surface temperature of about twenty-seven thousand degrees, five times as hot as the sun. As it expands, the total light-emitting area of the shell gets bigger, with the obvious result that the overall brightness increases as well. Within a minute of the explosion, the hot shell outshines its formerly much brighter companion, Sirius A. And still it expands.

Though it took only minutes for the shell to reach Sirius B's planets, the shell's next victim is much farther off. Even at a tenth the speed of light, it is only after some twenty-six hours that the shell slams into the larger star, Sirius A.

It was the internal instabilities of the giant star that set Sirius B down the long, complex path toward self-immolation, and now, in its death throes, the lesser star has its revenge on its tormentor. The outer layers of Sirius A's surface are ablated and stripped off by the violent impact with the fast-moving shell. The impact sets off incredibly energetic outbursts of all kinds. But it is not merely the outer skin of the shell that preys on Sirius A. The shell engulfs the larger star, traps it in the superhot radioactive furnace of the supernova's interior, and Sirius A is roasted alive. The greater star will survive, but it will be badly damaged by the assault.

Such matters do not concern the still-expanding gas shell. The impact with Sirius A does not even slow it down.

Chapter 5

May 1998
Santa Barbara, California

Francis insisted on daily walks. He was a great believer in evening constitutionals to get a bit of exercise,
a bit of air in the lungs, and he insisted on taking Desmond along. Weeks ago, Desmond had given up argu-
ing about it. Truth to tell, he had actually come to enjoy
the strolls himself. He had been healing here in California, recovering from wounds he had carried so long,
he had forgotten they were there. But still the shadows
of Dorothy's death, of little Jane's death, of the security
shelter, hung over him.

The evening air was warm. A sea breeze played with
the fabric of Desmond's short-sleeve shirt, played with
his now neatly trimmed beard, blew over his bare forearm. Spring had come to the seaside town, to the nearby
mountainsides, and summer was on its way. But such

things as seasons were of little consequence here, and
that bothered Desmond Potter not at all. He had had
enough of seasons, and change, and the cycles of life
and death.

*To every thing there is a season, and a time to every
purpose under heaven.* The quotation intruded itself on
his recollection, and there was something almost re-
proachful about the tone of the voice that spoke in his
head. It startled him. He glanced to Father Francis,
walking beside him, but the priest had not spoken. Indeed, the voice had not sounded anything like Francis.
Desmond shook his head as if to clear it, and pulled a
deep breath of air into his lungs. A momentary illusion,
a trick the mind played on itself. He was not hearing
voices, he assured himself, a bit too firmly to be convincing.

But whatever the source, the words held meaning.
They were a reminder that time had not stopped here,
that Life—all right, that God—still required things of
him. Desmond Potter still had a role to play. Otherwise
he could just as well have been left to rot in the security
shelter.

But what that role might be, he had no idea.

It was a beautiful day, calm and restful, and that was
the main thing. He looked toward the ocean, hidden
behind a screen of houses and foliage. He could smell
the fresh tang of salt air that blew from the west, and
from here and there, even in the middle of the town, it
was possible to catch a glimpse of blue. The mountains
rose up behind them to the east, stern and verdant
green.

"So, Desmond, have we managed to change your
viewpoint at all?" Francis asked as the two men strolled
the town.

"If you mean, is it still possible for me to think of
man as basically evil on such a lovely evening, when I
have food in my belly and I've had enough sleep?"

Francis smiled and shrugged. "Something like that,
yes."

Desmond let out a deep sigh and stuffed his hands into the pockets of his jeans. "Yes, it is, Frank. It is very much still possible."

Francis turned and looked at his friend worriedly. "You were a victim of a terrible crime; there's no denying that. You have endured a lot, and suffered greatly, and seen things most people would not choose to see. But—"

"But just because I do not see evil and madness *now*, there is no cause to believe them? Because they are not present in front of me here, now, I should conclude they have no power?" The two of them passed a line of newspaper dispensers and Desmond gestured at them. "Put fifty cents into any one of those machines and you'll see the power of evil at work. India and Pakistan at each other's throats again, Iraq and Syria ready to attack each other. Riots in Moscow and Bucharest. The latest fashion in New York is designer-color bulletproof vests. And right here, in Southern California. Waterjacking wasn't even a *word* ten years ago, and now it's the biggest crime in California. Diverting water, one town stealing it from another. Good God, black-market *water?* Letting your neighbor go thirsty so you can water your lawn? That's not evil and madness?"

Francis did not reply.

Their route this evening had taken them into one of the scruffier parts of town, though that wasn't saying much for Santa Barbara. Even the roughest parts of town seemed downright genteel compared to where Desmond had been recently. Desmond looked across the street and noticed a run-down building. He stopped to look at it, and Francis stopped with him. The place looked as if it might have been a bar or a restaurant in some previous incarnation.

In fact, it still looked quite a bit like a bar, a biker bar. There was a line of motorcycles parked outside, with long-haired, tough-dressed men sprawled across several of them. Bright floodlights glared down here and there along the side of the building, but the illumination seemed to do little more than accentuate the darkness that surrounded the pools of light.

The bikers' women—Desmond resisted the idea of women as possessions, but it was utterly clear in every posture and pose that these people thought that way—at any rate, the bikers' women brought the men fresh beers and sat on the men's laps. Loud rock music blared down from tinny public-address speakers bolted to the outside of the building. Desmond realized he had been hearing the music for some time as they walked along.

"Not quite my idea of a church," Father Francis said wryly, gesturing to the sign over the door.

Desmond looked up at it. THE CHURCH OF THE ROAD, it read. Over it was an elaborate symbol, a motorcycle wheel and a pair of handlebars below a crucifix. "My God," Desmond said in surprise. "The Christriders."

"You know much about them?" Francis asked. "They have a spotty reputation, to put it mildly. It looks like they're living up to it tonight."

"Oh, I know them," Desmond said. For no reason he could understand, his heart was suddenly racing with excitement. There was a feeling, somewhere deep inside, that reminded him of the moments as a child when the family was returning from a long trip and their own house would finally come into view. "Oh, I know the Riders," he repeated. "There were a number of Riders in the shelter. One of them was quite good with a needle."

"A needle!" Francis looked at his friend in shocked surprise. "They managed to smuggle drugs into a security shelter?"

"No, no, a tattooing needle. I even let him work on me, when I got bored enough." That sense of excitement still tingled inside him. "I heard a lot about these places in the shelter, but I never did get the chance to see one of them myself."

"You aren't actually proposing that we go in there,

are you?'' Francis asked. He raised his hand to his throat, and touched his Roman collar, no doubt wondering what sort of reception the Christriders would offer a Catholic priest. There had been stories.

"Why not?'' Desmond asked. "All they could do to us would be to throw us out.''

"They might manage more than that, Desmond.''

"Oh, Frank, where's your sense of adventure?'' Desmond asked. "Come on.'' He took the priest by the arm and pulled him across the street, deeper into the shadows on the far side of the road and up the three low steps into the building. Desmond pulled the heavy door open and they stepped inside.

If the exterior greatly resembled a biker bar, the interior resembled one completely. The music roared louder than it had outside. The room was dark, with patches of dim light supplied by a few beat-up overhead lamps strung here and there. A tiny dance floor was crowded with bodies. There was a tinkle of broken glass from somewhere.

As the priest and the psychiatrist watched, a lithesome, redheaded woman in hot pants and a clingy red top stepped up onto one of the tables. As the other dancers cheered and hooted, she stripped off her tight T- shirt and danced bare-chested.

Desmond jumped as a hand clamped down on his shoulder, and a pit formed in the base of his stomach. Bracing himself to be told in no uncertain terms by a surly bouncer that he and Francis were not welcome here, he turned around—

—To look into the warm and friendly smile of a tall, slender woman, modestly dressed in jeans and long-sleeve shirt. "Janny really gets 'em going in there, don't she?'' the woman shouted over the music, in a tone of voice that made it sound as if she were commenting on the antics of mischievous children. "But she's probably not what you came to see. You fellows looking to come inside?'' she bellowed into Desmond's ear.

More than a little confused by the situation, Desmond could do little more than nod dumbly. He glanced at Francis, whose face had gone completely pale.

The woman nodded and gestured for the two men to follow her down a long hallway that ran along one side of the bar. "I'm Emma, by the way," she shouted over her shoulder. "I'll be glad to show you around later, but you can see things are jumping right now. They need me on the outside, but maybe I can come on in later." The sound level diminished a bit as they moved away from the bar. She came to a heavily soundproofed door at the end of the hall. "Next time you come, head around to the back and you won't have to come through the bikers."

"Aren't, ah, *you* a biker?" Father Francis asked.

Emma's faced clouded for a moment, but then her smile returned. "Well, course you wouldn't know all our lingo. And maybe if you talk to some of the outside types, they might call themselves something they're not. I'm a *Rider,* not a biker. A Christrider. Everyone, well practically everyone in here"—she hooked her thumb at the door—"is a full-fledged Rider, and they don't take kindly to being called bikers. Bikers—they're the ones outside, the ones watching Janny dance. Some of them *call* themselves Riders, but they're not. Not yet, anyway, and a lot of them not ever. Bikers—they're our raw meat." She grinned, and it was not altogether a pleasant expression. Then she yanked open the heavy door and stood by it, ushering the two men past her into the next room. "Inside there is the *real* Church of the Road. Y'all have a good time. See you later."

Desmond went through, Francis beside him, a dubious expression on his face. The heavy door slammed behind them, and the two men found themselves staring at each other. They were standing in a dimly lit, narrow hallway, about twenty feet long, that seemed to open onto one end of a large room. By the looks of things, they were now in the building adjoining the bar, a place that had looked like a warehouse from the outside. The connecting door through the abutting walls of the two buildings seemed to have been knocked through fairly recently.

The first thing Desmond noticed about being "inside"—whatever that meant—was something that surprised him. With the door slammed shut, the blaring dance music faded to a mere whisper behind them. He had assumed that the music from the bar was going to be booming twice as loud on the inside.

Instead he heard a man's amplified voice over a background hum of conversation, the speaker's words not quite distinguishable over the buzz of the crowd.

Desmond hesitated, wary of venturing further into this strange place. He glanced at Francis's worried face and wondered just how smart and fair it had been to bring the priest here.

But damn it, he *had* to know. What the devil was "inside"? Desmond's curiosity got the better of him and he walked down the hallway, stopping just shy of the doorway leading to the back of the main room.

This room—the back room, the inside room—was brightly lit. Members of the "congregation" were sitting around the sort of tables that would have looked perfectly at home in any bar or juke joint. The people—at least the ones here at the back of the house—were drinking and eating, chatting among themselves, table-hopping. There was a low, constant buzz of cheerful conversation and laughter in the place, and it struck Desmond that he had never heard that in a church before. He found himself wondering why that should be so, wondering what was wrong with the sounds of happy people that they should not be heard in church.

And to be fair, most of the people were paying at least cursory attention to the unseen far end of the room, where, Desmond assumed, the service was taking place. At least the amplified voice was coming from there, a very deep, resonant male voice, though the words it spoke were muffled by the background noise.

None of this was as Desmond expected, but it was the deep and complicated smell of the place that sur-

prised him most. In the front room, geologic ages of
cheap beer, cheap whiskey and wine, and sweat had
left their mark, their odor long ago having seeped into
the floors, the beams, the walls of the place.

But here other, better, newer smells replaced the stale
odors: sweet incense, scented candle smoke, fresh
bread, tangy spices, the aromas of a dozen foods. And
good foods, their odors fresh and tantalizing—not the
stale, greasy slop he would have expected. The place
was cleaner than he would have guessed, as if someone
had been working very hard to keep the sordidness of
the front room bar from seeping in.

What sort of place was this? He looked at the faces
in the room, trying to read some sense of the people
who joined the Church of the Road.

They seemed *happier* than he had expected; calmer;
stronger than the surly, half-besotted bikers outside, or
the grim-faced, half-crazed men at the shelter who had
called themselves Riders.

But there were no fresh-faced, clean-cut types here.
Call themselves what they might, they *were* still bikers,
no doubt about that. Most sported well-worn leather
jackets with full regalia, and there were elaborately
decorated helmets on most of the tables. Yet it went
deeper than how they dressed. Not so long ago, Desmond had made his living from reading human beings,
and there was a great deal he could read here, in the
faces, in the way people moved and acted.

The Riders might be cleaned up, healthier, happier
than the crowd outside, but there was something under
the surface that told him they were no less dangerous.
He could sense that much just standing here, noting the
look in an eye, in the edginess beneath a smile, a slight
jumpiness. A hundred tiny signs whispered to him that
these people were still perfectly capable of the crazed
anger, the angry lashing out, that had typified a certain
class of his patients.

And that should not be surprising. Not from a group
that *recruited* from biker gangs. What had that woman

Emma called the bikers? "Raw meat"? Desmond shivered.

The Riders less dangerous than a regular bike gang? No, not so. These were clearly people capable of organizing, cooperating, setting a common goal, and working toward it. Grafting such ability onto, say, the Hell's Angels' capacity for violence, the *predilection* for violence that was part of their heritage, made them far more deadly than the thugs in the front, the outside.

All right, then, he would think of them as a different kind of gang, a *church* gang, somehow. And yet they tolerated the existence of the outside bar, and they were obviously much more similar to the people outside than they were willing to admit.

So how, exactly, were they different? Fine, they were cleaner and had better organizational skills. But what were the *deeper* differences, the core reasons? They were there, that much he could see even if he could not yet understand. Desmond shook his head, let it go. He had learned that, back in the shelter: Sometimes chasing too hard after a mystery only causes it to retreat before the pursuer. Let the unknown answer alone, let it come of its own free will in its own good time. He smiled, and forgot his anxiety. He was in a strange new place, confronted with a mystery of human behavior, struggling to understand others. There was a small voice inside him telling him that it was good to be home.

Standing right beside Desmond, Father Francis felt far more nervousness and far less curiosity than his friend seemed to feel. Here, indeed, he was a stranger in a strange land. He had been in all sorts of churches and temples and places of worship, of course. But this was like no church he had ever imagined.

It was one thing to see a religion with beliefs wholly unlike one's own, and see that *its* traditions were strange. But his understanding was that the Riders were *Christians,* his brothers in Christ—but here, apparently during the service itself, were waitresses (unless you wanted to call them deaconesses) in low-cut tops and short-short skirts selling beer, flirting with members of the congregation, accepting tips. Or did it all go into the collection plate?

Desmond seemed content to stay where they were, peeking into the back of the room, at least for the moment, and that suited Francis just fine.

The deep, unintelligible voice stopped talking. Music began, a hymnlike tune, but with a toe-tapping beat, played with a heavy bass line on an electric organ. The conversation faded away, but did not stop altogether, as almost the entire congregation—who finally started to act as such when the music began—turned toward the far end of the room, around the corner from where Desmond and Francis stood at the entrance. Some stood to sing, some remained seated, some raised their glasses and waved them back and forth in time to the music. The singing was loud, almost boisterous, boomed out with such enthusiasm that Francis could not quite make out the words. Apparently neither could Desmond, and he seemed eager to learn more, see more.

To Francis's alarm, Desmond stepped around the corner and looked down toward the far end of the long room. Francis hurried to join him, not altogether comfortable about being alone in such a place.

Once out in the main room, Francis could see the layout better. There was a low, bare stage at the far end of the room. To the right of the stage was an organist working a fold-out keyboard. A man stood in the center of the stage, dressed in a pair of slacks and a corduroy sport coat. It occurred to Francis that such an outfit was the very pinnacle of formality in this leather-jacketed, T-shirted, beer-bellied setting.

The man on the stage was thin, almost gaunt-looking. His eyes were alert, bright and nervous, almost pop-eyed, putting Desmond in mind of a high-strung, spirited racehorse. His hair was dark brown, close-cropped, bristly, shaped to conform to the curves of his skill. His skin was pale, almost translucent. He had a brown beard, neatly trimmed. He was conducting the singing, indicating the beat with a strong, fervent gesture of his arm, his hand clenched into a fist, his face animated and excited as he sang along with the others in a strong, booming baritone.

Francis noted Desmond looking around the back of the room. Then Desmond spotted an empty table toward the back of the house and sat down, sliding into a chair without taking his eyes off the man on the stage. He gave no sign of noticing when Francis nervously took a seat next to him.

The hymn wound down, a bit raggedly, and the organist, a wizened-looking little old lady with a cigarette dangling out of her mouth, added a final bluesy flourish to the end and cackled softly to herself when she was done, stubbing out her cigarette and reaching for the beer that sat on the top of the keyboard.

"Thank you, Martha," the man said, his voice clear and carrying. "Glad to have you back and belting them out again." He turned to the congregation and nodded his head at them. To Francis, it seemed his manner had as much to do with a nightclub emcee as it did with a church minister. "Now, what do you say? Why don't we settle down and really get this service under way?"

There was a burst of applause and wild whoops of agreement from the congregation. The man onstage grinned and nodded again. "Good enough. For those of you who are just coming inside for the first time, let me welcome you to the Church of the Road and introduce myself. I'm Reverend Hiram Goodman, and I've been running this parish since we bought out the bar, about six months now. We've been growing every day since then. That's the news from all over the country, in fact. Our numbers are swelling everywhere, as we reach for the excitement, the promise, the *blessings* of the Last Days!"

Francis blinked and swallowed. Dear Lord, they were millennialists. He had forgotten that. Again there were

cheers, whoops of delight, a rebel yell or two, and enthusiastic clapping.

"Yes, *that* is the good news, the news we want to
spread everywhere," Goodman went on. *"These are
the Last Days,"* he repeated with greater emphasis.
"Scripture promised it; our patron-prophet, the first and
only saint of our church, Nostradamus, predicted it;
and we are seeing it all come to fruition. All the signs
are there; all the events just as were foretold are coming
to pass. The end is *near.* "

More cheers and clapping. Goodman hesitated for a
moment, then strode to one side of the stage and looked
over his audience, making out as if he sensed some
doubt among his listeners. "Now, I hear some of you
saying, 'But, Preacher Goodman, why is that *good*
news? Why are you looking forward to the end of the
world?' you ask me." Goodman nodded thoughtfully,
acknowledging the worth of the question. Francis
watched carefully, admiring the man's skill in handling
a congregation. Granted, the Catholic Church didn't go
in for this sort of thing, but even so, Francis knew he
had never been this good at working a crowd. He felt
a brief, microscopic twinge of envy. He shook his head
to clear it and concentrated on the sermon.

"Well, why *is* it good news?" Goodman said. "Because of this: It is *not* the end of the world—but merely
the end of *our age.* The Earth shall still be here—but
we shall be gone, swept off the face of the world, the
planet scrubbed clean, ready to be reborn. Who shall
take our place? Will anyone? Or anything? Or will the
Good Lord see fit to let planet Earth lie fallow for a
while? I don't know, and I don't need to know. The
important fact is that *we* shall be gone."

He stopped again, looked about the suddenly silent
audience. He gestured toward all of them with both
arms, then gestured toward himself, tapping his chest
with the tips of his ten fingers. "We shall be gone,"
he said in a suddenly quiet voice. "And why is *that*
good news? Why is that something I'm glad to know,

happy to tell you?'' Francis found himself leaning forward, eager to hear the answer.

''Because there was an old promise, made long ago, a promise that has never been true until now—and at last it *will* be true. And you all know what that promise was.'' He paused, and when he spoke again, more than a few members of the audience spoke with him. *''Millions now living will never die,''* they echoed, in perfect unison with the preacher. Hiram Goodman nodded eagerly and turned to pace back and forth on the stage. Now his voice began to rise again. ''Throughout all time, it has been the common fate of all men and women to die. Even those who found salvation in the Lord, and were to be transported into Heaven, were first required to die, undergo the torments of leaving the flesh, before they could make the great transition. But not anymore. Not now. Those alive now, today, who believe, who repent, those who don't just mouth the words but truly *believe,* and accept Jesus Christ as their savior, who ask Him to ride alongside them all the days of their lives, to travel down all the miles of life's road—those believers shall *not* die. Nor, when the Rapture comes, shall they be vanquished, cast down into the pit. No! They shall be raised up, be transported bodily to the New Jerusalem, still alive, their flesh still firm, their eyes still bright, freed from the curse of death. *Those* believers shall be raised up to start a new and everlasting life in Heaven.

''When will it happen? We don't know, and that's the God's honest truth. Sometime soon, and that's all we really know. If you're looking for the signs, the proof, just pick up today's paper. It's all in there, happening every day. But when? That's the question. Because to God in His Heaven, time is a very different proposition than it is to you and me. So what is 'soon' to God? Maybe it's today, right *now,* as you sit in your seats. Maybe on the stroke of the millennium. But the men who figured out the calendars long ago got a date or two wrong. Some scholars believe Jesus was born four years one side or the other of the year we mark as the time of His birth. Or maybe the Day will come two thousand years to the second after His Resurrection. Or two thousand years from the moment of His baptism, or from His bar mitzvah.'' There was a flurry of laughter at that idea, but Goodman grinned and waggled an admonishing finger. ''Why not? It would be a significant moment in His life, the moment He became a man. After all, He was a Jew, and even if the Bible doesn't say He had a bar mitzvah, it doesn't say He didn't.

''Or else the Lord God doesn't care if the years come out to a nice round number when you use the sort of numbers we happen to use. Maybe He marks time in some completely different way, or measures time, not by the passage of years, but by the passage of events. Judgment will come not when the calendar and clock reach some arbitrary position, but when all the events prophesied have come to pass. Or else God decided that He'd better not choose a date in advance. Otherwise, we could all be having a fine old time, sinning our heads off, so long as we checked in with God or a preacher and got to a state of grace before five P.M. some Friday afternoon. God wants to keep us on our toes, make sure we try to get into a state of grace and stay there, full-time, just in case.

''So what's it all come down to? Just this: Maybe now, maybe twenty years from now, when your children and your children's children are here with you— the Rapture will come. And if you are in a state of grace, a believer, the sin washed from your soul, when *that* day of days comes, you will be transported, as a living soul, directly into Heaven.''

Wild cheers and whoops of joy filled the room. Hiram Goodman let it ride for a moment, and then raised a cautionary finger. ''But there's another question I have to put before you. You can go across the street, or down the road, or over to Los Angeles, and trip over half a dozen folks on every street corner who'll tell you the same thing. Lots of churches springing up in these days of fear and wonder. So why come here and listen to me, instead of the man on the corner with the sign that says REPENT in big letters?''

A smattering of derisive hoots and Bronx cheers came up from here and there in the big room. Goodman looked up sharply, stuck out a warning finger, and looked meaningfully about the room. ''Now, don't you go laughing at those brothers and sisters of ours. We are all on the same road together here. Some of us may be a bit further ahead, some of us a bit further back. But we are all headed to the same place—or to another place, if we're not careful,'' he said with a sly grin.

That brought a flurry of laughter. ''But the question I was asking is a simple one. What have we got that they don't? If they're our brothers and sisters in Christ, what makes the Riders special? You can get the answer to that one next time you look in a mirror. *You* make us different. *You* make us better. As to why that might be so, I'll get to that in a minute. For now, let me just tell you, before anyone thinks to ask one of our passed-out friends sprawled outside—no, it's not because we recruit from a better class of person.''

Another rumble of laughter. Goodman smiled at his own joke, but then his face grew serious. ''Glad to hear that you all still have that famous Rider sense of humor. But if you look at it another way, there *isn't* much funny about the way our friends live. And we don't dare laugh at those folks outside. Because *we used to be that way. We* used to be *them*. Drunk too much, bathed too rarely, cruel and thoughtless without need too often. About as far from the Road toward God as anyone could imagine. Almost off the road entirely. We *have* to stay humble, remember how low we were, to keep from thinking we're anything wonderful now. That's one reason we allow, and even encourage, the bikers to hang around outside, and welcome them into our services. To remind us just how bad we were.''

Suddenly there was a scuffle at the far side of the

room, from a table full of rather more disreputable types than seemed to populate the rest of the room. A bleary-faced man in a heavily studded leather jacket stood up and flipped his middle finger at Goodman. "Fuck you, man," he shouted, standing a bit unsteadily. "You can't invite us in and then talk about me and my buddies tha' way."

Goodman gave the man a wolflike smile. "Oh, yes, I can, my friend," he said in an icy voice. "You just look around this room and I'll prove it. Tell me, friends. How many of *you* were this man once? Biking around, looking for fights, joining some gang to act tough, maybe robbing and stealing, selling stolen goods and drugs, scaring people to hide how stupid and lonely the world made you feel?" There was a pause in the room, and Goodman looked around. "That's an interesting question, isn't it? Let me put it another way. How many of *you* pulled this stunt, or one just like it? Got good and stoned on Church booze and then stood up and shouted drunken obscenities at the preacher when he called you drunk and obscene?" He paused again. "How many? I know *I* did. *I'll* fess up. Maybe I could get everyone else who one time stood up like this fellow here, maybe I could get those folks to stand up once again, here and now." Goodman stopped talking, held out his arms, beckoned to the people in the room.

The silence hung heavy for a moment, and then there was the sound of a chair being shoved back, of boots on the floor. At the center of the room, a big man stood up. He had a scraggly beard and a big gut and a cross around his neck, a frightening calm in his face. He did not look toward the heckler, but to Goodman. And then another man at the same table rose, and another. Suddenly half the people in the room were getting to their feet, standing calmly, silently, looking toward Goodman. Father Francis Xavier O'Rourke felt a chill going down his spine. There was power here. Power and danger.

"Now," Goodman said. "Turn. Turn and look at

him.'' The silent crowd did as it was bid, shuffling around until it was facing the heckler. "Look at these faces, son," Goodman said in a carrying stage whisper. He stepped down off the low stage and walked toward the heckler. Francis was surprised at how slight the man was compared to some of the giants he walked among. "These are the people you don't want to see coming down a dark alley," he said, still moving forward. "Give them the right reason, and they can be the *worst* kind of bad news. You don't want 'em mad at you. One time, they all did what you're doing, trying to prove they were the roughest and the toughest and the meanest and the strongest. Now they don't have to do that. With Christ on their side, they *know* they're the toughest.

"And don't let that old saw about Christians always turning the other cheek bother you. We're Christians who ran out of cheeks to turn before we ever saw the light. We don't pick fights, but we don't run away from 'em. We don't fight to prove how tough we are— because we know just how tough we are, and just how to fight. We're not gonna turn into punching bags for the likes of you." Now he had crossed the whole length of the room, and was standing just a few feet away, looking up into the eyes of the heckler. To Francis's eye, the drunken biker had at least forty pounds and six inches on the preacher.

"But I've got a question about your life. A real simple one: what's it got you?"

Goodman looked steadily at the biker, letting the question hang for a minute. "What does all your cursing and stealing and hurting *do* for you? Does it make you feel better about yourself when you do it? Then you must feel great about yourself by now, 'cause you've done so much of it. Or if you *don't* like yourself so much, maybe your life does something else for you. Does it make you feel like you got a future, or like you've got people you can trust?" Goodman gestured offhandedly, almost but not quite contemptuously, to the heckler's friends. "Can you trust *them?*" he asked. Then he reached into his own back pocket and pulled out his wallet. He tossed it onto the middle of the heckler's table, all without breaking eye contact. "Now, I got about three hundred sets of eyes watching my every move right now, so I *know* that wallet's safe from you. There's no such thing as honor among thieves, not really. What there is instead is everyone watching everyone else because *no* one can be trusted. And I'd be willing to bet every dollar in my wallet that I've just described your life, how you think about the people you call your friends. But I don't call that trusting each other.

"Let me tell you what real trust is. I could leave my wallet, all my worldly goods, piled up in the middle of a room filled with my friends, filled up with *these* people, and never worry at all.

"In fact, just to make a point, I'm going to leave that wallet there, because I *do* trust my friends so much. I don't just trust them not to hurt me, not to steal from me. I know they will watch out for me. They'll keep an eye on that wallet for me, make sure no fingers at your table get sticky. Couldn't be safer in a bank vault.

"So let me ask you, how long would your money last if you left it where your friends might reach it? And how long would it take *you* to steal their cash, if you got the chance?" He turned back toward the congregation, his back deliberately to the heckler, demonstrating that he had no fear, that he was in such control that the move put him in no danger.

"See, that's the *real* question. And asking it *is* what makes us different," he said, speaking to the whole room. "Jesus Christ our Lord was put to death hanging on a cross between two thieves. Anyone in this room who wouldn't qualify to be nailed to one side or the other of Jesus? Who hasn't been a thief, a liar, an adulterer, an idolator, a *sinner?* That's what we mean when we ask someone else—are you on the side of Jesus? The Good Lord died alongside miserable sinners, to tell us that *we* could live alongside the Son of God. Even the least of us is good enough to stand beside the Highest of All—*if* we have the humility to see that in our needless cruelty is weakness, that in our selfish violence is fear. Strike and fight for yourself, for the satisfaction of a momentary desire, and you strike at yourself, endanger your immortal soul. Strike that same blow for another, for a greater goal, for the Lord, and Salvation is yours!''

He turned and faced the heckler once again. ''That's what we're here for, son,'' he said gently. ''Whoever invited you inside for drinks on the house thought maybe you were just about ready to hear that message, thought there might be just enough of a spark in you that you would be able to hear the Word and benefit. So you just sit back, and think, and maybe listen some more.''

He turned to the front and stepped back up onto the stage. ''Now, I bet that even if I hadn't started flapping my gums tonight, you'd all know the standard arguments for believing that the end is near. But let me tell you my own, personal reason. It's very simple. It's because we live in an age of miracles. Dark miracles. We do, you know.'' He looked around, as if expecting someone to disagree with him, though, of course, this congregation was so thoroughly in the palm of his hand that any such thing was impossible. *Another theatrical flourish,* Francis thought, with grudging admiration.

''Yes, friends,'' Hiram went on, ''an age of miracles. It's just that no one sees them as miracles because we have the gall to create them for ourselves. Lasers, space flight, computers that think like men. Babies born to women who are not their mothers, indeed babies with no true parents at all, their genes snipped from this person and that and then stitched together. Genetic wonders, they are called. But 'abominations' might be closer to the truth. There was a story in the paper just the other day about one of these multigene-source babies, born to a young surrogate mother who had never been with a man. A virgin birth, in literal fact, and one the doctors and scientists deliberately set out to create. Did they never stop to think that God might be angered by such overweening pride?

"New machines, new technologies appear every day, and they seduce us, defeat us just as the serpent did, by offering us temptation, proffering forbidden fruits."

Goodman was again pacing back and forth on the stage, and Francis could see the gleam of sweat on his forehead. "My own mother is walking around today, strolling the grounds of her trailer park—but if you put your ear to her chest, you won't hear her heart beat—just a low whir. She's got an artificial heart." Goodman let that statement stand by itself for a moment, and the room was dead silent. "I know what you're thinking," he said at last. " 'Did this guy just say he wanted his mother dead?' "

There was thin, nervous laughter in the back of the room. "Well, folks, the answer is—yes."

Someone gasped, and the room was silent. Francis looked around. Every person in the room was staring at Goodman. If someone had dropped a pin, the sound would have echoed.

"Now that I've horrified all of you, now that someone in the back is itching to stand up and say how dare I say that, how wonderful it is that my mother is still alive, let me fess up and say I'm glad she's still with us, yes. And that's what tears at me. Because, folks, her heart gave out. It stopped beating. Her time had come. She was *dead*. Her soul was on its way to Heaven.

"And they snatched her back, ripped that motionless heart from her chest, tore out the very symbol of life and love and caring, and instead they gave her a plastic and metal thing. They took the most basic sound of life away from her, and replaced it with a low hum. They played God, and decided plastic and batteries were an improvement on living flesh. How many of you can stand up now and say that was a righteous, God-fearing thing to do?

"How many other ways have we done that? How many ways have we decided to take God's place, decided we could do things better than He could?

"Dark miracles, my friends. And God's patience is not infinite. Sooner or later—and I think sooner—he's going to decide to take back all the power human beings have presumed to take upon themselves. That is the message of our Church, my friends. The time is near. The end is near. And we are *ready* for it!"

The room erupted into cheers, the wizened organist struck up a tune, and the congregation got to its feet and started singing with a lusty enthusiasm. Francis still couldn't make out much in the way of lyrics or a melody, but it sounded a bit like a heavily worked-over version of "Rock of Ages."

The hymn—if it was a hymn—ended, and the people clapped to their own singing. Then there was a general standing up and shuffling around, people gathering their belongings and heading for the exit. But not all the people left. A fair number seemed comfortable right where they were. The lights went down a bit, and a toe-tapping country-and-western song started playing from somewhere. Two or three couples got up to dance. Francis turned and looked at Desmond. There was excitement in his gaze as he looked around the room and he nodded to himself, as if agreeing with something.

Francis opened his mouth to speak, but a booming voice behind him made him jump.

"So, Father," it asked. "How did you like the show?"

He turned around in his chair to see Hiram Goodman behind him. The preacher seemed to have ducked out for a quick shower during the hymn. His hair was wet, he was wearing shorts and a sweatshirt, and there was a towel around his neck.

Francis and Desmond stood up. "Oh, most interesting," Francis said, trying to be diplomatic. Never in his life had he seen such a hodgepodge. How on earth could anyone believe in such a cobbled-together, incoherent mass of gibberish and folklore? How could it be considered as a philosophy, a theology?

"Glad you thought so," the preacher said. "I'm Hiram Goodman, though you probably know that. And you are. . . ?"

"Oh, my apologies. Father Francis O'Rourke, S.J. And this is my friend, Dr. Desmond Potter. He is a psychiatrist," he added, trying to impress the man, warn him off a bit. Why not let him know that there were a few people who would not be taken in?

"So, a priest and a head doctor. We can hear from all sides tonight. Well, Dr. Potter. What did you think?"

"Fascinating," Desmond said. "Downright fascinating. I've heard many of the same arguments before, of course—a lot of them from your own people, back at the shelter. But I've never heard anyone make it all seem so convincing before."

Francis looked at Potter, aghast. But neither of the other two men paid him the slightest mind.

"A shelter?" Goodman said, smiling. "You, a shrink? You've done time in a security shelter, too?"

Desmond nodded slowly, beaming proudly. He reached his right arm over to his left shoulder and pulled up the sleeve of his shirt.

And there it was, Francis saw. The wheel, the handlebars, the cross. Done with a deft touch, too, he was forced to admit.

"Bennie's work!" Goodman said eagerly. "You must have been in back East somewhere."

"Boston," Desmond said, "and yes, it was Bennie."

Francis cleared his throat. "Ah, Desmond . . . it really is more than past time for us to be getting back."

"Oh, seems a shame when you've just gotten here," Goodman said.

"You go back without me," Desmond said, clearly

indifferent to the details of who went home when. "I can find my own way back later."

"Unless you'd like to stay, too, Father?" Hiram asked, clearly expecting to be turned down. "If it gets too late, I could get one of the boys to run you home."

The idea of roaring back home on one of those monstrous motorbikes put a little stiffening in Francis's spine. "No, no, I don't think that would be wise. And, Desmond, you really should come along as well."

"I'm staying, Francis," he said, a bit harshly. "God knows by this time of day I know how to take care of myself. You go if you want to, but there's a lot I want to know."

"We didn't upset you too much this evening, did we?" Goodman asked.

Francis hesitated, but then at last he spoke. "Well, in a way, yes. One thing you said disturbed me very much."

"And what was that?"

He sighed and shook his head. He simply couldn't let it go. "Ignoring all questions of theology and philosophy—and believe me, I'm tempted to stand here and argue every point—I was bothered by the suggestion that you wished that your own mother was dead. Isn't that likely to get back to her? Wouldn't that hurt her terribly?"

To his astonishment, Hiram Goodman laughed out loud. "Oh, Mom died years ago. Three-pack-a-day smoker. Cancer. But doesn't that story make the point beautifully? Gets 'em every time. Nice to meet you, Father. Come on, Dr. Potter. You and I have a lot to talk about."

Chapter 6

June 1998
Honolulu, Hawaii

George Prescott fidgeted nervously in his seat and glanced at his watch for the tenth time in as many minutes. The wait was nerve-racking, bad enough that he almost forgot his stage fright. Almost. It was terrifying enough to be here in the seats, waiting his turn. But the idea that he was about to go up that aisle and talk to these people was simply unacceptable.

He glanced at the folder in his hands, and resisted the temptation to go over his notes again. He had done all he could to prepare, and now there was nothing he could do but watch the young woman behind the lectern gamely plugging away, explaining some obscure point concerning the spectra of red supergiants long after the audience had lost interest.

George wasn't paying much attention himself. He was

scanning the audience, the hundred or so vaguely bored and restless people.

The semiannual meeting of the American Astronomical Society was as crowded as ever. Most of the time there were five parallel sessions going simultaneously. The five-minute papers were being presented all day long, in one of the largest lecture halls.

Months ago, back in the safety and comfort of his own office, with Jessica there to cheer him on, it had seemed a sensible decision to present a five-minute oral report, rather than a poster presentation. Now he wasn't so sure. After all, lots of the younger astronomers tended to prefer the poster route, and right now, just before he was due to go on, George could not blame them. Standing by a poster was a lot less scary than speaking. A man in the audience asked a question that George couldn't quite catch. Damn it, he wished Jessica could have been here, instead of doing her postdoc work, safely back on campus at Harvard, thousands of miles away.

His attention had wandered, and he was brought back to the present moment by a burst of laughter.

Were they laughing at the presenter, or with her? He looked toward her, and got the answer from the stunned expression on her face. He looked back toward the audience, caught the amused look on the face of the man who had asked the question. Suddenly that man, that one man in the audience, seemed to take on special significance to George. He sat there, a red-faced man in a bright blue suit that seemed to clash with everything, starting with his own complexion. But that didn't seem to bother him. He was the very personification of loud, boorish self-assurance. A friend sitting next to him whispered in Red-Face's ear, and Red-Face laughed out loud.

George swallowed hard, and suddenly imagined that the entire audience consisted of Red-Face clones, all eager for the chance to slice the speakers into ribbons. What in the world was he thinking of when he volunteered for this nightmare? How could he give a summary of a complicated theoretical work in just five minutes?

The second bell rang, signaling the end of the presenter's five minutes. The young woman onstage stumbled back down the stair into the audience, tears welling up in her eyes, and yet clearly relieved and grateful that the ordeal was over. Suddenly the session chairman called George's name, inviting him up onto the stage.

He got to his feet and walked the short distance to the stage. He went up the stairs, and made a beeline for the illusory safety of the lectern. At least it was something he could pretend to hide behind. He fumbled for the switch on the overhead projector and flicked it on. In an errant, random flicker of thought, he wondered how anyone had ever run a scientific conference before they invented overhead projectors. Most of the presenters might as well have been surgically attached to the things. But George knew perfectly well he was just trying to keep his mind off his fear. He slid his first transparency onto the projector and swallowed hard.

"Ah, good—good afternoon," he said, his voice echoing weakly through the lectern microphone. He leaned in a little closer to the mike and spoke again. "Hello." This time his voice boomed out so loudly, half the audience jumped out of their seats.

He backed off again and decided he might as well launch right in, come what may. "I would like to present the results of my recent model calculations for Type Ia supernova progenitors. These calculations show the mass of a supernova-progenitor white dwarf could be as low as .95 solar mass . . ."

And somehow the words, the facts, the ideas, took over. George forgot himself, forgot his fear and embarrassment, and launched into his material with enthusiasm. He handled his overhead transparencies smoothly, pointing out the salient graph points and formulae clearly and precisely. And then came the moment of truth.

He had to talk about his other ideas, about the chancy stuff. If he didn't, all his work would have been for nothing, and he couldn't bear that idea. "Now, then," he said in a voice so firm and confident it surprised no one so much as himself, "I should like to present some data points I uncovered while researching this work. These data points suggest that the Sirius star system is by no means as stable as we have believed. I have discovered archival evidence that Sirius A undergoes various cyclical behaviors, all of which seem likely to come to a head within the next few years . . ." He launched into his carefully prepared summary of his Sirius instability evidence and kept one eye on the clock at the back of the room. He ended precisely on time, exactly as the five minutes were up, feeling quite pleased with himself.

Until he noticed the blank faces in the audience. No one said anything. Hardly anyone even applauded.

George had not expected thundering applause or lively debate when he was finished, but he hadn't expected virtual dead silence either. He felt his stomach tying itself into knots. At last the chairman took pity on him and asked, "Are there any questions?"

He stood behind the lectern and stared out in the giant hall, a room that seemed full of nothing but wooden faces. Nothing. Dead silence.

At last a hand raised itself, a voice called out. The chairman pointed to the questioner. "Will the questioner identify himself, please." George realized with sudden horror that it was the red-faced man in the loud suit who had ripped up the last presenter.

The man stood up, a smirk on his face. "Thank you. Robert Davison, Yale University. Forgive me if I don't have this straight, Dr. Prescott, but are you implying that Sirius A could undergo a period of sufficient instability such that *Sirius B* would be in danger of becoming a supernova?"

George stood there, clutching the lectern, the sweat standing out on his forehead. It was the one question he had dreaded, the one point he had hoped to avoid. He realized with a shock that he had never even fully admitted to *himself* that there was such a possibility, that such a connection was clearly implicit in his work. He had never let *himself* fully see it, admit it. Always that potential had scuttled around the inside of his head, but he had never allowed the idea full rein. But something of the confidence that had buoyed him throughout the five-minute talk still remained to him. Now he *did* consider it, and he *did* look for the answer. Not in his numbers, not in his formulae, but in his gut, in his instincts, in his feel for the data he had been living with all these months.

George blinked, and found himself still looking at Davison. Only a moment had passed, and now there was a hushed silence in the room. Then George nodded, stiffly, dumbly. A tittering laugh played over the room, but he ignored that, rode it out. "I don't know that I would use the word 'danger,' but yes," George replied. "I would say that the evidence I have collected makes it a possibility. I have shown that a white dwarf star of Sirius B's mass can become a supernova, and we have seen that Sirius may not be a stable binary." George found that he had the sides of the lectern in a death-grip, and he forced his hands to relax. "I would suggest it's a possibility we must consider," he said in a low, calm voice that seemed to carry effortlessly to every corner of the room.

The room was deathly quiet again, but then Davison laughed unpleasantly, and the moment shattered. "I would suggest," he said, "that it is 'possible'—and perhaps probable—that you are one hundred percent dead wrong." Davison turned to the audience and grinned. "Or do you all really expect Sirius to go off like a flashbulb tonight?" He brought his hands up to his face and pantomimed an explosion. "Boom! Just like that!" he said with exaggerated theatricality.

Laughter again, all across the room.

Suddenly George's resolve broke, and his body was bathed in a cold sweat. As the session chairman called the name of the next speaker, he gathered up his viewgraphs and his notes and stepped down off the platform. Somehow he found a side door to the room and avoided having to walk the entire length of that room, filled with people laughing at him. He stumbled blindly out of the meeting room and into the hallway.

He had walked a fair distance down the hall before he became aware that someone was behind him, calling his name.

He turned, half expecting to see Davison following behind to taunt him further.

Instead he saw the grinning face of Kenji Yamada, and surprised himself. Up until that moment, George would have said flat out there was no one at the conference he would have been glad to see. Everyone here seemed to be a stuffed shirt with an oversize ego.

But Ken was different. Ever since the day the two met for the first time in a classroom in Tucson, Yamada had treated George like a younger brother, not an underling.

Ken had been a visiting associate professor at the U. of Arizona during George's first year as a graduate student there, and had seen to it that George developed a proper appreciation of Japanese cuisine.

Kenji Yamada was a tall, gangly, unlikely-looking stick figure of a man. His suit fit his slender frame, and yet didn't *seem* to fit. There was something about his crisp white, heavily starched shirt that *seemed* rumpled and out of control. His red-and-white-striped tie was definitely askew. His lean, angled face was full of youthful enthusiasm, but George knew he had to be pushing forty.

Ken was carrying a thick notebook in his right hand. He shifted it to his left and stretched out his right to George. George took it mechanically and Ken pumped it vigorously before dropping it and slapping George on the back. "Nice work!" he said, his English well pronounced but slightly accented. "An extremely interesting piece of work you presented there."

"Well, ah, thanks. But no one else seemed to think so."

"You mean Davison? Forget him! A blowhard who likes to throw his weight around. Hasn't done any real work himself for years. But listen, about your work. Have you written it up for publication yet? I would be interested in having a preprint."

"Thanks very much, Dr. Yamada, but I can't publish yet. It's a part of my thesis work. I don't think Dr. Stowton will approve my sending it to a journal before his thesis committee accepts my dissertation. *If* they accept it. You know how it is."

"Oh, they'll accept it. Don't you worry about that." Ken Yamada nodded knowingly. "But," he went on, "the main point is, I'm eager to see your work. Could you send me a copy of the draft of your thesis? Whatever you've got done so far?"

George smiled sadly. "I'm afraid you've just seen all of what I've got done so far."

"Surely you're exaggerating."

George thought of the reams of material and stacks of computer tapes back in Arizona. "Well, maybe a bit. But I've been working so hard on getting the material *together* that I haven't had a chance to worry about getting it into a presentable form. It might take a couple of months. Can I mail it to you at your Cornell address?"

Yamada hesitated. "Maybe not. See, I'm considering an interesting job offer in Japan." He shrugged. "In fact, why hide it? I'll probably take it. Maybe I'm getting homesick in my old age. The thing is, the arrangements aren't quite settled yet, so I'd appreciate it if you'd keep it quiet. It's not going to be a secret much longer, but for the moment, I don't want wild rumors getting around. I doubt Cornell is going to be too thrilled with me in any event, but I don't want to make matters worse.''

George Prescott felt flattered by the trust this genial astrophysicist seemed to place in him. ''Fine, I'll keep it quiet,'' he said.

''Great. I'll send you my new address as soon as I have it,'' Yamada said. ''In the meantime—stick to your guns. Get that work done. I know some people in Japan who I think might be *very* interested in it.''

And with that intriguing remark still hanging in the air, Ken Yamada turned and walked away.

August 1998
Tokyo, Japan

Two months after the AAS meeting in Hawaii, Kenji Yamada sat before a massive teak desk, watching the man seated behind it as he carefully read one section over again. True to his word, George Prescott had mailed a copy of his thesis paper the moment it was done.

At last Noboru Hayashi dropped the neatly bound report folder on his desk and leaned back in his chair. The title was on the heavy blue stock of the cover, in English and Japanese, ''A Revised Model for White Dwarfs as Progenitors of Type Ia Supernovae.'' The text inside was in Japanese only, thanks to some fast work on Yamada's part.

''So, Yamada-san. You have brought me some most interesting reading material.''

Kenji Yamada sat before the industrialist's desk, not entirely sure of himself, or how formal an attitude he should take. Deferential, but not subservient. Back in the States, there had never been a need to worry over such minutiae. He repressed a smile. Two weeks home, and already he was chafing under the demands of the more orderly society he had returned home to enjoy.

"Yes, Hayashi-san, I translated it myself as soon as I received it. I knew that you'd want to see it."

And knew that I would receive credit and recognition as well, Yamada thought. But there was more to it than cynical maneuvering. Hayashi was an old friend, as well as an important contact. And Yamada knew Hayashi would just plain *like* to know about this. He might even like it enough to *do* something about it. Hayashi might run a huge industrial combine, but he was also one of the more noted amateur astronomers in the country. That was how he and Yamada had met in the first place: years before, Hayashi had buttonholed him at an astrophysics symposium and asked some surprisingly informed questions about the structure of black holes and Schwarzschild radii.

"Do you think he's on the level?" Hayashi asked. "Or—let me put it another way: do you think he's right?"

Kenji Yamada nodded. "Yes, I do. He's a good young man, a smart and honest one. His mathematics are accurate, and I believe he believes what he says. I can find no flaw in his thinking, or in his evidence."

"Then if what he is saying is correct, there is a good chance that sometime in the next two to ten years, Sirius A will brighten significantly."

"Yes, Hayashi-san. If George—if Dr. Prescott—is correct, it will represent a major advance in our ability to predict stellar activity, and at the same time it will overturn a great deal of accepted knowledge about the Sirius system."

"Then the man who detects this instability first will be making a true contribution to the field."

"Yes, Hayashi-san. That is so." Kenji Yamada struggled to repress a cheer. Hayashi was going to do it! He was going to take on the challenge. It was an effort, but Yamada managed to avoid even breaking into a grin.

A few expensive nights at one of George's poker games had taught him that skill. Indeed, he had learned that the game of poker consisted largely of figuring out what your opponent was thinking while concealing your own thoughts. But the main thing he had learned was never to play poker with George Prescott.

Or *was* Hayashi going to rise to the bait? His expression did not seem very enthused. Maybe Yamada should have mentioned George's hairbrained ideas that Sirius could go supernova. It wasn't in the paper, and it had seemed too wild-eyed a thought to suggest to Hayashi. But maybe the idea would have appealed to the man.

Now the industrialist leaned back in his chair and looked thoughtfully at his guest. "You know, a train of thought occurs to me, Yamada-san. First, that your friend Prescott here must have known that the professionals in his field would be most skeptical of his ideas. Second, that the only sure test of them would require the nearly constant monitoring of Sirius A's light output, which would require a commitment of time, effort, and resources that few professionals would be willing to make. Which must mean that he hoped some well-appointed amateur would take up the task.

"It also occurs to me that you, in your brand-new position at ISAS, would not feel it wise to bring them a proposal for such a long-shot project. Yet you would want it to be done. Indeed, you might well go through much the same thought process as our friend Prescott-san. You might even try to think of a well-equipped amateur and attempt to entice him into the project."

Keni Yamada felt his face reddening. Had he been that obvious? Would Hayashi be insulted, interpret it all as an effort to manipulate him? "I, ah, ah—"

But Hayashi cut him short with a mischievous grin. "If your thought did indeed take such a course, you have thought wisely and well. I will undertake the project. If I can find this instability, it will make news. I have an idea for establishing an automatic monitoring system on my telescope anyway. This will give me the chance to try it. Once the autosensors are in place, I can program my primary telescope to monitor Sirius on a nightly basis. If our sensors and equipment are used to make a major discovery, that will reflect well on the company. I want to do this.''

Kenji Yamada nodded weakly, relieved that it had all worked out. But he made a mental note never to play poker with Noboru Hayashi, either.

September 1998
Santa Barbara, California

It was a quiet evening in Santa Barbara, a good night to stay at home and get some reading done. Father Francis Xavier O'Rourke had intended to do just that, but there was a flaw. Desmond was headed out again.

He set down his book and watched as his friend put on his jacket and made ready to head out into the night. ''You're not going down there again tonight, are you?'' Francis asked, feeling oddly like a man remonstrating with his son to stay home on a school night.

Desmond Potter nodded happily. ''Oh, yes,'' he said. ''Hiram's asked me to come up with some ideas for expanding the Church's membership, and I think I really have some things for him.''

Francis sighed and shook his head. It had gone too far. It was time, past time, to say something. ''Desmond, I cannot countenance this. I brought you here to Santa Barbara, to this retreat—this *Jesuit* retreat—so that your soul might heal, not so you could help some Bible-thumping con man recruit for his cause.''

Desmond looked at him stiffly. ''If you object to my staying here, I can make other arrangements.''

''That's not the point,'' Francis said. ''Stay here as long as you like. But the Christriders, Desmond? Hiram Goodman appeals to you?''

''Hiram Goodman is a man with vision! He says the things that need to be said! Hiram Goodman—''

''—is a liar!'' Francis exploded. ''That insane story

about his mother with the artificial heart. How can you deal with a man who could say and do such things?''

"Because he dealt with me! Don't you see? He admitted to me that his story was made up, two minutes after he met me. He revealed that secret to me, made himself vulnerable to me, because he wanted to show that he trusted me, and even in that first moment saw something in me that he needed.''

"What?'' Francis asked snappishly. "Your gullibility? The guilt-ridden death wish that you wear pinned to your sleeve? Your anger at the world, your need for revenge against Gibbons?''

"Yes,'' Desmond said, in a voice that froze the blood in Francis's veins. "Yes, I think that is exactly what he saw, exactly what he needs from me.''

"Gibbons is beyond your reach, Desmond. He killed himself the same day he murdered your wife and daughter. Even if you could bring down the whole world, it would not serve to harm *him*. He has gone to his own hell, his own punishment.''

"But his evil is still here,'' Desmond said. "And no matter what little fictions Goodman spun to illustrate a point, he speaks the truth about the larger things. The world *is* moving very quickly toward a crisis, and there is a great deal to be found in the Bible—*your* Bible, *our* Bible—that speaks of such a crisis, before the Second Coming. Madness, violence, evil, are loose in the world, and it will *take* the coming of Jesus Christ Himself to defeat them. I believe that, Francis. It's been decades since I was anything more than ambivalent about the Catholic Church. Concerning the Church of the Road, I have severe doubts, and I am willing to concede that Hiram Goodman is something less than my idea of a saint. But his message, the message of the Christriders—that I can believe in.'' Without another word, Desmond turned and walked out the door.

"Oh, Desmond,'' Francis said to the empty air. It would be pointless, worse than pointless, to try and go after him. The priest stood up, went to the window,

and looked down to watch as Desmond hurried outside
and got on that damnable antique motorcycle Goodman
had loaned him. Sorrow in his face, the blackness of
failure in his heart, he watched as Desmond roared off
into the night. He had hoped to bring Desmond here
and give him hope, put the light of God back in his
heart, walk him out of the Valley of the Shadow of
Death and back to the land of the living.

Instead, he feared very much that Desmond was
rushing, headlong, into the deepest, darkest parts of
that valley.

Desmond leaned into the turn as the 1947 Indian
Warrior took the curve. A beautiful old machine, a
classic motorcycle. Strange indeed to ride a machine
older than he was. It had been a real kindness, a true
gift, for Hiram to give him the use of it. It had been
tremendously useful, not just in getting him back and
forth to the church, but in conferring a little status. The
Riders were deeply suspicious of anyone in their group
who didn't ride a bike. For Goodman to grant him the
signal honor of riding the Warrior meant a lot in the
Riders' eyes.

And, truth be told, it meant a lot to Desmond as
well. But tonight, he knew, might be the end of all
honors from Hiram, and that scared him. The links
were new, and tenuous, but he *had* established links,
connections, with Hiram and the Riders. Aside from
Francis, the Christriders were the only people in the
world who really cared one way or the other about him.
And Francis was a link with his past, a past that seemed
dangerous and frightening. The Riders linked him to
the future.

The part of him that was still a clinical psychiatrist
recognized that the need to rebel was a major motivation in his befriending Goodman and the Riders. He
had to strike a blow against his past, against the authority and demands of responsibility that Francis represented. Perhaps most of all, he needed to strike a

blow against rationalism itself. After all, it was rationalism that had destroyed his life and family. Once, he had believed that all problems could be reasoned out, believed that he could convince a madman to behave sensibly, that he could use logic to defeat insanity. Now he knew his folly, and longed for ways to assault his former viewpoint, his past.

The night winds whipped through his hair, and his heart beat fast with excitement. The Riders seemed part of an exciting future, bright with promise. Yes indeed! He wanted to Ride with them—or at least some of them—right into the Kingdom of God.

It was the ones he *didn't* want to ride with that he needed to discuss with Hiram.

He gunned the engine and headed down the road.

It was quiet in Hiram's compact little office, tucked away in a remote corner of the church. The late service had just ended, and the dancing had just started, but Hiram was a great believer in good soundproofing.

He also believed in comfortable seating. There was a standard desk and chair in the room, but Hiram rarely used them. He had two old overstuffed couches shoehorned into one corner. He was lying down on one of them, his feet dangling over one arm, his head propped up on the other, carefully nursing a beer, working hard not to spill it as he drank from a reclining position. Hiram very clearly didn't give a damn about appearances once the show was over. Desmond sat up on the other couch, hands folded in his lap, his own beer sitting unopened on the side table.

"So, Desmond," Hiram said. "What was it you wanted to talk about?"

"The reason you recruited me," Desmond said.

Hiram looked up in mock surprise. "Did I have a reason? I thought that was just at random."

"No, really," Desmond said seriously. "You took one look at me and pulled me in, like you knew something about me. Don't get me wrong—I'm grateful, and glad to be here. But I need to know why.''

"For real, huh?'' Hiram thought about it for a minute. ''To be absolutely honest, I don't know. I mean, I didn't look you deep in the eye and instantly know here was a man with a calling—though I might use that line onstage sometime. Sounds pretty good.'' Hiram raised his beer in a mock toast and winked. ''But I don't know why I did it, exactly. Maybe just because it was obvious you wanted it so much, and because you've got an education. We could use some brains around here. But hell, even that's making it more logical than it was. I saw you, I reached out, and there you were. Probably not the answer you were looking for,'' he said, taking a swig of beer and setting the can down on his chest.

"No, actually, that's about what I figured,'' Desmond said. ''You're at a stage of the game where you're trying to collect all the chips you can. Later will be time enough to figure out what to do with them.''

"And this is why you wanted to see me in private?'' Hiram asked.

"No, but it's something I needed clear. And I needed to know if you'd be straight with me, or try to butter me up. Because there's some straight talking we need to do.''

"So what is it that you *did* wanna talk about?'' Hiram asked evenly.

"The fact that you're an ambitious man,'' Desmond said.

"Yes, I am. That shouldn't be a major shock to anyone.''

"Okay, then. How would your ambition react to the news that this place isn't going anywhere?''

"Hell, man, you've only been around here a few months. How can you tell?''

"I've been around long enough to see a few things you might not have the perspective to see.''

"Such as?''

"Such as, you have a great organization here,'' Desmond said, "but it's static, and it's got a bad reputation. You need to change that."

Hiram grimaced. "Tell me about it. I've had it up to here with the cops hassling me. You got a way out, you gotta tell me."

Desmond grinned. "All right, I will." He stood up to pace the cramped office. "The central point is this: *your* Church of the Road can't grow, can't be what it has to be, can't say what it has to say, if it is only saying it to bikers, if it's part of *the* Church of the Road."

"What do you mean?"

"I mean other people need to hear your message. People who are ready to listen. You've got to branch out, you've got to see other people. Don't get me wrong; you should work to keep your core group. It shouldn't be too hard. Your congregation is loyal to *you,* not to the Church. Those people inside are there because of you. They'll pay their dues to whomever you say. Announce that your congregation is breaking away from the Church of the Road and you'll keep ninety-five percent of them."

"But why the hell would I want to break off?" Hiram demanded.

He didn't seem shocked by the proposal. Desmond suddenly found himself wondering if Hiram hadn't been toying with the idea already.

"You might want to for reasons that are a little intricate."

"So explain."

"Okay. Let's see." Desmond sat and collected his thoughts for a minute. "Back when I was a practicing psychiatrist, I did a study once on how cults work, on how they evolve."

Hiram looked up sharply, an angry look in his eye. "If you're calling the Church a cult, *Brother* Desmond—"

Desmond raised his hand, palm outward, gestured for Hiram to be calm. "Ease off, Hiram. Sorry, I shouldn't have used such a pejorative term. It's just that

I got interested in the subject because one of my patients was mixed up with a cult, and I wanted to know how that had happened. How about 'close-knit belief groups'? That suit you a little better?''

Hiram growled and shifted his position on the couch, but didn't seem ready to protest further.

"Anyway," Desmond said, "what I was going to say was that when I did this study, I ignored *what* the group believed and focused on *how the group developed.* I didn't do it for any particular scholarly reason, just for my own curiosity. I looked over a whole series of groups, read up on their origins and early history. The early Christian Church, the Moslems, the Nazi Party, the Communists, the Scientologists, the Republicans and Democrats, the Irish Republican Army, the Mormons, a few others. I'm not saying that I found any universal truths, but I did come up with some useful generalizations, some causes and effects that seem to crop up in any group that's based on members who gather together because they believe something, and want to change things.''

"Like what?"

"They start off small, obviously. But it often seems that there's a pattern to growth: a spurt in membership, followed by a plateau or mild decline, and then a new spurt. Slow, steady increase in membership doesn't seem to happen very often, or work that well. Either that cycle continues until the group is a major force, or else the group becomes moribund, even falls apart. Sound familiar so far?''

Hiram nodded reluctantly. "Yeah. Christrider membership doubled three times in the first year, and then faded off again. Then it picked up steam when we started getting some publicity about doing charity work and busting up gang fights—though most of the recruits seemed more interested in fighting themselves. Now it's slacking off again—but don't expect me to say *that* in front of the congregation.''

"Okay. Let's look at a few other patterns from the

other groups. One: If the cult—sorry, the closely knit group—if it is to grow and flourish, it must at some point step outside its natural source of recruits and bring in people who are at least closer to the general population. Two: The organization can survive, even flourish, even as the purpose of the group changes—or even gets stood on its head. In fact, most groups *do* turn their purposes on their heads a few times.''

"We haven't,'' Hiram protested.

"No? If I'm not mistaken, the Church of the Road started as a group of fairly standard evangelical Christians who wanted to convert fairly standard biker gangs. The idea was to make them pretty standard God-fearing Christians. Except *now* it's bikers running the show, and the original members are long gone. Your group has shoved aside the founders of the group.''

"They couldn't hack it, and the Church was losing membership,'' Hiram said defensively. "The new leadership turned that around, and made the Church into something that could appeal to the people it was trying to save. The weak sisters went off by themselves and tried to start up again. They didn't make it. But what's wrong with clearing out the deadwood and revitalizing the Church?''

"Nothing, but I'm not talking right and wrong,'' Desmond replied. "I'm just trying to get you to see that your group is behaving the way a lot of groups have before you. Belief-driven groups tend to have schisms, and the Riders have had one without even noticing it. Why assume they won't have another? Next on the list, belief groups tend to inner and outer circles. You've certainly done that. Once that happens, the outside group tends to be seen as the tool of the inner power center. You seem much more interested in coopting the bikers rather than converting them. They're second-class citizens, and they don't have much chance of moving up.''

"What do you mean?'' Hiram said.

"Well, do you get many more inside from the riffraff

thugs in the front of the house? How many actual converts do you get from them these days? Like that heckler you jumped on the first night I was here. I haven't seen *him* around getting saved.''

''So he hasn't been back inside. Big deal.''

''But how many *are* coming inside, and staying there? A few years ago, sure, there were savable souls in the biker gangs—but the ones willing to be saved are all inside already. You've scraped the bottom of the barrel. By now the outside is just a biker bar with booze that happens to be cheaper than down the road.''

''So they get cheap booze. How does that mean we co-opt them?''

''Come on, get real. They ride with you. When you show up in a town to do a revival, and those guys show up as your 'security' team, you don't think that intimidates the local cops, makes the local church and business people think twice about asking you to move on? You know damn well having them around increases the collection, but let's just say they don't raise the money by appealing to the giver's higher feelings. I know it works for you, but not many other churches let the guy who passes the plate keep a percentage.

''And that leaves you open to two big dangers. One, you have a large, potentially restive underclass in your organization, an underclass that has a very different agenda from yours. Two, that *they* are co-opting *you,* using the Church of the Road as a cover for what they want to do. They're still bikers, and Christ isn't in them. They mouth the words and then lean on the parishioners for larger donations. They're in it for the money, and for the fun of busting heads with a little protective coloration. The cops don't hassle Christriders as much.

''And yet this underclass, these outsiders, *call* themselves Christriders, even if you people on the inside don't. The public thinks of *them* when it thinks of the Riders. Big, tough, hairy bikers with crosses on their necks. Even the people inside like that image. They get to hang out with big, tough bikers, ready to bust heads for Christ. That's the myth. But it's holding you back.

"And are you really recruiting from bikers anymore? Who comes inside, becomes a real Christrider? The bikers from the front room? Or just plain old-fashioned blue-collar guys, with a few oddballs like me sprinkled into the mix? Your new members have to go out and buy motorcycles *after* they join."

"Or get one given to them," Hiram suggested with a sly grin.

"That, too," Desmond laughed. "But the point is that now you have a belief-driven organization with an underclass majority that doesn't share the organization's beliefs. Guess what happens next?"

Hiram nodded slowly. "Nothing that surprises me. Sooner or later, probably sooner, the bikers, the ones who don't give a damn about Christ, will take over."

"Exactly. Now think about this: there is another term besides cultist you might use for the members of a close-knit, belief-based group interested in changing the existing order."

Desmond stood up, moved across the room and crouched down in front of Hiram. "You could call them revolutionaries. *You're* looking for the end of the world. I'd say that qualifies as change. You're running a revolutionary group."

He looked Hiram right in the eye. "And there's one more generalization about groups you need to hear. Revolutions kill their leaders. Robespierre. Trotsky. A lot of them don't make it. Or else the leaders get overthrown, or someone else comes in and steals the revolution from them."

"So what do you suggest I do? Surrender? Die? Resign?"

"No, no, not at all. What I'm trying to say is that it would be smart if you got ahead of the curve. Belief groups tend to have schisms in their formative stages. So don't wait for it to happen—run the schism yourself. Break away from the bikers before they break away from you. Kick the riffraff out of the bar. Tell the rest of your people it's time they became shock troops for Christ. Go down to those Los Angeles street corner churches, take away their business. Open up your own church in L.A.''

"And be just like every other flytrap hole-in-the-wall Bible-thumper in town,'' Hiram said. He set his empty beer can on the floor and sat up on the couch. "Why would anyone come to me instead of them?''

"Because you're going to be more sophisticated than they are. You're going to do more than just shout at the mob. I've seen you work in a crowd; I know what you can do. So think what you could do with a more sophisticated group, a larger group. You owe it to people. If these are the last days, there is a need for speed. Folks don't have much time, and you have to get to as many of them as you can. The more people you can bring in, the more people you can save. You're salvaging souls for Christ—you have to think *big.*''

"So all I have to do is what I'm doing, just do it better?''

"No. You'll need more than that. You'll need ways to communicate to other groups. Newsletters, pamphlets, books. You have to have something more to say than that the world is full of proof that the Last Years are here. You have to *show* them. Dig out the specific prophecies, and match them up with specific events. Instead of lying about your mother, find some real philosophical arguments to oppose transplants as trespass into God's realm.

"Think big. Buy a satellite network two years from now—if we're all still here two years from now. Preach the Word of the Last Days from there. Start from square one establishing your Church on a good, sound business basis. Take in money so you can spend money to send the Word out so you can take in money. But the most important thing is that you run the show yourself. Don't be a branch office for someone else. Make sure the new Church is *your* organization.''

By now, Desmond was pacing again, speaking in excited tones. *"That's* the sort of organization you need. And you need me to help you get it started. I've got money from my insurance settlement. It'll do for seed money. I've got the ideas you need. You out front, speaking the truth, me in the background running the organization. This is the reason you took to me that first night. Somewhere down deep, you knew you needed me, and this is what you need me for. You *can* start this Church. Let me start building it with you."

Hiram Goodman stood up and looked Desmond in the eye, a piercing gaze that felt as if it drilled straight down to Desmond's very soul. At last Goodman spoke. "It sounds like a bunch of damn fool nonsense to me," he said. "Real pie-in-the-sky stuff, wild dreams. But, well, the thing of it, Brother Desmond—the thing of it is, I've been praying every night for you to come here and tell me just what you have." His face broke into a wide grin and he offered Desmond his hand. "Put her there," he said. "We've got work to do."

Desmond smiled and laughed and took Hiram's hand, and they shook on the deal, their gazes still locked on each other. There was genuine enthusiasm in Goodman's face, but there was that ever-present reserve as well, as if the real Goodman were in there, a cold, calculating observer, watching the show, pulling the strings. For just a split second, it crossed Desmond's mind that each man must be thinking he was using the other, and knew the other was using him.

But that was all right, as long as the cause was served.

If only he could be absolutely certain they were both interested in the same cause.

Chapter 7

December 1999

Time passed. Fifteen months went by.

Much to Father Francis's concern, Desmond Potter moved out of the Jesuit retreat in October 1998. He and Hiram Goodman found a storefront in Los Angeles and opened their church.

After George Prescott spent the summer of 1998 at U. Arizona, sweating out the acceptance of his thesis, word finally came that it was approved. After endless political maneuvering and backbiting, his thesis paper even got published. But the wheels of academe grind slowly, although not particularly smoothly. He officially received his degree only in January 1999. In the meantime, however, with Dr. Stowton's help, he had landed a postdoc job at Caltech, in Pasadena in the fall of 1998. The fact that Jessica was going to be at Caltech at the end of 1999 played no small role in his motivation for chasing a job there. Days, he did someone else's research. Nights, he fine-tuned his stellar modeling system, and wondered if he had wrecked his career before it had started.

Jessica Talmadge completed her own postdoc at Harvard in November 1999, and took up her position at Caltech effective December 1.

Kenji Yamada happily settled back into his life in Japan, dividing his time between research at ISAS and work on the Siberian gas pipeline sensor project for Hayashi Industries.

Norboru Hayashi installed the auto-monitoring system on his telescope, and left it running every night that he was not using the instrument for some other purpose. For the most part, he forgot all about it.

And from the nine light-years in the past, the light rays carrying the first hints of changes on Sirius were headed toward Earth.

December 9, 1999
1:45 A.M.
Tokyo, Japan

The squeal-alarm blasted its way into Noboru Hayashi's sleeping mind, shattering the still of the night. The shrieking noise filled the room for two seconds and then shut off.

Noboru Hayashi snapped awake, sitting bolt upright in bed, eyes wide open, his heart pounding wildly. He ran a hand through his jet-black bottlebrush hair and tried to calm himself. What the hell was—

The squealer shrieked again. Hayashi jumped out from between the covers, and hurried across the room to shut off the alarm unit. He held the alarm in his hand for a moment and looked at the neat *kana* character stenciled next to the single button on the otherwise featureless cube of plastic. *Sirius*, it read. Still numb with sleep, he stared at it, not quite awake enough to understand. Hayashi had never truly expected to hear this alarm blast its news into his bedroom. This alarm was not connected to any clock. It was hooked into a modified subcircuit of his home's security system, though it could give no warning of a burglar. This alarm was connected to a sensor seventy kilometers away, and the only intruder it could alert him to was a celestial one. *Sirius*, he read again, as the last cobwebs of sleep swept out of his mind.

And then he truly awoke, and let out a delighted curse. It had happened—it had actually happened. That crazy Yankee astronomer had been right all along, bless his heart. It was really happening.

He set down the cube and rushed for the cordless phone by his bed. He punched in the speed dial code for his corporation's situation room, and headed for his closet. *Clothes*, he thought, focusing on the trivial as his subconscious whispered that he would earn his place in history tonight. *It will be a long night, and a cold one. Heavy winter clothes*. The phone chirped and an alert, stolid voice answered on the other end.

"Hayashi Industries Situation Room."

Hayashi spoke as he started pulling clothes off the hangers. "This is Hayashi. I want a helicopter on the roof of my house in ten minutes, with a flight plan to my observatory from here. No, belay that. Locate Yamada Kenji-san and ask him to stand by for pickup as well. Order the pilot to land here first, then collect Yamada. Once we are both aboard, we fly to the observatory."

Hayashi shut off the phone and tossed it onto the bed without waiting for an acknowledgment of his instructions. He knew the quality of the people he employed. The idea that his orders might be misunderstood or disobeyed never so much as entered his head. Still, it was a sign of his excitement that he neglected to put the instrument back on its cradle. Pants. Heavy shirt. Parka. Yes, the gloves were in the pocket. He gathered up the clothes and carried them back to the bed, stripped out of his pajamas, and started pulling undergarments out of his bureau drawer. For a frustrated half minute or two, he could not find proper socks or shorts or undershirt for a night on the mountain. That was the flaw in relying upon servants; a man was left unable to fend for himself. But at last he found everything and was able to dress himself.

Five minutes later he was shoving open the rooftop door and standing in a blistering cold, crystal-clear night. Hayashi looked up. The sky was black velvet, studded with fat bright stars that swept across the night. But there was only one star he had eyes for, and he found it in a moment. There. Sirius, in the south. To the naked eye, the star seemed serene, unchanged.

But either his specialized equipment had failed or else *everything* about Sirius had changed.

A gust of wind came up, and the cold brought tears to his eyes, breaking his concentration. He thought how fine a thermos of tea would be at the observatory. Perhaps he should rouse the servants, order them to prepare it—but it was too late. There was the helicopter already, rushing closer, its running lights strobing red and white across the star-blanketed sky.

The noise of the machine seemed to come after it, though that was mere illusion. Suddenly Hayashi felt himself surrounded by the thundering racket of a helicopter landing almost on top of him. Supposedly, modern helicopters were designed for reduced noise, but there was nothing that seemed reduced about this roar. Hayashi indulged himself with a pang of guilt. Surely the roar of the copter's engine had wakened half of his very exclusive neighborhood. But then the landing skids of the machine touched down, and Hayashi forgot all about such matters in his rush for the opening hatch.

Two strong arms pulled him aboard even as the pilot lifted off again. The lights in the copter's interior dazzled him for a moment, but then his eyes adjusted and he recognized Kenji Yamada's smiling face.

"Yamada-san! What the devil are you doing here?" Hayashi demanded, his astonishment plain.

Kenji laughed out loud, but the sound was washed out in the thunder of the copter's ascent. "I'm a mere company consultant, Hayashi-san, and it's only midnight," he shouted in Noboru's ear. "Naturally I was still at the office."

Hayashi found himself grinning back, though the joke was at his expense. Hayashi Industries might be quite modern in other respects, but it was positively old-fashioned when it came to expecting a full day's work from its employees. Kenji had been overseas too long; he made no secret of his belief that the Japanese workday was absurdly, counterproductively long. It was far from being the most heretical of his ideas.

"Seriously, though, what *were* you doing there?"

"Just working the mainframe computer," Yamada explained. "I wanted to see how well my latest theoretical model matched the actual gas flow patterns of your Siberian pipelines. When you hung up on the operator, all he had to do to find me was turn around. I sprinted for the helipad and here I am. What is it, Hayashi-san? Is it Sirius?"

Hayashi nodded, but did not try to speak. Helicopters were no place for conversation, and he allowed himself to be cloaked in the noise, used it to gather his thoughts.

Sixteen months, he thought. Sixteen months since Kenji Yamada had brought him the news of this fellow Prescott's work. Sixteen months since he had hooked a photoelectric monitor to his telescope and programmed the telescope's computers to track Sirius whenever the telescope was not in use, whenever sky conditions permitted. Sixteen months since he had programmed the photoelectric monitor to trip the alarm that had wakened him this night.

Noboru Hayashi was the proud owner of a forty-five-centimeter refractor telescope, a very powerful instrument for an amateur, but one that he did not get to use much; hence the automated systems built into the telescope. But had it really worked, or was it a bug in the system, some foul-up of the sort that bedeviled sensitive electronics?

There was a sudden change in the sound of the rotor, and Hayashi felt the copter beginning to descend. He looked out the window and he could see the open dome of his observatory.

As soon as the helicopter touched down, Kenji shoved the door open and hopped out; Hayashi followed suit. The copter leapt back up into the sky the moment they were out, but the aircraft had vanished from Hayashi's thoughts before it flew out of sight. Now he only had one thing in mind: Sirius. Hayashi hurriedly opened the locked gate of the fence around the observatory dome, then stepped inside to unlock the door of the dome proper. There were no lights, no heater inside the dome, for light and heat disrupted observation. The two men stepped into the chill, dark dome and looked up to see the metallic tube of the refractor telescope trained on the south, locked on Sirius.

Yamada and Hayashi both knew their way around this place, even in the dark, and they hurried toward the computer terminal on the opposite wall of the dome. Kenji made a move to sit at the keyboard, but then checked himself and accorded the honor to his employer. Noboru smiled in the darkness and nodded at his friend. This was a discovery, an honor, that Hayashi wanted for himself. He powered up the terminal screen and worked the keyboard, ordering it to bring up a brightness-over-time display of the night's data on Sirius. The graph appeared on the screen, and both men swore in amazement. There it was, just as the American scientist Prescott had speculated. There was no possible doubt: Sirius's luminosity had increased by a full five percent.

Hayashi shook his head in wonderment. "Excellent, excellent night," he said. "Come now, Yamada-san. We must work to confirm this, determine which of the two stars in the Sirius system is brightening, and then confirm that the machinery is functioning properly. It would not do to announce such a discovery with insufficient detail or announce it and then find the readings were caused by a flaw in the equipment." Calmly, solemnly, Hayashi Norboru stood up from the control console and started to run a check on the telescope and the dual-channel photometer.

Dawn was not far off before Hayashi leaned back in his chair and nodded in satisfaction. "All correct," he said. "There can be no question that it is Sirius A that is brightening, and that the brightening is real. Now, Yamada-san, we can send our telegram to the International Astronomical Union. We have the proof, and it is time to claim priority."

Kenji Yamada found himself shivering and forced himself to stop. It might be cold in the observatory, but that was no excuse for losing control. He looked at his watch, and forced his tired mind to think. It had taken time to get to the observatory, time to make the observation, time for Hayashi to confirm the effect as real. But time was moving still, here, and in other parts of the world. And if his tired mind was calculating the time zones correctly, time was working against one friend in particular.

Kenji Yamada looked to the older man and offered a slight, formal bow. "Hayashi-san," he said in a quiet voice. "Before we send the telegram, there is another call that we must make first, most urgently."

December 9, 1999
1:00 P.M.
California Institute of Technology
Pasadena, California

Jessica laughed and set down her wineglass. "So, Dr. Prescott," she said. "How's life with a doctorate?"

George smiled, felt his spine relax against the chair. It felt *good* to be here. A quiet restaurant, a slightly long and somewhat liquid lunch, no rush to be anywhere, nothing he had to do—for once, no deadlines looming—and a very pleasant reunion lunch with Jessica well under way. "Good, Dr. Talmadge," he said at last, getting just as much pleasure from using her new title as she had from using his. "I might ask you the same question. You haven't had yours much longer."

"Gee, thanks for making me feel like an old-timer," she said with a smile. "How much did I beat you by? Eight months?"

"Something like that," he said mildly. "But to make matters worse, you outrank me." He saw the smile fade from her face, and knew instantly it was the wrong thing to say.

But Jessica spoke before he could offer up an apology. "So I got a tenure-track job before you did. You've got your doctorate."

"Barely," he said. "There are a few people out there who wanted to give me a rubber room instead of a doctorate." That much was barely an exaggeration. His thesis work had received scant recognition from the astronomical community, although that did not surprise him. He was still just nobody from nowhere. His thesis paper, "A Revised Model for White Dwarfs as Progenitors of Type Ia Supernovae," hadn't exactly rocketed to the top of the charts. He had decided to go for broke with the paper, offering not only his modeling work, but all his more speculative ideas as well.

When he'd submitted it to the *Astrophysical Journal*, he drew a referee who didn't just probe it for weaknesses. Instead he fought tooth and nail against its publication in any form. After a huge struggle, it saw print, but only after some of the offending parts had been expurgated. Gone was any suggestion that the white dwarf star Sirius B might someday become a Type Ia supernova.

George shrugged and sipped his wine. "I dunno," he said, apropos of nothing in particular. "That paper caused everyone a lot of trouble. Sometimes I think they gave me the Ph.D. just to get rid of me."

"Maybe they did," Jessica said. "But since when did breaking new ground *not* cause trouble? You're a square peg in a profession full of round holes, George. You're already a brilliant astrophysicist. It's just that no one knows it. If they were willing to look at your *work*, and not your seniority or their own preconceived notions, every university in the country would be falling over itself trying to snag you. Ten years from now, there will be students entering astronomy because they were inspired by your work. You're an original, George. A genius at what you do, if you want my opinion. And if the world is slow to recognize that, that's the world's problem, not yours."

George smiled sadly. "Maybe you're right, but sometimes I have the nasty feeling they gave me a non-tenure job at Caltech because of a clerical error. *You,* they were falling over themselves to give a tenure-track job. Arizona didn't even want to offer me a postdoc job."

"Well, they were fools," Jessica said, with real spirit.

And George looked up at her and smiled. As long as one person believed in him, it was going to be all right.

Life, George decided as he walked across the Caltech campus, was good. Lunch with Jessica had certainly done nothing to hurt his mood. He was mightily pleased that the gods of luck and academia had seen fit to land them both at the same school. It was good to get caught up with her again. Two years ago, back in the old days when they were both working at U. Arizona, it had always been a pleasure to meet her for a bite to eat—once he worked up the nerve to talk with her. It was good to be slipping back into the old habits, the old ways—and feel the old feelings rekindling themselves.

Of course, she outranked him now, and that might make things awkward. She was tenure-track, and he wasn't. Postdoctorate work just didn't have much status. People didn't take him as seriously as they would if he were a tenure-track.

None of that mattered to Jessica. She had made that clear the first moment she spotted him in the restaurant, and that was a comfort. George frowned. The trouble was, it mattered to *him*.

Still, lunch had been good. That was a nice bonus to working in Pasadena; lots of excellent places to eat. But such idly cheerful thoughts evaporated as he stepped back into the astronomy building. Time to get back to work. There was a whole series of projects he needed to get caught up on. He was only halfway down the hall when he heard his phone ringing insistently.

George hurried into his office and reached across his desk to snatch up the phone. "George Prescott," he said, in his best clipped, professional voice. More than likely it was one of his poker buddies confirming the game for next Friday night, but it never hurt to sound businesslike.

There was the split-second speed-of-light delay of a transoceanic long-distance call via satellite, and then he heard an excited voice on the other end. "Hello, George!"

It took George a moment or two before he recognized the slightly accented voice. "Dr. Yamada!"

"Ken to you, George, please. Unless you want me to call you Dr. Prescott?"

"All right, Ken; how have you been? I haven't heard from you in months." George glanced at his watch and made a quick calculation. "And what are you doing calling at this hour? It must be early morning out there." He maneuvered the phone cord around the edge of the desk, pulled his chair out, and sat down.

"Yes, it is morning here. We've been up all night. And that's why I'm calling now. I wanted you to be the first to know. We haven't even sent the telegram yet. It's happened!"

George leaned forward, pulled the phone toward him. "What's happened?" he asked in a half whisper.

But Ken Yamada obviously wanted to tell things his own way. There was something formal and careful in his voice, as if he were speaking for the history books. George thought there might even be a recorder running, and perhaps there was. "I am calling from the mountaintop site of the automated forty-five-centimeter telescope owned by the amateur astronomer Norboru Hayashi, a noted industrialist. After hearing about your work from me, he decided to monitor Sirius's luminosity. Earlier tonight, his remote monitoring equipment told me that the brightness of Sirius was increasing. He phoned me immediately and we traveled to his observatory.

"There can be no question about it. The Sirius system had brightened by five-hundredths of a magnitude, or approximately five percent on a linear scale. We immediately adjusted the equipment, and used a smaller photometer entrance slot to isolate Sirius A from B.

"It is Sirius A, the larger star, that has brightened, just as you speculated. Hayashi-san is sending a telegram to the International Astronomical Union's Telegram Bureau in Cambridge, Massachusetts. The telegram, of course, credits your predictive work, but we both wanted you to be the first to hear this."

George was speechless. He could hardly believe his

ears. At last he recovered enough to speak. "That's fantastic. Wonderful."

"I thought you'd be excited. This is the start of big times for you, George. You were the one who predicted this."

"And big times for you and Hayashi-san as well," George said. "But it might be that things will happen fast at Sirius. Can you manage continuous observation there, every night the sky is clear? And is there any way you can get some spectra as well?"

"That's the plan," Kenji said. "We weren't set up to get a spectrum last night, but we'll be back to take some tonight. But don't you worry about getting observation and spectra. As soon as our telegram hits the IAU e-mail systems, there'll be people observing Sirius all over the world. I guarantee someone to the west of here will be taking visible light spectra in the next few hours. You'll probably be getting a spectrum faxed to you from an observatory in the Soviet Union before you get local night in California."

"That's exciting, but damn it," George said. "It'll be forever before I can get a direct look at Sirius!"

"It doesn't seem right. An American did the predictive work, and the States will practically be the last place to get a look at the event. What about an American-run orbital telescope? Is there any chance of your getting time on the Hubble observatory to observe Sirius before you can see it direct?"

"Not a prayer of time on Hubble," George said sadly. "Even if they *did* let me on, the ground-control technicians would have to program the experiment, and then simulate it to make sure it was doable, and then cancel the scheduled observations and feed the new setup to the Hubble's on-board system. By the time they got all that done, Sirius would have risen over my local horizon and set again. Besides, Sirius is much, much too bright for the Hubble. It was designed to observe faint objects. There's no way to step down the brightness on its spectrographs." Finally over its endless teething troubles, the Hubble Space Telescope had matured into a superb instrument, but by virtue of that very fact, it was in heavy demand, and almost impossible for someone like George to get any time on it.

"Is there any other way you could arrange some observation time *somewhere* before California sunset?" Kenji asked. "Someone else you ask a favor of overseas?"

"I just don't have any real connections with any observatories outside the States. And besides, a lot of the information I'll need will be in the ultraviolet. A ground-based telescope won't do it, and God only knows how long it would take to get an ultraviolet payload off the ground." Most of ultraviolet light could not penetrate the Earth's lower atmosphere. Ultraviolet sensors needed to be carried aloft, by balloon or sounding rocket, or on a satellite, before they could pick up incoming UV.

Satellite. Wait a second. George had never done anything that rated time on an orbital observatory—but this was big.

"Maybe there is a way. There's another spaceside observatory, in geosynchronous orbit. The Kepler Ultraviolet Observatory. It's run by NASA out of Goddard Space Flight Center in Maryland. They could observe Sirius right now."

"Yes, that's right. The Kepler," Kenji said. "I forgot about them."

"Maybe I can get the director's discretionary telescope time on it." George glanced at his watch and figured time zones. "It's close to quitting time now on the East Coast. I'd better call them up right away."

"Okay, you do that. We'll keep in touch. Hayashi-san says *yoroshiku*—hello. So long now, old friend. I think maybe you hit the jackpot this time."

"Thanks a lot, Ken. Good night!"

George set down the phone and felt his blood racing. This was almost too much to believe. It was happening. It was actually happening, just as he had predicted. There was a strange feeling in the space just under his heart, a twinge of pain, a pang of pride and astonishment. Here he had played God, predicted the movement of the spheres, the actions of the stars— and been right. He found himself at a loss for words to describe the feeling, even to himself. He had played God—and won.

Jessica. He had to call Jessica. She should have gotten back to her office by now. He picked up the phone again and punched in her number.

"Talmadge," her voice announced on the second ring. George smiled to himself. He wasn't the only one who tried to sound businesslike.

"Jessica! You're not going to believe this."

"George? What's going on? Are you all right?"

"I'm fine, more than fine. I just got a call from Ken Yamada in Japan. They've just observed Sirius A brightening. Exactly as I speculated." George felt a moment of hesitation and decided not to pat himself that firmly on the back. "Well, I don't know if it's exact. It's too early for good numbers, but—"

"But nothing! George—are they sure of the brightening? It's not some instrument fluke?"

"No, not if I know Ken. They were just about to send a telegram to the IAU when we hung up, and he'd never commit himself that far if he wasn't sure of his ground. Now I've got to scramble and see if I can scrounge up some observations of my own."

"George! Oh my God. Congratulations! Now, get the hell off the phone with me and start calling observatories. Damn it! I'm right in the middle of a big computer run on the Delta network right now. It'd be the end of my job if I dumped it early. Listen, I'll get it done as soon as I can and get over there. It might be an hour or two, but I'll try and hurry."

"You're coming over here? But why? I mean, I'm glad to have you and all, but—"

"Shut up, George, and get on the phone with some telescopes," Jessica said, a surprising brusqueness in her voice. "By the time I get over there, and that IAU telegram hits, you're going to need all the help you can get."

There was a click as Jessica hung up, and George found himself staring at a dead phone. He still doesn't see what help Jessica could be, but never mind that. He was, to offer a tiny paradox, worldly enough to know he wasn't worldly enough. He knew he wasn't good at managing things, but he knew it was important that *someone* knew how. For now, if he was going to trust in Jessica's advice, then he'd better get started making those calls.

But nothing works quickly when you're in a hurry. The Kepler project director could not be reached right away, or for that matter, at all. George left a message with the resident astronomer on duty and on Goddard's voice-mail system, asking the director to return his call as soon as possible. Then he started working the phones in earnest, with little regard for the office long-distance bill. He tried half a dozen numbers at Goddard, but there seemed to be nothing and no one at the Space Flight Center but answering machines and receptionists. At last he gave up on the phone and sat down at his computer keyboard. He typed out a hurried message explaining the situation and requesting observation time. He sent the message to Goddard via fax and e-mail.

But after that, there wasn't much else he could do to get time on the Kepler. He gave up on Goddard and started calling elsewhere, anywhere, where he might be able to wangle telescope time, but his luck was no better. Nothing. It seemed as if the entire astronomical world was at a conference, or on vacation, or out of the office with the flu.

But it was Goddard that finally came through, an hour and a half after Kenji had called.

George was pacing the floor, frantically trying to think who else he might try and call. When the phone rang, George snatched it out of the cradle. "Prescott here," he said.

"Yes," a slow, careful voice began. "I'm returning a call from a George Prescott to the Kepler Observatory director's office. The director is out of the office at a conference at Johns Hopkins for the rest of the day. Practically the whole office is there."

"Yes, this is George Prescott. An associate of mine in Japan has detected a distinct brightening of Sirius A. It's most urgent that I arrange for some observation of Sirius, and start taking spectra of Sirius A immediately. Is there any way I can get access to the director's discretionary time on the observatory?"

"Yes, sir," the slow voice went on. "The director called me just a minute ago. There's an IAU telegram that arrived at Hopkins just a few minutes ago. I checked, and we got it, too."

"Yes!" George said excitedly. "That's what I'm calling about." Maybe there was hope.

"Anyway, the director ordered that the Kepler immediately target Sirius."

"Yes, yes," he said, "That's great news. I appreciate your call. But if all my models are correct, things should be changing very rapidly for Sirius. We need to start getting spectra immediately, and take them repeatedly, as frequently as possible over the next few days. Not only on Sirius A, but on Sirius B as well."

"Right. The director is on the way, and I'll tell him that. I'm sure he'll arrange it."

George gave the caller a few technical details, said his goodbyes, hung up and breathed a sigh of relief. Getting someone to do the work had been tough; but the job itself wouldn't be easy. Even before the brightening occurred, Sirius A had been too bright for most telescopes. It would only take the Kepler satellite a fraction of a second to gather sufficient light to get a good high-resolution spectrum in the ultraviolet. The tricky part for Goddard would be to get the exposure time short enough.

He hadn't gotten much further than that thought when

the phones started to ring. His department head wanted to know if he had heard the news. Stowton, his faculty advisor from the University of Arizona, called in his congratulations.

Then the first reporter phoned in. It seemed that the IAU telegram had been released to the wire services. Naturally the reporter got the basic facts wrong, and seemed to insist on the idea that Sirius A had become a supernova. George made the serious error of trying to explain why only white dwarfs could become Type Ia supernovae to someone who was unfamiliar with the concept of there being different kinds of stars.

He found himself pacing the floor behind his desk, politely trying to disentangle himself from that muddled confusion of a conversation, when Jessica came in. She stood by the door and listened for a moment, and saw the bewildered look on George's face.

There was something solid, grounded, clear-eyed, and sure about Jessica as she stood there, as if she understood what was going on and knew what was needed. At any rate, it didn't take her long to figure out what was happening on the phone. She went to the vacant desk on the other side of George's office, picked up the phone there, and punched up the extension George was on.

"Excuse me," she said, "but I'm afraid that Dr. Prescott has several rather pressing engagements right now." The title seemed to make an impression on the caller, and that was all that mattered right now. She looked toward George and made a throat-cutting gesture across her throat. George hung up his phone with a distinct feeling of relief. Jessica listened on the phone for a half second or so and then shook her head. "No, I'm afraid he's been called away already. However, if you like, I can help you with some of your questions."

Again, she listened for a moment, and then answered, a bit brusquely. "Well, let me see. There are several reference works I could suggest." She rattled off the titles of a half dozen highly technical books.

"Any of those should contain the background material you require. Is there anything else I might—Well, yes, that's fine. Good day to *you*."

She dropped the phone into the cradle and shook her head. "Incredible. Why is it that not one single newspaper seems to have a science reporter with a science background? This guy wasn't even clear on why you couldn't see the stars during the day!" She shook her head and looked over at George, sitting behind his desk, feeling more than a bit shell-shocked. Her face lit up into a smile.

"Oh, George, you *did* it! You called it. No one in history has ever gotten this kind of prediction right before, and you did it."

Suddenly she was across the room and he was standing and her arms were around him. George stood there in a state of acute embarrassment for a second before it occurred to him to return the embrace. Jessica's body felt good against his. Not just in a sexual way, though that was certainly there. It was more that she seemed to fit, seemed to *belong* there. She looked up at him, and George thought he could read something of the same idea in her face.

But then the phone started ringing again, both lines at once. Jessica stepped out of the embrace, perhaps a bit too eagerly, and crossed the room to take one call while George took the other.

"George Prescott," he said.

"Yeah, this is Phil Clarence from the Arizona *Leader.* We got a call in from the university press office that you're involved in some kind of exploding star. Ah, you *did* go to U. Arizona, right?"

"Ah, yes, I did—"

"Great, great. My editor loves the hometown-boy-makes-good angle. So you can fill me in real quick on what star blew up?"

George winced in frustration, wondering how the hell he was supposed to make up for this man's ignorance, or where it was written that he was required to do so. But no, damn it. Jessica had taken the right tack. It *wasn't* his job to do this reporter's job. Let him call back when he had his facts straight. Probably, if he ever did get the facts cleared up, he'd conclude—correctly— that there was nothing of interest to the general reader in a star that happened to brighten infinitesimally. The real story was that someone had managed to predict a star's behavior, but how could he possibly explain how important that was? What could he say?

Besides, Jessica seemed to be trying to get his attention. "I'm sorry that I can't help you," George said, "but I'm terribly busy right now. But I can tell you that no star has blown up. Good day." He hung up the phone with a feeling of real satisfaction and looked toward Jessica.

Jessica had her hand over the phone as she spoke. "George! It's a Dr. Sheffield, the Kepler project director at Goddard Space Flight Center. He said they've already got a spectrum and they want you to have a look at it."

"Listen in," George said excitedly, and punched in the other line on his phone as he picked up the receiver.

Jessica took her hand off the phone for a moment to speak. "Here he is," she said before clamping her hand back over it.

George cleared his throat and tried to speak calmly. "Hello?"

"George Prescott?" It was a friendly voice, very urbane and courteous.

"Yes, this is George Prescott. My colleague tells me you have a spectrum of Sirius A already?"

"We certainly do. I broke all records getting back here from Hopkins, and it was worth it just to see this data. The magnesium and iron resonance lines show P-Cygni characteristics. That suggests an active mass flow to us. We assume the flow is from the larger, Sirius A, toward the dwarf, Sirius B. We're rushing the data processing, so we'll probably have a fully processed tape by morning. We're doing a spectrum of Sirius B right now, though that's going to take a while."

George nodded, not at all surprised. Sirius B was thousands of times dimmer than Sirius A, and even with the Kepler satellite's supersensitive detectors, it would require an hour or more to get a good exposure.

Dr. Sheffield kept talking. "If you're in a hurry, we can send you the tape by Federal Express. If you're *really* in a hurry, you can catch the red-eye from L.A. to Washington tonight. That will get you here at about six tomorrow morning, bright and early. If you fly into Baltimore-Washington International, we're about a half-hour cab ride from the airport. Or else you could rent a car."

George blinked in surprise. "Ah, well, ah, thanks very much. I'd like to fly there, of course, but I've already used up my travel funds for the current year." That was a slight bit of face saving: his job didn't *have* contingency travel funds. But Jessica was gesturing frantically for his attention with one hand as the other stayed clamped over the mouthpiece of her phone. "Hold on just a moment." He put his hand over his own handset's mouthpiece. "What is it?"

"George Prescott, have you gone out of your mind?" she demanded. "This man's offering you the data you need on a silver platter, and you're worried about *travel budgets?* Get there if you have to crawl on your hands and knees!"

George opened his mouth to object, but then he thought about it. She was right. He had to have ultraviolet data, and the sooner the better. It dawned on George that he had better start looking over his shoulder right now. Once word about Sirius got out, the race would be on to interpret what was happening, and gain the recognition for it. With the professional stakes as high as they seemed likely to be, George couldn't let his credit rating stand in the way of his whole career. "Ah, ah, never mind. I'll be there. I'll have to travel on personal funds, but I'll be there in the morning."

The director responded easily. "Oh, don't worry about the money, Dr. Prescott. We'll take care of all your travel expenses. You've put us onto something very exciting. Just keep track of your receipts. See you in the morning. And congratulations! I know what this means to you.''

George mumbled something in the way of a good-bye. Confusion seemed to be swirling around his head today. How many times this afternoon could a phone call turn his world upside-down?

He blinked and thought for a second. And how many observatory directors magically granted wishes to brand-new Ph.D. graduates? It suddenly dawned on him just how important this event was going to be to him. His cockeyed speculations had worked out, and he had just experienced, for the first time in his life, the sensation of being taken seriously.

''I could get used to this,'' he muttered to himself.

''What?'' Jessica asked.

''Nothing, nothing,'' George said. He turned and grinned at Jessica. Things, it seemed, were definitely looking up.

Sleeping on an airplane was never very pleasant, or even very easy, but George managed to do it for about three hours of the flight east. As a working astronomer, he was used to catching sleep piecemeal at odd hours and in odd places. But it wasn't the cramped seat or the muted roar of the engines that kept him awake. It was the excitement in his heart, as if he had been a child on Christmas Eve, knowing full well that the next day would be full of wonder and surprises.

Years before, George had been lucky enough to wangle a pass into the Jet Propulsion Laboratory when the *Galileo* probe arrived at Jupiter and dropped its atmospheric probe. The thrill of that day echoed through this long night as he napped fitfully, high over the darkness of the great plains. Dream and reality, aware thought and sleep-twisted imagining, intertwined in his head. Again, there he was at JPL, walking hurriedly down the long corridors toward the main room as the news came down from the Sirius probe. Jessica was by his side, running the controls on *Galileo*, operating the luggage carousel as he walked down the long halls, struggled to collect the bags he didn't have in Chicago, because he had only brought a carry-on, but it was all right, he had remembered to bring his claim check and his data tapes. But no, that was a dream. He had already landed at Chicago, walked the chilly concourse from one end to the other, one plane to another, taken off again.

He opened his eyes and stared at the long, darkened interior of the plane, the deeper darkness of the sky outside the window. *That was just a dream,* he told himself again, a bit foggily. But there was no time for dreams. He had to think. Think about the day ahead, the data he was flying so far to see. Yes, that was it. Think about the spectra. Think. Suddenly it was all clear, crystalline and perfect. He could see it all. Now he could download the image of Sirius right into the reporter's brain, while Jessica ran a perfect simulation of his entire life on the national Delta supercomputer network, and all the phones rang at once, with Professor Stowton in his new job as an editor demanding to know why George was so rude to his reporters. But then, abruptly, it was all perfect and sharp. The dream images were perfect. All he needed to do was remember that one detail, that one point, when he woke up, and it would all be so simple—

And the flight attendant was shaking his arm, telling him to wake up and put his seat in the full upright position for final approach into Baltimore-Washington International Airport.

He blinked, pulled himself awake, and felt the pangs of waking, of losing the illusory crystal clarity that he had dreamed of having.

George followed the other refugees of night off the plane, yawning and stretching with the best of them as he tried to bring himself awake. Time to get back to reality.

He negotiated the endless hallways of BWI, rented himself a car, and drove out onto the Baltimore-Washington Parkway without untoward incident, thankful that he had been to Washington and Goddard often enough to know the area even while half-asleep.

By the time he had his car and was out on the road, it was still only 7:15. There wasn't much point in getting to Goddard at that hour. George decided to freshen up first. He drove to the suburb of New Carrolton, close by Goddard, and checked into the Sheraton.

Determined to look and feel his best, in spite of the all-night flight, he grabbed a quick shower, changed into a rarely worn suit and tie, and wolfed down a bacon-and-eggs breakfast in a Bob's Big Boy across the street. Then he drove to Goddard, arriving just before 9:00 A.M., congratulating himself on managing time so well.

The guard at the gate was ready with a visitor's badge for Dr. George Prescott. George drove over to Building 21 and was met at the front door by an excited-looking young man, the resident astronomer on duty.

The duty astronomer had obviously been up all night himself. His bleary eyes, weary-looking blue jeans, and rumpled shirt testified to that. Stiff and uncomfortable in his shirt and tie, still fresh from his shower, it crossed George's mind that he looked a lot like George had two hours before.

The duty scientist stuck out his hand and shook George's with enormous enthusiasm. "So glad you're here," he said. "I'm Bill Robertson. The director asked me to meet you here this morning."

George introduced himself and promptly forgot his host's name. But as he followed the man down into the building and into a somewhat scruffy hallway, he had the distinct feeling that *his* name wasn't uppermost in his host's mind either. As he walked through the gray-fluorescent halls of Goddard, George got the strange and disturbing feeling that he was still on the same stumbling, all-night, half-waking journey he had begun the evening before, still making his awkward way down the endless corridors of night. Less than a day ago, he had been enjoying a leisurely lunch with Jessica.

He blinked, tried to focus his eyes. The last eighteen hours had gone past in a fog, in a bewildering patchwork of excitement and confusion, emotional peaks and physical lows. Walking down that one last hallway, he felt tired as he never had in his life, his soul drooping with exhaustion. But then, somehow, as he reminded himself where he was going, the load lifted. His host—Robertson, wasn't it?—handed him a paper cup of coffee from a pot brewing in a hallway niche. George burned his lip on the hot, bitter stuff and he was suddenly awake, feeling stretched, pulled tight—but awake, and ready, eager.

Robertson, still talking on with endless enthusiasm, led him at last to the data analysis room. George sat down at a console. The brand-new Sirius data tape was already mounted on the computer's drives. Robertson typed a series of commands into a keyboard, and the monitor displayed the high-resolution mid-ultraviolet spectrum of Sirius taken sixteen hours before. Complex lines marched across the screen, displaying the star's absorption spectrum.

"There," Robertson said triumphantly. "There it is."

George stared at the data and drew in his breath. "It sure is," he agreed, and leaned in closer to the screen, examining every detail of the image. "You have got one hell of a mass transfer going there. This matches the upper range of my models perfectly."

There was no question about it. To the man in the street, to a reporter—even to astronomers who didn't study stellar spectra—the spectral lines were meaningless. But to George, they spoke of huge forces at work. The spectral features of the resonance transition of once-ionized magnesium atoms at twenty-eight hundred angstroms showed clear indication that mass flow was occurring at a prodigious rate. George looked at them again and whistled, a single low tone. No wonder Sirius A had brightened suddenly.

He checked the spectral features of once-ionized iron near twenty-six hundred angstroms, and the story was the same. "Show me the far-ultraviolet data," he said. The far-ultraviolet spectrum would give him a look at the spectral features of thrice-ionized calcium and silicon atoms; even there he saw evidence of gas outflow. He shook his head in amazement. If the gas could be three-times ionized in quantities that large, the leading edge of the turbulent plasma had to be ferociously hot. George's model predicted temperatures that high, but there was unquestionably something different about seeing the real data from a real star.

"That's from last night, from before you left," Robertson said. "We've taken three more spectra of Sirius A since then, target-of-opportunity shots. Here's the rest of the data." Three new sets of images snapped into being on three more screens, one right after the other. It was plainly obvious that every line that signaled mass flow was getting stronger with each spectrum.

George swore under his breath in astonishment. "Have you tried to estimate mass flow rate?" he asked Robertson.

"No time yet. We just got the last of this data reduced an hour or so ago. I've arranged time on our Delta node to run a computer simulation later. We won't have any really solid numbers until then. But there's no doubt that there is a lot of mass getting pumped out into space. We see that directly. We don't have to guess or estimate."

George looked sharply at Robertson. "How do you know that?"

"Because there's a hell of a lot of mass being accreted by Sirius B. The spectra for B were actually easier to do than for A, because Kepler was designed to handle dimmer objects. It took a one-hour exposure, but that's no big deal. Anyway, the long and the short of it is that we got a pair of high-resolution spectra of the white dwarf." Robertson worked the keyboard again and cleared the first two screens to bring up new spectra, wildly different from the shots of Sirius A. George stared at them intently. Yes, yes, he could see what Robertson was talking about. It was difficult to spot in the unexpanded raw data, but George could see clear signs of mass accretion in the faint absorption features of several ionized atoms. They were red-shifted with respect to their normal wavelengths, a sure sign that they were moving away from the observer—which meant, in this case, that they had to be falling into Sirius B.

"Any guesses on the amount of mass Sirius B is absorbing?" George asked.

"Lemme see." Robertson jotted some numbers from the spectra on a notepad, and started working over the figures with a pocket calculator. "Okay, figuring from the doublet absorption lines we've got, and if the scale is linear and assuming it's an optically thin case, giving us a lower bound—hold on, lemme plug in the formulae—" Robertson stopped and stared at the result that appeared in the calculator's display. "Wait a second. That can't be right."

"Why not?"

"Because if you assume that B is absorbing a proportionate amount of what Sirius A is pumping out, then A has to have been pumping out many orders of magnitude more mass than we thought it was. More mass than it *could* pump out."

"I bet Sirius B isn't just capturing proportionate amounts," George said. Suddenly the lines on the spectrum chart were speaking to him, and a new jolt of adrenaline seemed to rocket through him. He leaned back in his chair and stared at the screen. "I bet the mass is moving preferentially toward Sirius B."

"What makes you say that?" Robertson asked.

"I've spent the last three years modeling this type of system," George said, a hard edge to his voice. "The mass coming off Sirius is a highly ionized gas. If Sirius

B has a good-sized magnetic field, assuming it is connected to the magnetic field on Sirius A, the ionized matter will flow along the magnetic lines of force. What you get is a magnetic bridge, practically a conveyor belt taking a large fraction of the mass Sirius A is blowing off, and pulling it into Sirius B.''

''And you think that's what's happening? That's what these numbers mean?''

George pointed at the screen. Somehow his tiredness was becoming part of him, shaping him, making him feel stronger about his own gut feelings. ''All I can tell you is that I would expect to see this sort of result if I assume a very strong magnetic field for Sirius B. That's what we seem to be observing, if my model is correct. You can't get past the uncertainty that's inherent in the mathematical modeling of a physical process. We can't *know* for certain, but if you held a gun to my head, I'd say those spectra are telling us there is a massive, preferential infall of matter onto the white dwarf.''

''Can you confirm that somehow?'' Robinson asked. ''Feed this data back into your model and see if you get a good back-fit?''

George shook his head. ''Maybe. But the level of uncertainty isn't going to drop that much until you have a hell of a lot more data to analyze. But I would guess there is a significant mass influx onto Sirius B. And maybe something more than just significant. Maybe massive.''

Robertson looked at his calculator again and shook his head. ''My God, just how much mass can a little white dwarf like Sirius B *take?*''

George shook his head wearily. He knew what his models had said in answer to that question, even knew the models were probably right, but he wasn't quite ready to go that far out on a limb. Not just yet. He knew too well the limitations of models—and there were some possibilities you just didn't talk about until you had them nailed down.

Like, for example, the possibility of a supernova explosion a lousy 8.9 light-years from Earth.

"How much mass can it take?" George repeated. "That," he said, "is exactly what I'm wondering."

Chapter 8

December 15, 1999

There were four days at Goddard, four days of watching the spectra and brightness of Sirius shift and change, wildly at first, and then more sedately, until the changes became steady, predictable. Four days of too little sleep, of too many phone calls, too many hallway conferences and computer runs and formulae scribbled on wallboards, scraps of paper, on whatever flat surface seemed handy. Four days of dealing with reporters who tracked him down at his hotel. None of them understood the situation, and all of them insisted that George explain it to them in impossibly simple terms. George never saw anything more than a one- or two-paragraph story about the events of Sirius in the papers, and he never saw anything on TV. Given the amount of fuss generated merely to produce a few brief and inaccurate stories, he started to wonder what it would be like to get *real* press attention.

But after four days, the ultraviolet spectrum of Sirius had settled down into predictable behavior, and it was time to go home. George was eager to get back to Caltech and plug all the newly established accretion rate data into his computer model for Sirius B. Already the real star's data closely matched one of the cases in George's model. He was eager to see what his model would do with the refined and far more detailed information.

The flight back was a pleasant anticlimax, with nothing more exciting or stressful than a change of planes and the discovery that one could get Maker's Mark on an airplane. Maker's Mark . . . George smiled, and thought back to that day; what was it now, two, three, years ago? After all, it had been the simple desire for a taste of Maker's that had led to the dustup with the Christriders, and *that* had led to the broken arm.

And it had been the broken arm that had put him in an ornery enough mood to stick to his guns when Stowton demanded that he change his thesis topic. If he had been feeling reasonable that day, probably he'd be in some safe little job somewhere right now, studying galactic centers and bored out of his mind.

Instead, here he was, sipping Maker's Mark, savoring the idea of being at least a footnote in the history of astronomy. How many people did even that well?

It was a good flight back.

Back at Caltech, bright and early the next morning, George set to work, struggling to incorporate the flood of new data into his theoretical model. The only trouble was that new data—not just from Goddard, but Sirius B data from Hubble, from Hawaii, from Arecibo, from seemingly every telescope working in every waveband in the world—was pouring in. The e-mail computer nets were buzzing with information.

Over and over again, his theoretical model was made

obsolete even before the calculations were complete. Each new burst of data made the stars in the box more accurate, more predictive, more like real stars. But each refinement only led him back to the parts of the model that weren't working, that still needed more data, more refinement.

He sat at his computer and used the mouse to bring up the visual simulation again. He knew it was perhaps the least informative, least useful part of his model, but it gave him the important feeling that the things he was working on were real, substantial, not just arbitrary numbers racing around inside the memory circuits. He could look at the stars he was simulating, not just perceive them as lines of program code. Besides, the simulation was pretty to look at.

The oversize screen went black, and then two flaming spheres appeared. George adjusted the time control, set the star system inside his computer moving a thousand times faster than the real system. The greater and lesser suns began to pirouette about each other. Filaments of fire bloomed up from the larger star, and a glowing cloud of gas formed around the smaller one, flattening itself into a classic accretion disk.

The lesser of the two stars in the computer screen suddenly pulsed, blossoming into a flare of light before settling down again. George had seen dozens of such flares as he ran his simulations. It was a surface thermonuclear runaway, in effect a baby nova that blew off the overburden of accreting matter and left the star core intact. *But that was then,* George told himself. *This is now.*

George was face-to-face with the virtually impossible job of *real time* theoretical modeling. He desperately needed the use of a supercomputer, something with the vast capacity and speed of the Delta net, the nationwide supercomputer network that was on-line across the country. Every university was panting to get hooked up to it. And it was the only system with anywhere near the power to do the sort of job he needed to do on his model. But he couldn't think of any way to tap into that power.

Until he remembered that Jessica had mentioned something about a Delta account the day Kenji Yamada had called. He reached for the phone and punched her extension. It was answered by the familiar voice after barely two rings.

"Jessica Talmadge speaking."

"Hello, Jessica. George."

"George! Welcome back! You've certainly caused a stir. If there's a wall around here without Sirius spectra stuck to it, I haven't seen it."

"Thanks. It's good to be back. Listen, there's something I need to talk about with you. How about a sushi dinner at the Seven Samurai? My treat this time."

"I never say no to free food," Jessica said cheerfully. "You've got a deal."

"Terrific. What time is good for you?"

"Pick me up around seven, okay?"

"Perfect. I'll be at your apartment right at seven."

"See you then," Jessica said, and hung up.

George hung up the phone, got back to staring at the wall, and wondered if he was falling in love with Jessica. No, Jessica was a friend, a colleague, and that was the beginning and end of it.

Except, truth to tell, he was acutely aware of the twinge of jealousy he had felt when he ran into a visiting Dutch astronomer as the two of them went out for dinner a few weeks before. Was it even remotely realistic to think he might have a chance with her?

He smiled to himself and gave up worrying about it for now. No matter what his circumstances, or motives, or goals, *he* was the one taking her to dinner tonight.

Kenji Yamada had introduced both George and Jessica to the more sophisticated areas of Japanese cuisine, taught them that a serving of the most exquisite forms of sushi was called a *nigiri,* that the true test of a *nigiri* was the freshness and quality of the fish and the way it was put together with the carefully cooked rice. George had chosen a Japanese restaurant in his honor. But George would have plenty of reason to toast him with a Sapporo beer even if Ken had never taught him a thing about food. After all, if not for Ken Yamada, and the way he had sold the idea of monitoring Sirius to the industrialist Hayashi, they all might have missed Sirius's initial brightening.

But there were limits. No matter how grateful George might be to Ken, he could not bring himself to go the whole way on sushi. Raw octopus, for example. He objected to eating anything that seemed to contain still functional suckers. George played it safe and ordered the tuna. Jessica, on the other hand, went for the gusto, and ordered a nigiri of *tako,* aka raw octopus. As a rule, George tried not to notice what Jessica was eating when it came to sushi.

But George found the sight of the food a bit less distracting than usual tonight; he had other things on his mind. Such as finding some way of busting through the small talk to broach the subject of filching some computer time.

It was no small issue. Delta time was a precious resource, and much sought after. Those favored few who possessed accounts on the Delta net were an elite, an upper crust. People horse-traded for Delta time, did favors for it, paid off in the coauthorship of papers for it.

But all that being said, how to wheedle Delta time out of your best friend without sounding like every other academic sponger in the world? They were down to the sake stage before George figured that out—or more accurately, before Jessica figured it out for him, after polishing off her last *nigiri* of octopus and snitching a bite or two of George's tuna.

George was a slower eater than Jessica to start with, and he was a bit nervous tonight. The waiters had cleared Jessica's plate while he was still working on the last of his main course. "So, what sounds like a good deal to you?'' she asked casually, pouring herself more rice wine from the porcelain sake bottle. ''Use of my Delta account in return for coauthorship on the resulting papers?''

George stopped with his chopsticks halfway to his mouth and stared at her openmouthed for a full ten seconds before he could recover. Even then, he wasn't able to come up with anything more expressive than ''Huh?''

''The deal, George. The deal on getting Delta time to enhance and extend your model of Sirius. The reason you're buying me dinner tonight. You *are* buying, aren't you?''

''Ah, yeah, sure. But, ah, how did you—''

Jessica laughed and shook her head. ''George, George, George. You're a brilliant theorist, but I don't know how you keep from losing your shirt at those poker games of yours. I could take you, and I don't even play. I can read you like a book.''

George frowned and shifted in his seat, feeling more than a bit uncomfortable. ''Well, maybe I act a little different at a poker table.''

''This,'' Jessica said, still smiling, ''I believe. But come on back to the deal. What do you think? You willing to share credit on your magnum opus, let someone else get some of the credit if she does her share of the work?''

George nodded slowly. ''Absolutely. But there's another angle on this. I want to stick my neck pretty far out on this one. *Really* far out.''

The smile faded from Jessica's face and she set down her sake glass. ''How far out?''

''Remember way back when, the first time I talked about all this with you? Back when we both thought it was daring as hell for me to even suggest that Sirius A and Sirius B might be unstable? Well, it seems like I keep swallowing hard and taking the next step—but good old Mother Nature stays one step ahead of me. I thought it was daring to discuss the instabilities, but I did it. Then I found out there was long-term evidence for Sirius A being unstable. Then I figured out how I might use the old instability events to predict the next one—and I got that right. Then I went ahead and worked out how these instabilities would affect Sirius B.''

George reached for the sake bottle and poured himself a long one. ''About a week ago,'' he said, ''I was sitting next to a very intense young astronomer who had been up all night and needed a shower. I got one look at one spectrum and I knew exactly what mechanism was transporting those tremendous amounts of mass from Sirius A to B. I saw that *one* spectrum and knew, without looking at anything else, what was going on. It was a perfect fit with one of the assumptions in one branch of my model calculations.'' He looked Jessica in the eye and leaned toward her. ''I *knew* what was going on,'' he said again. ''I could tell him what it meant. But what I didn't tell him was what happens next.''

''What?'' Jessica asked. Her eyes grew wide as she looked at George.

She knows, George thought. *She knows what's coming. She sure as hell knows how to read me.* He swallowed hard, and whispered the word.

''Supernova,'' he said.

The word hung there between them for a time before George spoke again. ''I can't prove it,'' he said. ''Not yet, anyway. But I *know* this data now. I've been so deep inside this whole situation that it's down at the level of intuition.''

Suddenly he knew why he had such trouble asking this favor of Jessica. It wasn't just that he was taking advantage of friendship—though that was certainly part of it. It was the danger, the career risks, that getting involved would entail for her.

This thing was a high-stakes gamble. He was reasonably confident of his theoretical model, but whether or not the actual sequence of events would lead to a Type Ia supernova explosion in a white dwarf star nine light-years away—how the hell could he truly be certain of that, no matter what his gut feeling or the numbers said?

There were too many variables to be sure he had a handle on all of them: The mass accretion rate and how it varied. How long the mass influx would continue. The process that started the mass outflow from the primary star. Suppose it stopped, or just tapered off? Then there would be no supernova.

Or suppose the accretion rate became excessive? If too much matter hit too fast, the matter accumulating at the surface would blow off before the interior developed enough heat and pressure to produce a global core explosion. There would only be a thermonuclear runaway at the surface of Sirius B. In other words, it would be merely a nova, thousands of times less spectacular than an authentic supernova.

Even if he allowed for those possibilities, and put them in his paper, the astronomical community would only remember that his harebrained supernova predictions did not pan out. They'd forget all of George's ifs and buts. He couldn't ask Jessica to entangle her promising career with such a risky venture.

George looked down at the table. He picked up the sake bottle, passed it from one hand to another, and set it down again. "I'm not saying this well," he said at last. "Let me put it this way. Right now I don't know. Instead of knowing Sirius B is going to go supernova, I *believe* it. But believing is what the cultists and the people who follow astrology and wear quartz crystals and play with tarot cards do."

George looked up at Jessica again, and suddenly realized her hand was in his, without his knowing how it had got there, which of the two of them had reached out for the other. "But believing isn't good enough for me." He squeezed her hand tight and shook his head. "I have to *know*. I have to run the numbers and see what they say. And if the numbers say nothing's going to happen, then I'll accept the numbers. But if I get the figures I *think* I'm going to get—then I am going to do a paper predicting a Sirius B supernova. That's what I want the Delta time for—to squeeze the most out of the data and my model and publish the results, come what may. But that's for me," he said. "That's my choice, my decision. Whether I'm right or wrong, I can choose to risk my own neck. I can't risk yours. I can't pretend this is going to be *safe*. I can't ask you to come in on it."

"But what happens to you if I don't come in and you don't get the Delta time from me?" she asked.

"Then I get it some other way, or come up with an alternate," George said. "Or else I go with the results I can get out of the old one-lung VAX computer in our lab." He smiled sardonically. "Or else I do the calculations by hand. I'll manage somehow."

"But you're going to do this thing," Jessica said. "Somehow, by hook or by crook."

"No matter what happens, I'll do what I have to do."

"So you're asking me if I want to be part of it."

George shook his head slowly. "No. No, I'm not. You can ask yourself that, but *I* can't. I'd welcome you to the project, I'd be delighted to *have* you—but I can't ask you. I speculated on the remote possibility of Sirius B eventually becoming a supernova in my thesis and almost lost my shot at a doctorate. They only let me publish after I removed all mention of the idea from the paper. Now I want to predict it as a real, forthcoming, specific event. Never mind getting on a tenure track—if this goes wrong, I could have trouble getting a job teaching junior high school. They could take my head off."

"Well, couldn't you hedge a little bit? It seems to me that there are other possibilities—nothing happening, or just a plain nova event. Could you couch it in terms that would get you at least some credit for anticipating the possibility of a nova instead of a supernova? Talk more about the mass flow itself and less about the consequences."

"Assuming I get the results I expect, I couldn't do that and be true to my data," George said. "Besides, if I put that in a paper, I wouldn't be saying anything new. I've already seen papers from several theorists suggesting that Sirius B could become a nova if the ongoing mass flow from Sirius A continued unabated— and none of them referred to my work. All of those guys believe they were the first to come up with the idea."

"Whereas your real claim to fame is making a Chicken Little–type fool of yourself by publicly suggesting the idea that Sirius B might become a supernova," Jessica said. "You've said it in public, and now you want to say it on paper." She hesitated for a moment, drummed her fingers on the table, and thought. "Okay," she said at last. "I'm in. But it's a package deal. If you want Delta time, you get me, too—as a real, working coauthor."

"But what—"

"But nothing. George, there are bigger issues at stake. *Think* about it. Not as an astronomer examining some interesting measurements from out in space, but as a person. As a resident of this planet."

George cocked his head and looked at Jessica in confusion. "Huh? What are you talking about?"

Jessica leaned closer to George, and her hand reached out for his. "I'm talking about danger," she said. "Sirius is 8.9 light-years away, and that might seem like a great distance. For most purposes it is. But we're talking about the single most energetic event that can happen to a star, the most powerful form of explosion this side of the big bang. If it happens, every kind of energy, radiation, and particle there is will be thrown at Earth, in massive quantities."

George leaned back in his chair, stunned. That side of the question had never entered his head, any more than he would have thought to worry whether or not the full moon posed a threat.

Jessica kept on talking. "We can't sit around worrying about the risk to our *careers* on this thing. We've got to figure out what's going to happen to the *planet.*"

Chapter 9

December 31, 1999
Pasadena, California

Two weeks. Two weeks of day-and-night work in the
Caltech labs, loading the model onto the Delta network, running it, evaluating the run, changing the variables, running it again, plugging in new data as it
came down from Kepler and the other observatories.
The Sirius system model was more than a research effort now. It was a pursuit of the truth, a race against
time. Because if they were right, if the supernova was
real—what would happen to Earth?

They split the project, and the paper, into two sections: a prediction of the supernova event with docu-
mentation for that prediction, and a much more
speculative section suggesting some of the possible climatic effects on Earth. It did not take more than five
minutes with a pocket calculator to confirm what they

both knew: If it came to that, Earth itself would easily survive Supernova Sirius. At the range of 8.9 light-years, even supernovae were not powerful enough to melt planets.

But a supernova would certainly affect the planet in serious ways. Depending on where in the range of possible intensity values the supernova hit, it would, for some weeks or months, be somewhere between three and eight percent as bright as the sun. That did not sound like anything much, but there were any number of studies in the literature confirming that even minor fluxes in the sun's output of light could have drastic effects on the Earth. It would get hotter, that was for sure, but by how much and for how long? With more energy pumped into the atmosphere, would there be massive storms, wild weather, ocean warming?

And there was a second wild card in the deck: If Sirius did go off, where would it be in the sky relative to the sun? If, for example, it went off sometime in May or June or July, it would be fairly close to the sun in the sky, a brilliant object in the daytime sky, but with no major effect on the day-night cycle.

But if it happened in December or January, night would be virtually banished. There would be brief periods of darkness between the sunset and Sirius's rising, but in winter, even those would not be complete—atmospheric scattering would keep the skies at least partially light even when both were below the horizon.

The supernova would be thousands of times brighter than the full moon, bright enough to read a phone book, bright enough to turn the sky blue and drown out the other stars. How would animals react to a world that never got dark for weeks on end? How would the oceans' algae react? Would they release more oxygen? If so, how much? What effects would an algae bloom have?

In normal times, the planet absorbed heat on its daylight side and released it on the night side. What would happen to the weather patterns if there was no night side? How much additional heat energy would it absorb? How much more heat would the planet retain?

Neither of them were climatologists. They could scarcely think of the right questions to ask, let alone come up with the answers. Both of them knew the real issue was what questions they had missed altogether.

They needed to get the news of the possible supernova out to the people who would know the right questions, who would have the data and the resources to find the answers. And they had to hurry.

Christmas barely happened, so far as George and Jessica were concerned. Time was too short, the work too daunting. They celebrated the day by sleeping an extra hour. When they met at the lab for breakfast, George gave Jessica a book and a pair of earrings; she gave him a pair of binoculars. If the gifts were not inspired, it was because their minds were on other things.

Besides, if Christmas couldn't serve as a deadline, the New Year could. George had sent out invitations to a New Year's Eve party weeks before Sirius brightened, and it would be impossible to cancel at this late date. The two of them agreed they would have to get done by then, or be working over their printouts in a roomful of partygoers.

And then a miracle occurred: they made their deadline.

December 31 dawned with the paper—or at least a semicoherent first draft of it—written. They sent out e-mail copies to friends.

They split the rest of the day between sleeping and buying supplies for the party.

Everyone was there at George's place for the New Year's party. More people than he had ever imagined knowing, and somehow they were all crowded into his apartment. Half the Caltech astronomy faculty, a whole mob of graduate students, even a few faces from the past—Professor Stowton for one. And everyone seemed to have brought someone. It was a cheerful madhouse, and the climax of the evening was upon them.

Such was not the case everywhere, of course. The more established churches were holding prayer vigils to usher in the new millennium. Others looked not at beginnings, but toward The End. Various sects of Enders were holding their own services, more than half expecting and hoping that their solemnities would be cut short by the end of the world. Others were facing the universal doom in less respectful ways. The bacchanals had started two or three days ago, huge parties, thousands of people convinced that (a) the world was about to end, (b) they were already doomed to hell anyway, and (c) therefore, they might as well enjoy the end of time by committing as many sins as possible. Naturally, all of the above was being eagerly reported by the news nets. There were reports of looting and arson in a half dozen cities across the country.

"Twenty—nineteen—eighteen—" The crowd shouted out the numbers. Clearly they were all determined to make this a night to remember.

The noise in George's living room was deafening. The music was blaring. The television's sound was cranked up full blast to see the celebration live from downtown Los Angeles. Firecrackers were going off in the street, and every person in the room was shouting out the countdown. Most New Years only rated a five- or ten-second count, but this was the big one, and the count had started at sixty.

The newspapers had been full of retrospectives: year's end, decade's end, century's end, millennium's end. It seemed like everyone was offering up predictions—some tongue-in-cheek, some deadly serious, not a few of them warning of the world's end.

George felt a strange tension in the pit of his stomach. Suppose—just suppose—they were right? Suppose God was up there, and did have some bizarre hang-up about numbers, and was waiting for a nice round number to finish the place off? Suppose that this one arbitrary night, this one microscopic slice of time out of all the billions of years in eternity, was truly *it?* The idea was crazed on the face of it—but just suppose. George had just enough liquor in him to wonder.

"Eleven—ten—nine—eight—"

Just suppose, he thought blearily, that the Doomcult and the Christriders and the Last Church and all the other sects that had sprung up overnight like so any mushrooms—suppose they were actually right. Yes, all of them made it clear that The End need not happen tonight—but it was clear that the Enders—as they were collectively known—were more than half hoping that tonight was The Night.

Well, suppose it was? Shouldn't the end have come already—when midnight came to Jerusalem, say, or Greenwich mean time? Or would it happen as midnight swept over the international date line? What was God's pleasure? What would it feel like? Or would God have seen fit to end each chunk of the world at midnight local time? Had Jerusalem, Rome, Paris, New York, Chicago, already vanished, the news suppressed by God Himself so as not to spoil the surprise when The End came here? What would it feel like to have the world end?

The whole idea became more and more absurd the longer he thought about it, but George was in a fog, thanks to the way his glass never seemed to empty, and the idea gathered strength inside him, until he found himself utterly convinced that it was real, that The End would come at midnight local time. And it was only seconds away—

"Seven—six—five—"

Suddenly his heart was pounding, there was a tightness in his chest, and a thrill of fear surged through him. Yet somehow he kept counting down with the rest of them, the grin fixed on his face even as his heart and soul braced for doom and nothingness.

"Four—three—"

The voices grew louder, more manic, as the moment came, and it seemed to George that he caught a look, a wild panic, in more than one person's expression, and suddenly he knew he was not the only one caught wondering, not the only one who would deny worrying tomorrow—if there was a tomorrow.

"Two—one—"

Like a leap over a precipice, the moment came on, unstoppable—

"Happy New Year!" the people in the room, the city, in this part of the world, all shouted in ragged unison—

And the moment was over even as it began. And the world went right on as if nothing had happened—as indeed nothing had—the raucous cheers of the people thundering over any chance for contemplation, wonderment, thought. *The world survives,* George told himself. *From day to day, from year to year, from century to century, all the wonder of life and nature goes on, and always has—and isn't that miracle enough? Is not continuance of the universe in all its wonder a greater miracle than any mere parlor trick of making it all vanish on cue?*

But suddenly he realized that Jessica was in his arms, her hand pulling his head down to hers, as she kissed him on the stroke of the New Year, with far more passion than tradition demanded. Surprised, unsure, he kissed her back, held her tight, willing *this* moment to last, hoping beyond hope that this embrace was something more, something real. He had had enough of illusions.

The kiss turned long, languorous, taking its own time in the midst of the crowded, noisy room, and Jessica seemed as willing as George for it to go on.

But a surge of movement went through the room, and someone backed into George, knocking him off balance, forcing him to break off the embrace. He stumbled, and Jessica released him.

The two of them looked at each other, and George

could read all his own emotions in her face—surprise, happiness, confusion, a little fear. He reached out his hand to hers and she took it. "Happy New Year, Jessica," he said.

"Happy New Year," she agreed, her eyes shining.

But then someone was popping a bottle of champagne, and a crowd in the corner was starting up "Auld Lang Syne," and the ebbing and flowing tides of the party drew the two of them apart.

The party waxed and waned as parties do, the crowd moving inexplicably from one room to the other. At one point the living room was empty and the kitchen was packed to the rafters. Then the tide would turn, and the dining room was suddenly the place to be. People started to trickle out, headed toward home, headed toward other parties. The evening was a success, George had no doubt of that.

But the apartment was still loud and hot, and George had sobered up a bit, and he couldn't seem to find Jessica anywhere. He'd had enough of noise and warmth for the moment. He made his way through the crowd that seemed to have repopulated the living room, and to the sliding glass door that led to the balcony. He stepped out onto his narrow balcony for a breath of air and the sound of quiet.

He was surprised to find he was not alone. A man was leaning over the railing, smoking a cigarette and staring into the darkness. George had to give his eyes a moment to adjust before he could recognize the man. It was Wilton Stowton, his old thesis advisor, the one who had tried to talk him out of supernova research in favor of galactic cores. The two had kept in touch with letters and phone calls, and the old relationship of advisor and student had transmuted into one of older and younger colleague. Calling Sirius A's brightening had helped a lot of people take him more seriously, accept him more.

"Hello, George," Stowton said.

"Hello, Wilton. Sorry I haven't had a chance to really visit with you tonight."

"Oh, that's the way these parties go. Although there'll never be another one like this for us, will there? End of a millennium."

"Not for another year," George said with a smile, leaning over the rail next to his friend. The old debate had revived itself, as it did at the turn of every century. Did the new century and millennium start at January 1, 2000, or a year later on January 1, 2001? Each side thought it had irrevocable logic on its corner. As with most astronomers and other scientists, George actually favored the second date, but there wasn't much choice but to bow to the will of the majority. The whole world was bound and determined to celebrate tonight, and that was the beginning and end of it.

Stowton laughed and took a drag off his cigarette. "True, not till next year. Well, maybe we can all come back and have another party just like this one then."

"Hey! You up there!" A voice came from the darkness below.

George's apartment was on the second floor, his balcony overlooking a small park, a nice change from the endless vistas of parking lots at his old apartment in Arizona. George looked down and saw Jessica looking up at him. "Hey, what are you doing down there?"

"Too hot in there for me. I went for a walk. Hold on, I'll come on up." George was about to ask how when Jessica scrambled up a set of ladder rungs set into the exterior wall of the apartment building, no doubt on account of some fire or earthquake regulation. No wonder the locks on the sliding door were so good. *Typical for both of us,* he thought. *I've lived here for months and never noticed those rungs. She spots them at two in the morning and uses them to go for a walk.* Jessica reached the top and neatly swung herself over the railing onto the balcony. George helped her down from the rail, though it was quite clear to both of them that she needed no such help.

Stowton turned around and leaned back against the railing, propping himself up on his elbows. George and Jessica turned to face him, and George was as much astonished as pleased that Jessica snuggled herself up against him, in front of God and Stowton and anyone who could see them from the apartment. If *that* wasn't a public pronouncement that the kiss at midnight was more than tradition, George didn't know what was. He was distracted enough that he didn't quite hear the beginning of what Stowton said next.

"—you two stirring up more trouble, I see," he said.

"Huh? Ah, what did you say?" George asked, still a bit distracted.

"With the latest damn fool paper you've cranked out," Stowton said. "I checked my e-mail this morning, and guess what I found. I was glad to see it before you published it, and it's fascinating, but dammit, the subject matter! You've really got a talent for shoving your face in a hornet's nest, don't you, George?"

"So far he hasn't gotten stung," Jessica said proudly. "You told him supernova studies were a dead end, and he brought them back to life. They told him Sirius A and B were stable, and he showed that A's light curve bounced like Ping-Pong balls and Sirius B had gone through a pseudogiant stage in historical times. They told him no one could predict when Sirius A might light up again, and he did." She turned to him and grinned. "You just won't listen, will you?"

"Well, if you're wrong this time, all those hornets are going to make up for lost time," Stowton growled. "Jessica, *you* were always a sensible person when you were back at U. Arizona. How did he convince you to put your name on this paper? Predicting a *supernova* explosion? On *Sirius?*"

"He didn't convince me," Jessica said. "The numbers did that. I had to hold a gun to his head before he would even let me work with him."

"I didn't want to ruin her reputation," George said with a laugh. "But seriously, we're both very much convinced—by the evidence, not by the chance to pump our egos or the chance to thumb our noses at the establishment.'' George grinned and shrugged. "Though, mind you, those are nice bonuses.''

"The science, though,'' Jessica said. "The actual numbers in the paper, the report on our computer model. How did it seem to you?''

Wilton Stowton dropped his cigarette to the concrete floor of the balcony and stepped on it. He breathed in deeply and shook his head, then let out a sigh and lit a fresh cigarette. "Dammit,'' he said at last. "The hell of it is, I'm convinced. You made a believer out of me, and I hate to admit that.''

"Oh, that's wonderful!'' Jessica said. "If we can convince you—''

"That doesn't mean a damn thing. I know you two. I have reason to believe that you are honest, conscientious, careful. Who *else* knows that? Neither of you has a solid reputation yet. Well, George does—but as a wild-eyed boy wonder. Maybe someone would listen to this if some boring old sobersides submitted it. Someone known for being slow, careful, deliberate.''

Jessica laughed. "Is that a hint?''

Stowton looked up, astonished. "What do you mean?''

George was surprised, too. The idea had never crossed his mind. But why not? He looked at Jessica and saw her nod. "She's right, Wilton. It's a brilliant idea. If you put your name on this paper, that would give it tremendous credence.''

Stowton looked hard at George. "You're serious.''

"Absolutely. This thing is important. Anything we can do to get people to pay attention, to believe us, we'll do. Hell, I'd be happy to take my name *off* this paper if you think that it would hurt its chances if it was associated with me.''

"No, no, I don't think we need to go that far,'' Jessica said. "Your name on it for notoriety, but you on there, too, Wilton, to lend it some authority," she said firmly.

Stowton was silent for a moment, and at last he asked a question. "Well, there's one or two sections where I might want to tone down the language a bit, but, oh, hell—where are you submitting our paper?"

Jessica grinned and squeezed George's hand. "We were thinking of *Nature*," Jessica said.

Stowton grunted. "Well, your odds—ah, *our* odds would be better there. I don't think the *Astrophysical Journal* would touch this thing with a ten-foot pole. Neither would any other professional astronomical magazine. You need to get this to a more general audience magazine that will afford you more flexibility."

"There's that, too, but that's not why we were thinking about *Nature*. We need to get this information out to as many people as quickly as possible if we are to do any good. If Sirius B *does* go supernova, and if the more pessimistic of our predictions should be borne out, the world will need to get ready in a hurry. *Nature*'s circulation is way up, and they've gotten to be very fast in their response and publication times in the last few years."

"Hold up a second," Stowton said. "I didn't say that you could get *Nature* to take it, but even if you managed to get it published, there's no guarantee that anyone would pay the slightest attention to it. The world doesn't listen to something just because it makes sense and the numbers fit. Millions of people were willing to believe that the end of the world was due two hours ago, because they listened to a bunch of crackpots and their garbled interpretations of a packet of myths." He shook his head. "Sometimes I think that if they hadn't named it 'Revelations,' we'd be in better shape.

"The point is, people like to believe in solutions, not problems. Even if the solutions are literally incredible, they still insist on believing."

"But the end of the world?" Jessica asked. "That doesn't sound like much of a solution to me."

"Oh, but it is if you belong to one of the Ender cults," George said. "If it's all over, then you don't have to deal with life and your crabby neighbors and your credit card bills anymore. And you're part of the chosen few. You get to live forever in Heaven as a close personal friend of Jesus Christ Himself. That sounds better than everyday life."

Stowton nodded. "At the same time, people are very reluctant to believe in bad news and impending disaster, no matter how compelling the proof and the reasoning."

"So we might fail. That doesn't mean we shouldn't try," Jessica said.

"No, of course not," Stowton said. "I just didn't want you to get your hopes up. But for now, let's not worry about it. Just tell me what Chicken Little is thinking. Sum it up for me," Stowton went on. "If your numbers are right, how much time do we have, and what are the odds?"

George glanced to Jessica and then spoke. "There are three possible outcomes, based on what happens to the mass outflow from Sirius A. There is a substantial chance that nothing at all will happen. That's the result if Sirius A settles down and stops ejecting matter in time. Sooner or later it *will* stop, it's just a question of when. If Sirius A stops putting matter out, then obviously Sirius B would stop taking matter in. Sirius B could safely absorb the mass it's already taken on, and then settle down itself. We'd estimate about a thirty-five percent chance of that."

"What happens if Sirius A *increases* its mass outflow and Sirius B takes on more matter?" Stowton asked.

"No supernova then, either. Instead of a core event, you'd get a surface runaway and a plain old nova. It would be bright, and interesting to look at, but it wouldn't do anything much here on Earth. We clock that at about ten percent odds."

"Leaving about fifty-five percent residual odds of the third outcome—continued mass outflow from Sirius A at about the current rate, resulting in a supernova,'' Jessica said.

"Okay, but when?" Stowton asked.

"According to the numbers we got in the last run yesterday, it could pop anytime in the next five years. Probability peaks at about three years out, but it might even happen within a year or so," Jessica said.

"So a sixty-five percent combined probability of a supernova or a nova," Stowton said. "You—I mean we—could cover ourselves a bit that way."

"Yeah, true," George agreed. "But you were right, Wilton. If nothing happens, even with all the caveats in our paper, they'll only remember that we got it wrong. It could destroy our careers."

Stowton laughed grimly. "Not mine, friend. Mine's almost over and I have tenure—and reputation enough to survive being taken in by an unscrupulous ex-student. And Jessica's got a tenure-track job. She's got several outstanding and useful papers out already. She's not quite fireproof, but she's close. *You're* the only one who has to worry."

"Jessica's not all that safe," George said.

"Oh, phooey! Don't you go all male and protective on me now. Even if you want to live forever, I don't. I'd rather live a dangerous, interesting life than a safe, boring one. You can bail out if you like. I'm staying."

George looked at Jessica and smiled. Maybe Stowton thought Jessica was merely indulging a flair for the dramatic, but he knew better. Jessica meant every word. A successful career was not a goal for Jessica, but merely a convenience. Having the right pieces of framed paper on her wall opened some doors for her, got her simple access to some tools that were useful in her work—such as the Delta computer network. But beyond that, she was only interested in exploring the universe, setting her mind on the challenge of understanding how it worked. If the price for finding out was losing her job, then so be it. Of course, Jessica's talent and her ability to get along with people had smoothed all ways before her. A little corner of his mind had to wonder how she would handle it if life did hand her a disaster of one sort or another.

But none of that mattered now. George had worked all his life as a loner. Now suddenly he had not one but two highly useful allies, a most encouraging turn of events. "All right, then," he said. "We'll try for *Nature.*"

"How soon?" Stowton asked.

"Immediately," George said. "As soon as we hear back from our other prepub readers."

"Who have you got?"

"Well, there's you, and Kenji Yamada over in Japan, and two or three friends of Jessica's back at Harvard. But we hope to get their comments back in a week or so. Then we submit."

"Could you hold off maybe one more week?" Stowton asked. "If my name is going to be on this, I really have to work my way through it in greater detail, and get a close-up look at your modeling. And I already know there are a few changes I'll have to make. Minor things, really, but I'd feel better."

George nodded dumbly, as he discovered, rather abruptly, the downside of having partners and allies. When he had been working alone, he hadn't needed to keep anyone else happy.

"Good," Stowton said. "But don't worry, George, I'll work fast. Because if we get this done before about, say, January tenth, then maybe we can do something more for this paper than just get it published."

Jessica frowned. "What do you mean?"

Stowton grinned. "You two *have* been working too hard. The semiannual American Astronomical Society meeting is in two weeks. In Tucson. And I'm the chairman of the local organizing committee. I was in Pasadena to cover some AAS business. As the local chair, I can arrange to have an extraordinary paper presented, and see to it that it gets proper press attention."

George opened his mouth and shut it again. Maybe there was something to be said for working in a team.

Wilton Stowton moved faster than he himself had expected, and trod far more lightly on the paper than George had feared. Most of the changes he insisted on were grammatical nitpicks, not matters of substance. Strange that a man would send out a work that could make his place in history or wreck his career, and yet be worried about the proper use of the serial comma. The other prepub readers were equally gentle, though Kenji Yamada did make a few pointed remarks about ignoring gamma ray behavior in the supernova model.

As of 9:00 A.M. Pacific standard time on January 7 of the New Millennium, George was in his Caltech office, staring at his computer screen. It had been a busy week for the world. But by now, most of the world's-end vigils had broken up, the doomsday orgies had sputtered down to nothing, and the riot corridors were back under control. Of more immediate interest to George, the final draft of "Predictive Modeling of a Nearby Supernova and Its Terrestrial Effects," by Prescott, Talmadge, and Stowton, was ready to be e-mailed to *Nature*'s editors, along with a cover letter requesting expedited evaluation, given the timely nature of the material.

George brought up the *send* command, but then hesitated. If he had been on the edge of an imaginary precipice at midnight on New Year's Eve, he found himself facing a real one now. The moment he pushed that button, events would be out of his hands. Hit that one key, and his world was going to be turned upside down.

But the time was long past when he had any choice in this matter. He could not imagine simply standing up and walking away. Sooner or later he would get over his nerves and send the thing off. If he didn't, Jessica certainly would. And Stowton had pulled all sorts of strings to have the paper presented at Tucson. Might as well do it now and get it over with.

He could no more resist pushing that button and sending his work on its way than he could resist getting up in the morning or loving Jessica. He would not be himself if he did not do this thing.

He stabbed his finger down on the button, and the fruits of his labor were on their way, off to seek their fortune.

January 20, 2000
Tokyo, Japan

It was a cold day for a walk in the park nearby, but the air was fresh and clean, and that made it worthwhile. Noboru Hayashi and Kenji Yamada had gotten into the habit of walking the grounds at least once or twice a week. The torrent of data from Sirius always gave them something to talk about, and somehow it seemed right to leave the office and talk outside, under the sky, in private, without phone calls and urgent messages threatening to interrupt.

"You said that your American friends had sent you a new paper," Hayashi said as they walked along.

"Yes, they have. I'll try and translate it for you in the next day or so. It is a rather remarkable document. In it, they go so far as to predict, with a fifty-five percent probability, the occurrence of a supernova in the Sirius system."

Noboru Hayashi stopped dead in his tracks. "A supernova?" he asked. "And your opinion of this—this prediction?"

Kenji Yamada looked his friend in the eye and spoke in a calm, dispassionate tone. "I have the highest regard for their competence and ability. I have examined the paper carefully and found no substantial flaw in it."

"Then you agree with the prediction."

"I would agree that there is a strong probability, even a likelihood, of the supernova, yes. But I do retain a reservation."

"What is that?"

"They also address the question of the consequences for Earth if they are correct. They bring up the issue of climatic results, and freely admit they are not qualified to predict what will happen."

"What is your objection, then?" Hayashi asked.

Yamada made a gesture with his hand, indicating uncertainty. "I believe they have missed something," he said. "An effect of the gamma ray emissions a supernova would produce. I am so unsure of my ground that I have not communicated my fears to them. But I do feel that I must discuss them with you, for I may need to call upon your company's resources."

"What resources?" Hayashi asked. "And what will you need them for?"

"Research material," Yamada said. "Some of it perhaps classified. It may also be that I will need to perform a few laboratory experiments to confirm my ideas. And I will need to do it all very quietly."

"Why quietly?" Hayashi said. "And what is this effect you say they have missed?"

"It must be quiet to avoid needless panic in the event I am wrong," Yamada said. "Our friends are to present their paper in Tucson next week, and their initial report will cause enough consternation without my confusing the issue with a rather remote hypothetical possibility. As to what they have missed—Hayashi-san, it concerns a phenomenon I know you have dealt with when manufacturing electronics for the American military and our own self-defense forces.

"It is called electromagnetic pulsation."

Hayashi's eyes widened in shock. "Panic indeed," he said. "You shall have whatever you need," he said. "And let us both hope that you are utterly wrong."

Chapter 10

Los Angeles, California

As was his custom, Brother Desmond Potter got up at sunrise. Actually, it wasn't so much the hour of the day as the street noise that got him up. The Last Church of the Apocalyptic Revelation was located in a rough and noisy part of town, and the garbage trucks came through early.

Not that he had gotten much sleep last night. One thing Desmond had predicted correctly—Hiram's congregation had been loyal to Hiram, not to the Christriders. And they had all been here last night, making quite a party of it. Again. Desmond shook his head. He had thought the newly formed Last Church would be a bit more sedate than the Christriders, but if anything, breaking away from the Riders' biker image had been a casting-off of inhibitions. Certainly the Last

Church was a rowdier group than most of the other Ender sects.

Which reminded him: sometime today he had to head down to the hospital to visit with a few parishioners who had gotten into a rather spirited discussion with a gang of Doomcultists. Brother Desmond took but little comfort from knowing the Doomcultists looked worse. There were days when he wondered exactly what he had helped to create. This wasn't quite the Last Church he had envisioned.

Desmond sighed and got out of bed. He and Hiram Goodman split a run-down two-bedroom apartment on the second floor of the old storefront that housed the Church. Desmond didn't much care for having a roommate, but on the plus side, Hiram was a night owl who could sleep through anything. He wouldn't emerge from his room for hours yet.

Desmond had hoped for a better location for the Church, but this place was the best they could prudently afford, even as a rental. Which, of course, brought the new Church's money worries to his mind as he stepped into the shower. He still had most of his insurance money and his savings tucked away, but he knew full well that the ministry's day-to-day expenses would soak that money up quickly enough without spending it on a massive mortgage or rent. Granted, the Last Church hadn't joined with some of the other Ender sects in designating New Year's Day as the big day, but even so, the fact that the world survived unchanged was getting to be bad for business. Money was coming in, but the start-up costs had been heavier than expected. Right now, they were just about breaking even, in spite of their growing congregation. If contributions didn't improve soon . . . Brother Desmond smiled to himself and shook his head. Amazing. Even running an Ender church, half his worries were about money.

He stepped out of the shower, dried himself, and carefully combed out his beard. He took some pride in it. It was growing out nicely, now that he had started taking care of it. And he himself was filling out a bit, putting back more of the weight he had lost. He was starting to *look* like someone who should be called Brother. Maybe he should invest in a set of monk's robes.

That was worth a chuckle. He slipped on his bathrobe, went back to his room, and got dressed in a sensible pair of jeans and a work shirt.

He made his way down to the street and over to the newspaper racks on the corner. In this neighborhood, home delivery was neither practical nor reliable.

Back at the church, he went upstairs to his apartment, put the paper on the breakfast table, and fixed himself a cup of instant coffee before sitting down to read. The first page was covered with the usual gloomy stuff. A new crisis in the Mideast, another round of terrorist attacks in the Philippines, a congressman busted for cocaine possession. He sighed and shook his head in discouragement. Yes, all of the events were bad news. But were any of them *signs?* Oh, he had no doubt that half the Ender clergy in the city, including Hiram, could find some way to shoehorn each and every front-page item to fit something in Revelations or Nostradamus, but Brother Desmond was getting tired of such games.

A sign should be just that: a sign, a big, clearly readable pointer that led you where you were going. Not an everyday event that could be tortuously entangled in some piece of vague mystic prophecy. For a man in a religious order, even one he had made up himself, Brother Desmond could be somewhat hardheaded. He just didn't see the point of God working in riddles.

The trouble was, nothing ever jumped out the way it seemed to him a true Sign should.

Then he opened the paper to page A14, and a headline caught his eye.

ASTRONOMERS PREDICT EXPLODING
STAR MAY DESTROY CIVILIZATION

He stared at the headline for a full ten seconds before he really understood what he was seeing. At last he pulled himself together enough to start reading.

Tucson, Arizona (AP)

In a seeming bow to the millennial fever that has swept the globe in recent months, a young Caltech astronomer has predicted that one of the nearest stars to Earth will soon explode in a massively energetic display called a supernova, with possibly dire consequences for the Earth's climate.

Dr. George Prescott, who received his doctorate from the University of Arizona, last year made a name for himself in astronomical circles by successfully predicting that Sirius A would brighten measurably. He and his colleagues, Dr. Jessica Talmadge and Dr. Wilton Stowton, now say that Sirius A's brightening is likely to serve as a catalyst, touching off a massive explosion in that star's nearby companion, Sirius B. Dr. Prescott states that Sirius B could become a supernova within the next five years.

In a paper delivered at the semiannual meeting of the American Astronomical Society, Dr. Prescott said that Supernova Sirius B, as seen from Earth, would be between five and ten percent as bright as the sun, in effect adding that percentage of energy to the solar energy that drives the Earth's weather and controls its climate. While the large number of variables make it impossible to predict the precise effects of such an increase, Dr. Barry Stewart of the World Climate Institute speculated that the effects could be "cataclysmic."

"Obviously there hasn't been time to run

any definitive simulations, and there are
several contingencies that our programs
were not designed to handle. But we have
done some quick studies," Dr. Stewart said.
"If Dr. Prescott is right, and if we assume
his worst-case scenario, then we could be
looking at massive, if temporary, disrup-
tions of weather patterns. There is also a
chance that the additional heat would lead
to significant melting of the polar ice caps.
Every sea-level city in the world could be
flooded, wiped right off the face of the planet.
And I doubt very much if the global economy could survive that."

There was more from Dr. Stewart, but frustratingly
enough, no quote from the man doing the work, George
Prescott. Brother Desmond read through the rest of the
article quickly. The article seemed typical for a piece
of science reporting as done by a general-assignment
reporter: the main points pretty much correct, but one
or two points a bit garbled.

Brother Desmond leaned back in his chair and sipped
at his coffee, trying to restrain his excitement. Okay,
he had asked for a sign and there it was. As clear a
sign as anyone could want. But he needed to know
more about this supernova. What could it really do, and
what had the reporter, or this climatologist, gotten right
and wrong?

Clearly, George Prescott was the one to contact. Just
as clearly, Desmond wasn't going to be the only one
trying to do that today. And, not to put too fine a point
on it, Dr. George Prescott was not going to have much
time for Brother Desmond Potter of the Last Church of
the Apocalyptic Revelation.

But maybe he would have time for Dr. Desmond Potter. Especially if said Dr. Potter were willing to spring
for dinner. He remembered his own life in the days

when his degree was brand-new. Money was tight, time was short, and there was never a chance for a good meal. So how to swing it? He glanced at the clock on the bookshelf. Just after 7:00 A.M. Not much point in trying to reach Prescott just yet. And maybe it would be smart to be a bit more educated before he did try tracking him down.

He finished his coffee and went back to his bedroom. Maybe he could make some progress on the phone lines. He sat in front of his desktop computer and fired it up. Desmond was always searching the various online news services, sifting the reports from around the world for possible clues to The End. He had gotten good at tracking down leads and tracing a story.

And this particular morning, his practice paid off. Within two hours he had found three mildly contradictory accounts of Prescott's paper, and he had downloaded a copy of the paper's actual text to read later.

None of the other news accounts went anywhere near as far in suggesting world-threatening danger from the supernova, though they seemed to agree that the temporary increase in Earth's heating and cooling patterns would have tremendous weather effects. That was disappointing. Worse was the result of a data search that indicated that the grandly named World Climate Institute was little more than a newsletter shop, and that Dr. Stewart didn't seem to have any expertise whatsoever in the area of climatic modeling. There were one or two scientists who mentioned the idea of dangerous heavy particles, whatever that meant. In any event, it sounded promising. In fact, the more news accounts he read, the more lost he became. Were the predictions reliable? Was George Prescott legitimate? If so, how powerful would the supernova be? And how badly would it affect the Earth?

Never mind all that. Here was a young man prophesying the advent of a great new star in the heavens. What more could he need?

Now he had to get hold of Prescott. The question of

how intrigued him. The man would be deluged with calls right now, from people with legitimate reasons to call, to curiosity seekers and plain old-fashioned lunatics. The problem was how to pose as a member of the first long enough to demonstrate he was an entertaining member of the second group, while taking pains to seem nothing like a member of the third.

All right, if Prescott was buried in calls, then he wouldn't make one. Instead he'd write a respectful, courteous, direct letter, saying he was interested in learning more about Prescott's work and wanted to help him celebrate his discoveries. He would offer to buy dinner for Prescott. Better still, for Prescott and a friend of his choice. That ought to make him feel safer, less likely to be trapped somewhere hearing some nut-case harangue him. Better let them choose the restaurant as well. And send the letter Federal Express so it would stand out. Dr. Prescott would get it tomorrow, and that would give Desmond time to read George's scientific paper.

Brother Desmond smiled as he turned back to his keyboard to start work on the letter. Well, it would have worked on *him* when he was George's age.

George got the letter a little after 9:00 A.M. the next day, and was greatly pleased. It was the first communication related to the supernova paper from someone who wanted to do something *for* George, rather than the other way around. The phones had been ringing off the hook again, and there was a fresh blizzard of faxes and e-mail messages coming down on his desk, all demanding more information, or expecting George to interpret this or that observation, or asking him to grant another interview.

And not all of the people contacting him were exactly respectful either. He had half hoped that people would take him seriously this time, given his track record, but that was fast fading. He was very rapidly getting tired of Chicken Little jokes, and crank calls, and splutteringly indignant letters from senior astronomers chewing him out for degrading his profession with yet another cheap stunt. Those were what hurt the most. He could understand it if he had come up empty the last time, but he had been right, and his new work was based on his old. Why were they so hostile?

Well, at least this time Jessica and Stowton were on board. Let *them* handle some of the mail.

George looked again at the letter from Desmond Potter, M.D. A free dinner, and he could bring Jessica along if he liked. Why the hell not? He had worked hard. He deserved it. There was a phone number along with a return address. He picked up the phone and dialed.

It was answered on the second ring. "Hello?" It was a low, kindly-sounding voice, the voice of a man who had been through life.

"Yes, my name is George Prescott. I was trying to reach a Dr. Desmond Potter?"

"This is he," the voice said eagerly. "I'm delighted that you called back. Will it be possible for me to take you to dinner?"

"It sounds like quite a treat to me," George said. "The only trouble is that I will be a bit tied up for the next several days. I don't think I'd be able to get away until Friday evening."

"Well, Friday would be fine with me. I can't tell you how glad I am you're saying yes. I must admit I was wondering how you'd react to an invitation from a total stranger."

George laughed out loud. "I'm sitting here looking at a whole deskful of invitations from total strangers. Invitations to do their work for them, to go soak my head, to hand back my doctorate, and a few more unpleasant ones. Yours is the only one that I might actually enjoy."

"Well, I must confess I have ulterior motives. I want to hear about your work."

George liked the gentle way Desmond spoke, courteous but to the point, a rare combination. He found himself warming to the man. "Well, I'm delighted to accept your invitation."

"Wonderful. Have you given any thought to what restaurant you'd like to try? Would you care to come into Los Angeles, or is there a spot in Pasadena you'd prefer?"

"Would you mind driving out here?" George asked.

"Not at all. It would be a treat for me to get out of the city for an evening."

"All right then. There's a new Cajun restaurant called the Old Bayou that just opened up in Pasadena. I hear that their gumbo soup is heavenly. In fact, Dr. Talmadge and I had been talking about giving it a try." *The minute they triple our paychecks,* George thought. *But the man said our choice of restaurant. He can't be expecting us to suggest Burger King.*

"Will she be able to join us, then?" Potter asked.

"I would expect so, though I haven't had a chance to talk with her this morning," George said.

"Well, if she can, that will be a double treat for me. I'll call the Old Bayou and make a reservation for three in my name. Then, unless I hear from you otherwise, I'll be looking for you at about seven on Friday."

George hung up the phone and found himself wondering if saying yes had been a bright move. Dinner with a total stranger who had tracked him down through a newspaper article?

Oh, what the hell. It had to be safer than sitting down to a meal with certain of his more infuriated colleagues.

Jessica was more dubious about the whole enterprise, but the idea of a free dinner at the Old Bayou was a strong draw for her as well. Maybe astronomers loved good restaurants because they were one of the few compensations for the long hours and often grueling travel the job sometimes required. A good meal on the road, or just before heading up to the mountaintop for a long, cold night of observation, could make the tougher parts of the job much more tolerable. Stowton was fond of saying astronomy lived on gastronomy.

Besides, it paid to know the good spots in your own town for those times when an out-of-town colleague came through on an expense account.

They drove into Pasadena in good time for the meal, arriving at the restaurant a few minutes early. George possessed exactly one suit, bluish gray, rather standard and perhaps a year or two out of style. He looked perfectly respectable, if somewhat nondescript in it.

But Jessica was breathtaking.

She was wearing a slightly daring version of the classic little black dress. It was not quite tight enough to be overly revealing, not quite short enough to turn walking and sitting into modesty-saving contortions, not quite low-cut enough to be ostentatious. She wore a short open red jacket over it, and a single rounded, polished piece of amber hung around her neck on a silver chain, with matching amber earrings. Her short hair was carefully styled, and a bewitching scent trailed behind her in the air. George was bursting with pride to be her escort.

George gave Potter's name to the maître d', and was informed that their host had already arrived. They were led to a table in the back of the house. Potter—at least George assumed that it had to be Potter—stood up as they joined him, and moved quickly to pull a chair out for Jessica. "Dr. Talmadge, Dr. Prescott," the man said. "I am Desmond Potter. I can't tell you how delighted I am to meet you." He took George's hand to shake it, and then Jessica's. "Welcome, welcome," he said. "Please, Dr. Prescott, take your seat."

The two men sat down, and George Prescott took a good hard look at their host. He certainly wasn't the sort of man George had expected. He had envisioned Potter as a small man with thinning hair, an expensive suit, and something a bit precise about his movements. Instead here was a big man, expansive in his gestures, with a thick mop of dark brown hair and a very full beard.

He was wearing a suit somewhat older than George's, which didn't fit as well. Somehow George got the impression the suit had just been purchased at a next-to-new store somewhere. Yet Potter's face held nothing of the pinched and worried look of a man down on his luck. He was a big, solid man, well nourished. His complexion was clear, his eyes bright and merry. Not a poor man, then, but one who had little use for a suit and saw no point in spending too much money on one.

Yet there was something behind those eyes, something that George could recognize all too easily: a deep and abiding loneliness. This man had suffered loss, and survived.

"Thank you once again for agreeing to see me," Potter said. "I can't tell you how much it means to me."

"We're delighted to be here," George said.

Jessica nodded slightly and said "Yes, delighted," but it was obvious that she was far more suspicious of their host than George was. "I understand the food here is excellent."

"Well, then, let's get a look at the menu and find out, shall we?" Desmond asked.

They started off with the house specialty, a thick, pungent gumbo. It was almost enough for a meal by itself. That was followed by escargot for an appetizer. George ordered crawfish for the main course. Jessica had the trout, and Desmond the veal. They managed to keep the conversation general throughout most of the meal, with Potter asking a series of fairly intelligent questions about supernovae in general and George's predictions in particular.

Jessica didn't do much talking, preferring instead to sit back and listen as the two men talked. She amused herself by trying to figure out what it was that had brought Potter here. He wanted something from

George, that much was obvious. But what? It was clear from the tone of his questions that Potter had no real grounding in astronomy, but that he had done a lot of intensive cramming about supernovae in the last few days. There were remarkable gaps in his knowledge. He understood all about accretion disks, but couldn't quite get the idea of redshifting. Who was this guy? Once or twice he made references to being a retired psychiatrist, but he seemed a bit too eager to get that information across, tossing it in a bit too casually for it not to be contrived. So if he wasn't a shrink anymore, what was he now, and what was a supernova to him?

By the time the after-dinner cognac was served, George and Desmond Potter were on congenial terms, calling each other by their first names. George was clearly being taken in by Potter, warming up to him, almost forgetting Jessica was there now that he had such an eager audience.

Jessica found herself getting restless, tired of just sitting there and being talked past. Besides, she had to look out for George's interests.

"Excuse me, Dr. Potter," she said, leaning in toward the table.

Desmond turned toward her, all smiles, and took a sip of his cognac. "Yes, Dr. Talmadge, what is it? I'm sorry. I've just been going on and on. You must forgive me for forcing George to talk endlessly about your supernova."

"Oh, you're not forcing George. He loves it. But I would like to change the subject a bit. I know this is going to seem a bit rude, but I've been sitting here waiting for the answers to a couple of questions, and so far I haven't got a clue."

"And what questions are those?" Desmond asked, still all smiles.

"One: who the hell are you? Two: what are we doing here?"

"Jessica!" George was plainly annoyed with her.

"I could understand your buying us this dinner to

hear about the supernova if you were interested in astronomy, but I bet you barely would know which end of the telescope to look through. It's obvious—by what you do and don't know—you've been boning up on supernovae all week, just getting ready for this meal, making sure you knew enough to ask George sensible questions and make him happy.''

"Jessica! How can you be so—''

"Because this guy wants something from you, George. And if he wants it badly enough that he's willing to act out this whole charade, and if he needs to go *through* this charade to get it—then I say something's out of kilter and you have to be damned careful.''

Desmond Potter looked at her in numb surprise. "There isn't much that gets past you, is there?'' he asked at last. "And I suppose you do have to be careful. Very well, be it confessed, I do have an ulterior motive. I would like to offer financial support to your work, if you need it.''

"And do what, buy Palomar Observatory for us?'' Jessica asked sarcastically. "Or maybe the Brooklyn Bridge?''

George frowned and looked toward Jessica. "Ah, thank you, Dr. Potter, for your generous offer. I think that the point Jessica is trying to make, however bluntly, is that I can't think of anything where private money could help. Not in our line of work. Our expenses and work are paid for by Caltech and the observatories.''

"Perhaps Dr. Talmadge was also trying to suggest a legitimate potential donor would know that much,'' Potter said. "And perhaps she has a point. I'm not doing this very well.''

"So if you're not a legitimate donor, who are you?'' George asked.

"And I spent the whole drive over here telling myself there could be no harm in an innocent deception,'' Desmond said. "Here it has already bred tremendous suspicion. Very well. Let me tell you the truth then. Up until about two years ago, I was a successful clinical psychiatrist. Then I started treating a man named Conrad Gibbons.'' Anger seemed to wash over him as he said the name. ''Gibbons was a dangerous psychotic, but I believed that I could help him. I ignored the threats he spouted all the time, ignored his history of paranoia.''

As Potter told the story, all of his previous volubility disappeared. His gestures were suddenly small, his face almost motionless as he spoke. ''One day, Gibbons decided I was the Antichrist. He blew up my house and killed my wife and daughter. He was trying to kill me, but I wasn't even in the house at the time. Later the same day he committed suicide.''

Desmond Potter didn't even notice the stunned silence at the table, the expressions of horrified shock on Jessica and George's faces. Eyes downcast, he was staring at the tabletop, seeing nothing at all. ''After that, I couldn't be a psychiatrist anymore. I couldn't pretend that I understood the human mind—or my own mind. I fell apart for a long time. I wound up in one of the security shelters, until an old friend, Father Francis O'Rourke, came and took me away from that place. It's funny, though. Even after all he did for me, I've fallen out of touch with O'Rourke again. I wonder what *that* should tell me about the human mind.''

Potter looked up suddenly at Jessica, looked her straight in the eye. ''Francis tried to bring me back, to show me that there was hope for the world, even though it contained such evil and insanity. I say tried, because he failed. There is no hope for our world as it is, but only in a new world, or in this one reborn.''

''Oh my God,'' Jessica said. ''You're an Ender.''

''I'm an Ender,'' Potter calmly agreed. ''I was with the Christriders for a while, but a group of us broke off to form our own congregation. I am Brother Desmond Potter of the Last Church of the Apocalyptic Revelation,'' he said with a touch of pride.

''And you want to know if George's supernova is going to cause the end of the world.''

"Oh, no, that's where you're wrong, Dr. Talmadge," Potter said. "I already *know* it's going to end the world. What I hoped to learn from you is *how.*"

"It won't. It can't," Jessica said. "It can disrupt the weather, and perhaps cause some storms and some ice cap melting. That's it. If you saw one of those quotes from that Dr. Stewart character, every climatologist I've talked to says he doesn't know what he's talking about. The supernova could cause a lot of damage and trouble, but it's not going to destroy the planet."

"I have been researching the question quite seriously in the last week, and I think you're underestimating the potential damage. But ignoring that issue, what about the heavy particles?" Desmond asked. "If the supernova happens, a massive barrage of atomic nuclei, intense radiation, will slam into the planet. You can't tell me *that* will be harmless."

Jessica and George exchanged another look. "You *have* been doing your homework," George said. "But even if there is a supernova, those particles would be moving far more slowly than the initial light-blast, at something on the order of a tenth the speed of light, maybe a bit faster or slower. They would arrive at Earth somewhere between eighty to one hundred fifty years after the light-blast, and yes, in the worst-case scenario, they could roast the planet alive. Any person or plant or animal that was on the surface of the planet when they struck would be harmed. But if the supernova strikes, we will have a century's advance warning of that. It would be tremendously difficult to protect the planet, but certainly it would be possible."

"Then perhaps it will merely be a sign," Desmond said. "I don't pretend to know all of God's plans. He may choose to bring the end some other way—or perhaps the end shall indeed come in a hundred years time, and the supernova itself is a signal for us to repent."

"You're not going to do this," Jessica said suddenly. "I am very sorry to hear about the deaths of your wife and child, and I can even understand how that might lead to your religious conversion, but it does not give you the right to suborn our work and turn it into some sort of sideshow attraction for your Church."

"A sideshow?" Potter looked at her calmly, still refusing to be baited. "I suppose I can understand your thinking that way. But can you understand me? I entered a seminary for a while, before my career as a psychiatrist. I nearly became a priest, and now that I have entered a religious life, I realize that it is my true calling. Though I doubt my friend Father Francis could agree. He doesn't approve of my behavior any more than you do. Dr. Talmadge, Dr. Prescott—I don't suppose either of you are Christians? I doubt that many people in your profession would be. A certain level of healthy skepticism is required to do good science, and that tends to get in the way of faith. I doubt many astronomers believe in God."

"I was raised Christian, but it never really took," George said. "Though many astronomers do believe in God. There is so much of Creation, and it is so complex, that they figure there must be a Creator of some sort. But by the same token, the universe is so large that most astronomers who *do* believe don't think God would pay much attention to our little corner of it."

"I'm no Christian, and I don't believe in anything I can't measure or detect," Jessica said flatly. "And, to be honest, I've always had trouble with a large part of the Christian message."

"What part is that?" Desmond asked.

"Frankly, I fail to see how somebody being nailed to a piece of wood two thousand years ago is a solution to the world's problems."

"That story has inspired countless billions of people to live better lives, hold themselves up to Christ's example," Brother Desmond said. "Isn't that point enough?"

"Not if the whole thing was a sham, a put-up job, if God was calling all the shots, manipulating everything toward the conclusion He had preordained. Besides, if

God set up that set of circumstances, it suggests to me that He could have set up any other situation He wanted. God could have set things up some other way and avoided the need for anyone to be nailed to anything. So why didn't He?''

''That's just a way of recasting the old question of why God created evil.''

''Maybe it is,'' Jessica agreed. ''So why did God create evil?''

''He did not. He merely made it a possibility, a road that we could choose. In order to permit true freedom, God had to permit the freedom to do wrong. God must have decided that a world where evil was possible was to be preferred over a world where freedom was impossible. Jesus and Mary and Pilate and the Roman soldier all *did* have the freedom to choose their own actions. If Jesus had been allowed to live, perhaps He would have founded the Kingdom of God on Earth two thousand years ago. Just because that did not happen does not mean it was not a possibility. God saw the *likelihood* that His son would be murdered, but it was not inevitable.''

''And yet the end of the world is inevitable,'' George said.

''Though it seems you've missed your deadline,'' Jessica added. George kicked her under the table and she gave him a dirty look.

''I have been speaking in a rather unfortunate shorthand. Some Enders do expect the actual, physical planet to simply pop out of existence. I think that is not true. The end of the world is not coming—but the end of human mastery over it is. When Gibbons slaughtered my family, I knew we had reached the point of no return,'' Desmond said. ''It could come through nuclear war, or pollution, or the greenhouse effect, or overpopulation, or through a rain of heavy particles from a nearby supernova, but it is coming. It's my own personal view that God will end it all in His own way, before we drag it out and damage the Earth irretrievably by doing it our way. I think He has sent the supernova to punish us.''

''In that case,'' Jessica said, ''you have an interesting theological problem to deal with, *Brother* Desmond. If the supernova blooms tonight, it must be due to something we did no later than 1991. After all, the light from Sirius takes that long to reach us. Couldn't God in all His power find some way of smiting us a bit more promptly?

''So if, as you say, it's in just the last few years humanity reached the point of no return, became so debased and evil that it must be scourged from the Earth by means of the supernova, then God must have arranged the punishment long before we ever committed the crime, and we're right back to God seeing our predestined futures, which He himself creates, and punishing us for doing the deeds He compelled us to perform,'' Jessica said.

Potter looked at Jessica long and hard. ''You're good, Dr. Talmadge,'' he said. ''You are very, very good. I suppose I should assume that you aren't going to help me, Dr. Prescott, but hope does spring eternal. What are you going to do?''

George sat there, silent, for the better part of a minute. ''Regular reports,'' he said. ''I write up a summary of the work I've done for myself at the end of every month. I'll send you a copy. It will be confidential at my end, and it had better be at your end. Now, I can't reasonably expect you to ignore the supernova talk when everyone else will be discussing it. But bring *my* name up even once, associate yourself with me in any way, and it's all over. I'll do everything I can to make it clear your ideas are nonsense.''

Jessica looked at George, completely shocked. ''But—''

''No, Jessica,'' George said, his voice hard and firm. ''The knowledge I gather is meant to be shared, not hidden. I think we can trust Brother Desmond not to betray our trust.''

Desmond's eyes were shining, his whole face alight. "Oh yes, yes, you can indeed. This is most generous of you. Now, before we go, might I suggest a coffee? It will be a long ride back for me."

George looked toward Jessica, and saw her glaring at him. *And for me as well,* he thought.

George and Desmond exchanged addresses, and Desmond paid the bill—in cash, using small bills no doubt taken from the collection plate—and got a receipt. Jessica wondered how he would enter the expense in the church ledger. *Dinner with Drs. Talmadge and Prescott. Discussed end of world.*

The three of them walked outside into the brilliant, star-bright night and said their good-byes. Potter offered his hand to Jessica and after a moment's hesitation, she took it. The man's views were strange, but he had been a perfect gentleman and a splendid host. But she could not resist raising one or two more points.

"Good night, and thank you for a lovely dinner," she said. "One last question for you, Brother Desmond. I get the impression that you're still pinning your hopes on the supernova melting the ice caps and drowning the world. Endless storms, the water swallowing the land. Right?"

"Well, yes."

"Isn't that the one disaster you know is *not* going to happen? Don't you remember God's covenant with Noah, and His promise never to send a flood again? And if it is the heavy particles that get us, then it will happen a hundred years from now. They will kill the sons and daughters, the innocent grandchildren, of the people who so displeased God. They will die in agonizing pain of radiation sickness. Would He truly mete out such punishment on the heads of children for the sins of the fathers?"

Desmond Potter blinked in surprise and looked at Jessica very thoughtfully. At last he nodded and pulled a long, expensive-looking cigar from his jacket pocket and made a bit of a show out of lighting it up. "My dear," he said at last, "you are exactly right, and I don't see how I could have missed those very obvious points. But you make the unwarranted conclusion that you have considered *all* the possibilities and eliminated them, and that there will therefore be no disaster. How can you be certain of that, when dealing with such a powerful, complex phenomenon? No, it would be far wiser to assume that then there is some other disaster, a hidden one," Desmond said. "One that we, in all our arrogant efforts to outguess God, have missed. Good night to you both. George, I thank you once more. I know we will talk again soon."

And with that, he turned away and walked into the night, trailing a cloud of fragrant smoke, the burning ember of his cigar a tiny spark in the darkness.

They were barely out of the parking lot before Jessica turned toward George. "Okay, spill it. Why? Why on earth offer any assistance at all to that man? He can't do anything with the information but cause trouble. Why let yourself be used?"

George pulled the car out onto the highway. "I'll tell you why. Desmond—Brother Desmond—gave us *his* life story in there, but did you ever think about mine?"

"What are you talking about?"

"I saw a lot of me in Desmond Potter. He's been a very lonely man for a long time, and he's finally found some people who want him, who will take him in. Do you know what it feels like to be out in the cold that long, and then finally be accepted? Don't you think they would be angry with him for failing tonight? Even if it's a nut church that gave him that feeling of acceptance, it is not something I feel the right to mess with. Not when I can help him by printing out an extra copy of my progress log and sticking it in the mail.

"But it goes deeper. I've spent practically my whole career so far believing in things everyone else thought were absurd. I've been rejected, laughed at, over and over again. I fell in love with you the day you didn't laugh at my crazy ideas. I know how that laughter cuts.

"Maybe Desmond spends his days on Hollywood Boulevard waving a sign that says *The World Is Coming to an End*. Maybe people point at him and make jokes, hassle him on the street, run up and pull his beard to see if it's real. Or maybe he sits in an office and pushes paper. Who knows?

"No matter *how* he expresses his beliefs, sooner or later he gets laughed at for them. You laughed at him tonight. I don't blame you—his ideas are *crazy*. But I've *felt* that kick in the belly. I know how it hurts. Who am I to inflict it on anyone else, when there can be no harm in being kind?"

Jessica looked through the shifting light and darkness of the car's interior, the streetlights sweeping past outside, and saw shadows flashing across George's face. "George, I'm sorry. I didn't know. I didn't think."

"It's all right," George said. "There was no way you could. But there's one other reason I'm helping him. It's a million-to-one shot . . ." George stared out into the darkness, guiding the car with a sure but careful hand. "But there is always the chance that he's right."

Chapter 11

May 2000
Los Angeles, California

Hiram Goodman strode back and forth across the
stage, waving the latest copy of *Nature* in his hand.
"Now the scientists are saying it, too, brothers and
sisters! When we were promised a great new light in
the sky to signal the end of all days, we all thought that
meant a comet, or a great meteor, or maybe a huge
asteroid coming down to smash the Earth.

"But God outsmarted us again, the way He always
does, warning us away from the sin of pride. A supernova! That's what's on the way. The pure light of a star,
made as great and powerful as a thousand suns, coming
down to smite the wicked, coming down as a signal to
all God's children that the Time of the End has indeed
come. Praise God that we shall be here to witness it.
We shall see those who have scoffed at us smote down

by God's wrath, punished for their wickedness, drowned in the deepest of floods—''

Desmond watched Hiram work the crowd. The small storefront church was filled to bursting. The crowds were getting bigger, night after night. More and more "insider'' Christriders were leaving the Church of the Road and re-joining Hiram. They had opened their third congregation just the week before, and brought in another preacher who knew how to give a real Hiram Goodman-style fire-and-brimstone rendition of the Gospel, with the sacramental wine and beer flowing freely.

He no longer had any worries about the collection plate. The first five months of the New Millennium had been good for the Last Church. Unless the millennium started in 2001, of course. *That* argument showed no sign of letting up among the various Ender sects, though it seemed like the general public was tired of it and quite content to score it as a tie.

Among the believers, of course, it was a matter of vital importance, and would be up until the precise moment of midnight, Jerusalem time, on December 31, 2000 Anno Domini.

At which time, of course, exactly nothing would happen. Nothing would happen until the supernova came. Desmond did not know exactly when he had come to that conclusion, but he had. As to whether or not the supernova represented divine intervention or merely a natural disaster, he was no longer sure. Something had changed for him that night with George Prescott, something he could not yet define.

He had *lied* to that young man, or come as close to lying as made no difference. He had gone in there hoping to use George, to trick him or bribe him into providing the information he had ended up giving him freely.

There was something about that evening, about that contact with another human being. It had been the first time since the death of his wife that someone had done something for him out of simple kindness. Oh, Francis O'Rourke had pulled him out of the shelter and put him back on the road to sanity, and he would be eternally grateful for that, but there had been the bonds of friendship, of old days together and debts to pay. Hiram Goodman had taken him in as well, but it was obvious that Goodman helped Desmond because Desmond helped *him*. Goodman needed him.

But George Prescott had no reason to help, and every reason not to lift a finger. Indeed, he should have regarded Desmond as his enemy.

And yet those summaries came the first of every month, and there was always a friendly, personal note tucked in with them. Each month the news grew stronger, more certain. The chances for Sirius A to stop expelling mass were virtually down to zero now. Now it was a question of nova versus supernova, a question of when it would happen. Desmond now understood far more of the processes involved, the intricate, violent, complex, but perfectly straightforward and natural processes that could turn an Earth-sized ball of compacted gas into a flame of light that could outshine the galaxy.

And it was coming. Now George thought it might even come before year's end. Which perhaps meant that nothing would happen December 31 because there would be no human beings left for it to happen to.

But no, that was ridiculous. Even if the supernova did its worst, it would not magically wipe every human being off the face of the Earth. The floods, if they came, would take time to form, time for the ice to melt and the oceans to rise. The heavy particles would take generations to arrive. And certainly there would be people, probably quite a number of them—probably most of them—who would manage to survive both of those disasters, if they came. He remembered being vaguely disappointed when he reached that conclusion. But why? The total destruction of the human race was not good news, no matter what Hiram preached. Why had he ever wished for it, devoutly prayed for the destruction of the race?

Had he hated the world that much? Had he hated himself that much, wanted that much to punish himself and all the world for the crime of surviving when his wife and daughter were murdered?

Had he been that crazy?

It was too much to say that one tiny gesture of kindness from a man who should have hated him was enough to have turned Desmond's world view upsidedown. Hiram's gleeful promises of horrible destruction for those who did not believe had bothered him, and all his denials to Francis to the contrary, the knowledge that life could be lived in places more pleasant than a shelter helped as well.

But it was George Prescott, who was no Christian, who turned his other cheek, that made up his mind.

Life, it turned out, was good after all.

June 2000
Tokyo, Japan

It was a lovely summer night, mild and warm, and droves of young couples were taking advantage of the weather. Hundreds of them had spread their jackets out on the expensive lawns in front of the moat of the Imperial Palace. The air pollution in Tokyo had cleared up quite a bit in recent years, and tonight the sky seemed especially clear, the stars fat and bright in the velvet darkness. The full moon hung high in the eastern sky.

But Hideo Nakano was not aware of the spectacular sky. He was too absorbed in Toshiko's beauty, in the taste of her lips, the eager warmth of her body. She had driven any thought of other women clear out of his mind. He bent over her, and kissed her again.

He had met her at work, at Hayashi Industries, where they both worked. Hideo worked as a technician in the

research department, and Toshiko in procurement. It
had been two months since they had first met, but
work had been a mad rush since March, when Hayashi-
san himself had brought in that scientist Yamada and
started up on some huge new mysterious project. They
had started ordering all sorts of oddball equipment,
with no obvious thread explaining how it all fit together. Vacuum tube radios, old cars in good condition,
shielded computer equipment, new cars, military communications equipment. It didn't seem to make any
sense. Hideo and Toshiko had met in the midst of the
tangled effort to track down some of the more obscure
items. They had spent a pleasant lunchtime trying to
guess what the old man was up to. Whatever it was, it
certainly required a lot from both procurement and research.

But mystery projects were the last thing on Hideo's
mind as he kissed Toshiko. A long moment later, they
broke the embrace and let out quiet sighs of content-
ment. It was a magical night. Hideo rolled over on his
back, wrapped his arm around Toshiko, and snuggled
close to her. The two of them lay there in silence for a
long moment, staring at the sky.

But Hideo's mind was not on the stars, or on romance and poetry either. He was thinking in terms of
tactics and strategy. He had no vast experience of
women, but one thing he had learned over the years:
There was a hardheaded, practical side to romance, one
that required careful scheduling, one that no woman of
his acquaintance even seemed aware of. Baldly put, in
Japan, in the year 2000, it took a good bit of planning
to find a time and place to make love. In crowded Tokyo, that was especially true.

Women never seemed to concern themselves with the
worrying, the planning—all right, the downright
scheming—required to get two people alone in a comfortable, private place, at the moment when both were
in the mood. Rather, women seemed to take for granted
that either the man—or fate—would arrange things.

Fate! As if blind chance could arrange a vacant room at a busy hotel, as if fate could see to it that an apartment just happened to be vacant, and put the spare key in the man's pocket besides. Women seemed to think it was done by magic. Over their beers after work, his friends from the office all described the same experience.

No, the women seemed to regard the whole thing as some happy, magic chance—unless and until they took it as a grand insult to discover the man had made any such plans. There was no way to win. That was the way women were.

And yet, deep inside, Hideo knew that wasn't true, that he was selling women short, and maybe men as well. It wasn't the people themselves who took the act of love and turned it into something to be won or lost by tricks and stratagems, but the circumstances of their lives. He couldn't flatly conclude that all women were the same—not while he was looking into Toshiko's eyes. She was herself, an individual, who made her own choices.

Which led to a point of some delicacy. What choice would she make tonight, when he presented her with the chance to choose? Hideo, sensing that this might be *the* night for Toshiko and himself, had made certain arrangements. Now seemed like the ideal moment to make a delicate hint.

But Hideo still wasn't quite sure where he wanted to take her. He had the reservation at a nearby love hotel—but would that be too crass, too obvious? There were whole districts of love hotels, all of them carefully designed to maintain the anonymity of their clientele. The front doors were screened from the sight of the street, the receptionist hid behind smoked glass, and they expected you to pay cash, and pay on an hourly rate. You paid dearly for a room that was yours and yours alone, with no relatives or neighbors behind too-thin walls. Yours, that is, until your time was up and you went out the back way, never having seen another human being.

All very discreet and quiet and carefully designed to prevent scandal.

That was the trouble. It afforded a couple privacy, but the love hotels worked so hard to hide their clientele. It made the act of love seem like a shameful, sordid thing. It turned love into something that had to be hidden away.

Perhaps he should invite her back to his condominium apartment. But no, damn it, his condominium was just too far away and too small. His bed was barely large enough for him to sleep by himself. Besides, if they went to his place, he would never be able to get her back to her parents' home at anything approaching a decent hour. It was the love hotel or nothing.

That choice made, it came down to a question of time.

Hideo glanced discreetly at his watch. It was getting late, and the love hotels were probably already filling up. They weren't likely to hold his reservation long if he and Toshiko got there late. It was now or never.

He swallowed hard and spoke. "Toshiko—I don't mean to be forward, but . . . well, why don't we take a cab and go someplace a bit more private? This just feels too public. I can count a dozen couples without turning my head." He hesitated for a moment and then spoke again, awkwardly, trying to find a retreat when his suggestion was met with silence. "Uh, unless you'd rather stay here. I wouldn't want you to do anything you didn't want . . ." His voice trailed off into the darkness and he cursed himself for being a fool.

At last he saw her smiling in the darkness. "I've been half expecting you to ask," she said. "So I told my parents I might be out a bit late tonight, just in case."

She turned and looked at his lean profile in the moonlight, reached out a hand to touch his face.

Hideo was amazed. So much for women never planning ahead in matters of the heart. He tried to think of something to say, something that would express how he felt about her. But words would be little and too much. Instead he bent down his head and kissed her again. After a few moments they broke off the embrace. He stood first and extended his hand to help Toshiko to her feet. They walked the few hundred meters to the street without talking, carefully threading their way among the other couples on the lawn.

"So," Toshiko said, "where are you taking me?"

"Well, um—" Hideo was feeling deeply embarrassed.

"Aha!" Toshiko said with obvious delight. "Then it *is* a love hotel. I've always been curious about those places."

Hideo stopped and looked at her in astonishment. "You *want* to go to a love hotel?" he asked.

"Why not?" she said, laughing. "It's an adventure."

Hideo laughed, too, and they hurried out of the park to emerge on the main street by the moat. He flagged down a passing cab, climbed in after Toshiko, and told the cabbie, "Utamaro-so in Shin-Okubo, please. And hurry."

The cab driver grinned broadly. "Need to get there quickly, eh?" Obviously he had made this run before, and probably made the joke as well. He seemed quite amused by it all until he caught sight of Toshiko's stony expression in the rearview mirror. Hideo looked over at her and saw that she had turned beet-red with embarrassment.

"That's enough of that," Hideo said firmly. "Have some respect for the lady."

The smile faded from the driver's face. "My apologies, ma'am," he said. "Very good, sir. I know a shortcut around the congestion in Shinjuku district. I'll get you there in no time."

Hideo looked over at Toshiko. She was sitting up in the far corner of the seat, hands on her lap, staring straight ahead, the picture of demure and modest womanhood. Hideo sat back in his own corner of the seat, suddenly angry and frustrated. He longed to reach out and touch her, but he dared not. Not in front of the driver. Why did it have to be that way? It was different in the parks; you could touch and kiss there, but only because of the unspoken agreement that all the couples would pretend that no one else was there. And even in the park there were very strict limits. Outside the parks at night, it was scandalous to be seen so much as holding hands. Hideo shook his head. He had been abroad, seen places where people touched and kissed in public without the world coming to an end.

But not in Japan. Even when two lovers were obviously on their way to an assignation, it was considered ill mannered to express their desires too openly. The cabbie knew where they were going, and why, and *they* knew that he knew it, and he knew they knew, around and around and around in a weary circle, and yet they all had to pretend they were headed off to drink tea with Toshiko's grandmother.

At least the taxi driver knew his work. He got them to their destination with miraculous speed, considering the Saturday night traffic in Shinjuku, and that made up for all. Hideo broke with Japanese custom and not only tipped the cabbie, but did so generously.

They got out of the cab and looked around. Both sides of the street were lined with love hotels, their neon signs gaudily announcing their trade, but they were headed for one of the biggest and best, and Hideo took a certain pride in that. Utamaro-so was a multi-storied building that dwarfed its neighbors.

Hideo and Toshiko went inside, and were greeted by a discreet matronly voice that came from a speaker set in the wall by a smoked-glass partition. They could just make out the receptionist's silhouette. That way, any shamefaced lovebirds who came in need not feel embarrassed by being seen by the receptionist.

"Hello," Hideo said, feeling a bit foolish speaking to the shadowy figure behind the glass. "You are holding a reservation number 1147 for a Mr. Suzuki?" Suzuki was the Japanese equivalent of Smith or Jones; no doubt a whole parade of fictional Suzukis had been through tonight. That was why the reservations were numbered.

The matronly voice spoke obsequiously. "Ah, yes, we have your reservation, Mr. Suzuki. Your room will be equipped with the usual amenities. Would you like anything special?"

Hideo hesitated for a second. He did not want Toshiko to think he used love hotels like this all the time, but on the other hand, he did not want to seem unsophisticated. Unfortunately, he wasn't quite sure what the "specials" were, and he certainly didn't want to spend time just now finding out. "I don't think we will be needing anything special. Uh, we will only be 'resting.' " That much he knew, and was rather proud of the knowledge. The word "resting" meant that he wanted the room for three hours, rather than overnight.

"Very well, sir. Your room is number 315. The elevator is through the door on the right. That will be nine thousand yen including the tax."

Hideo paid in cash, pushing the money through a slide-drawer under the reception window and getting his key-card back the same way. He took the key and ushered Toshiko through the heavy steel door. He stopped to test the door after they had stepped through it and it had swung shut. Sure enough, it had locked behind them. They would not be able to burst in on the next couple who came through.

The elevator ride to the third floor passed in an embarrassed silence. Hideo did not know what to say, and Toshiko was not helping matters. She was standing as far away from him as possible, her face expressionless, her eyes downcast.

Hideo felt increasingly nervous. What was this place going to be like? They found the room, and Hideo opened the door with the key-card. The two of them stepped inside. Hideo turned on the light as he closed the door behind them.

There was a large mirror on the ceiling, and two of the walls were also mirrored. There was a huge circular bed in the center of the room, pink and white. In fact, everything in the place was pink and white. The carpet was a thick white plush, the walls done up in plush pink velvet.

A video camera stood on a tripod in one corner, with a cable leading into a VCR and a TV set into the adjacent wall. That much Hideo had heard about. Some couples liked to record their lovemaking and then play it back to get a second thrill out of their passion, and maybe stimulate themselves for a second round. Hideo stepped into the bathroom and looked around. The tub was big enough for two. He stepped back out, for some reason more embarrassed by the tub than by anything else. Toshiko seemed to be examining the video equipment with some alarm. The place was huge, absurd, ostentatious.

Toshiko and Hideo looked at each other and then laughed out loud. Suddenly, as if laughter had been the cue, Hideo pulled Toshiko tightly into his arms and kissed her voraciously. She responded just as hungrily.

She let him undress her, though she seemed more eager than he to get her clothes off. He worked hastily, albeit clumsily, first on her dress, then her underwear. Then he undressed himself, stripping his clothes off with reckless haste. They embraced and fell onto the circular bed.

Hideo was a bit startled when the bed started rotating slowly. A drippily sentimental love ballad suddenly started to play, and the room got dim as the lights automatically faded.

Suddenly he had to laugh. Toshiko looked at him in alarm. "Hideo! What is it? Have I displeased you?"

"No, no, not at all. But look around you! The bed senses when we're on it. The lights dim when we lie down. The music starts when we start to make love. Even the damn video camera is panning back and forth, automatically keeping us in view. If you had put a tape in it, it would be recording us right now. Think for a moment. How is it that the room is so smart? How can it tell what we're doing? Who makes the environmental sensors that make this possible?''

Toshiko frowned for a moment, and then blushed prettily as she laughed out loud. ''Hayashi Industries! The Remote Sensing Division! *We're* the only ones making that equipment.''

''Exactly. We ought to send Hayashi-san down here to see this place. It's practically a demonstration center for his products.''

She laughed again and kissed him before snuggling up beside him. Hideo was lying on his back. He opened his eyes and looked up at the ceiling. There were the images of his naked body alongside Toshiko's, their reflections caught in the ceiling mirror, slowly spinning around on that absurd bed. Their two naked bodies seemed to be whirling around in midair, suspended on a pink and blue cloud.

The spinning made him dizzy, and the sight of his naked self seemingly hanging from the ceiling was far more disorienting than erotic, but somehow that fit. It made the whole night seem even more dreamlike, more like an imaginary adventure than something that was really happening.

This is life in one of the richest nations in the world, he thought. *This is accepted and normal—your apartment is too small for privacy and quiet, so you go to a gaudy, overdone fantasy bordello to have the privacy and quiet that should be the normal right of every couple. We dive into a fantasy land in order to grasp at normalcy. In the old days, there was room and peace and quiet enough for a man and a woman to be together in their own home. But not now. Now this is what we have to do. And then we try so hard to see all this as normal, as natural. How much of Japan is like this room, how much of the world? How much is balanced atop a crazy hodgepodge of technology that seems to do little more than make it harder to live life?*

But even if he had to go to such a strange place as this to be with Toshiko, the important thing was that he was with her. He forgot the mirrors and the sensors and turned to his love.

Later they bathed together, washing themselves outside the tub as was customary, but breaking with tradition enough for each to wash the other, paying meticulous attention to the most sensitive parts of their bodies. The bubbly slipperiness of the soap added greatly to their tactile sensation. They slipped into the deep tub and luxuriated in the hot water, the steamy air, the passion of the night. And then they made love again, in the tub.

If Toshiko had been as eager as Hideo to go into the bathroom, she seemed to share the usual woman's trait of being in no hurry to come out. There was her hair to dry and comb, and a whole collection of exotic powders and scents to try.

Hideo, feeling a bit at loose ends, turned on the video recorder. He picked an unmarked tape off the storage shelf and put it in. He had expected to find a commercial erotic tape. They were commonly, if illegally, produced and distributed in Japan. Instead, he found himself staring, in some surprise, at the tape left by the previous occupants. The man was apparently in his early twenties, and the woman looked to be a very good-looking forty or so. He was about to switch it off when Toshiko joined him, her skin still pink from the hot bath. She did a double take at a sight on the screen.

"They did that? Here?" She stared in openmouthed astonishment. "How could she let herself be taped like that? I'd sooner die than let anyone see me like that. Why in the world didn't she make sure that they erased the tape before leaving!"

Hideo shrugged, trying to show a little nonchalant sophistication. "Who knows, maybe she got a little kick out of knowing another couple would be watching her performance.

"Besides, I've heard that some of the video cameras in these rooms pipe whatever they pick up to a central control room. They can record it, or patch it through so the other guests can watch the show. Do you want to try some of the channels on this thing?" Hideo grinned what he thought of as a devilish grin.

Toshiko turned bright red. "Do you mean to say that someone else could be watching us *right now?* No! That just can't be!" Suddenly she seemed close to tears.

"Easy now, Toshiko. I'm sure it's just a rumor," he said, though he was sure of no such thing, if his friends at work were to be believed. He reached over and grabbed his pants off the floor. He threw them over the camera lens. "There, now it can't see anything. Come back to bed."

It took a little urging, but at last she came to lie down beside him, and before very long at all, she had very clearly forgotten all about the camera. As he pulled her toward him, Hideo congratulated himself on not mentioning the rumor that some of those mirrored walls were made of one-way glass, with an audience on the other side.

Toshiko pushed him over on his back and started to nibble on his neck. The bed started spinning again, and Hideo looked up toward the ceiling, watching the two of them whirling through their overdone fantasy land.

Can this really last? he wondered. But he didn't know whether he meant his happiness or the techno-wonderland that surrounded them.

Chapter 12

September 2000
Tokyo, Japan

Kenji Yamada stood watching through the plate glass as the technicians set up the last of the monitors and powered up the last of the devices to be tested. Or perhaps "test" was the wrong word. They had done this before, and everyone here knew what was going to happen. "Demonstration" would be more accurate. This run was not about doing science, but about convincing someone of the facts. And it had damn well better do that.

There was a bustle of activity behind him, at the entrance to the cavernous lab. Noboru Hayashi was arriving, surrounded by the usual entourage of a busy executive on an official visit. He strode directly up to Kenji Yamada, and the scientist went over to meet him. The two men bowed to each other with a bit more formality than the occasion would require if this were merely the routine test all were pretending it to be. Then Hayashi and Yamada shook hands, making it clear to all present that they were equals, partners in this.

"Welcome, Hayashi-san. We are just now ready for the test. If you'll come to the observation station, I think we can proceed."

"Excellent. I need to see this, Yamada-san. I know your work is valid, and I know the danger is potentially real, but I have invested a tremendous amount of money preparing for this contingency. I need to *know* that it could all be worthwhile."

"Absolutely. If you would just take your seat by the window."

Hayashi nodded, walked over to one of the rather severe folding chairs, and began to sit down. "There is no danger, sitting this close to the glass—"

"No, Hayashi-san. The test chamber is well shielded, but that is more for the protection of our monitoring equipment. You could stand in the center of the chamber itself during a run and never feel a thing, though I wouldn't recommend it as a steady habit. Come, I will sit by you. Now take a good look, Hayashi-san. It is all about to change."

Through the observation window they could see a large room full of a rather eccentric collection of equipment, all of it on and running. Televisions, radios, electric mixers, refrigerators, car engines, computers, telephones, fans, electric lamps, a traffic signal, a large water pump sitting by a tank of water, busily pumping the water out the bottom up to the top of the tank.

A 2001 Honda sedan sat next to a battered old Honda Civic from the 1970s. A technician ducked into one, then the other, starting the engines, flicking on the headlights and the windshield wipers.

Front and center were a collection of antiques: muzzy-pictured televisions and radios from the 1960s. Yamada could see the tubes on one radio glowing. Next to them were several rather severe-looking pieces of military-specification equipment—a computer with a razor-sharp monitor displaying a grid pattern, a portable satellite audio receiver.

The test chamber was blazing with flickering, glowing light from all the machinery. There was a low buzz of noise that came through the soundproofing. Yamada reached out and turned up a volume control set into the test chamber's outer wall. The observation area was drowned in a cacophony of sound.

"All right," Yamada said. "Now we shall simulate an electromagnetic pulse. We have shielded cameras and other recording instruments, of course, but watch carefully. It will happen quickly." He turned toward a technician standing by the observation window and nodded. What was his name? Nakano, that was it. Rumor had it he was dating one of the prettier girls over in procurement. Yamada blinked and shook his head. Why was he distracting himself with such inconsequential trivia? "Nakano-kun, you may proceed."

Nakano picked up a phone and punched in a number. "Generator room, this is test bay three. Engage main pulse generator." The lights in the observation area dimmed for a moment.

"Was that the—" Hayashi asked.

"No, no, just a power surge as the generator came on-line. It takes a few moments to build up the required force. You can see a cone-shaped device in the ceiling of the test chamber. That is the actual pulse simulator. The generators downstairs must develop enough power to activate it."

"Will I see anything the pulse simulator is doing?"

"No, no visual phenomena from there." The man on the phone gestured to get Yamada's attention, and then gave him a thumbs-up. "Ah, now I think we are ready." He nodded at the technician again.

"Generator room, engage on my mark. Commencing countdown. Engage in five, four, three—"

Hayashi leaned forward, staring intently. Yamada watched him, not the demonstration. His reaction was what this was all about. Hayashi knew what he was going to see, but Yamada understood that didn't matter. It was his gut reaction to seeing it that was important, that would steer the decisions.

"Two, one—MARK!"

The sleek, modern hardware in the test window instantly went dead. The water pump stopped its pointless efforts. The radios went silent. The computer screens scrambled as the machines went mad, then died. The traffic light went out. The new Honda, that smooth, sleek epitome of Japanese manufacturing, suddenly shuddered, its motor seizing up. It stalled out in a cloud of smoke.

The boxy, worn-out, thirty-year-old car next to it puttered along sedately.

Suddenly the tube of one television set exploded, and then another, and another. A computer screen blew out next. A powerful ham radio with a long whip antenna blew up. The technicians had deliberately left a few tufts of flammable padding scattered about the floor. Sparks from the explosions landed on a few of them, and fire sprouted up.

But in the front of the room, the elderly radios and TVs, the military-specification gear, all continued to operate as if nothing had happened.

Suddenly Hayashi stood up. "I have seen enough."

Yamada stood as well and waved his hand, and technicians sprinted into the test chamber with fire extinguishers to douse the flames.

Hayashi looked toward Yamada. "What is your current estimate of the probabilities of—that?"

"Little changed, sir. There are so many variables, it is almost impossible to make a useful estimate. I am not as convinced as our American friends that the primary event will even take place. They talk about it as if it were a certainty, but, with all respect to Dr. Prescott, my model calculations do not reach the same conclusions.

"Every astrophysicist in the world has an opinion on this one, and all of them are different. Half of them still refuse even to consider the idea that anything will happen, but that is more a denial syndrome than a rational reaction to the data. Then there is the question of gamma ray and X-ray intensity, both at the source and upon arrival here at Earth."

"An answer, Yamada-san. I must have an answer." Hayashi looked stern, and worried. He watched through the observation window as the technicians popped the hood on the brand-new Honda, releasing a cloud of smoke. They shot a fire extinguisher into it. "We have decisions to make. How much further shall we go in our preparations? We may well be running out of time."

"Very well. At this time, using my figures for the likelihood of a supernova, and the likelihood that it would touch off an EMP, and the chance that Japan would be struck by the burst, I would estimate the overall chance of an EMP strike on Japan at about five percent. If we use Prescott's figures on the likelihood of a supernova, that value is closer to eleven percent."

Hayashi turned toward the observation window again and shook his head. "Five percent, eleven percent. Those numbers are too high to do nothing, yet too low to shout warnings from the rooftop."

"How too low? What risks could there be in warning people?"

"Have you never read the Western myths and fables? The tale of the little boy who cried wolf when there was no wolf? He was distrusted and scorned ever after. I do not wish to discredit my business and be made a laughingstock in front of the entire world. And yet even five percent is by no means a microscopic probability. Certainly not when the stakes are so high. If the worst does happen, the price could be terrible.

"There is another Western myth to think of," Hayashi went on. "One that Dr. Prescott himself has referred to more than once. Chicken Little, who warned the sky was falling, making a panicky prediction of a disaster that never came. Only fools listened to her."

"What is your point, Hayashi-san?"

"Rather than be thought of as fools, most people would refuse to believe. You may warn the world all you want, but unless we can develop more compelling evidence that this danger is real, I doubt that anyone will listen, or act. Even I still hardly believe George Prescott, and I wonder if that is the failure of his data or my pride."

Yamada frowned deeply and nodded. "Yes, I see that."

"Very well," Hayashi said. "We shall continue our preparations, but we shall not yet issue any public warning. I shall see to it that Hayashi Industries continues to stockpile the needed supplies and replacement parts, to hold them ready for distribution."

"And I shall continue to work on determining if the danger is or is not real," Yamada said wearily.

Hayashi looked at the burned and broken things that had been such bright and gleaming machines a few minutes before. He had seen it happen, yet he had seen nothing. One moment the machines worked, and the next they were ruined beyond all repair. It might as well be magic, or a curse from on high. And perhaps it was, or would be. "Find that out, my friend. We must know—are we pursuing imaginary ghosts, or about to be destroyed by a ghostly monster that is far too real?"

Kenji Yamada shrugged helplessly. He did not know. But he did not feel equal to the task of finding out by himself. Besides, there were others entitled to the knowledge, even if the time was not right to broadcast a warning.

There was a call he needed to make.

Pasadena, California

The phone rang next to Jessica's bed and she reached out a fumbling hand to answer it. A bleary eye peered at the clock. Two A.M. Who in the world?

"H'llo?" she said.

"Jessica, it's Kenji Yamada. Forgive me please for calling at this hour."

"Kenji?" She sat up in bed and rubbed her eyes. "Where are you?"

"In Tokyo. Forgive me, but there is a matter we must discuss."

There was something in his tone of voice that worried her. Besides, Kenji would never call at such an hour without good reason. Suddenly she was completely awake. "What is it?" she asked.

"There is a—a *possibility* I wish for you to look into. I do not wish to influence your thinking on it whatsoever, but merely bring your attention to it. I want you to investigate it, see if your results match mine."

"But why not publish it if you need to see if your thinking is right? Let lots of people test your—"

"No, I can't do that," Kenji said hurriedly. "I do not wish to affect your thinking, so I can't explain why. But you must do this, Jessica. It is most urgent."

"All right, Kenji. All right. What is it?"

"Gamma rays," Kenji said. "I want to ask you the question: what will gamma rays do to the Earth?"

"Gamma rays, right," Jessica said, even more confused. What the hell was he talking about?

"Be diligent, Jessica," Kenji said. "It is most important."

And then, with a click, she heard him hang up.

October 2000
Palomar Mountain

"And this is the one they let you have," Desmond said, his face a vague smudge in the darkness. "This is the twenty-four-inch telescope, right? And it's all yours.'' George had promised him a nighttime tour of the premises a long time ago, insisting that was the proper time to see an observatory. It was just after one in the morning—prime time for an observatory.

''Oh, I wouldn't quite put it that way,'' George said, but the pride in his voice was hard to hide. George had been able to persuade Palomar's director to let him have a priority access on the twenty-four-inch. That amounted to a monopoly on the instrument. ''It's the smallest telescope here, but it's powerful enough to monitor Sirius A and B. We're on it nearly every night. Besides, it's not in much demand because it's small. But its resolving power is fine for our purposes, and the light gathering is more than enough. In fact, the biggest problem we have observing Sirius A is trying not to gather too *much* light. We used neutral filter to block as much as we can, but even so, Sirius A is tremendously bright. It only takes a second or two to get a good spectrum. We're not used to making exposures that short.''

''What about Sirius B?''

''Much more our style.'' Astronomers had been working for centuries trying to make more and more sensitive instruments so they could observe dimmer and dimmer objects, with the result that Sirius B was actually a fairly bright object in comparison to a lot of other targets. George's team was using a high quantum efficiency charge-coupled detector. ''We can obtain a high-resolution spectrum of Sirius B in less than an hour, and then view it immediately on the computer monitors. This telescope is getting a spectrum on Sirius B right now. That hardware there is the CCD unit. We pull the data through that cable there and back to the data reduction center. It sure as hell beats standing out here for five or six hours waiting to expose a photographic plate, the way they did it in the old days.

''We really need fast exposures. Sirius B's spectra can change significantly in a few hours. We're monitoring both stars, taking spectra of each one three times a night whenever the seeing is good enough.''

"That should give you enough data.''

"Well, it gives us a lot in the visual spectrum, but we can't get all the wavelengths we need. Ultraviolet light is especially important. There's a lot of information there, but UV gets blocked by the atmosphere. That's why we need the satellites. We're getting UV spectra of Sirius A and B from the Kepler spacecraft at least once every twenty-four hours.''

"It sounds like you're doing all right," Desmond said.

George turned to Desmond and smiled. He was so very tired, but he felt good. He was doing what he was supposed to be doing, working on something worthwhile, and at long last he was getting the support he needed.

"Yeah, I guess we are. Come on," he said. "It's getting too cold to stand around in an unheated dome if you don't have to. Let's head back over to the office—I'll buy you a cup of coffee. The telescope can take care of itself for a while.''

Desmond smiled back at the younger man and slapped him on the back. "Besides which, it's time to kick me out so you can get back to your work.''

George grinned and shrugged. "Yeah, I suppose. But it's been good to see you.''

"Same goes for me. Thanks for giving me a tour. I appreciate it. But maybe I should skip the cup of coffee and just head on back.''

"Okay," George said. "I'll walk you to your bike.''

The two men stepped out of the dome and started back across the compound. It was a cold mountain night, a real autumn nip in the air. There was something strangely invigorating about being there—reassuring, as if the night were a promise that had been kept.

Desmond stopped halfway to the parking lot and looked up at the sky. George could see him tracking his way across the firmament, finding the three stars of

Orion's belt hanging in the east, then tracking southeast toward the horizon from there, until his eyes found the brightest star of all, hanging just over the horizon.

"Sirius," he said happily.

"Yes," George said, gazing at it himself.

"It's funny," Desmond said. "The whole world is talking about that star, but always as though it were hypothetical, imaginary. People treat it as if it's some unseen, intangible thing, like global warming or the state of the economy. But anyone in the world can go out and look up at the sky, and see it, point at it, and know where it is. It's *real.*" He shook his head and shrugged, his face scarcely visible in the darkness.

"I know what you mean. I don't think we astronomers do the stars justice either. The stars are *there,* they exist. Somehow we almost manage to forget that. We almost always think of them as imaginary objects, impossibly far off, a symbol for our unreachable aspirations. They get to be nothing more than the collections of statistics we gather in our experiments. Every once in a while, I realize I haven't gone out and just *looked up* in a long time. I forget what real stars are. Then I do go out, and I do look, and there they are, as big and bright and clear as you could want." George sighed. "It's a sad state of affairs when not even the astronomers go outside and look at the stars enough."

"Neither do preachers, George. Neither do preachers."

As the two men started walking again, George turned toward his companion. "So do you still think the supernova will signal the end of the world? I mean, if it comes?"

Desmond hesitated over his answer for a long time. "No," he said at last. "To tell you the truth, I think I've lost my faith in that regard." His laugh was quiet, rueful. "Strange way to put it. Losing one's faith is supposed to be a very negative thing, but I've lost my faith in the idea of the whole world being destroyed, of its being such an evil place that total annihilation would be necessary. And here I am running the Last Church of the Apocalyptic Revelation.''

"So why are you still there?" George asked.

"Because the Church does some good. It pulls people together, pulls people who have lost their way back to a feeling of belief, and belonging. And because if I left, Hiram would have it all his way, and I shudder to think what *that* would be like. He needs a moderating influence, especially as we become more successful. I try to provide it.''

"Okay, so the world's not coming to an end. Have you held on to the other parts of your faith?''

"Oh, dear God, yes. I see now that my belief in and my hope for its destruction were merely my own anger, my own hatred. As to still believing in God—you said it about astronomers the first night we met. To look at the wonder of the universe forces you to believe in a Creator. It's just as true for me. I feel as if I am rediscovering the world, and every day I see another miracle that proves God exists. An act of kindness, a perfect sunset, Sirius gleaming down. What more proof could a person need? It's just that I believe in a God that is closer and more personal than yours. And I believe in Jesus Christ and all His gentle miracles.''

"Well, maybe the universe is large enough to have room for supernovae *and* Jesus Christ," George said.

Desmond chuckled. "I'm sure it is. Which reminds me—what are your probabilities at the moment?''

George made a thumbs-up gesture. "Still increasing. Right now we're at eighty percent, and we're looking at a much earlier date than we were before. We're coming to a crisis point. It's going to be make or break time. The mass transfer rate is increasing again.

"If it accelerates *too* rapidly, Sirius B's surface will blow off before there is enough internal pressure built up to force a supernova. We'd just get a nova.

"But if the mass transfer rate slacks off a little and Sirius B accumulates matter until it can no longer accept more mass—well, about the only thing that can happen is a supernova. My guess as to when is sometime in November or December. Possibly as late as January.''

"My heavens. I didn't realize it could happen so soon. Next month, or the month after . . . Are you prepared up here?''

"Very much so. If the supernova happens, we have priority over every instrument on the mountain from the two-hundred-inch on down, and communications tie-ins to every astronomical facility in the world. In other words, if the supernova blows, and we have something to look at, it's all ours. Whoever is using the two-hundred-inch telescope at the time would have to yield it immediately. There will never, ever be a supernova this close to Earth again—there just aren't any progenitor stars of the right type close by us, and Sirius B was a thousand-to-one shot anyway. We've tried to think of everything. There's been a lot of worry that the supernova might touch off some heavy weather, so if some damn tree falls on a power line, we've got auxiliary generators ready. We've got the direct satellite link if the phone lines go. There's a backup for everything.''

"But what good does the two-hundred-inch do you if even Sirius A is too bright to observe with it?''

"Special detection equipment," George told him. "We've designed and set up a detector that will let us apply high-speed imaging techniques, things that were first developed for spy satellites. We'll observe the expanding surface of the supernova shell with millisecond exposures. But the exciting part is that we should be able to see *structure* on it, the actual shape and surface and features of the supernova shell. We should be able to attain an image resolution of half an arc-second or better with such short exposures, and the supernova shell should reach that apparent size within a couple of hours of the explosion.''

"At this distance? I was assuming it would remain a

point light source no matter how much you magnified it."

"Desmond, you've got to think big. Once it expands far enough, it's going to have a disk discernible to the naked *eye!* Granted, you wouldn't be able to look at it for more than a second without going blind, but it will be a disk. We'll be using the wide-angle forty-eight-inch Schmidt telescope to keep from cropping its edges. At least, since the exposures will be so short, atmospheric blurring won't be an issue.

"If all goes as planned, we ought to see real features on the expanding shell within twenty-four hours of the initial explosion. But we're going to have to use every trick we know to step down the brightness significantly."

Desmond shook his head. "Amazing." They had reached his motorcycle, and the two men shook hands good-bye.

"And what will you do," George asked, "if the supernova comes?"

Desmond reached into his pocket, pulled out his keys, and jangled them nervously in his hand. "I don't think you realize, I don't think anyone realizes, what sort of monster I've created down there. Hiram Goodman is a dangerous man, and the Church is growing. The people who come in—sometimes I don't think they worship God at all. I think they worship Hiram. His control is that good. He could use the supernova in a lot of ways. If he were offered that sort of opportunity, that sort of attention-getter—" Desmond stopped, looked up, and took one more look at the close, fat stars in the sky. "It would drive people toward him, move him forward to a whole new level of power and ambition. If *that* happened, about all I could do is pray."

Gamma rays. Jessica Talmadge stared at the computer screen and felt the cold sweat of fear break out

anew on her forehead. No wonder Kenji had wanted
her to check this. Damn it, yes.

Gamma rays. Why hadn't they *seen* it? It was such a
tiny probability—and, by her figures, diminishing as
their model of the supernova improved. If the supernova came at all, the odds were much against the supernova shell splitting open in the right places at the
right time to create an electromagnetic pulse on Earth.
Even if the shell did crack just right, the supernova
might not provide enough energy to cross the gamma
ray intensity threshold needed for EMP . . .

No. Kenji Yamada was right. With odds this low, it
was wholly irresponsible to raise a warning.

Besides, even if it happened, a warning might well
be useless. How could it be defended against without
crippling the world economy?

Jessica shivered and looked out her office window at
the sky, and that was what decided her. She, better than
anyone, knew the ranges involved, the huge distances
in question. Even to her, it seemed incredible.

For how could the stars—the far-off, friendly stars—
do this?

Interlude

On the scale of the stars, time is distance. The two are directly and intimately linked, one an aspect of the other.

Consider the image of Sirius as seen from Earth, 8.9 light-years distant from the star itself. From Earth, there has been only the slightest flickering increase in brightness in the star, completely unnoticeable by the casual observer. Indeed, the star had undergone many such fluctuations in the past, all of them utterly undetected.

But draw closer to the star, and perceptions change. At the same moment of time, and a few tenths of a light-year farther off from Earth, a bit closer to the star, an observer would see younger light, the image of Sirius as it has been more recently. Here the image is of the star as it explodes, blossoming up from a pinprick of light to a brilliant flare, all but blindingly bright.

Closer still to Sirius in space, and thus closer to it in time, Sirius blossoms further upward in brightness—

and then starts to fade, to begin the long process of guttering down to nothing.

To an observer hard by Sirius itself, the story is all but over. The light of the first explosion left this place almost nine long years ago. Where once there was a star, there is now nothing but a expanding cloud of cooling gas.

But back at Earth, 8.9 light-years away, the supernova that is here long dead has yet to be born.

On Earth, the first light of the explosion is about to be seen.

Chapter 13

Sunday, December 10, 2000
3:05 A.M.
Los Angeles, California

Hiram Goodman paused in his preaching to take a breath, and looked out over the crowd in the newly acquired room. Yesterday a warehouse, tonight an auditorium. Tomorrow—who could say? He grinned. This place held six times as many people as the old church, and still it was full to overflowing. And the place was still packed, three hours into the midnight Sunday service. Though not many churches would characterize a meeting of hard-drinking folk like this as a church service, that was for sure. And in truth, it had more of the feel of a rowdy nightclub or roadhouse, well into the late show. There had been singing, and witnessing—and now there was the sermon, Hiram's beloved chance to shine.

"It was a new star over Bethlehem, my friends! That is all the word nova means—'new star.' Don't let the scientists get you all confused with their fancy talk about dwarfs and giants, saying that nova-stars are there all along, that they just get brighter. What good is a star that is too dim to see? A nova is a new star, sent by God to tell us of wondrous things to come. Two thousand years ago, God sent a nova, a new star, the Star of Bethlehem, to signal the arrival of the Son of God. It was a pretty thing, the Good Book tells, a lovely light in the sky that guided the Three Wise Men.

"But now the so-called Wise Men of our era say that is not good enough for them! They must have a *super* nova, bigger and brighter and more important than the star that marked the very birth of Jesus Christ himself. Brighter, more powerful, more frightening. Bright enough to banish night, perhaps bright enough to melt the polar ice caps—though now the climate scientists and meteorologists are saying not to worry about that. It won't be that severe, that dangerous.

"Not *dangerous?* Have they not asked themselves how they shall pay for this arrogance of prediction, what a new star, a new superstar, in the heavens might mean? Haven't they asked what this mighty beacon shall be a sign *of?* Have they not asked what price they might pay for knowing the future of God's plan for the Earth?

"Sisters and brothers, we were cast out of the Garden of Eden for knowing the difference between Good and Evil. Might not these scientists cause us to be cast off the Earth altogether, for having forced upon us the knowledge of times to come?"

Brother Desmond Potter watched from his usual post at the back of the room. Incredible. Here was a man who quoted the biblical prophets endlessly, and prophesied himself, and yet could stand there and call prophecy blasphemy. Logic and consistency were not Hiram's strong points.

Equating the supernova with the Christmas star was

a new angle. Hiram had just thought of it that morning over breakfast, and he was quite pleased with it. He liked the idea of equating the threat of a supernova now, exactly two thousand years after the birth of Christ, with the Star of Bethlehem.

Never mind that Christ was certainly *not* born in A.D. 1, but a few years earlier, and probably not in winter. Never mind that there had been at least three supernovae in the Milky Way Galaxy since then—in 1054, 1572, and 1604. For that matter, never mind that some scholars believed the Christmas star to have been nothing more than a close conjunction of Mars, Jupiter, and Saturn. Hiram Goodman wasn't going to pay attention to the facts. He was on a roll.

Desmond watched as the collection plates moved up and down the aisles, eager hands stuffing them with change, dollar bills, fives, tens, twenties, checks. He saw one woman pull off her rings and earrings and drop them in.

But it was too much for Desmond. He turned and walked out of the auditorium into the crisp, clear night, shoving his way past a few hangers-on leaning up against the door.

He was so tired of it all, he thought as he went down the low steps to stand on the sidewalk. There it was against the velvet sky: the star, the perfectly ordinary star that had started all this, or at least restarted it. Desmond had gotten to be quite the star watcher over the last few months. He knew the sky well. There was Orion again, the grandest of all the winter constellations. A full moon shone down from just over Orion's left shoulder, north and west of the mighty hunter. It was a bright moon, the only source of light around here bright enough to cast a shadow, as this neighborhood didn't go in much for streetlights. They tended to get shot out. Desmond glanced down at his feet, saw the squat patch of darkness cast by the moonlight.

But the beauty of the night could not drive his worries from his mind. He had started this thing, and he had known what he was doing when he began it. Desmond had gone out searching for something Hiram could hang his speeches on, and the supernova had done them all proud. Just the idea of it was all they needed to play their games. And games were all they were. Perhaps once Hiram Goodman had been genuinely interested in saving souls, but that time was long past. Now he had become little more than a caricature of himself, a figure on the stage, calling the faithful to himself, eager not for their souls, not for their faith, not even eager for their money, but hungry for their power. Goodman wanted to speak for them, not to echo their fears and hopes, but to further empower himself.

Desmond sighed and looked up again at the sky.

How were they—

Wait a second.

Desmond looked at Sirius again. There was something strange about it. He had seen it night after night, in clear skies and clouded, watching, wondering, until it was habit that set him to looking, and the meaning was gone.

But tonight it looked different. As if it were—

Brighter. Sweet Jesus God in Heaven, it was *brighter.* Desmond glanced up and down the street, and noticed two or three little clumps of people standing around, looking up. They saw it, too. He wasn't imagining it.

Suddenly his heart was pounding, his palms were sweaty, his throat was dry. Good God, it had happened. It *was* happening. More and more people were coming out into the street, looking up. Cars were stopping, people were pointing up, there was a faint whispering of hushed conversation that seemed to come from all sides.

Desmond looked up, slack-jawed. There it was. George had told him it would start like this, just a simple brightening of the star, but one that would not stop, but go on and on and on. Perhaps it had started just as he looked up, perhaps it had been going on ten minutes before while he was inside listening to Hiram. Silently, calmly, gradually, it had arrived, quite unnoticed. There was something disturbing and otherworldly about the silence of that starlight, the quiet, self-assured way it simply blossomed into the night.

It was here.

He looked over to the knot of people loitering at the entrance to the building Hiram was using for his service and spotted an elderly, somewhat musty-looking man. "Charlie!" he shouted. "Go in there! Tell Hiram, tell them all—it's here!"

"Whaz here?"

Desmond said nothing, but simply pointed up. Charlie turned his bleary eyes skyward, and then he saw, and his eyes widened in fear and amazement. The rheumy old man stood there, rooted to the spot for an endless moment, before he lurched back to self-awareness and stumbled inside the building.

Desmond promptly forgot all about Charlie as he turned his gaze skyward once again. *There it is,* he repeated to himself, his heart pounding, a feeling of great wonder and excitement growing inside him. *Sweet Jesus Lord if it isn't a miracle.* True, humans could explain it and describe it and predict it—but was not such a mighty light a miracle just the same?

Brighter and brighter, moment by moment.

The crowd surged out of the church, shouting, laughing, crying out in fear and astonishment. Suddenly Hiram was standing in front of him, grabbing him by the shoulders, grinning ferociously, throwing his arms around Desmond.

"It's here!" Hiram shouted, struggling to be heard over the suddenly deafening roar of the crowd. "Praise be to God, it is here! Now we can really go to work." He turned to the crowd that was spilling out into the street.

"Behold, brothers and sisters, the sign that I foretold. It is come, it is here, it dawns. This is the First of the Last Days!"

A wild cheer erupted from the congregation.

Desmond did not join in. He felt a cold, hard spot at the base of his stomach as he turned his gaze back to the furnace-bright fleck of brilliance in the sky.

It was here.

3:06 A.M.
Palomar Mountain

A hand grabbed at George's shoulder and yanked him out of sleep. But George did not wake easily. He muttered something and tried to roll back over. It wasn't fair. He had just gotten to sleep. Everyone on the mountain knew he had been planning to catch some much-needed rest tonight.

That made it more than a bit annoying for him to be awakened. There could be no point in waking him unless—

Suddenly he was wide-awake. He rolled over on his rickety cot and looked up to see Jessica's excited face grinning down at him.

"It's here!" she said. "It's happened."

George swung around to sit straight in bed and pitched himself clean out of the cot onto the floor in his underwear. He scrambled to his feet and grabbed his pants off the back of the chair.

"When?" He didn't need to ask anything else. It was all in her eyes.

"We had the twenty-four-inch tracking Sirius, and the brightness-increase alert went up about two minutes ago. The twenty-four-inch dropped right into its alert program and started squeezing off one image every second."

"What about the two-hundred-inch?" George asked, pulling on his shirt and stumbling into the little washroom in the back of the office. He splashed water on his face, cupped his hands to catch more, then took a mouthful and gargled, trying to get the rumpled taste of a catnap out of his mouth.

"We're on it," Jessica said. "The astronomer who was using it scrammed his observation, and the technicians are plugging in our observation pack now. We should be ready to observe by the time they can repoint the telescope."

"Wonderful." George dug a comb out of his pants pocket, ran it through his hair. Together they rushed out into the night.

But there *was* no night, not anymore. Not with that blinding-bright full moon, soon to be rivaled and overtaken by this new and sudden jewel in the sky. The moment George stepped out of the office building, he stopped to stare up at the sky, transfixed. *There it is.* His knees felt weak and there were tears in his eyes. It was so beautiful, so perfect—and in a strange, special way, it was *his*.

He stood there and looked up, remembering the road that had led him to this moment: ambition, curiosity, a determination to rebel, to show them all—

But now all those desires were swept from him in an overpowering wave of wonder, delight, a deep and abiding affection for the incredible sight hanging calmly in the sky.

He could only stand there, rooted to the spot. Part of him told him to hurry, that he needed to rush forward and get busy—but doing what? With a shock he realized that the telescope technicians wouldn't let him get near their precious two-hundred-inch instrument. They would install the instrument pack themselves, then run the observations themselves—under his direction, yes, and maybe they would let him work the controls himself, but he wasn't going to get near the telescope. And the twenty-four-inch was operating in automatic mode. There was nothing he could do there but watch the computers display their images on the screen. Later, that would be useful, but it was too early for him to have enough data to work with yet. Not for a little while.

Here it was, the climactic moment of his life, and there was nothing for him to do but sit and watch.

And it dawned on him that the situation suited him just fine. He wanted to see this. He sat on an outcropping of rock and simply *watched*.

Jessica was rushing toward the two-hundred-inch dome, and for a moment did not notice that George wasn't keeping up. At last she glanced behind her and saw he wasn't there. She stopped, turned around, and rushed back over to him.

"George! What are you—"

"I'm stargazing," he said, suddenly calm, very much at peace. "Take a moment," he said. "We're not going to have any time to do it later, once we really have some data coming in." He offered her his hand. "Come here. Sit down and look. Just look. That's our job, after all."

Jessica gave him an odd look and approached him hesitantly. At last she reached out and took his hand, sat down next to him as he slid over to make room on his rock. "What do you mean, that's our job?" she asked.

"We're astronomers," he said. "And ours is the oldest science."

"So?"

"So think about it. Five thousand years ago, they did it just this way. One person alone, or maybe two or three friends sat together outdoors and *looked*. Nothing more. They just *looked*, watched the sky at night, and wondered. That's all we do. We're connected to those people. They watched the same stars we do. They would have sat on a rock, and stared up at the sky. They would have looked at this supernova and wondered how it happened, wondered what it would mean in their world."

"And we have to wonder what it means in ours," Jessica said.

They sat and watched, not long, but long enough. Until they knew, truly, deep in their bones, that it had happened, that it was a part of their world. But then it was time to go to work. They stood, and walked through their brightening star-shadows to the telescope dome.

Sunday, December 10, 2000
8:08 P.M.
(Sunday, 3:08 A.M., Los Angeles time)
Tokyo, Japan

Hideo Nakano sat on his couch and admired Toshiko's silhouette as she stood by his picture window. She in turn was admiring the view out that window, the forest of high-rises and the city beyond. *Beauty admiring beauty,* he told himself.

He reached out, picked up his glass, and took another sip of wine. *Tonight,* Hideo told himself again, *is ours.* Toshiko's parents were away for a visit to relatives. They weren't going to be at home to wait up for her.

But the grandest prize was Hideo's fine new apartment, easily twice the size of his old place, a high-rise with a fine view toward the east. True, it was on the far outskirts of the city, but on the other hand, it just happened to be rather close to Toshiko's parents' house.

The old place had barely been large enough for Hideo to stand up and turn around—but *this* place had a separate bedroom, large enough for a double bed.

And, therefore, no more love hotels. Both of them were glad of that. The hotels had been an adventure at first, but all too soon they had turned into a dreary, sleazy routine. They were places for people who were ashamed to love, who wanted, or needed, to hide it. The layers of pseudosophistication and sleek mass-produced hedonistic luxury were only there to hide that fact.

But love was for home. Hideo nodded to himself and decided he liked that thought. He stood, crossed the room, and joined Toshiko at the window.

The moon was just clear of Tokyo's glare and haze,

thick and heavy over the land. The three stars of Orion's belt were visible below it, and two or three brave bright stars higher in the sky, but the lights of humanity washed out all the other lamps of heaven.

But there was one new light, toward the harbor, a bright gleam of white just climbing clear of the horizon haze and the clutter of buildings. At first Hideo thought it must be a low-flying aircraft, its running lights aimed straight at them. But this light was unmoving. It just hung in one point in the sky, a stabbing-bright point of—

Starlight. A star shining through haze and city glare so thick that no star had any right to be there.

Sirius. The supernova.

A sudden jolt of fear swept over him. He thought of all the work they had done at the lab, all the experiments. He did not pretend to understand half of what Yamada-san did, but he knew perfectly well that the actual arrival of the supernova made all the dangers real. Not certain, not absolute, but the risks were greater.

"Hideo!" Toshiko turned her face toward him and smiled. "Do you see it?"

"Yes. Yes, I do."

"I've been watching it, and it doesn't move. It just gets brighter. Is it the new star they have been talking about?"

"I think so," Hideo said. "But it's not a new star, just Sirius getting brighter." He hesitated, realizing just how much he was understating the point. "A lot brighter."

Toshiko turned to him in some alarm. "It can't hurt us, can it? The scientists all seem to think the weather problems wouldn't be as bad as they thought at first."

Hideo shook his head and thought about gamma rays. From what he understood of the work at the lab, the danger was still slight. There was an excellent chance Earth would escape unscathed. "No, the weather can't hurt us."

Toshiko smiled and threw her arms around him. "What a magical sign, Hideo, for the first night we spend together. It's a blessing over us."

Hideo smiled, trying to hide his worry. Maybe, indeed, that was all it was. He kissed her under the fast-swelling glow of nova light, and suddenly the embrace became passionate. They began to undo each other's clothes, their bodies casting a double shadow under star and moon.

They lay down on the carpeted floor, forgetting all about the double bed that Hideo had been so proud to get. They made love as the supernova banished the last real night much of Earth would know for many weeks.

9:45 P.M.
Hayashi Industries Building
Tokyo, Japan

There was quite a crowd on the roof, watching the fantastic sight. The city below seemed to have made itself quiet as well, as people stopped their endless rushing about to watch the birth of a second sun. Noboru Hayashi stood on the roof of the building and fancied that he felt the warmth of starlight on his face. No, that had to be his imagination. But a thing so bright, so brilliant, surely it must cast heat along with light. At first, Hayashi had burned with the desire to rush out to his telescope again. But reason, in the form of Kenji Yamada, had prevailed. As Yamada pointed out, by the time they got a helicopter called in, boarded it, and flew to the observatory site, the supernova would be far too bright for any of the instruments Hayashi had.

Already it was almost too bright to see with the unaided eye. Several of the crowd on the roof were sporting sunglasses, a strange thing to see at night indeed.

But there would be no night, not anymore, not while Sirius glowed with greater and greater brilliance with each passing minute. If Yamada-san and that Prescott fellow and all the rest of the scientists were right, it would not reach its full brilliance for days or weeks yet, but already it almost outshone the full moon with which it shared the sky, putting the proud empress of the night sky to shame, making her seem but pale and dim by comparison.

Already there was a circle of dark blue sky about Sirius, washing out the light of other, lesser stars. The rest of the constellation Canis Major would soon be blotted out altogether. By tomorrow night, the next at the latest, all the night sky would be washed out, with a strange dark blue sky from horizon to horizon. Soon after, Sirius would peak at about eight or ten percent the brilliance of the sun. Night would be gone, replaced by a strange, brilliant twilight, a clear night sky offering about as much light as a heavily overcast day, but with the sharp shadows and contrasting light of a cloudless day. There would be just a brief band of partial darkness at sunset and sunrise. Later, in the spring months, as the earth moved in its orbit, Sirius would seem to travel across the sky, closer to the sun, the two sharing the day. But for now, in winter, Sirius was almost exactly opposite the sun. One would rise in the east as the other set in the west. For all intents and purposes, there would be no night.

A strange thought, inspiring and frightening all at once: for now, and the weeks ahead, any sky that held a sunset would also hold a dawn.

Day would never end. Exciting, and inspirational. But then Hayashi thought of the experiment Yamada had run for him two months ago, and shivered. If things went wrong, if they were all very unlucky, then the world might yet see an endless night as well.

Sunday, December 10,
5:02 A.M.
(Sunday, December 10, 10:02 P.M.*, Tokyo time)*
Santa Barbara, California

Father Francis Xavier O'Rourke was an early riser of long habit, but this morning he awoke to a world of far less quiet than usual. Awake but with eyes still closed, he could hear voices in the hallway, people walking back and forth outside, the snap of camera shutters. The Jesuit retreat seemed abuzz with conversation. He opened his eyes to a room filled with a strange light.

Father Francis instantly knew something was wrong. The light. It was the light of a muted sunset gleaming through the French windows in the west side of his room.

But sunset? At this hour?

He rose, pulled on his robe, stepped to the windows, and threw them open.

Glowing over the western horizon, reflected in the calm waters of the Pacific, a brilliant bloom of light was setting into the sea, framed in a strangely dark blue sky.

Father Francis looked, and knew, without a moment's wondering or hesitation, what he was looking at. It was the supernova. It could be nothing else.

The dimmer light of a strange-colored full moon was hanging a bit lower in the sky, farther to the northwest, to the far side of Aldebaran. Another bright point of light, Jupiter, lined up alongside the moon.

But even mighty Jupiter was easily lost in that sky. Francis had eyes only for Sirius and the moon. Both star and satellite were reddening as they slipped below the horizon.

With a strange feeling of calm, Father Francis watched the remarkable event. *Call it not sunset, but starset,* he thought. He felt no excitement, no surprise. It was the realization that he felt no shock that made him feel surprised. He found that he had been expecting this. Not just the supernova, but this moment, this sight. Some part of him had known there would be this to see if Supernova Sirius came in winter. This had come, this he had foreseen.

He thought of Desmond and that preacher Goodman, off in the wilds of Los Angeles. He set his hands in a firmer grip on the handrail, and braced his feet square and strong on the ground, as if he had expected some great force to try and knock him over.

For from this vantage point, it was easy to see other, more frightening things which had yet to be.

Chapter 14

December 12, 2000
12:30 A.M.
Pasadena, California

If there was no night, then neither was there any day.

Before the explosion, George and Jessica had been spending virtually all their time at Palomar. Now they lived on the mountaintop, and almost never went outside. Forty-eight hours after the initial explosion, it seemed to George that he had never had any previous existence. Surely his entire life had been spent in this semidarkened room, staring at the malevolent glowing-red image of Supernova Sirius as seen in the light of the first Balmer line of hydrogen.

He looked toward Jessica, hunched over the computer keyboard next to him. For both of them, time was passing in a dim blur, the moments connected to one another not by the measures of the clock, but the demands of their work. Every waking moment—and there were few of any other kind—was spent observing, analyzing the observations, or examining the torrents of data coming in from other observers with whom they had collaborative agreements. Both of them were averaging less than three hours of sleep a day.

And yet—there was something about Jessica. Something about the way she focused on her work, on the points she concentrated on, that bothered George. She seemed more than excited and motivated.

She seemed scared. What was worse, she did not want to talk about whatever it was.

George blinked, shook his head, and rubbed the bridge of his nose. Never mind. He had long ago learned that if Jessica was not in the mood to talk, there was very little anyone could do to change her mind. Nonetheless, it made spending twenty-four hours a day with her a bit tricky.

But there was one advantage to their situation: There were very few ways for the outside world to intrude. Had they been back down at Pasadena, the press would have been all over them. George could spare little time to look at the news reports, but what he could see suggested that there was little else being talked about.

Up here, at least, they were more or less safe. The observatory director had all incoming phone calls monitored and intercepted to protect George and Jessica from the onslaught of the reporters. A constant stream of them made their way up the mountain in person, but the director kept that under control as well. He set up a press center well away from the main installations. George and Jessica were trotted out for one or two briefings and were otherwise left strictly alone.

And that was good, for they had a lot to do. For the first time in history, astronomers could observe the expanding shell of a supernova and resolve its image. For the first time in history, there was an object at stellar distances large enough to show surface features, and all Palomar's telescopes were busily recording just that.

The two-hundred-inch reflector was in constant use, monitoring the rapidly expanding shell, taking a new visible-light image every five seconds, taking a fresh spectrum every sixty seconds, cycling through various interesting color filtrations between the visible light images. All the other telescopes on Palomar were just as busy, taking every imaginable measurement of the supernova. Every observatory on Earth was doing the same thing, of course, for in truth, there was virtually nothing else to observe—Supernova Sirius had turned the black skies of night to blue, making the sky too bright for any other potential object for observation.

It was possible—perhaps even likely—that they were collecting far more data than anyone could ever use. But there could never, ever, be such an opportunity again. They needed to take images to last humanity a very long time indeed, images for scientists yet unborn to use. No one wanted to take any chances.

But no one on Palomar had any doubt that, of all the telescopes in the world, it was the two-hundred-inch that was doing the best work. There might be newer, larger, more powerful telescopes—but no other observatory in the world had done so much to prepare in advance. The custom-built supernova observation pack Jessica had designed was installed in the focus cage of the big telescope, and it was pulling tricks no one had ever dreamed of doing with an astronomical telescope.

The telescope technicians had rigged up a specialized high-resolution imaging device adapted from spy satellite designs. It could catch an image in less than a thousandth of a second. Even that was too much light; they had to use neutral filters to cut down the amount of incoming light to something like a manageable value.

The fancy gadgets allowed them to make supershort exposures, virtually eliminating all the blurring effects of the Earth's atmosphere. The images pulled off the two-hundred-inch were as sharp as tacks. That, combined with the computer enhancement, made it dead easy to see the actual surface features of the supernova shell.

George and Jessica were spending a great deal of time staring at video display screen images of the supernova shell itself. The screens in Palomar's data reduction center were showing nothing else. In combined visible light, in hydrogen light, in calcium light, in radio frequencies piped in from Arecibo and the Very Large Array facility, in ultraviolet spectra piped down from Kepler, and in every other frequency anyone could manage to use to get an image, the glowering face of Supernova Sirius shone from every screen in the half-darkened room.

But getting the image was merely the first step; for not all the screens were showing true images of the supernova. Several showed displays of George's computer model.

In the crudest, simplest terms, George and Jessica were trying to make the simulation look more like the real thing. By tweaking the variables inside the model, adjusting them to what was now known about the supernova, the model would provide both a better predictive tool for what the supernova would do next, and prove a more accurate historical tool later, by better telling them what did happen.

By now, the simulation and the reality were almost identical. The model was superbly good. It would be a research tool for years to come. But even so, it was the images of reality that drew George's notice. There was something deeper and more emotional about looking at the images of the actual, tangible, object. George Prescott stared at the face of reality.

There was something brooding, angry, about the outswelling images of the expanding shell. When the various frame sequences were set in motion, in effect creating a strip of movie film, the sense of something angry and violent became even more pronounced. The sight of Supernova Sirius swelling out from its center at those terrifying speeds made it seem a brutal, greedy, living thing, eager to swallow all of space into itself. The motion of the shell's surface seemed clearest in the red false color, and that was the image that beat down on George's face now, a swollen red wound in the sky, staring at him in its surly pride.

Damn it, he couldn't go on thinking in these terms. This was only an object, as impersonal as a wave on the shore. It had no goal in mind, no desires, no emotions. It was no more purposeful than the water in a river as it goes over a fall, or a volcano spewing lava onto a living hillside. He tried to get a grip on himself and focus on the job at hand.

He reached for his trackball controller and called up a model image sequence from the previous day, during the period when the supernova shell had engulfed Sirius A. In his updated theoretical model, the shell could be seen swelling up and over the star, a hole gouged in its surface and then healing itself as the supernova shell flowed around and over the obstacle. It was a classic example of hydrodynamics. No doubt the event set up extremely elaborate shock wave patterns.

George leaned back and thought about the maelstrom of particles surging around inside the shell. The shell was made up of the white dwarf's former surface layers blown off into space, with its surface features giving hints on where fissures and weak spots might develop. For now those layers were still just as opaque as ever. There was no way to see past them to the interior of the shell. Whatever energy was inside the shell could not get out. Instead it was being kicked back and forth off the shell's interior wall, literally bottled up.

Soon, in six days or so, the shell would thin out enough to allow cracks to form, permitting leakages of those interior particles and energies out into open space, where George could get a look at them. But damn it, it was frustrating to have to wait that long. He had run simulations of the breakout, but he wasn't satisfied with their accuracy. Something was missing; he wasn't sure what. He brought up the latest version of his simulation and started running it through its paces.

No, damn it, it wasn't right. It was on the level of intuition, but he could tell he was missing something. He needed someone to bounce ideas off of.

"Jessica," he called. "I've got a little problem here. Could you take a look at it?"

Jessica nodded without taking her eyes off her screen, its light casting a strange reddish glow on her upturned face. "Just a second," she said. "Let me just get this squared away." She typed a few commands into her keyboard and then slid her chair toward George's station. "Okay, what?" she asked.

"This," he said, running the image sequence again. The two of them watched as the brilliant white visible-light image of the supernova shell expanded out well past its present bounds and started to fragment, a huge gap suddenly forming almost in the precise center of the simulated shell's image, and a flash of light emanating from it as the bottled-up high-energy radiation broke out. "I've been running simulations of the shell's breakup," George said. "If my numbers are right, that's exactly what it should be like. I've done a very detailed run, and it should get us right down to the position of the breakout gap. The numbers all seem right, but I just get the feeling I'm missing something."

Jessica looked at George with a strange expression and, with trembling hands, took up the controls. She ran the sequence backward and forward two or three times, at higher speeds and lower. At last she pulled her hands back from the controls and folded them in her lap.

"I've been simulating it myself," she said, "but not with so much detail. But from what I know, I am very much afraid that you have it right on the money."

She turned toward George and looked him in the eye. "George, there are things you don't know," she said slowly and carefully. "I think it's time we had a talk."

George looked at her carefully. There was a forced

flatness to her voice, as if she had been holding some great fear down. "About what?"

She shook her head. "Not here," she said, keeping her voice down. "Not in front of all these people. Walk me back over to the office center. There's some things I have to show you there."

She stood abruptly and headed for the door, snatching her coat from the rack without breaking stride. George was left to scramble after her to keep up. She was already down the hall and headed through the outside door before he could grab his coat and get to the entrance.

Stepping outside was a disorienting shock, like the moment of confusion he always felt after stepping out of a movie matinee into the bright light of day. He breathed in and out deeply, and his exhalation was a cloud of white vapor.

He looked around, still disoriented. It was light out, seeming broad daylight—and yet something was strained and thin about the light. George checked his watch. Just a few minutes before one. He had to stand there and think, really *think* for a minute, before he was sure that it was nearly one in the morning and not the afternoon. He was going to have to switch his watch over to twenty-four-hour mode.

No wonder the sunlight seemed bright and weak at the same time. Full daylight was far brighter than what the human eye needed, or could even accept, so the eye would contract its pupil, letting in less light. Supernova Sirius was currently about one percent as bright as the sun, but that was light enough to illuminate the landscape with something like the same brightness as a well-lit room. The trouble was that George's eyes, trained by a lifetime of experience, were taking the cues of sharp shadows and clear sky and interpreting them as meaning normal full daylight. But the light was too dim, the shadows too deep, the air too cold, for it to be daytime. His hindbrain was confused, getting mixed signals about what time of day it was.

He heard the mournful cry of an owl, and thought about all the other animals on Earth who must be even more confused than humans were. Nocturnal animals especially had to be completely baffled.

He looked up into the sky, and saw the brilliant sun-point of light that was Sirius, too bright to look at, hanging in the southeast, the nearly full moon hanging incongruously nearby. No one had ever seen a full moon in a blue sky before, except in the Arctic and Antarctic regions, for the moon was only full when it was directly opposite the sun in the sky. George frowned. These nights of day were strange indeed. It would take some doing to get used to them.

But never mind that; Jessica was well ahead of him on the path leading away from the data reduction building toward the main office building. He had to sprint, and he was almost breathless by the time he caught her.

"Jessica," he panted. "What is it? What's going on?"

"Trouble," she said, her voice flat and hard. She started walking faster, deliberately moving too fast for easy conversation.

George felt his temper getting the better of him. "Damn it! Will you hold still and talk to me!" He reached out, grabbed her by the arm, and glared down at her, expecting to see an angry face staring back up at him. Instead he was stunned to see a face full of fear, eyes bright with tears. "My God," he said. "Jessica, what's wrong? What is it?"

Suddenly her arms were around him, and she was crying. "Oh, God, George. I'm so scared. I've been trying not to see it, I really have been. But I can't help it. The proof is there. The effect is real. Your simulation of the shell rupture—oh, God, that puts the last nail in the coffin. It's real, it's going to come."

George looked down at Jessica, reached out to her face with a hand made stiff and clumsy in the cold. He pushed a strand or two of hair away from her face, wiped away a tear. "What's real?" he asked gently. "What's going to come?"

But Jessica did not seem to hear. "We know they'll break out. Our one hope was that they wouldn't come toward us," Jessica said. "That depends on where the first cracks in the shell develop. Wherever that first break opens, virtually all of the pent-up energy will rush out through it, like air from a popped balloon. But now you tell me it's all going to head straight for us. Oh, George, what will it all do to us?"

"What? The gamma and X-rays? Yeah, if the initial gap faces Earth, they're going to break out of the shell moving toward us. What did you expect?" He looked at her a bit worriedly. "Is it the gamma rays and X-rays you're scared of?"

Jessica nodded stiffly. "Yes."

"What the hell are you talking about? Gamma and X-rays can't even penetrate the atmosphere. There's no way they can affect us."

"But why can't the high-energy photons penetrate the atmosphere? What happens when they hit it?"

George shrugged. "The individual photons strike the atoms that make up the exosphere. The gas atoms absorb the energy and that's it."

"No, it *isn't!* That's the whole point. Electrons get knocked out of the gas atoms. The upper atmosphere accumulates free electrons."

"Okay, so what? Free electrons in the upper atmosphere. It isn't the end of the world."

Jessica broke free of the embrace and moved a step or two back, a strange, panicky look in her face. "Isn't it? George, maybe you'd better just stop for a second and ask if it isn't exactly that."

"Jessica—"

"Quiet! Just be quiet and follow me. I'll show you." And with that, she turned and walked away, through the bright darkness of the day that was night.

* * *

Jessica was at least superficially more calm by the time they got back to her office. She sat behind her desk, wrestled her coat off, and started pulling out paper files. "I've been working on this for a couple of months," she said. "And I've kept it damn quiet until now. But now—now we have to go public with it."

George pulled off his coat and sat in the chair opposite her. "Go public with what?"

"About two months ago Kenji Yamada called me up in the middle of the night and told me to take a good hard look at gamma ray effects on our atmosphere. He didn't tell me anything else, because he didn't want to influence my thinking. Maybe if he had said more, I would have worked faster, but now it's too late. Just before the supernova blew, I finished double-checking the numbers I came up with in my first pass. The results scare the hell out of me."

"What results?" George asked.

"If that initial crack in the supernova shell develops facing Earth, we'll get a flood of high-energy radiation coming right down our throats. When the gamma rays strike the upper atmosphere, they'll knock loose *incredible* numbers of free electrons. The electrons will pile up along the magnetic field lines and then release their energy in an electromagnetic pulse.

"If it all breaks the way it could, the upper limit of the gamma ray flux striking the Earth's atmosphere will be in excess of what's produced in the atmospheric blast of a multimegaton hydrogen bomb! And that means a major EMP effect!"

George stared at her in shock. He knew a little about EMP, half-remembered details from a popular article he had read years before. EMP had once been talked about as a military weapon. The military found out about it way back when they were still doing atmospheric A-bomb tests. They set off a bomb test eight hundred miles from Honolulu and accidentally knocked out all the phone service in the city. Then they started looking into what had happened. They established that you could touch off an EMP by setting off a nuclear warhead about four hundred kilometers high. The bomb blast would shower the upper atmosphere with gamma rays, and the gammas would set off the pulse. EMP didn't hurt people directly, but what it could do was hit electronic gear and overload it.

"Wait a second. You're telling me that with the supernova taking the place of an upper-atmosphere nuclear bomb, we're going to get an EMP?"

Jessica nodded wordlessly and stood up. She started pacing the room, kneading her hands through each other.

"Wait a minute, that can't be right," George protested. That same feeling of disorientation he had felt outside came over him again. This couldn't be real. There had to be some mistake.

But he knew there wasn't. It all fit together. It was the missing part of the puzzle he had sensed in his simulation of gap formation in the supernova shell. The moment the gap opened, it would let loose a swarm of gamma ray photons. When the highly energetic photons hit the atmosphere, they would knock loose vast numbers of highly energized electrons. The electrons would stream along the magnetic field lines. The free electrons would absorb further energy from the gamma and X-ray photons that would still be coming in. At last the free electrons would give up their energy in the form of an electromagnetic pulse.

And a surge of electromagnetic energy would pass invisibly, harmlessly, through people and living things and rocks and water, and yet wreck electronic equipment, especially anything that used microchips or integrated circuits.

That strange selectivity was dictated by basic physics. The pulse would move through every completed circuit and generate a huge pulse of electric energy in that circuit. If it had enough energy behind it, the pulse could force the electricity to jump any break in the circuit. But in a vacuum tube, the two sides of the circuit were too far away from each other for a spark to jump the gap. Modern electronics, though, had thousands of microscopic gaps, all of them easy to jump. An EMP could fuse an integrated circuit into a useless blob of silicon.

Anything with an antenna, or something that could serve as an antenna, would get hit extra hard. To an EMP, power lines would serve as nothing less than giant antennae. They would act almost like lightning rods, attracting the pulse, directing it down into whatever was connected to them.

"Good God," George said. "How can this be right?"

Jessica looked up at George, visibly fighting off hysteria. "It is right, George. Over half the Earth, over that half of the Earth from which Sirius is visible at the moment of gamma ray breakout, virtually every electric circuit in use will be overloaded, and destroyed. Virtually everything that uses electricity or electronics will be destroyed."

"My God." George sat there, stunned. He wanted to say *no, that can't be,* but he could not. The last few years of his life had been nothing but the act of proving, over and over, that the unbelievable could happen. And the problem, over and over again, had been not that the evidence did not support him, but that people refused to accept the evidence.

Not this time. If the evidence supported what Jessica was saying, then so be it.

At last he looked up at Jessica, still pacing back and forth. "Show me," he said.

Jessica gestured toward the thick file. "Good," she said. "I was praying you'd say that. I want you to check my calculations, George. Use my terminal to run any simulations you need." She stood up and headed for the door. "I'll leave you to it," she said, and left.

George reached for the file and started to read.

* * *

An hour later, George Prescott hit the enter key and watched as the computer model of the supernova explosion ran itself again, the stages of the catastrophe playing themselves out in calm perfection. But this time he was running the simulation for a different reason—to get some hard numbers on the power and duration of any gamma ray burst. He could not get a precise figure, but he could develop a range of values.

That was enough to plug into Jessica's model of the electromagnetic pulse scenario. Hers was no set of pretty pictures thrown up on the screen, but instead little more than a forest of numbers flashing up in neat, dry columns. And those numbers revealed all that he had missed, the terrible truth that had passed him by altogether in the torrent of congratulations and backslapping he had so joyfully soaked up in the last three days.

The gamma rays. The goddamn gamma rays. They had broken out of Supernova Sirius's interior nine long years ago, and had been on their way ever since. But however long or far they traveled, they would arrive at Earth very soon.

George shook his head, tears of fear and exhaustion swimming in his eyes. He had thought of the gamma rays as just one more interesting feature of his model. No one had worried about them, or what they would do in the real world. No one except Jessica and Kenji. Until now.

The figures were right, there was no getting around that. The gamma ray intensity would spike high at first, and then decay over a period of a day or so. If the lower estimate in the gamma ray flux should actually obtain, the EMP effects on the ground would be marginal. On the other hand, if the higher-end estimate should prevail, people directly under the initial gamma ray blast would be in for serious trouble, but the gamma ray intensity would drop below EMP threshold within minutes. But based on what he knew, George felt strongly that the high end was more likely. The initial pulse would almost certainly be powerful enough to cause an electromagnetic pulse event. Event, hell, they would cause an EMP blast.

Any place the blast touched, it would be like standing three feet from a lightning strike. Half the electrical devices on Earth would be destroyed, or at least disabled.

George had imagined the supernova—his supernova, the Prescott Supernova, as some press people were already calling it—as a bright but harmless light in the sky, a plaything for scientists. He had thrilled at the idea that it would bear his name, at least informally. But he fancied himself as winning against the odds, showing the whole world he was right and they were wrong. But now—now his victory was won at the cost of a terrible defeat for all humankind. Now the supernova was something more, something far worse. It was a thunderbolt from the gods, already flung, already on its way, its impact inevitable.

There was no way to be sure, no way to know until it was far too late. But there was an excellent chance that the first major gap in the supernova shell would form just as his model predicted—pointed straight at the Earth. And if the gamma ray intensity was as high as it *might* be, then—

George tried to calm himself. Moving automatically, he hit the save key on his computer, told it to run his standard summary creation program. He crumpled up his notes, swept them off the desktop, and swiveled around in his chair to stare out at the nightless day.

Take all the models, all the calculations, at face value, insist on accepting all data, instead of denying whatever parts of it were frightening or hard to believe, and this thing was going to happen.

And yet there were so many variables. He thought of the incredibly complex programming that had gone into that model, and the way it had grown over the year, not through any sort of planning, but almost of its own volition. At the core of the program that was now predicting a massive, disastrous gamma ray burst directed at the Earth was a program of only a few dozen lines he had written years before to estimate the patterns of instability in a hypothetical white dwarf star. That was madness on the face of it. It was as if someone had taken one of the earliest, crudest, video arcade games and gradually modified it into a full-fledged battle forecaster, with the fate of nations depending on its reliability. He was, in effect, using a souped-up copy of Pac-Man to predict the end of the world.

Damn it, why had he done it that way? He knew he wasn't any genius as a programmer, that his code wasn't as tight, as seamless, as it ought to be. He should have junked the whole model program eighteen months ago and started from scratch, with a modeling program specifically designed for the job at hand, instead of fooling around with this jury-rigged mess.

He thought again about his programming. There were so many places he could have made a mistake in that forest of numbers and formulae. So far, it had proved accurate—but just suppose one value in just the right little-used subroutine was off just enough to render his shell-gap prediction useless. How could he justify panicking the entire world because of a typo? He needed time to think, to consider, to check his work.

But there *was* no time. For if his model was right, then in three days Supernova Prescott would pound the Earth and shatter the works of humanity.

Chapter 15

Desmond Potter sat in front of his computer screen in the early morning light, watching as George Prescott's latest update report scrolled up the screen. He had been getting them via e-mail ever since Hiram had upgraded the Church computer system. George had been writing daily progress reports since the supernova had hit, and still saw to it that Desmond got all of them. Or maybe he did not see to it, maybe he had forgotten the arrangement altogether, but his computer system was remembering.

In any case, Desmond got the information. Whatever his original motives for wanting it, now he was fascinated by the knowledge, the wonder itself. Desmond had come to realize just how parochial his view of God's

262

universe had been. Geocentric, that was the word. What blind arrogance to assume that this one little world was the center of God's whole universe. What arrogance on his part to imagine that God would see fit to destroy one star and seriously damage its companion just on account of Earth. It was so wasteful, if nothing else. If God wanted an impressive sign in Earth's sky, he could have sent a great comet.

Or, if he wanted to destroy humanity in all its wickedness, an asteroid ten miles across would do the trick—or a perfectly simple plague virus, something just as fatal as AIDS, but a hundred times faster-acting and more contagious.

Ghoulish thoughts, horrible. He could not, would not, accept that God would do anything so wicked. And yet he had been hoping, not so very long ago, for God to wipe out humanity with the clean flame of a star. Was that what had made it acceptable to him? That it would be a hygienic, tidy destruction? What in the world had let him imagine being incinerated as a clean and painless death?

But never mind. He was now convinced, wholly and unalterably, that this supernova was no miracle, no sign from God, but merely a part of the natural world, no more or less a miracle than sunrise or the changing of the seasons.

Enough woolgathering. He yawned, switched on his printer, and made a hard copy of the report, taking a sip of his coffee as the pages came out. He picked up the first page and started to read, at first with nothing more than mild curiosity, then with mounting astonishment and alarm. He sat upright in his chair and started from the beginning, reading more carefully.

Most of George's reports were far too complex and scientific for Desmond to follow completely, but not this one. Good Lord, not this one. At least not in the broad strokes. There were details he did not follow, but the main facts were clear. The Earth was in peril. If it had been anyone but George issuing such a warning, he would have refused to believe it. But this was George Prescott's daily report to himself, and George Prescott was honest and careful.

Desmond leaned back in his chair again and read over the hard copy one more time, going over it slowly and carefully, step by step. Yes, yes, he could see it. It made sense to him.

But what to do about it? *There* was the problem. He had first approached George seeking proof of something he no longer believed in—the end of the world. Now, here in his hands, was, if not proof of world's end, then something very close to it. If Jessica Talmadge and this Kenji Yamada were right, then many people were about to die, and civilization was about to take all the damage of a world war—not one large disaster, but a million minor catastrophes, each making all the others worse. He could see that, hidden in the cautious words of science.

Or would it be even *worse* than he imagined? Could this disaster be even more deadly than expected? It seemed that every time someone had stated that Sirius could hold no more surprises, Sirius had astonished the world all over again. Suppose the supernova did manage, somehow, to emit strong gamma rays for twelve hours instead of just a few minutes? Suppose it managed to send that wrecking surge of power over all the globe, not just half of it? Suppose the damage was so great that civilization did totter and come close to falling? Or truly fell?

With a shock, Desmond realized that he was not playing with hypotheticals anymore. Civilization could fall, if things went as badly as they might. What sort of global depression might result if half the world's industry was stopped at once? How many would starve and freeze? How fast and how far would the effects cascade across the globe? He should bring this report to Hiram immediately.

He stood up, still holding the printout, and made a start toward the door. Then he stopped, turned, and began to pace the room. *Should* he bring it to Hiram? He had promised George to keep all the updates confidential. But this seemed so urgent, so vital. Surely they would be releasing the news in a few hours anyway. On the other hand, he could only imagine what Hiram would see in Prescott's words. What use would Hiram make of the news? What knots would he tie in this information? Goodman was growing wilder, more uncontrollable.

Suppose that the scales were so closely balanced between survival and catastrophe that it would take but the touch of one man's hand to send it tumbling one way or the other? Suppose Hiram getting this news just a little bit too soon could do it? Desmond snorted, irritated with himself. This was no moment for flights of fancy.

But other dangers besides the fate of the world could be eliminated—or brought on—by one man's act. Suppose that a choice he made resulted in saving one life— or causing one death—that could have been avoided?

Desmond stopped, turned, and happened to catch his reflection in the wall mirror. What nonsense. How could *his* actions shape events one way or the other? He was just one man, without any particular position or importance. Just an assistant to a preacher in a one-lung fringe-group church.

Yet still he feared what Hiram could do with this information. Maybe they would choose not to release it. Maybe it was in error, or was merely some sort of hypothetical study.

Nevertheless, he still felt ties of loyalty and debt to Goodman, and certainly a theory suggesting the potential destruction of half the world's economy would be of interest to the Last Church of the Apocalyptic Revelation. This was the very sort of sign Hiram had predicted. How, Desmond asked himself, could he justify this sin of omission, the act of not revealing this news to Goodman?

Desmond resumed his pacing and tried to think. He

was afraid of making choices, wrong and dangerous choices, in these times of crisis. Hiram could take this news and rouse the congregations, but surely he would cause panic as well, and be pleased by it; would see the panic itself as a Sign the end was near, rather than see it as something he himself had caused.

What path was Desmond to choose? Perhaps here and now was the time. Perhaps this was *the* choice, the point where the paths split for him. Perhaps this was *the* decision for which he would ultimately be judged, and found worthy or wanting. He looked again at the papers in his hands. What should he do with this information?

Which side do you want to be on? he asked himself.

Why have you remained at his side so long? Desmond looked around, startled. The second question had seemed to come from outside of him, from a voice unknown and unseen.

There was no one there.

But the question was still valid. Desmond sat back down at his desk and thought for a moment, and suddenly he was at peace. He had his answer. After all, he had stayed with Hiram Goodman in the hopes of being a restraining influence.

He pulled open the desk drawer, dug around until he found an old disposable cigarette lighter, left behind in the furnished room by some previous tenant. He walked down the hall to the bathroom, closed the bathroom door, and pulled open the window to give the smoke a way out. He flipped open the toilet seat, ignited the lighter, and set fire to the hard copy of the report.

He held the papers carefully, watching them shrivel away into black ashes. The smoke caught him in the face as a blast of cool morning air came in the window. Suddenly he found himself thrown back in time to another burning of papers, back on the cold driveway of his old home in Boston, three thousand miles away. But that seemed the act of another man. Had not that burning been an act of purgation, a destruction of the old

self and the making of a new man? Was he doing that
again, now? Was he leaving behind this life, too, cutting the ties to Hiram, the Last Church, and the Christriders who had fallen in with them? If he was, what
sort of new person was he to become this time? He
found the questions exciting, invigorating.

Then the flames got near his fingers and he dropped
the burning papers into the toilet. They hit the water
with a gentle hiss.

Desmond smiled to himself as he flushed the ashes
away. If this moment symbolized the birth of a new
man inside him, the old one wasn't getting much of a
send-off. Maybe he was trying a bit too hard to find
symbolism in every moment. He pulled a towel off the
back of the door and flapped it around for a minute,
trying to flush the smell of smoke out of the room. At
last he hung up the towel, closed the toilet seat, shut
the window, and opened the door.

But there was still one job left before the report of
EMP was well and truly gone.

He went back to his room, sat at the computer, and
typed in the command to erase the file.

And stared at the computer monitor in shock.

ERASURE NOT PERMITTED
ANOTHER COMPUTER IN THE LOCAL NETWORK
IS ACCESSING THE FILE

Desmond's computer was just hooked up to a standard
modem to use the phone lines. It wasn't on a network.

Or was it? There was the warning, right on the
screen. Suppose he was on a network without knowing
it? Suddenly his heart was hammering. He stood up and
gently pulled the computer forward on the desk by an
inch or two.

There it was, coming out of the back, out of the
minute gap between the backplate and the baseplate. A
wire, no, a bit of fiber-optic cable, as fine as a human
hair. If he had pulled the computer forward just another

inch or two, it would have snapped clean off without Desmond even noticing. No doubt that was the whole idea. As long as the computer stayed right where it was, the cable was all but invisible. Move it, and the tap snapped.

Inside the case of the computer, the cable probably terminated on the standard optical cable link somehow. Switch the motherboard's standard read-only-memory chips for an identical-looking chipset that had a bootleg copy of some network protocol burned into them, and the thing was done. It was a jury-rig, but a very smooth, slick jury-rig. The only way it could really be detected was in the way it just happened, if the tap operator happened to have a file open when the victim tried to delete it.

But who had done it?

Desmond knelt down on his hands and knees and carefully poked his head under the desk. He craned his neck up and peered upward, looking for where the hair-thin cable came from. There. Right there. It came straight through the wall, through a neatly drilled pin-hole.

And Hiram's room, Hiram's computer, was on the other side of that wall. Desmond stood up again, went out into the hall, and peered at the base of Hiram's door. There was an edge of light there, the gleaming yellow of a desk lamp, not the glow of the sun coming in at his window. He thought he could hear a radio playing music, very faintly. This day, at least, Hiram was not sleeping so late. Or was he secretly awake every day at this time, all but literally reading over Desmond's shoulder as he worked through overnight computer mail from the various branches of the Last Church?

He had to be in there, right now, reading the update from George at this very moment. That was why the network wouldn't let Desmond erase it. Desmond suddenly felt sick, felt as if he had been punched in the gut and kicked in the groin. He turned and made his way back to his room, sat down without noticing he had done so.

No wonder Hiram had simply given Desmond a computer instead of leaving him to the trouble of shopping for one himself. Desmond stared balefully at the traitorous machine. It must have come into the apartment already hotwired.

Hiram. Good lord, Hiram. When you thought about it, it suddenly made a great deal of sense. After all, the man had come to preaching by way of the back door, by way of petty grifting and a time or two in jail. He would have had plenty of chances to learn how to hang a computer tap, but maybe not so many chances to learn good programming, or learn a way to avoid this very glitch in the tap system. A really smooth pro would have fixed the network protocol to keep it from popping up that warning. Or maybe—indeed, more likely—Hiram had hired some old associate, negotiated just a little too hard on the price, and gotten what he had paid for. That would be in character for him.

But none of that mattered now. Five minutes before, he had imagined himself breaking away from his life, his role, in the Church. Now he discovered that his role had itself been imaginary. He had seen himself as Hiram's trusted second, the steady administrator who saw to it that all went well. Now he discovered that he was being used, watched, tested. He had thought that he had kept all the updates from Hiram. But clearly the man could have read them all for himself.

He had wanted to destroy the update because he feared what Hiram might do with the information. Now it was too late.

He had to warn George. Now, before Hiram could act. He reached for the phone and lifted the handset gently from its cradle, trying not to make it clatter or rattle and give the game away.

But instead of a dial tone, he heard a voice.

Hiram's voice.

"—es, yes, I realize it is very early, but I figured if

you guys were on the air right now, someone had to be there. Just please have the station's ad manager call me the moment he comes in. I want those ads to start this morning. I want people pouring into church tonight.''

"Ah, yes, sir, Reverend Goodman,'' another voice replied. "I'm just the engineer on duty, but I'm sure you can come on down and tape a spot first thing this morning. Believe me, a cash customer is always welcome. But you do understand that you'll have to pay a very substantial surcharge for placing the ads so late and asking for such rush work.''

Hiram laughed. "Oh, that's all right. Come another few days, and money's not going to be worth much anyway. Neither are television stations, for that matter. Might as well use both while I still have the chance. A friend of mine said a while ago that broadcasting was the best way to get people into church. This might be my only chance to see if he was right.''

Desmond pushed the hang-up button as gently as he could and put the handset back on the cradle. Too late for giving a preemptive warning. But George still had to know.

Suddenly it dawned on Desmond that he had nearly made a serious error anyway. If Hiram was tapping his computer, he would have to assume the phone was likewise unsafe.

A pay phone. He would have to call from a pay phone.

He rushed out of his room, out of the apartment, down the stairs, and out into the street, glad beyond words to be outside and away from the things he had just learned.

He rushed down the stairs, leaving everything behind except the clothes he was standing in. He thrust his hands into his pockets and dug out his keys. He hurried around to the alley in back, unlocked the shed, and wheeled out the red Indian Warrior motorcycle Hiram had given him so long ago. He swung himself into the cycle's seat and gunned the engine.

He turned and looked up at the rear of the apartment. This time he was not abandoning a home destroyed by a madman's bomb. This time the destruction was more subtle, but just as real. This shabby, tired little place had been his home for a while, but now it was wrecked by deceit, ruined beyond any hope of repair by betrayal.

He dropped the bike into gear and took off.

He would never go back.

Hiram Goodman, hunched over his computer screen, heard the roar of a motorcycle starting up. He stood up and went to the rear window, getting there just in time to see Desmond's back, the Indian Warrior thundering off down the alley. What the hell was he doing? Better go out and see.

Goodman unlocked the door of his room and stepped out into the hall. He went past Desmond's open bedroom door—and noticed that the computer was still on. That wasn't like Desmond. He stepped into the room, and read the warning message that still lit up the computer monitor. Suddenly he noticed that the computer had been pulled forward on the desk a bit, and things were pushed around a bit, as if Desmond had been trying to get a look at the back of the machine.

The Reverend Hiram Goodman swore angrily, stomped out of the room, and slammed the door. So much for one of his best sources of information.

But then, suddenly, he was calm. It was all right. It didn't matter.

After all, he could hardly expect to get much use out of dear old Brother Desmond after he paid his visit to the television station later this morning. Desmond Potter was used up already. He turned back to his own room, and got back to work on his script.

December 13, 2000
11:04 A.M.
Pasadena, California

Jessica and George stood, watching the television monitor, and Jessica found herself thinking this spot would never win any technical awards.

The lighting was bad. It made Goodman looked gaunt and sallow. The spot consisted of nothing more than Goodman staring into a camera and speaking his lines. The whole thing smacked of the amateur hour, somehow. But none of that mattered. Goodman was a skilled performer. His voice was strong and effective, and his eyes were fiery with passion.

"Hello, friends. I'm Reverend Hiram Goodman of the Last Church of the Apocalyptic Revelation, and I have an urgent message for you, one that could change your life forever. The scientists, the God-haters, have lied to you once again, my friends. They have told you that this mighty Sign will leave the world untouched, that it means nothing, that it is merely a bright and pretty light in the sky. But that is not so, and they know it. We have documentary proof from their holy of holies, from Palomar Mountain and that false prophet of science, Dr. George Prescott himself. I have given that proof to the newspapers and the other news outlets. Prescott knows, but will not tell *you*, that a new pulse of energy, a new form of energy, is coming from the supernova. It is called EMP, a form of energy the scientists have long known about and hidden from you. They fear it, for EMP harms not man, but machine, and these scientists love their machines more than they care for people."

Hiram leaned in closer to the screen, and his voice grew quieter. "They *know* what will happen, but they will not tell you. In three days the skies will crackle with new power, and God's Judgment, sent through the workings of the new star, will come.

"But you're asking, what does this EMP energy do?

And that is the remarkable thing. What it does is stop everything else.

"All machines will fall silent. Electricity itself will lose its power. Cities will fall into darkness, cars and planes shall be stilled. This and all other television and radio stations shall fall silent.

"And so mote it be. The history of this blasted and sinful civilization shall be closed, and the way made clear for a new beginning, for a Second Coming.

"*That* is what will happen in three days, my friends. It is time, and past time, to prepare for The End. I know that many of you do not, cannot, believe me yet. But come and listen. Come to our services tonight, and stay with us, stay through these days of peril with us in a place of safety. On your screen now are the addresses of Last Church locations throughout the Los Angeles area. Come stay with us and—"

Jessica reached out, snapped off the television, and let out a string of curses. "Well, I don't think he got a single fact right, but besides that, it was just great," she said bitterly.

George just sat there, staring dumbly at the blank screen, numb with exhaustion. It had been a long and sleepless night, half of it spent on the phone with Kenji Yamada. They had burned up the fax lines and computer links as well, getting all the facts straight, confirming that it was as bad as it seemed.

He had forgotten all about his arrangement to keep Desmond informed. Once told to put Desmond on the update distribution list, Caltech's computers and e-mail system had kept him on it. Before this latest disaster, he had not decided whether to go public with the EMP report, still unsure if the evidence was good enough.

Now he would have to do the press conference anyway, pretending he knew the evidence was right. He had been leaning in that direction even before Desmond's call. The price for being silent and right was far higher than that for issuing a warning and being wrong.

But Hiram Goodman had just made it that much harder to convince anyone. Up until five minutes ago, he had been hoping to beat Goodman to the punch, starting their news conference before Goodman began running his ads. But the earliest thing he had been able to arrange was a noon conference, an hour from now.

About all he could do was pray nothing else went wrong within the next hour.

12:00 noon

Dr. George Prescott stood on the podium on the stage of the Palomar Press Center and stared out again at the sea of faces. So much for being safe from the press on the mountaintop. But would they accept it? Would they believe him when he lined himself up alongside a religious fanatic?

He wished, devoutly wished, that Jessica were standing by his side instead of in the front row of the audience. But the press had latched on to him as the fair-haired boy, and Jessica had flatly refused to come up onstage with him. And maybe she was right. If there were too many voices speaking, maybe the words of warning themselves would be diminished.

He stared out at the sea of faces before him and was reminded, irresistibly, of that nightmarish day he had offered his five-minute talk on the seemingly incredible idea that white dwarfs in binary systems were far less stable than anyone had thought. He smiled to himself. Strange to think that presentation had scared him much more than this one was now. The stakes on getting this one right were just a bit higher.

The crowd seemed to be settling down, and the television lights came on in his face. George took the lights as a cue to begin and cleared his throat.

"Ah, good morning," he said. "I would like to present some rather urgent and important results that have just come to light in the last few hours. My colleagues here and in Japan have discovered an extremely serious threat to our planet, posed by the Sirius supernova.

"I know that the consensus has been that, aside from additional daylight and the probability of some bad weather, there is no danger. However, that is not so. One of the first, and most important, duties of a scientist is to be willing to admit it when one is wrong. I myself said there was no danger. I was wrong.

"Dr. Kenji Yamada of Japan was the first to recognize the danger, and he deserves all the credit you can offer him. What was at first a remote theoretical possibility has turned into a highly probable danger. When it was a mere remote possibility, Dr. Yamada refrained from publicizing it, for fear of spreading needless panic. He will hold a press conference in Tokyo in a few hours, and will make himself available for your queries. His contact numbers are on the press handout.

"My associate, Dr. Jessica Talmadge, developed a sophisticated computer model of the threat on very short notice, and she likewise deserves acknowledgment. She will be available for questions after I make our report.

"To be frank, my own contribution in this work has been extremely small. In fact, my largest accomplishment was in admitting that I had missed something I should have seen.

"Indeed, the only reason I am up here is that Drs. Yamada and Talmadge felt that the prominence I have achieved in the last few days, however undeserved it might be, would bring more of you out here to hear the news. Because the news is very bad, and it must be told.

"In brief, Dr. Yamada and Dr. Talmadge have established that there is a very high probability that, somewhere between forty-eight and seventy-two hours from now, the Sirius supernova will expose approximately one half of the globe to a major electromagnetic pulse, EMP."

George noticed a slight stir of surprise and laughter

in the audience. Some of them had heard Goodman and had been waiting for the magic word. A few other bored faces were startled into wakefulness, as if they had recognized the term but hadn't recalled much about it. He nodded and went on. "I see that more than a few of you are familiar with the term EMP. Good, that ought to make this easier. For the rest of you, check with any military source you can find to learn about EMP. We have prepared some detailed fact sheets for you all, which should be available in the back of the room. Suffice it to say for now that any intense burst of gamma rays in the upper atmosphere will result in an electromagnetic pulse, a surge of energy capable of disabling or wrecking many types of electric equipment."

Suddenly there was a forest of hands in front of him, and an unruly chorus of voices calling for his attention. He stuck his finger out at random and took a question.

"Dr. Prescott, what do you mean, half the Earth?"

"It's very simple. We expect Sirius to unleash a burst of gamma rays sometime between two and three days from now. The burst will peak almost immediately, then take several hours to taper down. However, it is only during the initial brief peak—a few minutes long—that there will be sufficient gamma ray intensity to present any danger. Those parts of the world from which Sirius is visible when that happens will be affected. Those places where Sirius is not visible, where it is below the local horizon, will not be affected."

Another forest of hands, another random selection.

"In those parts of the world where Sirius *is* visible, Dr. Prescott, what exactly will those effects be? You say many types of electric equipment will be disabled or wrecked. How do you mean?"

"What EMP does is induce electric current in a given electric device. If that current is strong enough, it will overload that device, damaging or destroying it. Some types of equipment are more sensitive than others, so not all electric gear will be equally affected," George said. "More sensitive equipment, such as computer equipment and other miniaturized electronics, will be most at risk.''

"Hold it. You're saying that all the computers over half the Earth could be destroyed? That sounds incredible.''

"I agree, but it is true," George said, a bit stuffily. "I might add that not only computers, but all devices that use an on-board computer or computer-type circuits, will also be at risk of being ruined or being caused to malfunction. A car that uses a computer to control its fuel pump and brakes, for example, might have the brakes lock on while the engine suddenly shuts down. An aircraft that uses a computer-driven fly-by-wire system would lose control of everything the computer system ran. The phone networks are nothing *but* gigantic computer systems, though they are somewhat shielded against EMP, and optical cable would be unaffected. Power-generating stations are built to handle massive overloads, but they would almost certainly be automatically shut down by the power surge—and their computerized control systems could be damaged.''

"Wait a second, Doctor," one rather irritable-looking reporter in the front row objected. "This is nuts. You're saying that *everything* is going to be knocked out? There's no way to stop it?''

George shifted uncertainly on his feet. "Well, yes, there are ways. As I said, some phone nets are immune. A lot of heavy-duty equipment is shielded in ways that will protect it. Most modern military equipment is shielded. And the more completely something can be turned off, unplugged, and shut down, the better.''

"So for three days people should unplug everything in the house? Go without electricity?''

"Well, yes," George said. "As a general rule, yes. But I am not an expert on protecting electric devices from EMP.''

"But you got us all out here to warn us about it,"

the reporter objected. "If you're not an expert, why should we—"

Suddenly George felt his temper flair. "I said I was not an expert on shielding. And no, I'm not an expert on EMP either. Not on the details. But I *am* an expert on supernovae. I can tell you that *this* one is going to blow a huge amount of gamma ray radiation out into space. Gamma rays are very high energy, very powerful. There is an excellent chance that the supernova will send that radiation straight toward *us*. In fact, if it's coming, it's been on its way for nine years. And I can tell you in general terms that a gamma ray strike on the Earth is going to cause a lot of damage through EMP. I have been shown the evidence, done my own checks on it, and I am convinced. I don't care if it sounds silly, or unlikely, it happens to be true. So if you people do your jobs and check this out, see what other scientists think, see if it's for real, maybe we can avoid some of that damage."

"But Dr. Prescott—"

"That's enough out of you. Let someone else have a chance. Yes, you in the back."

"Dr. Prescott, any comment on what an Ex-Christrider, a certain Reverend Goodman, is saying this morning on every cable or broadcast outlet that he can get on?"

Damn it. There it was. "No, I have no comment." Maybe that would make it go away.

But the reporter was still standing. She wasn't going to let him get off that easy. "Excuse me, Doctor, but most of what you've said, I heard from the reverend's broadcast an hour ago, though he was a bit more colorful and dramatic. Why won't you associate yourself with someone who is forecasting the same events?"

There was a two-edged sword of a question if ever he had seen one. Concede the point, and he was equating himself with a Bible-thumping con man. Argue it, and he would only be begging for follow-up questions from half the reporters in the room. George decided to play it straight and hope for the best. "My understanding is that this Goodman got his hands on a bootleg copy of an update summary I made late last night, and based his remarks—however confused and inaccurate—on that. So since he is basically garbling *my* information, it's not surprising my warning at least vaguely resembles his."

"But both you and he are predicting massive power outages and other problems."

"Yes, obviously. If he says what I'm saying, we're saying the same thing."

Suddenly a new reporter popped up, a rather hard-edged-looking young woman dressed in a black shirt and blue jeans, a gleam in her eye.

"The Reverend Goodman says that what is coming will be the will of God, the moment when the Lord will smite all the evil of our world so that it can be born again. Do you believe that? Do you believe that God willed this supernova in order to—"

Wonderful. A true believer, either from Goodman's crowd or from some other Ender sect. There had been a few of them floating around the press center, with credentials from this or that newsletter. George cut her off before she could gather any steam.

"Ah, excuse me," he said. "Let me make this clear. I have nothing whatever to do with Goodman, other than that he stole a copy of my work somehow. I certainly don't regard the supernova as anything but a large and powerful natural event. Next question."

"Dr. Prescott, is there any way you can give a firmer time window on when all this might happen?"

George breathed a sigh of relief, glad for an easy one. He shook his head. "No, I'm sorry. We're right at the limits of our accuracy now, and I'd much rather err on the side of caution. Yes, in the third row there."

"Dr. Prescott, assuming for the sake of argument that this EMP actually happens, have I got this straight? On one half the Earth, every electric circuit will be destroyed, but on the other half, nothing will happen?"

"That's oversimplifying, but yes," George said, refusing the temptation to take the Goodman bait again. "As I said, some electric devices will be immune, and others are shielded. And there may be localized areas where the EMP effect is stronger or weaker." George looked around the room for another question, and realized there was something wrong. George should have been in front of a room full of frightened people by now, but these people were calm, dutifully taking down his words, their faces placid and professionally neutral.

They would go back to the press headquarters and report, not that the Earth was in danger, but that he had gone over the edge, jumped in bed with that fire-and-brimstone biker preacher.

They weren't buying it. They didn't believe him. In the flurry of phone calls last night, Ken Yamada had warned him about Chicken Little, and Ken had been right. If it seemed too impossible, people just wouldn't believe it, no matter how solid the proof. With a feeling of desperation, he pointed to another reporter and took another question.

"Dr. Prescott—with all due respect, and bearing in mind that you have made a whole series of incredible predictions that have come true, you haven't given us much time. I infer from everything you've said that your colleagues have been working on the EMP problem for some time. If they were so concerned about the danger, why didn't they issue their warnings sooner?"

George slumped down, leaned a bit more on the podium. The truth, damn it. He had to tell the truth. "Because they didn't believe it could happen until now."

And then they laughed.

After that, the rest of the press conference could be nothing but an anticlimax. A disaster, perhaps, but an anticlimactic one. There were a few more questions, some of them even intelligent and useful, but George felt the heart go out of him. He went through the motions, but even he didn't listen to what was said. From where he was standing, the press conference didn't so much end as fall apart. A thin trickle of reporters heading for the exit turned into a steady stream. George could do nothing but stand behind his podium and watch them go, until he was talking to a room that was nearly empty, a rather large number of unwanted handouts left untouched by the door.

At last the proceedings ground to a halt and Jessica stepped up on the stage, came up beside George and put her arms around him.

"Ya done good," she said, smiling bravely.

"Are you crazy? That wasn't a press conference, it was a shambles."

"Come on, what more could you expect? You admitted yourself that it all sounded loony to you, too." She reached up and ran her fingers through his hair. "Frankly, I don't think you could have hoped for it to go any better. Especially with Goodman out there beating his drum, making us all look as crazy as he is." She gestured in the direction the vanished reporters had taken. "One or two of them will follow up. They'll talk with other researchers, and see that the danger is real, even if it does sound crazy."

George shook his head mournfully. "Hell, the whole story *does* sound insane. But it's *true.*" He picked up his briefing papers. "Oh, well, maybe Kenji will have better luck."

"Don't give up yet," Jessica said. "Come back to the office with me. We've got to start working the phones and the e-mail and the fax machines. You got one or two to listen here. We've got to find others who will as well."

Tokyo, Japan

Not very many hours later, Kenji Yamada watched the backs of a similar room full of unimpressed reporters as they filed out of the room, laughing and joking among themselves.

Noboru Hayashi stood by his side, clearly unhappy with the results of the briefing. "We have not reached them," he said.

"No," Yamada agreed. "It is as I feared. Our only hope is that fear and doubt will grow over the next few days."

"Perhaps a demonstration of the pulse chamber," Hayashi said. "Let them *see* what happens."

Yamada nodded absently, still watching the departing backs of the last of the reporters. "Yes, perhaps," he said, sounding unconvinced. "We'll try that. If we can get any of them to come, now that we have told them the sky is falling."

3:00 P.M.
Santa Barbara, California

The young seminarian stepped into the library and looked around. He spotted the man he was looking for and went over to him. "Father O'Rourke? There's someone here to see you."

Father Francis looked up from his reading. "What? Oh, thank you, Jeffrey."

"He's waiting in the vestibule."

"Thank you," Father Francis said again. He set down his book and stepped out into the hallway. *Who could it be?* he wondered. But in these days of wonder and fear, with this new and mysterious EMP threat suddenly hanging over half the world, with no one knowing *which* half, priests were much in demand. People needed comfort in these days. But who would have asked for him, specifically?

He stepped out into the vestibule, and got his answer.

Desmond. Desmond Potter, his eyes downcast, standing with his hands clasped together, his hair wind-blown and disheveled. Francis knew without being told

that his friend had driven his motorcycle directly from
Los Angeles, a hundred miles away.

"Desmond?" he said.

And his friend lifted his gaze, looked him in the eye.

"Forgive me, Father," he said, "for I have sinned.
Will you hear my confession?"

Interlude

Six days after the detonation as seen from Earth, the supernova approaches its peak brilliance. The thick, opaque shell swells outward, exposing more and more surface area. But even as it expands, the supernova shell begins to cool. The shell grows larger, but with the cooling effect taking hold, each given unit of surface area is dimmer.

From Earth, the shell is no longer just a point source of light, as all the stars are. Now it is just barely discernible as a disk, but so bright that looking directly at it for more than a few seconds can destroy a person's vision. A new term, *nova blindness,* will enter the languages of humanity. As the shell expands and dims, it will become both easier and safer to observe its disk with the naked eye.

But before that can happen, the shell must expand further, stretch itself, thin itself.

And develop cracks.

Inside the shell, the roiling power of the trapped radiation is waiting for its chance to burst free and out of its prison, unleash itself upon the universe.

Almost at the precise center of the shell's disk as seen from Earth, a weakness in the shell's fabric begins to unravel. The wall of superheated gases snaps, breaks.

And the bottled-up hellfire of the supernova's interior smashes through. There is a sudden and temporary up-pulse in the visible brightness of the supernova, but a bit more or less light is of no consequence at this point.

For the gamma rays have gotten loose.

The initial surge of high-energy gamma ray and X-ray photons hits the Earth's upper atmosphere, and then almost immediately falls beneath the danger threshold. Gamma ray photons will pound the Earth for twelve hours or more, but their intensity will drop off rapidly. It is only the first few minutes of the surge that have enough power to be dangerous.

But that is enough.

Far more than enough.

Chapter 16

Day had become night, night had become day, and both had become neither. George Prescott sat slumped over in a couch in the data reduction building, watching the row of monitors on the opposite side of the room, each over its own console. Jessica was curled up on the couch next to him, her head pillowed on his lap.

Other scientists were hunched up tight in front of those consoles, peering intently at the screens, acolytes seeking after the supernova's secrets. But not George. Not anymore.

Now he knew the secret, and he did not wish to know anything more. Now the supernova had lost all semblance of wonder for him. Once it had been a friend, a companion, a kindly god that told him wondrous secrets. Now it was a traitor, an enemy.

It was a time bomb, and he was waiting for it to go off. No, he could not stand any more watches over that monster. Let someone else sit in front of the screens. He would turn and walk away from this place, go outside and watch the damnable thing set, wait for the kindly rays of the true sun to rise and warm his face, and then he would go to sleep.

And yet he could not leave. Willingly or not, he kept his vigil, watching the real-time images coming down from the telescopes. He knew, deep inside, that he would remain long after Sirius had set, watching the playbacks, the analysis, watching the data come in from other observatories. He was trapped in this place.

Waiting for it to blow. They had done all they could to prepare for it here. Unneeded equipment unplugged and shielded as much as possible, the spare portable satellite link shut down, disassembled, and sitting in the deepest basement on the mountain, along with all the other portable gear they could scrounge up. The generator tanks were topped off, every battery-backup was at full charge. The primary computer systems and half the monitor gear were all shut down, and the backups were running in continuous backup mode, dumping everything to optical storage drives as it came in. The system was running as slow as molasses, but they were not going to lose any data, or be utterly crippled if and when the pulse came.

And maybe, just maybe, they had done some good. Companies were running backups of all their data. There were runs in the stores on batteries, freeze-dried food, firewood, bicycles, portable radios, fuses and replacement circuit breakers, first aid kits, candles, portable electric generators. Supposedly there was even a shortage of playing cards. Maybe people were worried about how they would entertain themselves after the balloon went up.

And the maximum danger period was over the weekend. That ought to help some.

But what about the ones who did not believe, who never even heard? He shook his head, knowing there was nothing else he could do to reach them.

George Prescott looked up at the monitors again, then glanced at his watch. Just after 5:00 A.M. Sirius would slide below the horizon soon, and that would be that for a while.

Let it set, he thought. *Let it go down, and maybe I can leave after all. Give Jessica a poke, walk her back to the dormitory, and get some real sleep. Maybe I can do it. I certainly can't get any real sleep here.*

Like a wall of baleful, sightless eyes, the multiple images of Supernova Sirius glared down at him from the monitor screens. Who could sleep when *they* were watching? He looked toward the false-color infrared image. He saw the mottled, leprous shell glowing an angry brick red, its face marred and mottled with twisting, rippling currents of gas flowing back and forth, its face pockmarked by gouts of orange fire pulsing and arching everywhere, as the outermost layers began to break up, revealing the hotter layers below. Hotter layers. He blinked. Lines of orange, and, almost precisely in the center of the shell's image, *a dot of white.* Suddenly the blood was roaring through his veins, thundering through his soul with fear and excitement. One spot of white. He pushed Jessica's head off his lap, not being entirely gentle. Then he stood and stared at the screen. The white-hot dot was growing, swelling even as he watched. That had to be the innermost layer appearing, spreading itself thin, succumbing to the pressure of the radiation below struggling to get out.

"Jesus Christ," he whispered, unsure if it was a curse or a prayer. "Jesus Christ." Suddenly he raised his voice and shouted across the room. "This is it! Everybody stand by. It's breaking open right now—"

And the image of the supernova suddenly flared over into white.

Saturday, December 16, 2000
9:50 P.M.
(4:50 A.M. Los Angeles Time)
Tokyo, Japan

Hideo Nakano and Toshiko Ogawa were finishing their dinner and starting the evening at a new Italian restaurant in the fashionable Harajuku section of Tokyo. It pleased Hideo tremendously that Toshiko had enjoyed the *linguine vongole,* spaghetti with red clam sauce, that he ordered for both of them. The waiter had just brought them each a dainty scoop of spumoni, served in graceful crystal bowls.

Between spoonfuls of the ice cream, Hideo shook his head. "Three times in two days," he said. "Three times we fill the pulse chamber with nice new equipment and destroy it for a fresh flock of reporters."

"Is it doing any good?" Toshiko asked. "Are they starting to believe?"

"Toshiko, I don't even know if *I* believe. I mean yes, we can run a pulse through a chamber—but does that mean it's going to happen to the entire world? Every time one scientist trots out a pronouncement that it's all true and we'd all better get ready, another scientist declares that it's nonsense. What about you?"

Toshiko shook her head. "I spent the whole week filling another rush order for Hayashi Industries. They've had us stocking up on all sorts of electronics spares and fuses for months, but now they've accelerated their efforts, and other people are getting in on it, too. It's even fouling up supplies. You can't buy standard household circuit breakers in wholesale lots anymore, and just barely on the retail level. Same thing with any kind of fuse you can think of, or batteries. They're gone."

Hideo was about to say something, but something in Toshiko's voice told him this was not what she wanted to talk about. Maybe it was time to get out of here before the mood bogged down. He gestured toward the waiter, signaling that he wanted the bill. But Toshiko reached out her hand to his. "I paid already, when I went to the powder room. That way I could avoid your making a fuss." She smiled impishly. "You wouldn't let me pay for anything last time, and this way we didn't have to fight for the check. So let it be my treat this time, okay?"

They left the restaurant and walked to the nearby Meiji Shrine Park for a romantic stroll. The supernova was already above the eastern horizon, casting the city in an eerie twilight. Sirius was shining like a mini sun, ten thousand times brighter than a full moon.

That was one trouble with the supernova: now, even in the depths of night, it was too bright for a couple to steal a kiss out in the open. Not with so many people around. Not with the hustle and bustle of the Christmas season. The Japanese people had no interest in the religious aspect of the holiday, but they were wildly enthusiastic about all its other trappings—the carols, the decorations, the tradition of gift giving.

But even that limited meaning was of no interest to Hideo right now. All he knew was that there were a lot of people around, and Japanese society did not approve of public displays of affection, to put it mildly. This park had no lawn open to the public where it was socially acceptable to pretend the other couples were not there. Here, they could not even hold hands. Hideo longed to make love with Toshiko, but instead he walked beside her, careful not to hold hands, careful not even to touch her.

They strolled around the strange-lit park. At last they rounded a corner and Hideo noticed that there was no one within sight. He turned toward Toshiko, and she was already in his arms, kissing him with eager passion.

"Not your place tonight," she whispered. "And not a love hotel either. I've made reservations at the Imperial Hotel."

The Imperial was one of the grandest, most elegant places in town, astronomically expensive. Hideo knew that Toshiko lived at home and banked practically her entire paycheck, but even so, the Imperial was an incredible extravagance. "You certainly are determined to make this a special night," Hideo said with a smile. "Why, Toshiko?"

She looked up at him, and he saw by super novalight that she was crying, silent tears streaming down her cheeks. With a jolt, he understood. *She believed.* She thought the EMP was going to happen. She wanted not a special night, but a last night that she could remember in the dark days ahead. She seemed about to speak, to try and explain. He put his finger to her lips, a gentle sign that no words were needed.

For suddenly he believed as well. He *knew,* with a deep-seated certainty, that it was going to happen.

"Ssshhh. Ssshhh. It's all right. Come on, let's go find a cab and get there," he said.

They turned back and had nearly reached the entrance to the park when something strange happened to the light. It bloomed brighter, as if someone had just twisted the power up a bit. Their shadows seem to deepen and darken.

And then the noise stopped.

Suddenly the light from the whole city blanked out, as if by magic. The ever-present background noise of a modern metropolis—the rumble of traffic, the subsonic hissing of the subway vents, the thousand hums and clicks and whirs and buzzes of machines—all faded away.

Then they heard the first of a new sound: the sickening squeal of tires, the cool, dead thud of collision, the sparkling shatter of broken glass. But even before the first impact was finished, a new one began, and then another, and another, until the night seemed filled with the sounds of cars crashing, the noise echoing in from all directions. Toshiko looked at Hideo, and he at her, horror in both their faces. They grabbed each other's hands and hurried to the park exit.

When they reached the city street, it was strewn with stalled cars, smashed into each other in every conceivable way. Two or three cars had left the road and slammed into the sides of buildings. One, just down the block, had flipped over completely, and the first tentative flames were starting to lick out from it. People were dragging the victims from what cars they could. Hideo glanced up and down the street, and spotted what looked like a fire in the window of an appliance store. Every television set on display had blown up. Now that he looked, there were signs of fire several place up and down the street. *Take this scene and repeat it,* he thought, *a thousand times over, and over again.* This is the whole city, the whole country, half the world.

He grabbed Toshiko's hand. "Come on, let's try the train station. They have their own power grid. Maybe they managed to stay on line. There might still be electricity there." He led her toward the Harajuku train station, past an endless line of smashed cars and the nascent fires. Hideo did not really expect the trains to be running, but at least it gave them a goal, someplace to head for. He was proved correct as they reached the station. Its interior was black and empty. People were milling around outside by the light of the supernova, suddenly the only source of light there was. Hideo wondered if the phone lines had survived, but then he saw someone try one, then another and another, of the station phones before giving up. These telephones were dead, at any rate. Probably the whole city system was out. He glanced up at the station clock and noticed it was stopped at 22:08, 10:08 P.M.

"What do we do now, Hideo-san?" Toshiko sounded worried, and Hideo noticed, though she did not, that she had used the formal honorific *-san*. She was deferring to him, putting him in charge, and he wasn't sure he liked the responsibility.

Hideo tried to think. Transit and communications

were both out. There was no point in trying to go to his high-rise apartment building. Even if they got there and made the exhausting stair climb in the dark, what waited for them there?

Then he thought of it. They could walk to the research labs in the Shibuya district. There were two small apartments inside for the employees who might have to stay there overnight. There usually were enough provisions there to last for several days. He had a key to the side entrance of the building. "Come on," he said. "I know a place. It's only fifteen minutes from here on foot. We can rest up there and make our plans for tomorrow."

Toshiko reached up and touched his face. "If there is a tomorrow." she whispered.

5:08 A.M.
Los Angeles, California
Interstate Five

Why the hell was traffic so bad? For God's sake, it was 5:00 A.M. on a Saturday, and the road seemed to be packed wall to wall. Barely doing forty. Walt Parks downshifted his eighteen-wheeler again, growled to himself, and reached over to his thermos for another cup of coffee. Damn construction. Had the interstate down to three lanes each way.

Walt wedged the wheel between his knees while he opened the lid, poured himself a cup, and resealed the thermos. He held the cup in his left hand while he used the right to toss the thermos to the passenger seat and flick on the radio. That done, he put his right hand back on the wheel, let go with his knees, and took a sip of coffee. The radio came on, playing a nice little country tune that instantly put him in a better mood. He liked that radio—a brand-new job, pulled in lots of stations, great sound. Okay, so there was a little traffic. Life went on.

Maybe someday soon he'd be able to afford a truck as new as the radio. This one was an elderly beast, easily ten years out of date. He was sick and tired of running everything manually. The new trucks did it all for you.

There was a pulse of light from the west, over toward the city, nothing like Walt had ever seen before. For half a crazy second, he wondered if some damn fool terrorist group had finally managed to get their hands on a nuke and do something about L.A. But there was no mushroom cloud, no pillar of fire in the sky. Everything as nice and normal as it could be with that weird supernova in the sky.

Suddenly the radio station died, faded away to static, and then the radio itself went dead with a funny *fup*. He glanced toward it with a frown, but then the road went crazy in front of him. Half the cars on the highway seemed to lose control all at the same time. A hundred yards ahead, a Buick slammed into a Honda, and a Saturn slammed into the Buick, spun out, and slammed into the guardrail right in front of him.

Walt dropped his cup and grabbed the wheel with both hands, ignoring the searing-hot coffee soaking into his pants. He slammed on his own brakes but hit the Saturn anyway, just as someone slammed into his rear. He felt his trailer jackknife and struggled to keep the truck upright. It began to spin out, slamming into one, two, three cars as the trailer swung through traffic like a scythe through wheat. Another car slammed into him from behind, but then the cab caught the guardrail, and the rear of the tractor slammed into the temporary jersey wall the work crews had set up. The truck came to rest lengthwise across the road.

Walt sat there for a moment, letting himself feel the shakes, letting them pass. Then, at last, he unbuckled and climbed out.

All around him, people were doing the same. One or two cars were on fire, two or three flipped over. Some poor bastard had been thrown through his windshield just ahead, and there were sure to be plenty of others who were just as dead. Things were no better on the opposite side of the road. Walt was stunned, amazed. He climbed up onto the roof of his cab to take a look around.

It wasn't just here: as far as he could see in either direction, both sides of the road were clogged with an endless sea of accidents and death, stretches of clear road interspersed with massive knots of smashed and tangled metal.

No one was going to get a car down this road for a long, long, time.

5:08 A.M.
Delta Flight 723
On Approach to Los Angeles International Airport

The great jet crossed over the land to the sea, finishing its flight from Chicago. Now there was just the turnaround over the ocean and the final descent onto the runway. Captain Sonya Hendricks was glad of it, and glad to let the autopilot handle the rest of the job from here. She was tired, and had been less than entertained by staring Supernova Sirius square in the face the whole flight. That was supposed to be one of the advantages of a night route—no sun glaring down in your eyes. Not these days.

The jet raced out over the water and turned back toward the airport, the light of Sirius slewing around as the jet turned, casting ruddy shadows on the cabin wall. Just before Sirius was lost to view out the side port, Hendricks thought she saw it give off an odd little pulse of light.

Never mind that; every astronomer in the world was watching that thing. Let them worry about it. She had a plane to land.

Ah. Yes indeed. There was United 1221, right in front

of her, just about to cross the end of the runway, just about to put her wheels down—

The cabin lights went dead, the computer screens scrambled and blanked, the background chatter between air control and the pilots fell silent. With a bump and a clatter, the entire bank of circuit breakers snapped over, one after another. Suddenly the whole aircraft was shuddering, bouncing around the sky. It felt as if the engines had been suddenly getting way too rich a mix of fuel. "Billy!" she shouted to her copilot. "Reset those circuit breakers, then raise the tower and report an emergency!"

"Roger!" He swung around in his seat and started throwing switches. Hendricks reached for the control stick, but it seemed welded in one spot, immovable. The safety circuit computers were supposed to switch over to manual if there was an electric power failure. Instead, it was simply jammed. She tried her pedals and throttles, with the same result. She could change neither speed nor direction. What had been an aircraft a moment before was suddenly a lumbering, unguidable missile headed straight for the airport. What the hell was happening to her plane?

"Circuit breakers won't hold a reset!" the copilot said. "They keep retripping."

"Keep trying! I'll notify the tower." Hendricks snapped on her radio switch. "LAX Tower, this is Delta 723 declaring an emergency. We have lost all electric power. We are in an uncontrolled descent. We have no control of the aircraft. Repeat, we have no contr—"

"Skipper! On the runway!"

Hendricks looked sharp, dead ahead to the threshold. Where United 1221 was piling it in, moving far too fast, about to gouge a hole in the runway.

1221 slammed into the ground in a ball of flame that shot halfway to the sky. Wings, tires, bodies, bits of fuselage, spiraled up into the air.

"Oh, my God," Hendricks said. "Billy, get me the

hell some power, or we're gonna end up like they did. Throw everything over to manual.''

''Yes, ma'am, switching all systems to manual,'' he shouted, throwing switches. ''I am getting no response,'' he said, panic starting to creep into his voice. ''I am getting no response. We have hydraulic power, but all electric systems are dead. Captain, I think the circuit breakers are all blown out, overloaded past reset.''

Hendricks tried the radio again. *Something* had to work. ''LAX Tower, this is Delta 723. We have no control, we have no control. We cannot throttle back our engines. I repeat, we cannot throttle back. Estimate current heading will give us an impact on the tower, repeat on the tower. Evacuate, evacuate.''

She gripped at the stick again.

Suddenly a flicker of control lights came on again. ''Okay, that's the backup stick control coming on,'' Billy said, almost sobbing with relief. ''You should have some control surfaces. Stand by, attempting to get you manual throttle control.''

''Way to go, Billy. Give it to me.'' She pulled in hard on the stick, trying to get their nose up. Now they were within a half mile of the runway threshold, almost over the fireball that had been 1221. The jetliner started to respond, the nose coming up. Sonya thought she had at least checked their descent, and maybe even started to gain some altitude, but with every damn instrument out, it was impossible to be sure. Now they were over the runway, coming up on the inferno below. Below— God, no, directly ahead of them—a pillar of smoke and flame stood directly in their path. ''Pull up, pull up, pull up,'' she chanted. With a shuddering roar, the jetliner slammed through the wall of flame and out the other side. But low, too low. Sweet Jesus, she was looking *up* at the tower. ''Pull up, pull up, pull—''

The jet's nose cleared the tower, but its belly caught a big piece of the roof, slamming hard into it, sending the aircraft tumbling out of control, down into the acres of covered parking lots behind, a pinwheeling ball of hell slamming down into the concrete, smashing huge sections of the upper level down into the floor below. Bits and pieces of the jet kept moving, the wings sheering off, the nose a shattered wreck, the tail rolling end over end across the access roads.

5:08 A.M.
California Aqueduct, San Gabriel Mountains,
California

The California Aqueduct was an engineering marvel, and no part of it more marvelous than the massive, elaborate, and newly modernized pumping system that drew the megatons of water out of the San Joaquin Valley, over the San Gabriels, and down toward Los Angeles. It was built to withstand earthquake, power failure, and terrorist attack. But even the most magnificent machinery has its limits of abuse.

With a rippling surge of power, the EMP burst smashed through the pumping station, knocking out the control computers. The pulse overloaded the turbines, setting them spinning faster just before the power died and the emergency cutoff valves slammed shut. A sudden backpressure built up in the pump chambers. The power grid tripped off just as the circuit breakers to the backup battery system slammed open. There was no electric power available to activate the shunts, but the sheer hydraulic power of the water moving through the system would not be denied.

With a sudden tearing roar, the massive turbine system spun down catastrophically, ripping itself to shreds. The turbine cases cracked and split open. Chunks of turbine spun off to punch into the concrete wall like so many bomb fragments. And the water broke free of its bounds, and cascaded down both sides of the mountain.

—And the pumping station was destroyed.

Indian Air Force Rocketry Command Bunker
Northwest India

Major General S. B. Vengurla stared at his ops boards in horrified astonishment. There went the last of his contacts with the outside world. The prime minister's office, the air force command center, all of them abruptly cut off the air. All nonhardened communications were down. For all practical purposes, the only lines now open were between this bunker and the launch sights. Hardened lines back to the central command authority had been scheduled for installation in another six months, but that was of little help now.

Tensions between Pakistan and India had been bad and getting worse for years, and on a virtual war footing for months now, both sides merely waiting for an excuse to start the shooting.

Of course, there had been tensions long before the present crisis, but things had been made no better when the damnable Paks had finally smuggled enough stolen technology to put together their own filthy stock of nuclear weapons. There had been some safety, some *stability,* in the situation when only India had such weapons. But not now.

Now it appeared that Pakistan not only possessed such weapons but Vengurla was sure they had *used* them, fired one high out in space over India to black out all communications with an EMP. It had been part of their war-fighting plan right along, according to what the intelligence fellows told him. EMP. There could be no other explanation. In fact, the command bunker had a sensing device for detecting electromagnetic pulsations, and it starting wailing the same moment the comm lines died. He had heard some damn foolishness about the supernova being able to jam communications, but that was obvious nonsense. The thing had been in the sky for a week without causing problems. No doubt the stories in the last few days had been Pakistani disinformation.

But the supernova could very well fit in with the Pakistanis' plans. They knew as well as Vengurla did that India had them all beat in night-fighting. What better time to strike than when there would *be* no night for weeks at a time, neatly bypassing the Indian advantage?

He paced the length of the bunker, studiously ignoring the nervous glances of the airmen on duty at the stations. He stopped by the tactical intelligence station, shooed the operator out of his seat, and sat down to check the latest information from the frontier himself. No change reported—but how much could he rely on that? This was the last information he could trust, and it was already hours old. *Large numbers of Pakistani forces massed and maneuvering*. That was the crux of it, and something he had already known. Possibly it was one of their regular maneuvers grown large, a show of strength. Or else, given the circumstances, something much more.

For an EMP strike by itself made no sense. It was supposed to serve as a decapitation strike, cutting off the commanders from their forces to cripple their reaction when a full assault began.

Full assault. Vengurla stared unseeingly at the computer screen as he considered what that meant. Pakistani troops pouring across the border, their missiles lofting toward New Delhi, or raining down on the Indian troops massed to face the Pakistanis.

No. It was not to be tolerated. He would not sit here and wait for orders, not when the enemy's first move had been to ensure no orders could ever arrive. Not when his *standing* orders, and the very purpose of this bunker and missile system, were to guard against just such a situation. They would strike, use their missiles against the enemy rear, to break up his formations. They would save this situation yet.

He stood up, straightened his tunic, and walked down the length of the bunker to where his executive officer waited, clearly nervous but doing a credible job of remaining calm. "Major Ponnami, we will extract our key cards and commence Case Shiva."

Ponnami snapped his heels together and saluted. "Yes, sir!" he said, his eyes wide, his face covered with the sweat of fear.

Good, Vengurla thought. If he was not afraid, then surely he was mad.

The first of the Indian missiles launched a few minutes later.

The last of the Pakistani rockets did not land for days.

Tokyo, Japan

Time had no meaning, and the night destroyed by the supernova was made anew by the thick, roiling clouds of smoke. The street was blocked by a wall of flame. Hideo turned around and stumbled back the way they had come, Toshiko's hand in his.

Gone. All gone. Three times now they had taken shelter, and three times the fires had come, driven them from their refuges one by one. Their clothes were little more than rags, and their faces were smudged and smeared with soot. Hideo had a bad cut on his scalp, and his hair was caked with dried blood.

But Toshiko was in far worse shape. Her legs had been badly cut in a fall when they rushed from their first refuge, the burning building collapsing around them. Hideo suspected that she had taken a bad sprain as well, but she was not willing to admit it.

Forward. They had to go forward. The way south down the street was blocked by a burning building collapsed into the street, but to the north were the fires that had driven them this way in the first place. They backtracked to the last intersection and started down the cross street, threading their way through the smoldering ruins of a half dozen cars wrecked in a horrific accident. Yesterday the roasted bodies caught in those cars would have seemed a horrible nightmare. Today they were merely part of the landscape. Toshiko and Hideo went past them without so much as a glance.

Suddenly there was a thundering roar behind them. They wheeled about to see a building behind them collapse into the street, cutting off their line of retreat. Hideo frowned grimly and faced front again. Now it was forward or nothing. They walked on.

One of the cars, the last one along, had flipped over. Somehow it managed to escape burning. It was not until they were alongside it that Hideo noticed the smell of gasoline. The car's tank must have ruptured. There was a small puddle of gasoline under the car, oozing out into the street. Hideo paid it no mind. They passed in front of the car.

But then, when they were just a meter or two past the overturned car, the wind shifted, and sparks from the inferno behind them were blown at the couple, catching in their hair, in their clothes. Toshiko's dress caught fire, and Hideo turned to help her.

But then a spark found the small pool of gasoline. Flame leapt up from the spark, ran up the tiny stream of gasoline seeping down from the gas tank.

The explosion ripped the car apart, and threw the shattered bodies of a young man and a young woman halfway up the block.

A half hour later, the flames of all the merging fires had spread far enough to consume the bodies.

Tokyo, Japan
Hayashi Industries Building

Noboru Hayashi stood and looked out the window at the great and injured city. Hayashi and Kenji Yamada had been camping out here for days, waiting in the apartments inside the building complex for the pulse to happen. *And now it has,* Hayashi thought. *And now we start the work of surviving.*

The view from the conference room on the forty-third floor of the Hayashi Industries Building in the Kasumigaseki section of Tokyo was eerie. Normally at this time of the evening, the nightscape of Tokyo was a panorama of lighted buildings, tall and short, their windows ablaze, the street canyons pulsating with the ever-changing neon signs. The supernova's change of night into day had cut back somewhat on the need for light in the past few nights, but now the reversal was complete. Virtually all the windows were dark. Nature had turned night into day, and humanity's artificial forms of daylight were cast into darkness.

But there was one other form of light easily visible here and there across the city: fire. The EMP had sparked thousands of electrical fires, and some of them were still gathering power. Here and there, whole city blocks were ablaze. But every street was an impassable obstacle course of stalled cars. Even if the fire department had been able to get its trucks started, they would not be able to make their way to the fires, let alone fight them. A pall of smoke hung over large portions of the city.

This evening, only a few buildings were lit, not by fire, but by electricity. Here and there lights gleamed in a handful of windows. No doubt a goodly number of buildings had emergency power plants, but what power they had was being used sparingly. No one knew how long it would have to last.

The Hayashi Building was one of those few that had some of its windows lit; indeed, it was probably the best-lit building in the city. Hayashi was well prepared to use some electricity. He had quintupled the usual stock reserves of fuel oil and brought in a spare generator. He had no desire to wait until the entire infrastructure of the power supply system was up and running again.

There was some word that one or two electric plants were back on-line again, but with so many transformers blown and lines down, there really wasn't anywhere to send the power. Worse, without an adequate supply of fuel from overseas, they would cease to operate in a few months. No doubt ships' engineers from here halfway to the Persian Gulf were struggling to get control of their vessels.

Their navigation computers destroyed, their control systems destroyed, their radios useless, they were adrift. Aboard some, the engineers would manage their miracles, restart the engines, rig a manual steering system, navigate by feel and by luck—for not even the stars could be seen while Sirius blotted them out—until they limped into some port or another. The U.S. Pacific and Indian fleets were out there, and the EMP-hardened ships had ridden out the pulse unscathed. Already Hayashi's radio operators had picked up a dozen reports of dramatic rescues at sea. Many a Pacific coast sea town would raise a monument to what the navy had done to save its sons today. Yet, though the U.S. Navy was performing heroically, across the great distances of the sea, even the largest fleet could do only so much. Many ships would not survive, but go aground, or simply lose themselves at sea, until all hands aboard died of starvation or disease.

The ships, at least, had a fighting chance. Ships did not sink when they lost power. But aircraft crashed. As best Hayashi could tell, virtually every airplane that had been in the sky over the Pacific at the time of the pulse had crashed. Even planes that had been on the ground when the pulse hit would most likely have suffered electronic damage. Nor would there be many places for an undamaged aircraft to lift off from. Every major airport they had raised reported at least one serious crash, and many airports had been closed—or destroyed—by crashes.

Both Narita and Haneda airports were visible as pillars of smoke, dim glows on the horizon. Hayashi watched the smoke in the direction of Haneda for a time, and wondered just how bad it could be.

But there was nothing he could do about Narita and

Haneda. He turned from the window and crossed the large open room to examine the situation board. There was something reassuring about this place, full of people bustling around, industrious souls intent on *doing* something, who *could* do something.

Hayashi examined the situation board. A huge electronic display was showing the greater metropolis of Tokyo. Another display showed the Japanese archipelago. The locations of the installations vital to the nation's existence, such as power stations, communications centers, water-pumping stations, and food distribution centers, were indicated clearly. Many of them were flashing red, meaning that, as best could be judged with communications so bad, they had been rendered non-operational by the EMP. Some had just been knocked out momentarily, while others had taken more serious and permanent damage that would require major repairs. But which was which? Who needed a one-hundred-yen fuse? Who needed a swarm of emergency technicians and a helicopter full of hardware?

The first order of business, then, was to restore communications, especially with those essential facilities. With the phone system out, with the cellular nets out, that was trickier than it seemed. The communication satellites, tens of thousands of kilometers above the atmospheric layers that produced the EMP, were for the most part all right, though a few were showing signs of taking a bit too much X-ray damage. But as long as they held out, the portable satellite stations would work. Line-of-sight radio worked as well, as long as you could find a working unit.

But it was the Self Defense Forces making it all happen now. They had been hit as hard as anyone else, yes, but they had shielded equipment and they were trained to move when no one else could. The SDF was like a fighter who had taken a punch to the face, shaken it off, and then gone to work. Communications parts and equipments were being shipped by the EMP-hardened helicopters and field vehicles of the defense forces. They were few and far between, but Hayashi Industries's own helicopters and motor vehicles, which had been given at least jury-rigged protection against the EMP, were also pitching in to help.

But it would not be enough. Hayashi had never thought that it could be. Despite their best efforts, it would be several days before a semblance of normalcy would be restored. There was a great deal of suffering and death yet to come. It could easily be weeks before electric power was fully restored, and without refrigeration, starvation was a real possibility.

Fortunately, there were emergency shelters with stockpiles of food, water, and first aid provisions throughout major cities in Japan, stored away against the danger of earthquake. They ought to be able to support the population for several days. *If the power, water, and communications could be restored quickly, Japan could get back on her feet,* Hayashi told himself, hoping that his confidence in his countrymen's ability to bounce back from a disaster was not misplaced. Still, he had done his best to foresee the dangers and prepare for them. And Japan was no stranger to natural disaster. The Great Earthquake of 1923, for example, had taken ninety thousand lives and left a hundred thousand injured. On the whole, society had held together then, although there had been some lawlessness, street gangs roving the night. And the Japan of 2000 was not that of 1923. Society was less disciplined, less controlled. If a breakdown started this time, things could be a lot worse. Hayashi did not want to see anything like that happening again.

Hayashi himself still had his childhood memories of a devastated Tokyo, the carnage created by the firebombing in March of 1945. Much of the city had been laid to waste, and over a quarter million people died in Tokyo alone. In his mind's eye, he could still see the ruined Tokyo of those days: nothing but burned-out houses and buildings in every direction. Yet, within a few days, some provisions were reaching the survivors. Law and order was maintained throughout. His family, like many of their neighbors, had to live out of the tiny bomb shelters for the next several months, but somehow they managed to survive and rebuild the city and the country. *It was not as bad this time,* he told himself. *The city stands.*

But the legends of 1923, and the memories of 1945, had left their marks. He was going to make sure that this time around, the rebuilding would be as swift and painless as he could make it. He was determined that his homeland would pull through all right.

But what of the rest of the hemisphere? There were even reports of war, nuclear war, out of India and Pakistan. He shook his head and rubbed his face with both hands. What of Australia, Hawaii, the West Coast of America, Siberia? Hong Kong, Singapore, China, Korea?

It must be the same as here—everywhere the same, over half the world: wreckage and smoke, cities largely intact but utterly paralyzed. Food running short, panic setting in, the roads clogged, the fires starting to grow, the people getting cold and hungry. Hospitals, fire departments, police stations, without power, struggling to cope and failing. Here a city would survive almost untouched, there the casualties to fire, starvation, disease, panic, riot, would be horrific.

And yet there was hope, surely there was help on its way. Half the world had escaped. Europe and Africa were intact, all of North and South America east of California unharmed, Asia west of India still there. *They will not leave us this way,* he told himself, watching the smoke on the skyline. *Will they?*

Los Angeles, California

Hiram Goodman stepped out into the middle of the street and watched his own home burn, a broad smile

on his face. Houses, possessions, did not matter anymore. Today was the day all debts were canceled, all
guilt was absolved, all sin was burned away by the
flames.

He turned his back on the fire and made his way
down the street toward the scruffy little park a block or
two away.

There was a scraggly knot of people in the park,
retreating from the burning buildings to the safety of an
open space. There were not more than twenty or thirty
at most, most of them with one sort of injury or another. He could hear a child crying, and the low moan
of a woman in pain.

But such things no longer mattered. The time of humanity was past. Hiram ignored the refugees. From
here, he could see the towers of downtown, the pillars
of smoke that seemed to rise from every quarter of the
compass. Exultation filled his heart. This was his hour,
the moment he had waited for all this time. The sword
of God had come down.

Now was the moment. Now his true people would
come to him. Now he would take his place at the fore-
front of the Armies of the Lord. He looked down at his
right hand, clenched it into a fist, and thrust it high in
the air.

He shouted at the top of his lungs, a cry of triumph
and delight that echoed down the burning streets.

Chapter 17

Tuesday, December 19, 2000
Scott Station, Mount Erebus, Antarctica

Bernard Samuelson stood on the frozen land and looked east into the driving snowstorm. The storm had let up for a moment, and he watched in horrified fascination as another huge mass of ice sloughed off the massive shelf and into the Ross Sea. The shelf was a mile off, a remarkable distance to see in this bloody weather, and it took time for the sound of the mighty event to cross to him. Then the ground shook beneath his feet with a mighty roar. Gigatons of ice were breaking away, smashing into the open ocean. If the damned weather would ever clear, you could see that the Ross Sea was dotted with enormous icebergs. Already, the old hands told him, twenty percent more ice than last year at this time had broken away. Not enough to cause a disaster, not yet, but still it was worrisome.

But of course, the weather was not *going* to clear, praise be. If it could stay socked in like this just a bit longer, then perhaps the danger would pass. The thicker the cloud cover, the more of the sun's light—and Sirius's light—would be reflected off into space, and the colder Antarctica would stay.

The storms were the children of Sirius, that much was clear. The increased sunlight on the southern oceans had stirred up new weather patterns, and drawn more water into the atmosphere. And when warm, moist air hit the frigid Antarctic landmass, the atmosphere gave up its moisture as snow. Lots of it. The snows were a well-disguised blessing in another way: The rate of snowfall on the landmass behind him was something like twenty-five percent ahead of a normal year. In other words, while more ice was breaking away from Antarctica than usual, even more snow than usual was falling onto it. If anything, the amount of water tied up in the Antarctic ice cap was *increasing* slightly.

Bernard shook his head and turned back toward his hut. At least the specter of supernova-spawned global warming and flooding was gone. The world had feared the ice caps melting, flooding all the coastal cities. That had not happened, and now seemed unlikely to do so. As for the EMP, down here at least, it had been a question of changing a few fuses. Most of their gear was military specification anyway, and therefore hardened against such dangers.

Up north, things were different. Bernard shook his head sympathetically. Up there, from all he could hear on the radio, they might be quite glad to trade their problems for a spot of global warming.

Sunday, December 24, 2000
9:00 A.M.
Los Angeles, California

Desmond Potter drove back into town, but it was not the place he had left eleven days before. The days with Father Francis had done him good, made many things clear, but they were not enough to prepare him for—this. He cruised slowly down the streets, horror clutching at his heart.

Los Angeles burned still, the pillars of smoke rising high over the proud towers of downtown. The pulse had touched off thousand of electric fires, and Desmond Potter doubted if the fire department had managed to reach a single one. How could they?—with all the roads blocked by wrecks and abandoned vehicles, with the phones out and with half their radio gear destroyed, with the water pressure low and dropping? Street gangs roamed at will, for the police were no longer even a factor in the equation. The cops were desperately over-burdened handling rescues, trying to restore islands of order around their own stations, trying to stand and hold on what ground they could until the army could be deployed. And it would have to be the regular army, for how could the National Guard be called up when there were no roads, no radio stations, no functioning transportation?

Los Angeles hungered, and the people were already on the march, looking for food, looking to escape. Pedestrians and cyclists were on every road out, hoping against hope to find a place safer, a place less burned, a place less frightening.

Los Angeles was near death. Brother Desmond saw that as he wandered the city on his antique motorcycle. Now Desmond was here to get a look at the man who would be its undertaker. Yesterday he had departed the safety of Father Francis and the Jesuit retreat, safe in the hills over Santa Barbara. Now he journeyed into the dangerous world of Hiram Goodman. The word had gone out: Reverend Goodman was going to talk, here, now, today.

Brother Desmond Potter of the Last Church of the Apocalyptic Revelation sat on his mud-spattered bike at the back of the crowd and watched the madness he had helped to unleash. Here it was, up and down into the street, in front of him, behind him, a collection of lunatics and fanatics and thieves, gathered in the name of the Lord, sure they had been blessed because they had survived, certain that the blessed could commit no sin.

Here they were, in their thousands, laughing and joking and cheering as if at a great celebration. More than a few were still carrying bits and pieces pried loose in their most recent looting. In fact, there were a few of them still working a store on this block, calmly walking in and out through the shattered hole where the display window had been, carrying out whatever bits of finery had survived this long. Others were working through the cars abandoned everywhere up and down the street. The air was thick with the smoky tang of the smoldering fires, with unwashed bodies, with cheap wine and spilled beer.

And there, almost a block away, on an improvised stage made out of the back of a stalled-out flatbed truck stopped dead in the middle of the intersection, was The Man. He had heard some of them call him that. Hiram Goodman, Reverend Leader of this mob. Desmond felt his anger surge up inside himself, felt his hands clench into fists.

He had not been sure at first why he had tracked that first band of Christriders he had stumbled across in the hellish chaos of the undarkened night just past, why he had followed them through the burning, rubbled chaos of downtown Los Angeles. Now he knew. Because they could lead him here, to this rally, lead him to Goodman, and Desmond needed to look on Goodman one last time, to give his anger a focus.

The figure on the back of the truck, holding a bullhorn in one hand, raised his arms over his head. Suddenly the crowd was cheering hysterically, applauding wildly, pumping its fists in the air, pounding on the hoods of cars.

Goodman lowered his arms and put the bullhorn to his mouth. "The city is ours!" he announced, to more wild cheers, more thumping and applause. "Do you want to keep it?"

"YES!" the crowd bellowed back.

"Do you want it under the tree for a Christmas present tomorrow morning?"

"YES!" the mob shouted again, and Goodman pulled the megaphone clear of his face long enough to smile. He put it back to his face and spoke again. "We are too many for the police," he said, "and besides, they are otherwise engaged, trying to revive the city as it was—but that city is dead. We can travel where we will, and they cannot stop us. We can go about our business of raising a new city here, a true city of angels. Do you want to be those angels?"

Again, the wild shout of "YES!"

"Well, good," Goodman said. "I *thought* you might."

Another shout of approval.

"This shall be the City of Angels, my friends, or at least a city of ghosts. It is nearly that already. It will be the likes of us that haunt it, until we have picked it as clean as a skull in the desert. All it needs is a little push, a little shove, a little parting of the waters if you will, and the old city will dry up and blow away. Those that are not clogging the highways already, fleeing however they can, will be soon enough, when we have done our work.

"This city will be the first to be shriven, stripped clean—work you have already begun, I can see," he said with that wild grin playing about his face. There were more wild cheers. "And yet your work is blessed, for it is the will of God that this city shall be no more. That is why He has struck at it so hard. But when that work is done, my friends, what then? What will become of this place, this city, when the rest of the populace flees, when you have picked over the rubble for all you can find, when the last of the fires have burned themselves out? When that has happened not just here, but in all the cities of the Pacific—what happens then? *There* is the question. Let me give you another little hint: do you know what happens seven days from today?''

Desmond thought for a second, and his blood ran cold. *December 31, 2000.* Suddenly he was beginning to understand. That was Goodman's deadline for destroying the city.

There were a few shouts and guesses from the crowd, but Goodman ignored them all. ''Surely there have been enough signs to give you a clue. God has sent his Sign, brothers and sisters. Now all we have to do is read it. He has sent his thunderbolt down to Earth, and where has it struck?

''The Bolt smashed down on the Pacific Basin! From Silicon Valley to the labs of Tokyo and the TV factories of Korea, the Bolt struck down at the breeding grounds of technology, of arrogant science. It has crushed the machines of the dark miracle that were the new Tower of Babylon, man's new arrogant challenge to God.'' Hiram Goodman seemed to sense that he was losing the crowd, and started over again.

''Brothers and sisters, the fall has begun, and by the dawn of the New Millennium, within one week, within the seven days it took the Lord to make this world, it must be complete. We must purge this world. God has given us this chance to be part of the work He has started. And if we do not join in that work, rest assured we will be swept away by it! Here is where we dared to take God's desert and make it bloom, and now we must move to turn the bloom back to desert. God's Bolt from the blue has already done two-thirds of the work for us, but there is still one more artery to cut. Will some of you come back to this place tonight and travel with me, aid me in finishing the job? Will you join the Legions of the Lord?''

The crowd's roar of approval was deafening. Desmond felt something very cold inside himself. Around him, he saw the faces of evil. These weren't just looters and thugs after all. They were believers, true believers, and they had just heard from their own personal God.

What was Hiram planning? The destruction of the city; but by what means? And what did he plan to gain from it? And why? Where had his madness and his ambition led him now?

Desmond couldn't figure it, but he dared not hang around to learn more. Already more than one face seemed to know him, and he had no desire to bring himself to the attention of Hiram or his hangers-on. And more than one of these soldiers of God had cast a covetous eye over his bike. This was no place for him.

But what could he do? Warning the police would do no good, even if they were willing to listen to him. They were outgunned and outnumbered already, even without trying to face down the Last Church. The army could help—but where in the city were their headquarters, and why on earth would they listen to a long-haired, bearded wildman on a fifty-year-old motorcycle, when he came in warning that the members of his Church were going to do something bad, but he wasn't sure what?

No, no, there was no one here in the city who would listen. In fact, there was only one place he could think of that he could do any good—if *they* would be willing to have him.

He turned his motorcycle around, gunned the engine, and pointed his front wheel toward Palomar Mountain.

Federal Emergency Management Agency Headquarters
Washington, D.C.

Brenda Marshall pounded away at the keyboard of her government computer, desperately trying to adjust the flow chart, rearrange the planning sequence yet again. How the hell to resupply Los Angeles? Only one out of six airports even partially open, the docks clogged with immobilized ships, the highways littered with wrecks, derailed trains on practically every rail line. And it had taken days just to get that information together.

The obvious answer was to use helicopters, but every flyable chopper was already in the air somewhere doing something.

Brenda worked to find a solution, while a roomful of other people chewed on their parts of the massive problem. The whole office was a sea of frantic chaos, with every FEMA coordinator and planner and programmer from every shift here every moment of every day. There had never been one like this—ever. In the history of humankind, no natural disaster so widespread had ever occurred. Nor had there ever been such a complete decapitation of so many systems all at once. Just barely, they had managed to pull back most of the major nodes that had been knocked out. Power stations were back on line, telephone systems functioning, medical supply depots established. Things were starting to come back to some sort of order. They were back in contact with pretty much all of the military centers in the West, and that was a big help. They had working vehicles, and some of them at least had airfields no one had crashed into.

But what good was all that when what they needed was ten million twenty-amp fuses, and the factories that made the fuses were all shut down? What good was a power station when half the step-down transformers and substations had blown? What good was a functioning central phone switchboard when virtually every phone

had surged out and blown all its microchips? Half the
ones that worked at all when you picked them up
wouldn't even ring anymore. What good were mountains of medical supplies when all the roads were
jammed with wrecks and there was no way to get the
supplies to the hospitals?

But they had to start somewhere. Slowly, agoniz-
ingly, as the death count surged into the millions, co-
ordinated rescuers would work it all out, get the people
and the hardware and the know-how and start to put it
together. They would rebuild, and come back, and
screw those twenty million fuses into place and get the
nation whole again.

But it would take time and work—incredible mountains of work. The undamaged part of the country was
perhaps in greater shock than the West was, for at least
those poor bastards out West had no real way of knowing how bad it was. East of Nevada, everybody knew.
The flyovers, the satellite shots, the refugee interviews
on the news every night. Everybody knew.

And everyone was working. Here and overseas, in
all the parts of the world that had gone untouched, they
were struggling to put a rescue together, and gradually
it would all succeed. Humanity would rebuild. Japan,
Australia, most of East Asia, were already starting to
make a comeback. But it would take so *long* to get it
fixed.

And, in America at least, Los Angeles would be the
biggest, toughest job of all. It was so big, so close to
ungovernable even in normal times, so fragile a beast
even before all this happened. The rest of the West
Coast would come back, there was no doubt of that.
But Brenda was beginning to harbor a secret fear concerning L.A. It would take so little to send it down.
One more little nudge, one more catastrophic failure of
a system that was just barely holding together—and they
could lose Los Angeles.

Noon
Interstate Highway 15, California

Desmond Potter throttled back his engine and threaded his way past another clump of burned-out wrecks. He forced himself not to see the staring corpse still at the wheel of one car. There were too many even to try to deal with any of them. He speeded up again, and passed another group of refugees on foot.

Palomar. George. He needed to talk with George Prescott. Desmond leaned into the handlebars and willed the antique Indian Warrior to go faster. The engine roared, and the clear skies seemed very close as the wind whipped through his hair and his beard.

Los Angeles. There had been ten million people in the metropolitan area before the Bolt. There was no way to know how many had died, or left. But what did Goodman have in mind for the city, and what would happen to those people if he had his way?

Desmond passed another burned-out, flipped-over, tangled mass of metal that had been a car. He saw a doll hanging upside-down in a shattered window. This time he forced himself to see. He had to know this reality.

He, Desmond Potter, had *wanted* this? He had dreamed of the world's end as a blessing, as something God would *wish?* Once, twice, a dozen times, he nearly turned back toward the city, back toward the suffering victims who needed his help. Surely there were thousands of ways an able-bodied man could do some good. A thousand years, a thousand lifetimes ago, he had earned a medical degree on the way to becoming a psychiatrist. Perhaps it was time to put that to use for the first time since he had burned his diploma.

No. Hiram Goodman was a greater danger. Desmond didn't know what Goodman was planning, but surely it was deadly. His speech had been full of exaggeration and bombast, no doubt, but he had promised to destroy the *city.* Even if he could not do that, surely

he was capable of doing major damage. Desmond kept
on toward Palomar. What good in saving one life if it
meant dooming hundreds or thousands more? Desmond
kept on his road.

But *why* did Hiram so wish to wreck the city? Hadn't
the Bolt done enough damage to suit him? Why enlarge
the destruction and disorder? Surely a God who could
send down such massive power would be capable of
destroying the Earth all by Himself, without Hiram's
help. Or did Hiram just want to help the end of the
world to come more swiftly than God willed?

Or did God even enter into it for Goodman? Did the
man even believe his own words? Did the man himself
even know? What was inside that mind? If Desmond
were to make a guess, he would put his money on
Goodman as a megalomaniacal sociopath, eager for his
own glory. Perhaps the adulation of the crowd has
turned his head. Perhaps by now he was even seeing
himself as God, and was planning to reveal himself on
December 31 as the embodiment of the Second Coming.

And how well did that bode for the people he led?
Desmond had bitter reason to know just how much concern Goodman had for using people well. Goodman
had used Desmond. By now surely Goodman likewise
saw the crowd as an object, a tool, a possession he
could use and discard at will.

Suddenly Desmond felt a chill drive through his soul:
Conrad Gibbons. The man who had killed his family.
Gibbons had seen Desmond as the Antichrist. Gibbons
at times had seen *himself* as Christ. On January 1, would
Lord Hiram Goodman of the City of Angels make a
similar announcement? Would that be the way the circle was closed?

No, no. He forced the idea away. It was madness
even to consider. One supposition on top of another,
guess piled on guess. He would end up with as many
delusions as Goodman and Gibbons put together if he
stayed on that course.

But what of Goodman's followers? Did they truly think that destroying one city would bring on the Rapture, the end of the world? Maybe, somehow, they were unconsciously reasoning by sympathetic magic. If their part of the world was destroyed, then so, too, would the rest of the world be wrecked. And if the world was destroyed, then the Second Coming would indeed take place. Except none of Hiram's followers could have performed that chain of reasoning consciously, or else they would have seen all the obvious places where it didn't make sense. Maybe they even made a semiconscious decision *not* to work through the logic, for fear of spotting the flaws. Wasn't it enough that it was Los Angeles, the City of Angels? Hurry, hurry, do the bidding of Goodman, be raptured, and be gathered to your reward in Heaven *alive*. Praise Be Unto the Lord!

Ultimately none of the internal reasoning mattered. No outsider would ever follow it completely. The plain and simple facts were what was important: Hiram Goodman, at the head of at least several thousand followers, wanted to render the Los Angeles area uninhabitable before mdnight December 31. And there was at least some reasonable chance that he could do it.

He slowed the bike at the turnoff to Palomar. Now all he had to do was convince George.

When he reached the entrance to the service road to Palomar Mountain, Desmond Potter was more surprised than he should have been to find it guarded by a nervous young man in a red down vest, a sporting rifle slung over his shoulder, and his right hand straying unnervingly near a holstered nine-millimeter handgun. Desmond looked past the guard and noticed that someone had done a pretty fair job of jury-rigging a swivel barrier across the road. There had been trouble here, obviously. That wasn't going to make this easier.

Desmond brought the motorcycle to a halt well short of the barrier. The young man with the guns didn't have the look of a guard. Somehow he had more of the look of a junior scientist pressed into duty in an emergency. Desmond doubted the man had ever held a gun before, or fired one. That made him far more dangerous than a guard who knew his business. After all, with a professional, the guns would only go off on purpose. It crossed Desmond's mind that the guard on duty was almost certainly backed up by a hidden partner. There was probably another edgy young man somewhere in the trees, doing his best to draw a bead on Desmond's heart. He raised his hands clear of the handlebars and showed that they were empty.

"Hello!" he called.

"Yeah, I see you," the man said, shifting uneasily from one foot to the other. "Who are you and what do you want?"

"My name is Potter, Dr. Desmond Potter. I'm a friend of George Prescott, and it's important that I speak with him."

"A lot of people feel that way," the guard said, making no other move to respond.

"Well, maybe that's true, but I need to speak with him, and I am fairly certain he'll want to speak with *me*."

"What makes you say that?" the guard asked.

"Because I have news about what Goodman is planning for Los Angeles."

The guard bristled and stepped forward a bit. "Are you with Goodman?" he demanded.

"No, no, not at all. I just have some information, and I need to talk about it with Dr. Prescott. Would you please let me through?"

"You stay right there and don't move," the guard said in a voice of half panic and half suspicious caution. He fished a small walkie-talkie out of his down vest's pocket and struggled to jam the earphone into his ear while keeping his gun more or less trained on Desmond. "Home base, this is front door; do you read me?" He listened for a moment. "Yeah, I got a guy on an old motorcycle who calls himself Dr. Desmond

Potter. Wants to talk with Prescott. Yeah, okay, we'll wait. Not much else to do down here.'' The guard gestured vaguely with his rifle, which Desmond found more than a bit unsettling. ''We're supposed to wait while they check,'' he explained.

Desmond nodded and concentrated on keeping his hands in view. He wasn't quite sure, but he imagined that he saw a flicker of movement, perhaps the glint of metal on sunlight, coming out of a spot of cover behind and to the right of the guard. *His backup,* Desmond realized. Very carefully he looked as hard as he could at every other part of the landscape but that one. He did not want to spook these people.

At last the guard in the road seemed to hear something over his earphone, something that seemed to surprise him. He stepped back to one side of the road and swung the swivel barricade up and out of the way. ''They say go on up,'' he shouted to Desmond. ''But take it easy on your way up. Couple of the watchkeepers might be a bit jumpy.''

Anyone you call jumpy, I'm going to watch out for, Desmond thought as he gunned the cycle's engine and eased it forward toward the barrier. ''What happened around here that you need all this security?'' he shouted over the engine noise as he rolled slowly past.

''Trouble a couple of nights ago,'' the guard said as Desmond drew closer. ''A mob tried to come up the mountain. They blamed *us* for the supernova. I think they figured if they smashed the telescopes, it would all go away. Had to chase 'em off with fire hoses and a few shotgun blasts in the air.''

Desmond nodded uncertainly and moved past the guard. There was, it seemed, a lot of that sort of thinking going around these days.

George Prescott stood at the top of Palomar Mountain and watched as the old red motorcycle gradually made its way up, vanishing around a curve in the road and then reappearing.

Jessica stood by his side, looking apprehensively at the lone rider who was climbing up the service road. He reached out and took her hand, shut his eyes, and breathed in the sweet air. He could not remember the last time he had stepped outside for the purpose of staying there, rather than just hurrying from one building to another. He had no idea what time it was, or what day, or even if it was day or night. Was that the sun in the sky, or Sirius? His mind was too tired, his eyes too bloodshot with exhaustion, to be sure. He could have looked at his watch and known. Like about half the electronic wristwatches on Palomar, his had kept working after the pulse. Yet somehow he could not bring himself to do it.

Perhaps some deeper part of him realized time no longer mattered, not really. And he knew that if he were not so exhausted that he could no longer feel, *that* thought would have terrified him. But it felt good to be out under the sun—yes, that *had* to be the sun. A gust of wind blew across his face, and he suddenly felt a bit better.

The motorcycle eased its way to the top of the mountain and pulled up alongside George and Jessica. Desmond Potter, his hair windblown, his cheeks flushed, stopped the bike, shut off the engine, and swung down the kickstand with a kick of his heel. He stepped off it and looked at his two hosts, obviously unsure how welcome he was or what to say.

Jessica stepped forward, smiled, and took his hand in hers. George breathed a sigh of relief. Was she truly glad to see him, or seething inside? Although he hadn't done it on purpose, Desmond had certainly caused a great deal of trouble. But whether her kindness was sincere or calculated hardly mattered. She was setting him at ease, and that was what was important.

"Merry Christmas, Desmond," she said.

Desmond looked at her in surprise. "My God, what day is it? Have I lost track?"

"No, it's the twenty-fourth. Christmas Eve. But Merry Christmas and welcome all the same."

"Thank you," Desmond said. "I wasn't exactly sure you'd be glad to see me. George—good to see you."

"Good to see you, Desmond," George replied. "I've been worried about you down there. Things aren't good."

"No, no, they're not," Desmond said, obviously trying to hold his emotions in check.

"Come on, then," Jessica said. "Let's get you inside and get you washed up and put some coffee into you."

Desmond looked at her in startled surprise. "Coffee! Now, that would be a Christmas present. *That's* something I haven't seen in a few days."

George laughed and took Desmond by the arm. "Well, come on to the cafeteria and let's get a look at some."

Both Desmond and George felt the need to catch the other up, but both could sense that time was short. Desmond gave a brief account of himself since what he called the Bolt, which seemed as good a name for the pulse as anything, and George caught him up on events at Palomar as Desmond wolfed down a late breakfast with the air of a man who hasn't eaten properly in a while.

"We watch," George said unhappily. "All of us know that it's important, that the world needs to know all it can about the supernova, but just watching the skies while the world is falling apart—"

"Except it isn't falling apart," Jessica said, "and that's the wonderful thing. People are pitching in, working to survive. In Seattle they already have plans to reopen the schools after the New Year. They have at least one lane cleared on every highway. Hawaii's got four radio stations back on the air. All the fires are out in San Francisco, and the main power grid is back up, and there are food supplies moving into the city again."

"What have you heard about India?" Desmond asked. "There were a lot of rumors down in the city."

George and Jessica glanced at each other unhappily. "Disaster," George told him. "Absolute disaster. Some damned madman in India assumed the EMP was a Pakistani attack and struck back. At least six cities have been wiped out. There's a fallout cloud blowing west. Riots, refugees. There's some kind of major battle going on, but no one seems to know much."

"But everywhere else, things are getting put back together," Jessica said. "We hear that in every radio and TV report that comes in off the satellite links."

"Everywhere but Los Angeles," Desmond said. "Things are bad there. Very bad."

"We've seen the refugees go past, but after that first little incident, we sort of keep our heads down and make sure they keep on moving," George told him. "We haven't heard much from any of them."

"You said something about Goodman controlling a mob," Jessica said. "What's that all about?"

"He's given his blessing to any robbing or looting anyone wants to do, and that's a pretty good recruitment tactic."

"According to Goodman, God says it's okay to steal?"

"I don't pretend to follow all the reasoning, and Goodman can contradict himself completely and still have it all seem to make sense. Sometimes the idea is that God wants all the sinful wealth that has been piled up to be redistributed to the worthy. Or else it has been decreed that the Lord Himself wants the city stripped clean of everything as the first step in its purification. Sometimes you hear some other story. But Goodman seems to have just about all the Enders under his thumb, plus the Christriders, and a bunch of the city gangs, though I bet *they're* just along for the ride, letting Goodman provide the cover while they go out and do what they'd be doing now anyway. A lot of opportunists out there."

"What about the cops? Can't they do anything?"

"Sure, they can get shot," Desmond said grimly. "There was a pitched battle near the Los Angeles Country Club on Wilshire Boulevard. The cops lost. Goodman's crowd has a lot of firepower. The people left in the city learned real fast to stay out of the way when Goodman's people go past."

"They can't control the whole city," George objected.

"They don't have to," Desmond said. "They just have to keep anyone *else* from controlling it, and they're free to do whatever they want. But Goodman is the key. Pull him out of there, and the rest of the organization will fall apart."

"But he has to know that," George said. "He's got to be doing whatever he can to hang on and protect himself."

"What was that stuff you told us about destroying the city?" Jessica asked.

"I don't know," Desmond said. "It was all pretty cryptic. Something about the job being two-thirds done, and parting the waters, and turning the bloom back toward a desert. He said something about cutting the last artery."

George looked up suddenly, and slammed his hand down on the table. "Oh God," he said. "It's obvious. I know what he's going after."

"What?" Jessica demanded.

"Water," George said. "Without fresh water coming in from the outside, Los Angeles isn't there anymore. The city is in the middle of the desert."

"So what's that got to do with the job being two-thirds done?" Desmond asked.

George let out a deep sigh. "Plenty," he said. "Water is half the politics around here. Before the pulse, there were three sources of water for the Los Angeles area. The California Aqueduct from the San Joaquin Valley—that gets pumped right over the San Gabriel Mountains. Then there's the Colorado River Aqueduct.

That crosses the Mohave Desert and gets pumped over the mountains to the east. *Pumped.* That's the key word. Pumped over the mountains. Both of those water systems *have* to have been shut down when the EMP struck, maybe even wrecked by it. There must have been a hell of a lot of water under pressure that didn't have anyplace to go all of a sudden.

"That leaves the Los Angeles Aqueduct from Owens Valley and the San Fernando Valley. It's the only direct-flow aqueduct into the city. The only one that could still be functioning. Cut it somehow, and there's no water in Los Angeles."

"Where is it? Where does it go?" Jessica asked.

George thought for a moment. "We need to look at a map, but as I recall it, the aqueduct ends up at the Van Norman Lakes. It goes under Highway Five near San Fernando."

"I know where you mean," Desmond said. "But what do you think he's going to do?"

"Cut the aqueduct. Maybe drop Highway Five *onto* the Aqueduct." George said. "Or maybe not cut the aqueduct, but just wreck it so it couldn't be repaired. Maybe blow the dams, empty the lakes. Then they could go back and do whatever they needed to do to the other water sources, make sure they can't be fixed."

"Then what would happen?" Jessica asked.

George thought for a moment. "Then there wouldn't be any more water in the city," he said. "Once whatever was in the reservoirs was gone, that would be it. You could bring in some water other ways, but not enough. Nowhere near enough. I think they might be forced to abandon Los Angeles, and fast."

There was dead silence around the table.

"I have to talk to him," Desmond said at last.

"What?" Jessica said. "Are you crazy? The only person we have to talk to is the local army commander, if we get in contact with him. Tell him to put a guard on all the water facilities in Los Angeles."

"Yes, yes," Desmond said. "I know, I know. But I

have been down in that city, and I have seen death, a lot of it. I have to prevent more if I can."

"What are you talking about?" Jessica demanded.

"I'm talking about waiting for Hiram Goodman on Interstate Five, right where it goes over the aqueduct. And trying to talk him out of it."

"Wait a second," Jessica protested. "Not if we call the army in. Believe me, they'll be able to talk him out of a lot more things than you can."

"Not without killing him," Desmond said. "Besides, I can get there faster than an army. I just have to hop back on the motorcycle and go. Armies have to get organized, loaded up, moved up—and they don't ride on motorcycles. I bet there's a helicopter shortage right now."

"Armies also need to be convinced," George said gently. "Jessica, I bet you'd be good at that. A lot better than I would be."

Jessica turned toward George and looked at him in utter shock. "Why can't you—" she began, but then cut herself off.

She stared at George in astonishment and then spoke again, her voice low and calm. "You want to go with him," she said in astonishment. "You want to go out with him and get killed because of your damn fool guilt over the supernova."

"Guilt?" George asked, a bit too disingenuously.

"Don't kid with me," Jessica said. "There's some part of you that still thinks none of this would have happened if you hadn't gone out looking for the damn supernova. There's part of you that's as nuts as the lunatics who came up here to wreck the observatory. You think that if you hadn't gone *looking* for it, then the supernova would never have happened."

George looked at Jessica, and breathed in deeply. It was time to speak the truth, and say the things he really felt. "Yes," he said at last. "Yes, I do want to go, and yes, I think you're right. I think maybe guilt is a big reason for it. And I *know* that guilt is crazy. But I also know it is part of me, and if I don't do something about it, something besides watching the sky and dreaming—if I don't do something out in the *world*, I won't be able to live with myself."

"And that's worth going out there and getting killed over?" Jessica's eyes were suddenly full of tears.

Desmond reached out to touch her hand. "Jessica, listen to a man who knows. I'm not asking George to come with me, but if he wishes to come, he is welcome. But listen to a man who couldn't live with himself for a long, long time. If the choice for George is between getting killed and spending the rest of his life regretting that he had not done what he could have done, then . . . yes. Trust me, it is very much worth getting killed over. I could have, should have, committed Conrad Gibbons. The knowledge that I did not will never heal. I will spend the rest of my life trying to make amends for that failure. If George feels the need to make amends, then he must do it. Because if he doesn't, it's not much worth staying alive otherwise.

"Trust me on that one, too."

Chapter 18

11:00 P.M.
Interstate Five
San Fernando, California, Northwest of Los Angeles

George Prescott shivered. The winter wind was blowing colder than it should have, there on the overpass. Los Angeles was supposed to be warm all the time. Maybe the supernova had something to do with it, screwing up the weather patterns. Maybe there wasn't any point to standing here in the middle of the undarkened night, worrying about water for Los Angeles. Maybe the supernova would skew all the weather patterns so badly that Los Angeles would get rain every day of the year. He looked down the road to where Desmond stood, a hundred yards or so closer to Los Angeles, watching the city, waiting.

George Prescott drained the last of the coffee from the thermos, pouring it into his cup, setting the thermos down on the ground, sitting back down on the edge of the motorcycle's seat.

He looked around at the interstate and decided that there was something grim and brooding about it, a still and yet unquiet graveyard for machines—and for people as well. Many wrecks still had corpses in them. When the wind came up from the wrong direction, the stench was staggering. George and Desmond were glad to find the overpass free of corpses, although here, as everywhere else, the road was littered with wrecks, with abandoned cars. But few other stretches of roadway had the lifeline of a city gurgling underneath. He couldn't see the water below him from here, though the Van Norman Lakes were clear and close. He could imagine their dams breached, their imprisoned waters cascading down, wiping away a hillside's worth of city, leaving a city without water.

The aqueduct itself was covered over, buried, as it crossed below the roadway, with something new and fresh about the work, as if it had just been done recently. The overpass, too, for that matter. Had they just finished up a refurbishment a few months ago? It seemed a shame that all that work would be wrecked just after it was done . . .

No, stop it, he told himself. His mind was playing games, desperately searching for anything else to think about besides the fact that a bunch of religious fanatics were on their way to blow up the spot on which he was standing.

Had they guessed right? Had Hiram Goodman meant what he had said? Could he do what he planned to do? And could the army get here in time, if they came at all? Jessica had still been trying to reach someone when they had left. Suppose they dismissed her as a crank?

He gulped down the last of his coffee and screwed the cup back into place on the thermos. *I miss the dark,* he thought. *I miss the stars.* He looked up at the slate-blue sky, tinged with haze from the last of the fires in Los Angeles. There Sirius hung, well up in the sky at this time of night, gleaming down proud and bright, as if it had had the *right* to blot out the night and make night a mockery of day.

Suddenly George felt unalterably tired, as if he would never again feel rested, as if he would never again be truly able to sleep until the night returned, until the dawn of the New Year, the New Century, the New Millennium.

Or would they dawn at all? he wondered. *Suppose, just suppose, Hiram Goodman was right?* Suddenly George Prescott laughed out loud, a bright, clear noise that seemed to challenge the gloomy near-silence, the secret whispering of the water under the ground.

If that *was* the way the universe worked, then let the end come. He had no use for a universe that worked by such absurd rules. He wanted no part of it, and good riddance when it was gone. He stuffed his hands into his pockets and walked down the littered road to Desmond.

The other man turned toward him. "Nothing yet."

George smiled and sat down on the hood of a 1999 Lincoln. "Oh, I don't know. It seems to me that quite a lot has happened already."

Desmond sat down next to him and smiled back. "Yes, I suppose so." He looked around at the wreckage that surrounded them. "If this isn't the end of the world, it'll do until the end comes around."

"I'll say," George said. "It's been a hell of a ride. And I'm glad I met you along the way." He put his hand on the older man's shoulder. "You've been important."

"And so have you, George. You sold yourself short, back on the mountain, when you said you were nothing but a watcher. People *did* listen when you gave your warnings. Maybe not all of them, or even most, but a lot. And you couldn't have made those warnings without doing all that watching and thinking first. There are lots of people who are alive today because of you. The ones who stayed off the road, or canceled their flights, or unplugged the television so it didn't blow up and burn down the house. Your sitting and watching probably saved millions of lives.''

''Hmmph.'' George leaned back on the windshield of the car and looked up at the blue skies of night. He pulled out his sunglasses and put them on. ''You know, that never even occurred to me. I suppose you're right, but it's still a very strange thought.''

''Millions of lives,'' Desmond repeated. ''Very few men get to do as well.''

''I don't know,'' George said. ''I think you'll even the score tonight. You're the one who brought the warning. If we've guessed right, and we can stop Goodman, there's a city of ten million down there. It might seem empty, but there are still a lot of people alive, hiding in their homes. And they'll all be in your debt.''

''Do you think they'll come?'' Desmond asked.

''Who—Goodman or the army?''

Desmond shook his head. ''Either one. Right now I'd settle for either one.''

And the two men sat in the too perfect silence of the highway, waiting.

The first sound came about fifteen minutes later, a growling mutter coming from the city, barely audible at first, but quickly growing louder. A plume of dust rose in the distance, and then, around a curve in the highway, they came on, at first not visible as more than shapes moving carefully through the wrecks strewn across the road.

''Which ones is it?'' George asked.

''I don't know yet,'' Desmond said. ''Let's get back to the bike. I've got some binoculars. Besides, if it's Goodman, I want to be with the bike when he shows. Don't ask me why, but I think that would help.''

''What are you going to say?'' George asked.

Desmond shook his head. ''I don't know yet. Oh God, let it be the army. Let them get here in time from wherever they are. Let *them* handle it. George, what the hell are we doing here?''

"All we can, if that's not the army getting here first," George said. "Come on."

They walked back to the bike, and Desmond fished the field glasses out of the saddleback. He put them to his eyes and took a long, careful look at the approaching group. "The good news is we did our guessing right. The bad news is it's Goodman." He lowered the binoculars and let them hang around his neck. "So now what?" he asked.

"Now we try and remember all the very good reasons we decided to come unarmed," George said, his voice nearly cracking. And they *had* been good reasons, too. No point to a pair of pistols up against a mob of hundreds armed with every imaginable weapon, and they certainly didn't want to give the Enders an *excuse* to shoot at them. But none of that seemed convincing as the vague spots of movement resolved themselves into a veritable fleet of motorcycles, fifty or sixty at least, slowly and carefully threading their way through the obstacles on the road, until the moment they shifted from *far* to *near,* and the noise of their engines shifted from a distant buzzing to a close, intimidating, thundering roar. Suddenly the riders were almost on top of them.

"There—there in the lead—that's Goodman on the Harley," Desmond said. "Oh God, he's spotted us."

The driver of the lead bike raised his hand, signaling a halt. He came to a stop about a hundred feet from George and Desmond. The riders behind him slowed and halted in ragged ranks behind him. They held there, revving their engines, staring intently forward. Goodman killed his engine, drew his bike up on its kickstand, and dismounted. He was dressed casually in blue jeans and a work shirt; no riding gloves, no helmet. Moving slowly, calmly, he walked toward the two men.

George felt his heart pounding. He wanted to laugh, to cry out to the world that the situation was absurd. How could this ragged band of thugs destroy the water system for an entire city? And yet here they were, and what other reason for coming here? Who could tell what tools, what stolen explosives, they might have with them?

And where the hell was the army?

Goodman approached to within about ten feet and stopped.

"Hello, Desmond. I missed you when you left. I guess you finally found the tap on your computer," Goodman said.

"Hello, Hiram. Yes. I did find it."

Goodman nodded, glanced at his feet, kicked some broken bit of a shattered car out of his way. "Is that why you're here now?" he asked. "Looking for an explanation, maybe?"

"No. Well, yes, I suppose. Mostly it's that you loaned me this motorcycle a while back, and I wanted to return it," Desmond said, nothing in his voice to show whether he was serious or not.

What is he saying? George wondered. *What was it between these two?*

Goodman shrugged. "Keep it. I got plenty." He grinned unpleasantly. "More than I got explanations. But you haven't introduced me to your friend." He turned to George and looked at him. "You know, without those shades on, you'd look a lot like that George Prescott who was in the papers."

"Yeah, I would," George said.

"And you know that all I have to do is turn around and shout your name and you'd be nothing but a skin bag full of hot lead."

George swallowed hard. "Yeah, yeah, I know that."

Goodman nodded thoughtfully. "And all I have to do is shout back to the boys, denounce Desmond, say he betrayed me, and he'd hit the ground the same time you did."

"So why don't you?" Desmond asked, and George thought his heart would stop.

Goodman shook his head. "I don't know," he admitted. "I really don't. Maybe just because there wouldn't be any point to it. But then, there hasn't been any point to a lot of this.''

"There was at first," Desmond said, his voice still firm and calm. "Back when I first walked into the Christriders, there was something there. When you and I opened the Last Church, there was something to believe. We were doing good.''

"Doing good never really did hold my interest," Goodman said.

"But destroying the water system for a whole city would?''

"I was wondering if you'd figured the whole thing out," Hiram said. "Yes, that's why were here. Shouldn't take more than an hour to set the charges and blow the dams and the aqueduct sky-high.''

"And that's your idea of something worthwhile," Desmond said. George found himself wondering if Desmond was truly trying to talk Hiram out of it, or if he was simply stalling for time, hoping against hope for the army to show up. "At the very least, thousands would die of sickness and thirst. Why, Hiram? What's the point?''

Goodman looked up and grinned again. "It seemed like the next logical step.''

"And that's reason enough to doom all those people—maybe starting with your own followers?'' Desmond asked. "Hiram, have you thought this thing through?''

"Don't you talk to me that way, you son of a bitch," Goodman exploded with sudden anger, his voice suddenly loud and fierce. "Don't you talk that way to a man who could have you dead in ten seconds.''

As if to emphasize his point, the waiting bikers reacted to the sound of his voice, shifting in their saddles, a few hands drifting closer to weapons. George felt his heart pounding again, fear-sweat popping out on his forehead. But the other two men ignored the bikers altogether.

"Kill us if you want, but it won't make any difference," Desmond said calmly. He shook his head, as if recalling a fond but long-lost memory. "It used to be that you and I could talk to each other. Just tell me—why wreck the city?"

Goodman looked him in the eye for the first time. "Because God wills it, as He wills the destruction of all wicked places," he said, in a voice that suddenly betrayed a sense of uncertainty. "Because I am the shepherd of this flock, and sometimes the shepherd is the one following the flock, and *my* flock seeks its own revenge on the world for the crime of being richer and happier than they will ever be."

"Come on," Desmond said. "Those are mighty weak reasons. Can't you do any better than that?"

"Because it is the next logical step!" Hiram said. "Because this is the place my life has taken me. God has led me to this place. What else would He have me do? Why else would He have put me at the head of His church?"

Logical step, George thought. "Yes, yes, it would be logical," he said suddenly. Something familiar had just dropped into place for him. "At least to you. Wrecking the city would be the next step to take *if* the world was coming to an end. An irrevocable act to draw your followers together, to prepare them for the acts of celestial destruction to come. A guilty act that would force them to stick together in order to protect themselves from punishment. But you don't believe in the world's end anymore, do you?"

"God is on His way," Hiram said. "And surely He shall smite the places of wickedness—"

"No!" George said. "No. You don't really believe that. I can see that on your face. It's a rote piece for you. It's obvious. Look at this destruction, breathe in deep and catch the stench of death in your lungs. Can you really believe that God would wish more of the same on the Earth?"

"Death doesn't matter anymore. Not in the Last Days."

"Then neither should life," George countered. "Surely

God could wipe out this city if He chose. Why take the job away from Him? Or is it that you have been moving forward so long you can no longer turn back?''

"What are you getting at, Prescott?" the preacher asked.

George looked at Hiram, and Hiram looked back at George with nervous, edgy eyes. But George had the feeling he was getting to him. At least he hadn't ordered George and Desmond killed . . . yet. But if he guessed wrong, took a wrong step now, that would change very quickly. "The next logical step, Reverend Goodman. Maybe it isn't always all that logical, even if it seems so at the time. That's how *I* got here. When I sat down to do my thesis, half the reason I chose supernovae was no one *wanted* me to choose them. I was being obstinate. But I did, and I started to study, never really expecting to find anything. But I did find things, and each discovery led me to the next logical step, the next discovery. I got more and more involved with it, until I got so wrapped up in what I was discovering, I started to feel *responsible* for the things I found. Your friends behind you over there aren't the only ones who wonder if I caused the supernova by discovering it.''

"That's ridiculous," Goodman objected.

George felt a flicker of hope. "Do you mean it's ridiculous that I *think* it's my fault, or ridiculous that it could be my fault?" George asked. "Never mind, it doesn't matter. Both statements are absurd. But I got to both of them, one seemingly logical mistake at a time. I believed it was my fault enough that I came out here to make amends.''

"What's all this got to do with me?" Hiram demanded.

"Just that I didn't end up out here on purpose, and neither did you. You didn't plan this. This wasn't your goal when you started out as a preacher, was it? The destruction of Los Angeles?''

There it was. That was it, the knife edge, George realized. If Hiram said "Yes," then there was nothing more George could say.

"No," Hiram said. "But this is where the Lord led me, logical step by logical step, to use your words."

George stared deep into Hiram's eyes, and knew absolutely he was looking into madness. How to reason with insanity, how to pull it back from the precipice it seemed so eager to leap over?

But it was Desmond who spoke, Desmond who found the words.

"How do you know it was Him, Hiram? How can you know for certain that it was the *Lord* who told you to come here, and not some part of yourself? *I* was sure that God wanted the world destroyed, until I realized that what I thought was faith was nothing but hatred and anger. How can you *know* you're not making the same mistake?

"Look around yourself, Hiram. Look around at the ruins, at the death, at the bodies rotting in the cars. Can you tell me for sure that God wanted it? Can you imagine God looking at this, and seeing that it was good? Can you think that God now demands *more* death? There's a nuclear war going on right now in India and Pakistan. Did God will *that* as well, or was it some fool in a bunker?

"Can you send thousands more to their deaths, let men and women and children die by your hand as sure as if you strangled them, one by one, *if you are not sure* God wills it?"

A spark of anger blazed in Hiram's eye. *Oh God*, George thought. *This is it. Desmond has insulted him*. Hiram glared at Desmond shifted his gaze to George, his arms hanging down by his sides, his hands flexing open and shut, open and shut. The three men stood there, silent, each watching the others. George did not dare to move.

"Can you make killing an act of faith, Hiram?" Desmond asked, his voice still low and steady. Hiram's head snapped around, back toward Desmond, and his ice-cold eyes locked with Desmond's calm brown gaze. George thought of Jessica, and said a silent good-bye to her, as he prepared to die. Hiram was going to raise his arm, give the word, and the men behind him would raise their weapons and—

"All right then," Hiram Goodman said, speaking at last, speaking quietly. His eyes flicked away from Desmond, locked on the horizon. He stared blankly over George's shoulder. "I won't do it."

He turned and walked back toward his men. Without a word to anyone, he got on his bike, started the engine, eased it back off the kickstand, and turned it around back the way he had come. He raised his hand in a signal, and started off down the road, his followers hesitating a bit before going after him.

A minute later, the last of them were once again nothing but tiny shapes moving down the distant highway.

And then, overhead, George heard it. Another muted mechanical noise, the sound of many powerful engines at once.

Helicopters. Army helicopters. He turned around and spotted them, coming in from the north, from behind him. At least a half dozen of them, coming in fast and low, roaring in until they were almost on top of George and Desmond.

With a thundering, roaring gale, the lead chopper set down on the highway, not a hundred yards away. Tired, mud-spattered soldiers leapt out onto the concrete, and George hurriedly put his hands behind his head before anyone had to tell him to do it. He nudged Desmond and got him to do the same. Law and order, at least of a very rough and ready sort, had returned to Interstate Five. Two more choppers came to a halt in mid-air, and the rest kept right on going, in hot pursuit of Hiram Goodman, his Last Church, his Enders, his Christriders, and whoever else was along for the ride.

George slowly lowered his hands just enough to glance down at his watch, and saw the numbers swing over to midnight.

"It's Christmas Day," he said to Desmond.

Chapter 19

January 1, 2001
5:00 A.M.
Mount Palomar Observatory, California

The New Millennium had arrived at midnight, right on schedule, and despite that provocation, the world nonetheless remained right where it was, once again stubbornly refusing to vanish in a puff of theological smoke.

George Prescott was glad of that. It was not a perfect world, perhaps, but it was a good place all the same.

But the Earth surviving into 2001 was old news: The third millennium was already five hours old, local time. Now George and Jessica and Desmond were sitting on the lawn of the observatory, watching something far more exciting than the passage of an arbitrary moment of time.

Sirius was setting; the stars were coming out.

Yes, there was that little patch of twilight just after sunset, but it was nothing like real night. This was. This was a chance for the stars of late night to well and truly come out, and offer their promise that the darkness was beginning to return. Now, at the tail end of night and the birth of the morning, just before the sunrise, a welcome darkness came just before the dawn. Sirius set at 5:10 this morning; the sun would rise just about 7:00, though it took time for the sky to grow truly dark, and the first streaks of dawn arrived long before the sun. Still, there was nearly a full hour of true night, and the dark period was lengthening a few minutes every day as the sun moved eastward around the background of the sky, getting closer to Sirius.

But night would not return completely any time soon. The sunrise was getting earlier every day as the day lengthened after the winter solstice.

Night's return would take some time, but by March, there would be five hours of full darkness every night.

But even the false daylight would be fading by then. The supernova shell was still expanding, and for now, that effect was neatly balancing out the gradual dimming of the shell's surface. Supernova Sirius would hold at its peak brightness, nearly one-tenth the brightness of the sun, for a few weeks more. But then the dimming effect would overtake the brightening effects of shell expansion, and Sirius would fade away, declining in brilliance slowly over the next several months. By June, when the sun had moved completely about the sky and stood almost precisely alongside Sirius, the supernova would be barely brighter than the full moon, rapidly guttering down.

George looked at the stars, and bid them welcome, and wondered. For the rest of his days he would wonder.

"I don't know," he told his companions. "I keep going over it in my head, again and again. My hearing is good, and even though Hiram was facing us, facing north, those choppers came in damn fast."

"So what's your point?" Desmond asked.

"There were at least two minutes between Hiram agreeing to leave and the time we heard the choppers. Did Hiram see them, or hear them, or sense them somehow, and leave because of them?"

"No, his attention was on me," Desmond said. "Those eyes were boring into me, not watching the skies. It was us, George. We talked him out of it. He responded to reason, not the threat of force," Desmond concluded, his voice firm and sure. Clearly that was the point that mattered to him.

George was not so sure. They had not been that eloquent, and he was certain Hiram was looking past them at the horizon, right at the end.

But let Desmond believe his version, if it helped him. Yes, it was the same old world with all its shortcomings. But if George was any judge, Desmond saw a better world than he had, one alive with hope, filled with the inner certainty that his life was worthwhile after all.

"Personally," Jessica commented, "I don't see what difference it's going to make to Goodman. One way or the other, he'll be breaking rocks at Leavenworth."

George shook his head and stared at the wonderfully dark sky. "Still, it doesn't matter. Jessica made a phone call and the army got there. They would have stopped him even without us riding clear across the city on your bike. We could have stayed here."

"Wrong again, George," Jessica said through the darkness, her voice gently mocking in the dark. "They would have had ten minutes, maybe fifteen or twenty, to get started laying their charges, taking cover. Maybe they would have been able to shoot back long enough to set the charges and blow the aqueduct. Maybe they could have shot down the choppers and finished the job. Or maybe not. But at the very least, because of you, they got caught in the open and surrendered without firing a shot. You probably saved their lives, and some soldiers' lives as well."

George smiled invisibly in the darkness. A funny world indeed when he, of all people, ended up saving Hiram Goodman's life.

But then, life these days was full of surprises. Caltech had wasted no time in presenting George with a slightly late Christmas present: the offer of a tenured associate professorship. Jessica, too, was to be promoted to the same rank. Desmond didn't seem that impressed by the news, but anyone in academia would know what extraordinary promotions they were. But then, George had to admit, their accomplishments were a bit above average as well. Nor was Caltech the only one making offers. Invitations had come through from a score of prestigious institutions in the States and overseas.

George had decided he would go wherever Jessica went. Let her decide if she wanted to stay here, and watch California rebuild, or go someplace new. But there was another question he wanted to ask her. And for once in his life, he thought he knew the answer to a question before he asked it—and that was a very pleasant feeling.

"It's not over, you know," Jessica said.

"What's not?" George asked.

"The supernova," she said. "The worst is yet to come. In about a hundred years, the heavy particles that make up the supernova shell are going to get here. Highly energetic radioactive particles are going to hit the solar system. It's going to last for months, and any living thing that gets caught out in it will be harmed."

"A hundred years from now," Desmond says. "There's time to get ready."

"How?" Jessica asked. "I have no idea. How do you shield the entire planet from a months-long exposure to killing radiation?"

"We have a hundred years to come up with the answer," Desmond said. "Come on. We haven't even had a *sunrise* yet in this century, and you're worried about what we'll do when it's over?"

"Do you really think so, Desmond?" George asked. "Do you think we have what it takes to start working on the problem before it's too late?"

"Oh yes," Desmond said. "I've got no doubts at all on that score. After all, the human race lived right through the *twentieth* century." He knitted his hands behind his head and leaned back on the ground to stare up at the zenith. "And if we could get through *that*, we can survive anything."

In the east, the first hints of dawn started to warm the sky.

Eric Kotani is the nom-de-guerre of a world-class space scientist who has done research on supernovae, among other cosmic events. He earned his Ph.D. in astrophysics, and is a professor at an Ivy League University. With John Maddox Roberts, Mr. Kotani has coauthored four previous novels: *Act of God, The Island Worlds, Between the Stars,* and *Delta Pavonis.*

Roger MacBride Allen is the author of *The Ring of Charon, Orphan of Creation,* and *The Torch of Honor,* as well as several other science fiction novels. Relying on the false assumption that a writer must live something before writing about it, various people who have read his previous books have assumed he was a defense contractor, British, black, a woman, an astrophysicist, a paleoanthropologist, a reporter, and/or a Baptist. As this book goes to press, he is none of the above. He lives in Washington, D.C.